ALMEDA GLENN MILLER

Tiger Dreams

POLESTAR
An Imprint of Raincoast Books

Raincoast Books acknowledges the ongoing financial support of the Government of
Canada through The Canada Council for the Arts and the Book Publishing Industry
Development Program (BPIDP); and the Government of British Columbia through
the BC Arts Council.

Edited by Lynn Henry
Text design by Ingrid Paulson

While some of the characters in this story are based on real people, the events that
take place are fictionalized and any resemblance to reality is purely coincidental.

NATIONAL LIBRARY OF CANADA CATALOGUING IN PUBLICATION DATA

Miller, Almeda Glenn, 1960–
   Tiger dreams

ISBN 1-55192-572-9

   I. Title.
PS8576.I5362T53 2002   C813'.6   C2002-910552-8
PR9199.4.M56T53 2002

LIBRARY OF CONGRESS CATALOGUE NUMBER: 2002105290

Raincoast Books   *In the United States:*
9050 Shaughnessy Street   Publishers Group West
Vancouver, British Columbia   1700 Fourth Street
Canada   v6P 6E5   Berkeley, California
www.raincoast.com   94710

At Raincoast Books we are committed to protecting the environment and to the
responsible use of natural resources. We are acting on this commitment by working
with suppliers and printers to phase out our use of paper produced from ancient
forests. This book is one step towards that goal. It is printed on 100% ancient-forest-
free paper (40% post-consumer recycled), processed chlorine- and acid-free, and
supplied by New Leaf Paper. It is printed with vegetable-based inks. For information,
visit our website at www.raincoast.com. We are working with Markets Initiative
(www.oldgrowthfree.com) on this project.

Printed in Canada by Houghton Boston

10 9 8 7 6 5 4 3 2

For Alice

Contents

Part One: Something Missing / 9

Part Two: The First Signs / 43

Part Three: Study of Collision / 121

Part Four: Interminable Prairie / 193

Part Five: India Gate / 247

Part Six: Confessions of an Old Woman / 289

Part Seven: The Tiger Dreams / 351

"If someone gives us pain through ignorance, we shall win him with love ..."

— Mohandas K. Gandhi

PART ONE
Something Missing

Tiger Dreams Film Opening Sequence

Sound FX. Steady drumming of wheels against railway tracks.
Music up and over.
Extreme Long Shot. 90 degrees. Train curving around a bend in the
    landscape.
Medium Long Shot. Arms dangling through open windows.
Medium Shot. I am pulled into focus through the barred windows of the
    train. I search through my bags. Pause. Medium Close-up. Touch my
    fingers to my ears, the buttons of my blouse, the pockets of my skirt.
    Cut.
Pan to the red coach car on a curve around grasslands of the Decca. Blur.

Something Missing

Something had gone missing. She was sure of it. For the five hours it took to get from Mumbai to Pune, Claire had searched every pocket of her camera bag, inside each sock, her money belt, even her pant legs, but nothing was missing. The coins Charlotte Blake had sent to Claire were securely packed into the side pocket of her camera bag. Her plane tickets were tucked in the zippered pouch of her daypack along with her passport and her medical records; photographs of her father's family were stuffed into the pages of her journal. Everything was where it should be.

She had come a long way for this and she grabbed for David's hand as the train slowed on its approach to the city she had been imagining all her life. Pune, India, birthplace of her father, population 2.8 million, was like every other city they had visited on the subcontinent. Despair and futility — even more so than in Mumbai — swarmed the train station as she and David stepped off the coach, gathered their backpacks and began to walk along the platform toward the gates. Cardboard homes, like the refrigerator boxes Claire and her brother had once used as forts, were littered with the excrement of children who crawled in and out of their mothers' arms, and their mothers, drawn and aged in skeletal configurations, held their dark oily palms into the air for spare change.

Claire and David paused to watch a raving snake charmer thump his sickly boa constrictor and shout incantations to the gods. Blind men and crippled women gathered around the couple, passing their hands from mouth to belly, mouth to belly, pleading for baksheesh. Three-legged dogs, half-lidded babes and listless children sat like gargoyles at the gates as Claire and David walked past everything and entered the frenzied marketplace of Pune.

Away from the main thoroughfares, which were typically grey and laden with diesel, the city began to expose its own style of provincialism and as their rickshaw crawled along the treed side streets, Pune transformed into the Raj city of Claire's imagination. Lanes were lush with foliage: there were topiaries in the shapes of elephants and tigers, sweet aromatic trellises surrounded shady courtyards, shallow clay-tiled roofs were draped with mosses and vines to cool the interiors of homes, and the thick plastered walls that encircled these gardens were dappled with broken glass and mirrors. These were the remnants of imperialism — the faraway places that had been pruned to mimic Cumbria.

The rickshaw driver pointed to a bridge in the distance. "Ahead," he said. "That is where they kept Mahatma Gandhi."

Claire leaned forward. "Yeravda? Over that bridge?" she asked.

"Yeroda," he replied. He pointed a twisted finger toward a vague location to the right of the bridge. "Yes," he said, "and the Memorial is only there, across the River Mula."

"You mean that is where we'll find the palace?" she asked.

He looked into his rear-view mirror and shrugged his shoulders, "I know only Gandhi National Memorial. Just there. If you want, I'll take you there."

David, who had been reloading his camera, leaned forward and placed his hand on the man's shoulder, "No thanks. We want to go for coffee first."

Their rickshaw turned off Koregaon road and pulled up to the Cosmic Enterprises German Bakery and Zen Restaurant, a destination the guidebook reputed to have good coffee — not the freeze-dried kind boiled with milk that they had been served since landing in Bangkok, but a true bean, ground and steeped in hot, potable water. "Call me weak," David had confessed to Claire earlier that morning, "but if I don't get some real coffee soon, there's going to be an incident."

"I'll wait for you." The driver swirled his head from side to side. "No problem."

"No thanks," David repeated. "We have other plans for this afternoon," and he paid the driver twenty rupees.

"I will wait here," the driver assured them, "to take you to hotel room."

"We want to walk from here, thanks anyway."

As David removed their packs and Claire's camera from the rear of the rickshaw, the driver leaned out of his seat and once again said, "No problem, I'll wait to take you where you want to go."

In India, David had become acutely aware of Canadian compliance; his initial instinct was to acquiesce to the hospitality of the driver. And though he had been well schooled in politeness — standing back to let others in line, offering taxis to others before himself, carrying luggage for women, or giving up seats on buses and trains to the elderly or the handicapped — he couldn't shake himself totally of what he considered "common consideration." In other words, David would never stop using his "pleases" and "thank yous" but he was learning to be more adamant in his daily struggle with Indian persistence.

"Do as you like, but we plan to walk from here," David said.

"Where you go? There is no place from here to walk."

"We're fine. Don't wait for us."

"I wait here. You ask for me. My name is Shyam."

David rolled his eyes at Claire. They picked up their backpacks and walked away from the rickshaw and into a terraced enclosure of the bakery.

The commune across the street from the German Bakery was more like a Club Med than a meditation retreat. Inside the ashram were tennis courts, a swimming pool, spas, yoga classes, shops and banquet rooms. Since Bhagwan Shree Rajneesh's death in 1990, followers had travelled halfway around the world to keep up the tradition of good, safe sex in a healthy environment. After some negotiation, David jumped over the counter of the bakery to show a young boy how to make a proper cappuccino. Claire sat down with her back against the wall and stared at herself in the mirror on the pillar to her left. She never thought herself vain, and had always assumed that those who occupied themselves with external appearances were simply avoiding an obvious lack of substance within themselves, but as she brought her fingers up to tuck the loose strands of hair into her braid she thought a little vanity might not hurt. Lines were beginning to form around the corners of her eyes and the sun had left spots on her neck and the backs of her hands. She stretched her neck up to see the soft healing of her scar blooming beneath her collarbone. She brushed the scar with her fingertips, wincing from the pain her body remembered.

David arrived with two well-foamed cappuccinos and some cinnamon twists. "They're not half as good as your mom's," he said. "Not that I'm complaining, because I'm not." He smiled and sipped his cappuccino noisily as he stared at Claire.

Claire clicked her tongue from the bitterness of the bean and stretched her hand across the table to caress his cheek. They had grown accustomed to not touching each other in this country and it was refreshing to reassemble themselves amongst the

Europeans and Americans who surrounded them in this little respite from the chaos.

David slouched forward onto the table and dabbed his large pulpy fingers into the crumbs from the cinnamon twist. "What do you think Charlotte Blake has in store for us?"

"More bloody tea, I suppose."

"Yes, more bloody tea," David said distractedly.

"This country is lousy with tea drinkers." Claire pulled out the bundle of coins she had tucked into the pouch of her camera, unwrapped the bundle and held her favourite coin — the one she had fashioned into a necklace — in between her forefinger and thumb. Then she placed it delicately into the centre of her palm. Her lifeline intersected the edge of the coin, disappearing briefly and reappearing in frayed strands below the blackened gold disc. She folded her fingers over the coin and turned her hand over.

David shifted in his seat. He reached across the table, took her chin into his hand and scanned her face: her warm, loving smile, her naturally red lips, a pale thin outline etching their fullness. Though Claire was relatively fair-skinned, she had the dark skin of the Indian around her deep-set eyes; her prominent nose, squared-off gently at the tip, intersected their unusual blueness. They were the colour of ocean water over a coral reef, and the iris of her right eye had a fleck of sun splashed into its web — an imperfection of the highest order. "Yes," he smiled, "lousy with tea drinkers."

Claire put down the coin on top of the cloth, reached across and wrapped her cold hands around David's wrist. "You? What's been going through your head?"

"You mostly," David sighed. He leaned against the wall and put his foot on a stool. A young Japanese girl danced in front of one of the mirrors. She wore a lace veil and the long maroon robe of the ashram uniform. A pretty child with a practised pout. Her mother, sitting in a corner smoking a bidi, caught David's eye. He nodded in the direction of her child and smiled.

"But are you glad you came?" Claire smiled and nodded at the woman while her cool hands circled the bones of David's wrist. Snakebite.

The child danced.

"India isn't a place you can ignore," David finally said. "I have a feeling it's going to repeat itself on me for a long time." He paused and focused on Claire. "It makes me miss home, though. And that's a good thing, isn't it?"

Claire smiled and released his wrist from her hands. "Of course," she said. "Of course," she repeated like an echo, quieter and more thoughtful.

They finished their cappuccinos and watched the hugs and kisses of all the well-intentioned stray Westerners who had occupied the other tables. Claire plugged another tape into her camera and began filming the young girl as she posed for herself in front of a mirror.

David, afraid they would never have another cappuccino while they were in India, ordered two more before leaving for Charlotte Blake's home. Charlotte Blake was the only living relative of Claire's father.

Tiger Dreams Film Opening Sequence.

Music. Drums.

Close-up Shot. Tiny bare feet stomp to rhythm of drums.

Medium Shot. Girl-child dancing. Loop image and gradually blur.

Jump Cut. Medium Shot. Shallow focus on reeds of grass. Blur. Pulling
   focus on grass, then stripes, then Tiger.

Close-up. Tiger hacking. Cut.

Medium Shot. Girl-child dancing. Fade.

Something Missing, Continued

As they stood on the front porch of Charlotte Blake's home and tapped on the wooden frame of the screen door, Claire thought about all the stories she had told David over the years and how, in the next few moments, they could very easily be proven false. What if everything had been a lie? She felt more vulnerable than she had ever felt with him before.

David whispered, "Take it wide and check your white balance."

"I already did that."

And David, standing beside Claire on Charlotte Blake's porch, reached over and squeezed Claire's shoulder as if to say, *It doesn't matter, Claire, these truths or lies don't matter to me. I am doing this: inhaling diesel, braving bucket baths and bad mattresses, doing this, not because it will change me, not even because I believe it will change you. I am doing this so that you can finally get your story straight.*

Claire shrugged her shoulder to release herself from David's hand.

Charlotte Blake had to swing her left leg by stepping back onto it, bending the knee and springing from the ground behind her to overcome inertia. It was as if she had to wind herself up like a toy in order to cross a room. In a big limping swagger — the furniture and lamps permanently pushed aside to allow for the wide path of her trajectory — she arrived at the front door of her home. The young woman standing on the porch before her was tall and dark; her black hair, pulled off her high forehead and woven into a thick long braid, draped like a tassel over one shoulder. Her two arched eyebrows framed the blue eyes Charlotte recognized immediately as those of the Spencer family.

"Come, come in," she said. "You must be Claire, William's daughter. I have been waiting for you."

"Yes," Claire said. "That's me. I'm pleased to meet you."

"And you must be David?"

David took the old woman's hand in his and carefully shook it. Charlotte stood back and motioned for both of them to enter her home. They stepped in, Claire first, David following, the screen door slamming behind him.

Inside Charlotte Blake's home were the mouldy remains of a parlour. The sour smell of age curdled Claire's stomach. She took short shallow breaths as she stood in the middle of the room. Her camera hung from her right hand as she slid her left arm through the straps of her backpack and let it drop to the floor.

Pallid, yellow walls and olive green throws were draped across an old Victorian chesterfield and chaise lounge. Pine rafters surrounded a cupola. Light from the outside, a murky, mustard liquid, shone through the window glass into the centre of the drawing room. Hanging on chains attached to the pine rafters, a long, narrow wooden box, carved with delicate filigree, housed a fluorescent light. Wires twirled in difficult tensions through the chain links and disappeared into a box in the ceiling. Surrounding the central parlour were lead-glass doors draped in yellowed white lace. These led to darkened enclaves, their contents indiscernible. Charlotte Blake's home was no exception to the general dilapidation that remained of the glory days of the Raj.

Giant spiderwebs floated over everything as Claire prowled around the room, deadly curious — a thief — wanting to take what wasn't hers, to hoard the remnants of her father's life. To this day, she had been unwilling to relinquish what little she had taken after his death — a book, a painting, a carving, a bookend — and at that very moment, with the pungent smell of neglect filling her nostrils, she felt in full possession of her father's past.

One, two, three fat cats swished their tails languorously as Claire, David and Charlotte crossed the room and entered a small outside terrace. Tea, already prepared, sat on top of a plastic table.

"Please, sit," Charlotte panted as she gestured to the chairs facing the table. "You've come a long way today, have you not?"

"We've just come from Mumbai," said Claire.

"Mumbai. Yes, that's what they are calling it now, isn't it?" Charlotte shook her finger at the camera, "Oh, dear, please put that down over there, hmmm?" and she gestured to a small table in the corner of the terrace. "That is your movie camera, I suspect. In your letter you said you hoped to do some filming of the prison. Is that correct?"

"Yes, that's the idea. If everything goes according to plan, which seems damn near impossible in this country." Claire glanced toward David. She stood up and placed the camera on the table, stealthily correcting the position of the lens before returning to her chair to sit down.

Charlotte, sitting in an excessively padded chair, reached behind her head to tuck a loose wire of hair into her bun. A large topaz ring on her right hand tossed amber light around the leafy walls of the shaded terrace. She returned her shaking hands to her lap and began twisting the stone around and around her bony finger. "It really is good of you to come," she said. "You know, your father, I called him Rikki. Rikki, the little mongoose in

Kipling's book? Yes, of course you know. Well, anyway, he brought you to visit me once while I was living in London. You were all freckled and pigtailed. Do you remember that?"

When the old woman spoke, a thin scar, slicing her right cheek into two equal hemispheres, stretched in vertical opposition to the rest of her face. This, and her eyes that constantly wept distracted Claire from the old woman's words. Neither intelligent nor stupid, their simple gaze beneath the sculpted folds of her forehead disappointed Claire; she had hoped for someone much more extraordinary.

Charlotte jutted her jaw forward and tipped her head back and looked down across her cheeks at Claire. "Do you remember London at all?"

"Yes, I do. Vaguely," Claire replied.

"Your father, he was a bright fellow, wasn't he?" Then she winked and nodded. "But I should think he was a bit of a tyrant with you, you being so lovely and all."

"He had his moments," Claire replied. Moments, she thought, more like years, if the truth be known. Claire smiled at Charlotte. It was such a relief for her to have her father's tyranny articulated by someone else. Claire felt for the earrings on her lobes, then brought her hands down to her lap as if she had been caught doing something she shouldn't have been doing. "Yes, he had his moments," she said, very unconvincingly.

"I think your father got his tyranny from his mother," Charlotte said. "Alice had some opinions." Charlotte slurred those words as if having an opinion was some kind of leprous affliction. "Oh yes," she repeated, "Alice had plenty of opinions."

Claire and David drank the sweet tea from their saucers, as Charlotte insisted they do, and after a few moments of silence Claire spoke. "You sent me some coins. Where did those come from?"

Charlotte stared vaguely at Claire. Then the old woman became flustered, fidgeting with the buttons on her cardigan and mumbling to herself. It was as if Claire had broken an enchantment. The old woman looked up at Claire as though she surprised herself with a memory and blurted, "The coins! Yes." She spoke quickly. "Yes, those coins! Oh yes, goodness me. I was clearing out some old drawers and came upon them. I'd forgotten completely about them and when I'd heard Rikki had died — I'm sorry by the way, how unfortunate." Her eyes moved slowly over Claire, their odd cataract irises viewing the younger woman peripherally. She told Claire that Alice had held the coins in her hands until the day she died, that she was very proud of that one of Nur Jahan, that she liked that one the best, she did — and when Claire heard the name, Nur Jahan, her relief was almost audible. She felt like she was surfacing into some kind of corporeal state.

"That's my favourite, as well." Claire fidgeted in her chair and asked Charlotte, "Who was this Nur Jahan?"

"Oh goodness, dear. I don't know. I never much paid attention to Alice's preoccupation with those old things. She was a great tiger huntress of some sort, slaughtered four in one day. Alice was very pleased with that find." Charlotte nodded, then leaned forward very deliberately and whispered, "Damodra, 1925."

Claire cracked her knuckles and asked, "Damodra, 1925? What was that?"

"Oh, it was something your grandfather never quite forgave your grandmother for. Nobody really knew what happened. She left for a month on her own." Charlotte dangled her index finger toward Claire. "Damodra was where she found that coin. When she came back from that expedition she never really was the same — the malaria, you know." Charlotte paused and then continued, "Shortly after that, your father was born." Charlotte snapped her tongue and cuffed her hands across her skirt. "Well, anyway, I have some things you might like to take home with you. I have kept them for half a century and I think probably I have had my time with them."

Charlotte leaned back and then threw her shoulder ahead to help engage her whole body into forward motion. "You know, an old woman must clean house eventually," she said and swung her leg to the side and wobbled into the house.

"You okay?" David asked Claire as he stroked a cat.

"I'm fine."

"Then quit cracking your knuckles."

Claire stretched her fingers out, shook them. "I'm afraid *you're* not going to be fine if you continue petting those creatures."

David clapped his hands and watched the cat hair hang in the air before him. "Asthma is the least of my worries in this country."

Claire walked over to her camera and checked the amount of tape left on her cassette.

Tiger Dreams Film Opening Sequence

Sound FX. Gunshots. A wild, keening yowl. Twigs breaking.
Close-up. Tiger prostrate. Laboured breathing. Steam from nostrils,
  so warm the spectator can smell it.

Something Missing, Continued

"Do you have enough tape left?" David asked.

"I don't know. Should I change it before she gets back?" Claire looked toward David.

"I don't know, Claire," David answered. "It's your project." She had been so full of indecision lately, immobilized by her distraction.

Claire patted the pockets of her skirt, felt for the earrings on her lobes, the buttons on her shirt. Again, everything was exactly where it should be.

David's chair wobbled as he stood up and walked over to Claire and the camera. Her distraction had forced him to become stronger and he thought this was maybe a good thing. Before they had left for India they had argued. She had wanted him to become more assertive, less accommodating. But Claire was de-evolving the further into India they travelled, and to prevent a complete disintegration of her sensibilities David remained aloof. In particular, he wanted to avoid taking over Claire's film. A complete alteration in her character — though he had to admit that he had fantasized, in the past, about her becoming more agreeable — could be more damaging than good. "Let me see," he said and kneeled to look through the window at the cassette. "These only last thirty minutes, right?"

She nodded.

"And you brought sixty tapes with you?"

"Yes, about that much."

"You should be OK, then. Put another one in if you think this scene is going to have any cool cuts in it. You can always tape over it."

"Do you think?"

"For Christsakes, Claire! I don't know!"

Claire snapped her tongue indignantly, put in another tape and returned to her seat.

Charlotte returned a few moments later with an old wooden box. "Denzil, your grandfather," she began to speak as she dragged the screen door across its tracks, "had wanted to send these on to Alice's parents but I just couldn't bring myself to part with them." She shrugged and stretched her lips over her teeth. "Confessions of an old woman," she mumbled into the open box, then looked up and stared blankly at Claire. She began again, "When Denzil died and I moved out of the Yeravda House, I took these with me. I suppose in a way I was keeping them for you."

Charlotte pulled out a long braid of shiny, thick black hair. A beautiful blue comb dangled like an afterthought from the braid's bound end. "Here you go, dear," Charlotte coughed. "This belonged to Alice."

Claire took the rope of hair into her hands and tucked the comb back into the braid.

"She cut that off shortly after Rikki was born." Charlotte leaned back into her chair and began twirling her ring around her finger. She continued, "Alice had an envious head of hair. Everyone thought so. Denzil wanted to send the braid to her parents after she died but I thought what on earth would they want to do with a clump of hair?"

The hair was as shiny and clean as Claire's and the lapis comb was fanned like the feathers of a peacock. "The photographs in my father's study," Claire said. "I don't remember this comb in them."

Charlotte reached into the box with the long, elaborate flourish of a magician, and brought out a necklace of creamy white pearls. "These will look lovely on you, dear," she said.

Claire glanced over at David, who uncrossed his legs and leaned forward to look at the necklace.

"Put them on, Claire," David said.

"Really?"

"Sure, dear," said Charlotte. "They belong to you more than they belong to anyone else."

"That's just because everyone else is dead," Claire said. And it was true; save for her brother and her mother, there were no other living relatives of her father's, none that she knew of. She examined the clasp and reached behind her head to slide the hook into place.

Charlotte added, "At least now, no one will argue with you about who it belongs to."

The pearls rolled over Claire's scar like cool beads of water and she enjoyed her own elegance as she moved her head from side to side, straightening her back, dropping her shoulders. She felt as if her body was being stitched back together, finished as a spine, essential. The whites of her eyes were clear. She knew this by the way David smiled. He had a thing for the clarity of her eyes, and she liked those moments when she could take his words away.

Charlotte sat and stared at Claire. The old woman's thin lips trembled and her hands rolled over one another in her lap as if she were washing them; the pale yellow topaz ring clustered light on the leafy ceiling. "You get your eyes," Charlotte said, "from your grandfather. He always had such a startling glare."

Claire slid her fingers around the uncultured pearls and pressed their imperfect roundness against her skin. "My father. My father, as well."

Charlotte took note of how Alice's granddaughter fidgeted across from her. The young woman seemed as restless as a cat in heat, like Alice had been, yes, as restless as Alice had been that final evening before departing to Karachi.

Claire held her grandmother's braid of hair in one hand and the string of pearls in the fingers of her other hand. All her life, she had struggled over her father — his ambiguities; that impenetrable, fearful silence — but now the idea of Alice enchanted her. *These pearls belong to me*, she thought. *This Alice, this grandmother of mine will be the one part of my father that cannot be apportioned — she is the one luxury my father will not be able to deny me.*

After a few moments of silence, Charlotte turned toward David, "You are a handsome boy. You look Indian."

At first, David had politely explained his origins to anyone who'd asked him in India, but due to the enormous population he encountered daily with the same observation as Charlotte's, he quickly tired of it and reduced his response to a nod and a smile, "Yes, yes, I do — don't I?"

"Well, are you?" she insisted.

"I'm Canadian," David said. Charlotte twisted her lips and squinted at him. He rolled his eyes and said, "My father was Cree."

"Is that what they call you people in Canada? Cree, is it?" Charlotte put on her glasses and began to flip through some papers inside the wooden box.

"First Nations is more accurate," David said.

Charlotte stared at David above her glasses, "First Nations? A bit pretentious, don't you think?" Shaking her head from side to side, she held up a bundle of homemade paper wrapped together with a thin string and as she tugged one of the pieces of paper from the bundle, she glanced toward Claire and tilted her head back to get a better look. Claire's long slender arms and thin wrists were as if someone had cut and pasted parts of Alice onto her. Of course, there were other parts of Claire that did not resemble Alice. Claire was broader across her shoulders; she was taller and more solid. She was well fed — not fat, not fat at all, just more robust than Alice ever was. We have all been cleaved, thought Charlotte, parts of us Indian, parts of us British, and inside ourselves still remains this constant conflict, two breeds battling for position. "You look like Alice, you know," she said aloud. "You have her contradictions."

Claire cocked her head to the side and smiled.

"Your great-grandmother was Malayali, from a tribe in the south. Alice was the darkest of all of us."

"Are you an Anglo-Indian as well?" Claire asked.

"Yes, dear. Most of us Anglo-Indians left the country after independence — ended up in Australia, Britain, and some, like your father, came to your country, Canada. I tried Britain but it wasn't my country. After your father's older sister and brother passed away I moved back to Pune. Better for my arthritis."

She handed the bundle of papers over to Claire. Yellow light flickered across Charlotte's cheeks as her bejewelled fingers jiggled and danced in the air. "These were letters your grandfather wrote to your grandmother when they first met. I found them in your grandfather's desk after he died. He never stopped loving her, you know. Even after he took another wife."

Claire's hands were oily and she wiped them on her skirt before taking the bundle from Charlotte. A cat circled around her bare ankles, straightening its tail, pushing into her, insisting. Claire casually lifted the cat with her foot beneath its belly and flung it aside. It returned, flopping its back hips against her calf muscle; its low rumbling purr was becoming increasingly difficult to ignore.

Tiger Dreams Film Opening Sequence

Music. Drums.

Extreme long shot. People — a dozen or so — dressed in mourning, walk placidly across open grasslands. Pull focus as they approach a fresh mound of rich, dark soil. No headstone. Close-up. They place offerings. Pan to people walking back across open grasslands. Extreme long shot. People, barely recognizable, continue to walk. Black specks on the horizon. Fade.

Mise-en-scène. Charlotte takes another sip of tea and points at the letters. She speaks to me. I am out of the field of focus.

Charlotte: "Your grandparents grew up in Nainital, a hill station in the foothills of the Himalaya. Alice's father worked for the railways — an unusually prominent position for an Anglo at that time. He worked out of Lucknow, I think."

Me: "I thought they lived in Bangalore."

Charlotte: "That, I believe, was in their retirement."

Me: "Seems everybody worked the railways back then."

Charlotte: "The Anglos — most definitely." Charlotte wipes her hands across her skirt. Jump Cut. Music under. Archival Stills of Anglo-Indians in various occupations.

My Voice-over: "The British had this knack for assigning different religious groups for different kinds of occupations. It was their way of keeping the country weak and divided. Sikhs were in the military, Hindus were in trade, and the Anglo-Indians were given offices in the Government Post, the Railways and the Prisons."

Last Archival Still of prison guards. Repeat and flow into footage of prison guards corralling prisoners into formation. Unmatched full-colour shot of girl-child being prepared for marriage.

Music Under.

My Voice-over: "The mixing of British blue blood with the dark red of the Indian was simply beyond contempt for the Indian. The Indian of today will deny that there was any prejudice but in the end, when pushed to the wall, they preferred things to remain as they were, that the Indian remain with the Indian and the British remain with the British. The British have another story — of course. They had even encouraged the men in the East India Company to marry the Indian — to integrate with the locals. Hindu girls of twelve and thirteen were married off to the British. They gave up their names for Christian ones and never saw their families again. The East India Company had promised these British merchants employment for their sons but when times got difficult in Mother England, those jobs were given to the sons of purebloods. So the Anglos eventually lost any status promised them and were stuck somewhere in the middle to create their own world."

Archival Stills of preadolescent Indian brides.

Something Missing, Continued

Beneath the arbour, slashes of sunlight on her jaw and cheekbone, Charlotte continued, "We were never really accepted as British and we were most certainly shunned as Indians. The Indian blood came from your great-great-grandparents; goodness knows how far your family goes back in this country, perhaps as far back as the Portuguese arrival on the west coast. That's how far my family goes back. In fact, I believe your grandfather Denzil, my cousin, had some Portuguese blood in him as well. Anyway." Charlotte snapped the word "anyway" like one of those social ticks used to punctuate pauses or moments of uncertainty.

In the silence, Claire's eyes widened. "Please, Ms. Blake," she said aloud, "you must go on." She said this with some urgency.

Her father had completely left all of India behind him; he had dropped his accent, burned his hankies, and aside from the rare occasion when he cooked curried eggs, there was little evidence of India left in him. It wasn't until her father had died that Claire even considered that he belonged to some history other than the one he had created for himself in Canada. He had spoken of his parents once or twice in the thirty-seven years she had known him, but his recollections were always shadowy and full of sadness and they often ended as abruptly as they began.

In the terraced garden of Charlotte Blake's home, time slowed and converged for Claire. She realized that all her memories of her father had been made from wish rather than truth, and in the year since his death she had conjured stories, lies really, of shared intimacies and mutual respect, claiming to have had a father who perhaps had indulged her, even overprotected her, but was deeply involved with her life. Her father's death had stretched and deformed her, made her seem distant from the person she thought she would be, and more complicated than she had hoped. She had become uncomfortable in her own skin and she carried her confusion like a blister, wincing from the pain.

He had been generous with his genes, there was no question about that, but he hadn't had the courtesy to share his losses — that of his mother, father, brother, sister — all of them young, all of them dead. He'd withheld evidence from her, omitted crucial details. Call it fear. Call it guilt. But now she sat with his history in her lap, stealing his story for her own. He could no longer deny her this part of himself.

Charlotte's voice became audible again as Claire tilted her head and swallowed, feigning deep thought. "I must say," Charlotte continued, her attention focused on David, "there were, indeed, advantages to our social condition, though at the time it was sometimes difficult to rise above the prejudice." She glanced toward Claire and back at David. "Anyway. Would you like some more tea?"

"Yes, thank you, that'd be great." David kicked Claire beneath the table.

Claire flinched. "Yes, that would be lovely, thank you."

While Claire fumbled with her grandfather's letters, Charlotte placed her empty cup and saucer on the central table. "I was a distant cousin to Denzil. After much controversy in my own hometown of Calcutta, I was sent to Denzil and Alice." She stopped and looked around the room. "Do you really want to hear this?"

"Please. This is why we are here."

Charlotte smiled, leaned back into her chair and adjusted the folds of her skirt, smoothing the fabric in long gentle kneading motions. "My family had been embarrassed by my inappropriate affair with a married naval engineer. They begged Alice and Denzil to take me off their hands. Pune is a fair distance from Calcutta, you see, and my mother, I'm sure, was relieved that they accepted. Martha, that was my older sister, was having severe bouts of depression, a 'general malaise' we used to call it. She drank and carried on like a whore and my mother blamed her behaviour on my affair. So, Mother bought me a one-way train ticket to Pune."

Charlotte stood up slowly and grabbed the back of her chair. She spoke with the wisdom and authority of someone who had already left her life, offering up her crimes to Claire as a relief to her crippling cataplexy. She massaged her hip, and swung it back and forth like the trunk of an elephant, her foot scuffing the floor, swish, swish, swish. "Jonathan was dashing, efficient and powerful and I thought he'd be just the sort of man to rescue me from idleness. But he was married to an equally powerful woman, and when the affair became known, his wife set out to destroy my family."

Charlotte, noticing Claire's distraction with the letters, bent over the table and righted her teacup, tipped over from its shaky descent. Then she leaned dramatically forward to oust her body from the room. "Come, young man, and help me with the stove. We'll give Claire some time to read through some of those letters while you regale me with stories of the exploits of your people."

David jumped up and circled around the table. Claire felt his big hand slide across her shoulder as he passed behind her; she tilted her head back and smiled up at him. She could hear the whir and click of the camera in the corner and the sliding screen door open and close as she shuffled her grandfather's letters in her lap. She had written many letters to her own father: on the insides of cereal boxes, the backs of programs, or around the daisy of a napkin. He had told her that he was saving those letters so he could hand them over to her teenage daughter, if and when such a beast should present itself. He had looked upon old age as revenge, and had filed her letters under Child 2.0 for future use. Those were only half the letters she had ever written him; the other half she kept in her own file labelled Father 1.0, thinking someday she might be able to threaten him with all the confidences they had never shared. Such were the complications of love for Claire and her father — his brooding intensity around her carefully crafted rebellion — and though her relationship with David was well established, she could still feel the waves of panic when she thought she might not know any other way of loving a man than the way she loved her father, the way she responded with only defiance and sedition.

She felt for her earrings again, touched each button of her blouse, fingered the pearls and the flimsy clasp at the nape of her neck. Something *was* missing. But what could it possibly be?

She opened the first of the letters. Their papers were flecked with parts of flowers and though the ink had been carefully applied and the pressure of the tip of his pen was obviously sensitive, the ribs of irregularity had caused her grandfather's handwriting to skip and waver, rendering his words almost indecipherable. She stilled herself long enough to imagine their life as a prelude to her, to her father, and in the thin branches of veins at her wrists she could feel heat like a story moving through her. She was fugitive. Migrant.

Tiger Dreams Film Opening Sequence

Sound FX. Chuffing of train.

Music Under. Close-up shot of young woman's face through dusty glass of
     train window. Deep focus on the reflection. Landscape of Rajhastan —
     west of Jaipur. Sitting next to woman and pulled into focus is a man
     in a topi. He is reading. Costumes — early twentieth century — fresh
     linens. Jump Cut. Woman's POV. Train and landscape.

Rajasthan 1917

When Alice Spencer was seventeen years old, she and Denzil married and moved away from their childhood home of Nainital. Denzil took a position with the Indian Civil Service in Lucknow while Alice continued her studies in archaeology.

In 1917, Alice was twenty-three and had been married for six years. She had continued to pursue archaeology and rather than return to Nainital for vacation that year, Alice convinced Denzil that the desert might be an excellent venue in which to conceive their first child. While the Decca revealed human remains and the coastal tides revealed dwellings, it was the desert that churned up the treasures of her most recent occupation.

They could suffer the hot for one season on the plains of Lucknow, and both enjoy the moderate climate of the desert in the wet season. "You can drink your gimlet in the shade," she said one evening.

"Whisky sour?" Denzil requested and then found himself on a train from Lucknow to Delhi and then to Jaipur.

The desert was a dangerous place. The hillsides hid tiger and elephant, hawks circled above rotting carcasses of camels and goats, snakes hunted scorpions, and mongoose hunted snakes. There was also evidence of human battle everywhere and below the fortresses, heavy with cannons, gunshots the size of eyeballs littered the ancient battlefields. Magazines were still stuffed full of muskets and gunpowder, spears and kangars.

The lofty fortresses of the last Rajputs contained within them coloured-glass murals — blue, green and red — inlaid to plaster. There were white marbled waterfalls, green and pink mosaic-tiled archways, and blue iridescent glass chandeliers. Marble shutters, tarnished by the fingers of women in Purdah, cast filigreed sunlight into narrow hallways. In this desert of capricious architecture, the source of all colours could be found in the olive green leaves, the pink sands, the red ochre cliffs, or the lime green of algal bloom on the oases.

"I have developed a sixth sense for treasure hunting," Alice told Denzil as she held a chip of blue glass into the sun and then held it against his eyes. "You see, Denzil, they take on their own special hue in order to be found."

In the desert, the sky was dusty blue and the curved horizon a milky white, but when the sun set and the moon appeared, the colours deepened to a thick black and the stars appeared even closer than they ever did in the foothills of Nainital.

They discussed, at length, the relative position of time. Did it have a fulcrum? A centre point? Did time terminate? Was there a culminating position? And Denzil read aloud, "Six respirations equal one vinadika, sixty vinadikas equal one dhata, sixty dhatas equal one day and one night."

"I thought there was no such thing as time in the centre of the sphere," Alice said as she strained her neck to see the constellations.

"We must be in the centre of the sphere right now."

"Isn't it true that we find our way by the altitude of the stars?" Alice asked.

"Thousands of miles from here, the star's declination would

be no different. If earth is at the centre, our measurement better be pretty damned accurate — that is, if we are going to use the stars to find our way home. I think a compass would suffice."

"On this wonderful evening, I never want to find my way home," Alice moaned. She was emerging into a world of great unrest, where the Anglo-Indian woman was at once expected to uphold traditional Christian values, protest the oppression of the Indian, and protect the world order of the British Empire. With Annie Besant in prison for her suffragist movement in Ireland, Gandhi practising satyagraha — his non-violent, passive resistance — in South Africa, and the outbreak of the first world war in Europe, Alice felt herself hyphenating, splitting into two. Her Indian roots were being diluted and her British heritage was becoming a great source of shame. India no longer seemed to be her country. Or perhaps, she thought, she was just waking up to the fact that it never had been.

Even though she was a careful observer of British law and custom, she continually battled the stodgy perceptions of the British. Still, Alice created her own rules.

After making a pass at Alice, a British officer told Denzil, "Vaishnivites, they are called, and I have heard that they travel in groups of twos and threes and offer their services for a meal or two."

"Perhaps there are women of such ilk but, I warn you, Alice is nothing of the sort and I won't protect you from my wife the next time you attempt to seduce her."

"Your wife?" the young officer had responded. "I beg your pardon, sir, but I thought ... I didn't think that sort of thing still went on between the British and the Indian."

Denzil never enlightened the officer about his own Anglo-Indian heritage and carefully omitted the young man from any further invitation to garden parties or tennis matches. It was clear to both Alice and Denzil that the laws of the British had not been created with the Anglo-Indian in mind. For a woman of Alice's ambitions, though, this had its advantages. She was able to occupy a space only imagined by British and Indian women, a space which — due to decorum — those of purer racial origins were prevented from exploring.

For his part, Denzil had quickly accepted his administrative position in the prison at Lucknow. He had soon discovered that there were breakdowns in the prison system all over India. To his amazement, and dismay, most of the ineptitude had come from the top and was trickling down. In his naïveté, he had thought that men in positions of power achieved those positions because of their brilliance; instead he discovered a rash of nepotism and incompetence in the ruling class. Though Denzil was considered amongst his colleagues to be a brilliant man, at work he had an arrogant and disagreeable nature. Consequently, strategic positions of power slipped away from him and he was passed over in favour of less able men of more amicable characters.

Position and bearings were crucial to Denzil though, and he was always conscious of the distance from which he came and the distance he needed to go. But with India in transition, he, like Alice, was becoming disoriented. The map of India was changing so rapidly Denzil was finding it difficult to locate himself in the political landscape. Where was the seat of power? Calcutta? Lucknow? Bangalore?

With his passion for accuracy, in the desert of Jaipur he measured his own zenith, hoping that somehow — and he knew this to be somewhat foolhardy — everything from that point onward would appear in predictable and reliable patterns.

"Let's not forget," Denzil said one evening in the desert, "let's not forget that the stars are in a constant state of collapsing." He sipped his gimlet and his cheeks spasmed from the sour lime.

"I thought they were expanding, burning out?" Alice asked.

Alice, thin as a curve, ripe as a fig, haughty as all hell, was everything Denzil had ever asked for in his life. She was emphatic, infuriating, restless and wild. He adored the controversy of her.

"It's not that I blame you," she joked with him. "But don't you find it particularly fascinating that amongst all this rebellion, the war in Europe, the Russian revolution, the Home Rule movement here, women are still without a voice? I think that, at least, our Mister Gandhi is addressing some of those issues."

"I should think I'd like to be in your position, organizing the servants, throwing parties, occupying oneself with the whimsy of ancient civilization. I'd say you've done all right by us men, and by the way, your Mister Gandhi took a child bride at thirteen, so don't give me all that suffragist banter you believe your Gandhi is so behind. He's just like all the rest when it comes to women, Alice."

"He has quite a following, Denzil. Women, all over, are talking about his reforms and what they mean for us."

"Us?"

"Women."

"I'm skeptical."

Alice sipped her drink and lay back on her cot, considering the peripheral. "By the way, darling," she said, "I'm carrying your child."

PART TWO

The First Signs

Tiger Dreams Film Part I Sequence

Music. Tabla.

Long shot circumnavigating the lime-green waters of Naini Lake. The hanging lake appears to be suspended above a scrim of clouds. Pine trees billow like green mushrooms above the silver wisps of cloud. Pull focus on the forests of oak and deodar. Pan the north side of the lake. Jump cut to south side.

My Voice-over: Here the rules of partial existence for the Anglo-Indian became a distant burden, the borders between people were temporarily forgotten on the plains of India far below. Nainital, a hill-station built by the Anglo-Indians during the middle of the 19th Century, borders the lake. Along the north side are the hotels, shops and hospital. Along the south side and perched on top of a steep escarpment are the schools and summer homes of its inhabitants.

Tracking shot of side streets.

Sound FX. Horse hooves on cobblestone.

Medium shot. The wide, shallow stairs to All Saints College. Tracking shot of walking into the front entrance and down the pillared outdoor corridor.

My Voice-over: The Anglo-Indians had built All Saints in the latter part of the 19th Century — it had been a way for the Christian missionaries to evangelize.

Medium shot of Chapel.

My Voice-over: Their thinking was that the Anglo-Indian was an ideal way to get at the Indian's religious sensibilities. Pause.

Medium shot of Classrooms.

My Voice-over: Regardless of the political motives of the colonists, the school provided an excellent English education for Anglo-Indian girl children.

Medium long shot of dormitory.

My Voice-over: My grandmother was one of these children.

Tracking Shot. Schoolgirls, in uniform, walk into and out of frame. Jump cut to lawn in front of All Saints entrance. Medium long shot of Sister Gwendolyn and myself deep in conversation. Medium shot of women sitting on stone steps. I help Sister Gwendolyn to sit. Close-up of Sister Gwendolyn's face. She is speaking.

Sister Gwendolyn: Yes, I do remember Alice. Not so much the young man she married, but Alice? Oh, she was a potent force.

Claire and David, One Year Earlier

Claire stopped by the liquor store and then the bakery next door and then Ronnie's Food Mart for black licorice and red hots on the way back to the apartment she shared with David. She walked up the four flights of stairs to their modest apartment. The building had the oranged look of seventies decor about it; mildew and nicotine stains mottled the walls in ascending and descending patterns and the carpet — a brown shag — was rubbed raw along the bull nose of the stairs and always tripped her as she entered the hallway from the fire escape. She opened the door of their apartment, walked into the room and placed the wine and bread on the coffee table before David. He was fast asleep on the couch. She kneeled beside him, quietly observing the deepening lines on his forehead as she worked her tongue over the remnants of licorice in her teeth. His glasses rested lightly on the tip of his nose. The book he read splayed open across his chest; its spine was bent awkwardly and ached to be closed. She placed the receipt from the wine in between the pages, rested the book comfortably on the table and removed his glasses. Her hands were cold, and when she slipped them onto his smooth warm skin beneath his T- shirt, David shivered and jolted awake. "I got the funding to make my film," she whispered. "You can make love to me."

She had come to David before, translucent-winged, a dragonfly in moonlight. She had crawled through his bedroom window or appeared before him in the shower; she'd begged him for some sort of confirmation that she was, indeed, a woman. He would fold her arms like wings into her sides and wash the dust carefully from her skin, whispering to her or maybe to himself, "Woman, woman," as if he too was convincing himself. He would beg her to stay; and she would, at least until her heart settled, and then she would sleep and wake and love him some more. All this, until the weather changed.

And now the sun was already forgetting them as they made love on an October night. She could feel him deep inside her, subtle and comfortable, all her emptiness swelling to meet his fullness, and she implored him to stop, to stop loving her so much. She lay beneath him with the weight of his body absent of fluid, the smell of lemon groves and their suffocating greediness for night air collapsing around her. She was sated. Citric.

Later, they drank her wine and ate her bread while Claire told David about her project. She knew very little about her grandfather, only what she had overheard from conversations on evenings when she and her brother, Ben, sat at the top of the stairs and listened to their father tell their mother stories of his adventures — the Six Day War in the Middle East, snakes and pestilence in the Amazon, boarding school in the U.K. Every so often, when enough Scotch had been consumed, her father would stand in front of the fireplace warming his hands and touch briefly upon his memories of India.

"Gandhi's jailer, imagine that," Claire said. "It's a story already made, a film already documented, the jailer and the prisoner, the liar and the soothsayer, the blinded and the sighted."

Claire revelled in the thought that her grandfather was notorious, and though her father had spent his life forgetting India, she would spend her life trying to remember it. She attached herself to the history of her father, believing that somewhere in his past were the indelible influences that would explain his struggle to love her.

"I won't apologize for my ideology," she told David as she explained her idea for the film. She was attempting to draw parallels between the current Native Land Claims issues in Canada and the Home Rule Movement of the 1930s in India. She had known the National Film Board would favour the project, and although she hadn't discussed it with David yet, she had used his name as the editor and assistant director. It wasn't unusual on grant applications to push a few edges, to suspend the plausibility of cash flows, to draw information from lofty sources. Using David's name hardly felt like cheating. After all, she was sleeping with the guy and the Board could hardly argue that fact. And he was one of the best editors in the business. People had found him arrogant and uncompromising, but everybody — it didn't matter how repugnant they found his methods — agreed his product was always clean and precise. He insisted on shaving surplus material from anybody's work regardless of how beautiful the image or how strong the metaphor. His work was seamless. Still, she hoped he'd permit in her work the oppositional style she preferred — unmatched shots, asynchronous sound — the kind of film work that drew attention to itself.

Not only did David have a good name in the business, but David also had Treaty Status, and money for the project was far more accessible to him than to Claire. And Claire was an opportunist by necessity. "We could use one movement to emphasize the importance of the other," she said to David, explaining the connection between Home Rule and Land Claims. It would be more of an editing job than anything else. "And that's where you come in. Simple concept really. Different nations, different peoples, European imperialism. Lots of cuts back and forth between archival shots and a smooth transition into some current footage of the prison in Yeravda."

David sipped his wine and raised his eyebrows over the rim of his glass. "Is that so?" he asked, then picked up a magazine and began leafing through its pages.

It had never taken much to send Claire into a tailspin of self-doubt. Suddenly she realized that David's opinion still mattered too much. He had, in the past, found Claire to be too organic in her process and he'd struggled to make sense of her storyboards and reality sequences. She wanted to believe they had grown since then, that their egos could cope with each other's style, but David's fondling of the magazine pages, his distraction, infused her with doubt and infuriated her. She thought it best to leave the subject until later.

David looked up from the magazine and watched her face fall with disappointment. He was undeniably relieved that she had dropped the subject. His enthusiasm could not match hers, not right now, and he could see her hardening to protect herself. A scrim covered her eyes and she spoke coolly, "Remember those coins I received a couple of months ago from Charlotte Blake?"

"Yeah?" he nodded.

In a letter accompanying the coins, Charlotte Blake expressed condolences for the loss of her father. Claire had written back to Charlotte, asking her about her grandfather. "I got a letter from her today. She invited me to go over there."

"Over where?" David asked.

"To Pune. Pune, India."

Claire brought out a tattered green cloth bundle that she had been carrying in her backpack for the last couple of months. The cloth was wrapped around a pile of cards. Each card contained a single coin. Thin paper had stuck to the faces of the coins. It had crumbled like pastry in her hand as she plucked her favourite one from its casement. David slid down onto his back and stared at the ceiling while Claire laid her head on his belly and played with the coin. It was the size of a dime and felt cool to the touch as she placed it on her eyelid, "This one's my favourite." She lay in the dark beneath the coin, listening to David's breath deepening. "David?"

David had fallen asleep with his chin tucked into his chest. He snored lightly. Claire rose quietly from his belly and covered him with a blanket. He was a big man, well over six feet tall, broad shouldered and slim hipped, and he had put some weight on since they'd met over a decade ago. He was solid, though. "That boy's got both feet on the ground," her father had offered when she first brought him home. "You need someone to help you level out a bit," he told her. "You've got too many peaks and valleys in your life." Her father liked to remind her of her inconstancy, of the January depressions and the June highs, the collect phone calls from obscure townships and the long silences. Like her father, she was grateful for David; his conservative prairie-boy mentality was a correction to all her wildness.

She kissed his forehead, rose to her feet and started toward the shower.

But waves of confusion were gathering in her head. Like an electrical storm, the arcing synapses were forcing her body to the floor. She knew this part. She was losing consciousness. Losing. And in this foreign landscape where everything seemed liquid she could hear the disembodied moan of a solitary voice.

Welcome,

I am Nur Jahan: It took me six years to build this tomb for my father. Pietra Dura, the i and e are independent. I took the idea from the Italians. On the walls outside here, most of the designs are geometric, but come, come inside. Here, the jeweller has fashioned images of ewers. You can see vases, and creepers, grapes and trees. Notice the inlay of jasper and cornelian; even some topaz and onyx have been cut into the smooth surface of white marble. I brought the marble in from the hills just west of here.

Six years. That's how long it takes to lose a father.

Claire's lips tingled and she felt the coolness of the floor on her cheek. The room began to take on a familiar hue as she slowly raised herself onto her elbows, leaned against the wall and gazed at someone's arm across the room. Time had passed and she felt as if her body had aged. Her hips ached and her knees and ankles clicked as she straightened them.

I am Nur Jahan. I am a voice so finely composed you can hear it like a heartbeat in a poem. If you try to get back here, you will have to re-enter your own death.

Claire's nose twitched from an awful smell.

That odour of sulphur and soot will always remain on your fingers.

She began to methodically reconnect all the parts of her life that had dropped away in her absence: the lamp she'd bought at an auction, the tattered couch she wanted to throw out, her piano with the chipped keys, books on the shelf she was going to read some day, *The Raw and the Cooked*, a biography of St. Exupéry, *Philosophies of India*, the Bible and a couple dozen more titles she couldn't make out from across the room. She struggled to remember her lover's name but found only a vague recollection in its place. She wanted to fill those lapses of memory with something, anything, a fiction or a falsity, something to fool herself with the promise of completion. She did, however, eventually recognize her own scent.

Yes, scent can be the most powerful memory at any elevation.

As she pulled herself up and along the wall and slowly felt her way toward the bathroom door, familiarity began to assert itself. For a few agonising moments, Claire could not negotiate the door-knob, she could not understand its function and she began to panic as she ran her fingers along the doorjamb searching for a way to get through to herself on the other side. Smelling herself with every movement, she felt the wetness between her thighs of — David, yes, David was his name. Thank God, she thought, as she began to feel real again. She calmly placed her hand on the knob, as she had done a thousand times before, turned it and stepped into the room.

Objects and their purpose were familiar to her now as she turned on the taps of the shower and slipped into the clawfoot tub. She pressed her face into the stream of water from the showerhead and let the water take parts of her away. To wash away her own scent as an animal does by rolling in death, she vigorously rubbed her hands over a bar of soap and covered her entire body with suds.

You do not want to be traced back to your life, but now that I am here I plan to stay.

David stuck his hand through the opening of the shower curtain and touched her breast. His hand fit perfectly and she was grateful for the contact.

"Are you coming in?" she asked to be polite, but in truth wanted more time to collect herself.

"No — you go ahead, I'll have mine later. Can I make you some tea?"

"That would be lovely. I'll be out in a moment."

The pipes cramped when she shut off the water and she thought about the way the weakened walls of an artery balloons before bursting and how her father's body, a building, was simply worn down by the abuse of its tenant. The blood had ripped through his cortex like a spring flood, a rush she felt every time she awakened. She wondered if in her father's death, he thought he was waking from sleep.

She stepped from the shower and began to towel herself off. David had returned and was standing in the doorway staring at her through the steam.

"What is it?" she asked.

His eyes were the colour of sea green glass and she was pleased with the way he looked at her, the way he sometimes couldn't speak. Until she had met him, she had felt too obvious — lovers always knowing more about her than she did, always playing smart with her — but with David, he didn't know all of her, and it seemed he didn't want to.

"Nothing," he said.

He shook his head and walked away. It seemed he was satisfied with the mysteries of her nature, and in his gentleness he unwittingly permitted Claire to reveal herself.

The following morning, Claire sat on her couch sipping coffee while she listened to the gathering speed of the day. David had already left for work. It was cold outside and only a matter of days before the snow would arrive. Frost, cold enough to rip a warm tongue of its flesh, dusted the spindles on their balcony railing. The grey sky held hostage the bony white branches of the poplar trees and the crackle of leaves on the lawn below was inside her, the brittle cold already on her nose. Steam from her coffee spread on the window as diffuse as the thoughts in her mind and she concerned herself with what had happened the night before. Like hiccups in time, her seizures — that voice — were increasing in frequency and duration.

The distance you travel during your absence, though, is ambitious.
"Your voice is as smooth as polished stone," Claire said aloud.
Colours will become more vivid, yellows and greens and blues will appear in formal, geometric patterns.
"They already are."

She dressed, brushed her teeth, braided her hair and threw on one of David's sweaters, grabbed a scarf, left the apartment, and walked the ten blocks to catch a direct bus to the university library. Cold air burned her nostrils. Leafless trees lined the streets. Sitting on the bus she wrote in her daily calendar: *call Mom re: Sunday, pick up loan application, phone for doctor's appointment.* She stared into the reflections in the bus window and wondered if the old woman sitting across from her knew that Claire was losing her mind.

As the bus moved out of the downtown core, across the bridge and turned left along Kensington, she thought how Calgary was really beginning to know itself, how it was becoming more metropolitan. Saturday's *Globe and Mail* or the *National Post*, a latte and a poppy seed brioche — these things had pretty much made her return from the mountains make sense. Most of all, she had returned because of David, because he had no interest in leaving the foothills and she had no interest in living without him.

The bus turned right and climbed onto the high banks of the river gorge. As with any place Claire had lived, she was okay as long as she could escape, and this city was easy to escape. One main artery connected Claire to a wildness in the landscape she had come to know intimately, the pure angles of mountains — their striations. There were forests that crawled up mountainsides and harboured the wildcats of her dreams. And though she had left simple fear behind with fairytales and ghost stories, she had cultivated a more earthly, bodily fear of landscape and beast, a kind of erotic fantasy she permitted herself.

On the highest point of land in the city, the university parking lots weathered some of the fiercest cold snaps of prairie winters. The university was perched on a plateau of ice and snow; "Siberia," she liked to call it. "Only the strong survive."

Claire got off the bus and dashed across the campus to the library. She and her father had spent their Saturday afternoons together in the libraries and bookstores all around the city. This library contained the articles and papers her father had written in the early years of oil exploration on the prairies. Claire shared his enthusiasm for maps and had worked tirelessly with him, stretching thin black tape along the contours of his suspicions.

Her father had observed the Pleistocene era as other men did religion. He had built models of the collision of plates and spoke eloquently about the glacial speed of deposition. He had drawn maps of his dreams, conjectures, speculations. Areas of the earth came into existence for Claire because she believed her father had invented them. "Quivera," he would tell her, "is the world we don't know yet." From him, she came to understand the creation of reality. And when she expressed a curiosity for rock, he drew circles around her, as if he knew someone, someday, would drill right through her.

Claire closed her eyes and attempted to recall an image of her father, but his face was as grainy as a poorly exposed photograph:

a collage of fractured memories bit the edges of his brow, the sides
of his jawline.

*You don't think much of it now and your father has been dead for
only a few months, but you'll realize later how quickly impressions
fade, how memory is not the simple truth. You'll have wished you had
taken the time to build a memory of him.*

She ran down the stairs into the basement of the library,
plucked the canisters Joan had left out on the counter for her
and locked herself in the small screening room. Joan, the archive
librarian, had already lined up some film clips from their meagre
collection and had called both Winnipeg and Toronto for more.
Claire had started an extensive reading list that both overwhelmed and intimidated her. She had already plodded through
histories and philosophies with dictionary in hand, pencilling
question marks in the margins and underlining interesting and
sometimes irrelevant material.

In the small screening room, she began to flip through the
collection of newsreel. Claire had hoped for a shot of Gandhi
standing waist deep in the ocean making salt, or shots of the
arrest and internment. Instead, she sat all afternoon in the dark
room viewing newsreels of famines, agricultural stations on the
Decca, and water projects in Rajasthan. The newsreels had some
interesting constructions — mostly traditional documentary
style, cinema verité with predictable transitions. She fell asleep
just as engineers installed a central pumping station in a village
near the border of Pakistan and she woke much later to the flicking of film around a finished reel. Bleary-eyed and uninspired,
Claire rewound the film, placed it back into the canister and
returned it along with the others to Joan at the front desk.

"How did that go, Claire?" Joan asked. Claire confessed that it wasn't going all that well. Maybe they could approach the whole thing from the other direction, maybe Joan could find some material on Land Claims? Joan thought there had been some UN footage of an Aboriginal conference a couple of years before. Perhaps there might be something useful in there?

Joan was a plump and able woman. She had a vigorous head of red hair, pencilled eyebrows and short straight eyelashes. She had been working in the archives for well over twenty years, and in many ways she had become the library. Her plaid skirts resembled bookshelves and her mole-eyes squinted out from her doughy cheeks like one of Beatrix Potter's rodent intellectuals. With an efficiency that came from years of repetition, she plucked the films from the countertop and returned them to the shelves in the back. Looking over the top of her reading glasses with a maternal smile, she said, "Don't worry, dear. You've got to start somewhere."

What had seemed absolutely clear to Claire when she was putting together her documentary proposal now seemed insincere. In both countries, India and Canada, land had been divided, burned, and fractured; it had been fenced and bordered. Those who owned land had the power, and by their systematic dispersion of property the British had successfully weakened the Indian opposition. Were land and power inseparable?

Claire tried to draw parallels between ownership and stewardship. She was reminded of her own fragile rootedness, of why her father's unequal division of his estate between Ben and her had severed her so dramatically. Had she appeared so fickle to him, so unconnected that perhaps she didn't belong? Was her father, by his final actions, attempting to weaken the bond between herself and her brother, to somehow reenact his own amputation from his family? From India? Or did he simply think her incapable of responsibility? Maybe he knew something of her transitory state, the seasonal rhythm of her engagement with life? Or was his reasoning so banal and ridiculous that he'd assumed the land should be bestowed upon the son and not the daughter? Surely they had come further than that.

Claire wanted her own piece of land, her own country. Not to be colonized and patronized by the well-meaning assumptions of a father. By his act — of ignorance, of control, of thoughtlessness, of malice? — he had caused her to believe their love was false. She wanted to leave the room.

Nur:
We push up through   grains
of
sand   women without men
without language

Deaf to the crack of a whip

We begged our fathers not to sell us
We begged our husbands not to lie with us
We begged our sons not to ignore us

While we lay beaten and lifeless the cow refused to give
*   the men milk*

our beauty thrashed out of us   our gold removed
*   from our wrists*
the cow and the calf
refused to eat

the men
they went hungry

We begged the tiger to take us

"Claire?" Joan coughed.

With an overwhelming sense of defeat, Claire grabbed the railing of the stairwell and turned to look back at Joan, who in the distance seemed to blend in with the shelves of canisters behind her. "Yes?" she answered.

"He was very proud of you, you know?"

Joan had attended her father's memorial, had wept profusely in the back bleachers of the hall, and had hung around at the family home long after everyone else had left. Her mother said later, when Claire mentioned Joan's distress, that Joan was mourning not just for Claire's father but for all that she had lost in her life. "Why would anyone want to go back to that despair?" Claire had asked her mother. "Because," her mother had said, "it is sometimes the only thing that makes us feel human."

Joan repeated, "He was, you know? Very proud, very proud."

"He had a really weird way of showing it," Claire said.

"He was always so kind to me."

"Yes, he was, wasn't he?" and Claire turned to leave.

It was like being the last one to know. Her father's colleagues had gone out of their way to offer her the same information, touching her on the elbow at her father's memorial, writing notes to her, sending snapshots with one line, *He was very proud of you*, as if they knew he had never shared his admiration with her.

Instead, she and her father had fought, and she wondered if the moments in his office when he seemed agitated with her were the times when he was trying to say he loved her. "What kind of father do you want me to be?" He had knelt before her on one of those occasions, the room in shambles from her throwing his office at him. "What kind of father do you want me to be?" And he had wept before her on his knees, clutching the folds of her skirt while she accused him of his infidelity, of loving other women, other women than herself and her mother. She wanted to change the way he loved others, the way he fathered her, the way he husbanded her mother. She boycotted him; she ignored his phone messages and remained silent when he questioned her about her politics. But her rejection of him only made him less capable as a father and more furious.

Gandhi had written that violence came from incompleteness and Claire had come to understand that the rage within her and her father stemmed from the fact that they were both half-baked and quarter-mooned, that they mirrored each other's deficiencies with the agility of mimes.

Oh, how we long for freedom from our father's yoke. We will not be crushed by the squeeze of our father's circumference.

Claire turned back and walked toward Joan; the light in the library was dimmed by the grey carpet and low ceiling. "My grandfather was Gandhi's jailer," she said, as if this infamy might tarnish Joan's memory of her father.

"Goodness me," said Joan. "Isn't that something? Well. Goodness me, that really is something," she repeated to herself.

"Yes, that is something, isn't it?"

Joan reached across the counter and pulled aside the strand of Claire's hair that fell in front of her eyes. "Well, dear," she said, "we can't be responsible for the actions of our ancestors. You'll just have to go and see for yourself, then, won't you? Have you ever been?"

"Been where?"

"To India. Have you ever been?"

"No. No, I've never been."

But Claire had been to India a million times in her imagination. She had travelled there in her childhood when her father had read to her again and again the story of "Rikki-Tikki-Tavi." Along with the thrill of the knowledge that her father was from an exotic land, she made up stories of his jungle adventures and his noble fights against the oppressive British rulers. Her father ate burnt toast, and butter dipped in sugar. He ate tablespoons of marmite, and sweetened condensed milk on buttered bread, and Claire had always imagined that these habits were the hangovers from his life during the Raj.

In your dreams and visions, you come up through grains of red sand, squinting into the glare of the white Indian sun. It will be as if you never left.

Until this moment, her curiosity for India had had more to do with the absences and shadows of her consciousness than with her father's birthplace. She tugged at the India of her mind, of her father's childhood, her grandfather's home, and like a reluctant animal, the story of India resisted, gave her no clues, surrendered no secrets. It was a peopled landscape in her mind, it swarmed with the bodies of a billion like her father; they were all so thin she could see their hearts beat through their ribs.

She left the archives and stopped at the telephone in the lobby to call her mother and then her doctor. She left the building, ran across the campus and caught the bus back downtown.

Tiger Dreams Film, Flashforward: Part II Sequence

Mise-en-scène. Shots busy with people. The train station in Pune. A side street in Delhi. The Fish Market in Mumbai.

Pune: The Early Years

Alice was not fond of infants and it was not until the children began to chatter in primordial English, walk around on two feet, and impress themselves on Alice with their own enthusiasms and curiosities that she became inspired by motherhood. Those early years were tedious for her and she found herself more often than she cared to admit standing in the middle of the garden pushing her cuticles back and gazing into the space around her.

The year Barbara was born, 1918, they had relocated during the hot to Pune and to the prison at Yeravda, which, just as Denzil had suspected, was a haphazard affair. Young boys arrested for petty theft were housed with middle-aged murderers; European offenders were thrown in with local tax evaders. It was a breeding ground for filth and pestilence, with no facilities for daily ablutions, no baths, and no system in place for feeding the men.

In one year Denzil cleaned up the grounds, separated the prisoners into categories based on the level of offence, set the young boys up with educational programs and assigned prisoners to various upkeep tasks.

Barbara, their first-born, had begun to announce herself to the world and Denzil and Alice took great pleasure in the engaging and often dramatic displays of her personality. Denzil taught her the alphabet forwards and backwards, "zyxwvutsrqp ...," while Alice sang nursery rhymes and showed her daughter simple tunes on the piano. In the evenings, while their daughter danced and played with the chuprassi's children behind the kitchen, Denzil and Alice walked the periphery of the garden searching the grasses and deadfall with their feet for the deadly Karait, a snake that had poisoned one of the servant's children the previous year.

When George was born, Denzil whisked him out of Alice's arms and returned him only when it was time to be fed. Later on, Denzil sang and played guitar while Alice and the children invented verses. As George followed his father around the gardens, Barbara and Alice enjoyed the pond, building paper boats and floating them with sails and sticks from one end to the other.

"I met your father in a sailboat," Alice told Barbara.

"Father sailed boats?"

"Oh, just little sloops on Naini Lake. He and your Uncle Richard always won the regatta."

"I think I should like to see Uncle again."

"I was sixteen and pretty cheeky and your father, well, he was so exotic to me."

"I'd like to see Aunt Estelle and my cousins, as well."

"The week before the regatta your Aunt Estelle and I had climbed up Tiger's Ridge to catch a glimpse of the Himalayas before they clouded over."

"I should like to see the Himalayas, Amma."

"You will some day."

Barbara's boat began to take on water. Alice guided the paper craft to the edge of the pond with a stick. She lifted and placed it on a stone to dry in the sun.

"We had to rise very early that morning and when we arrived the light had oozed onto the highest peaks, burning white onto the snowy dips and crevices of the mountains. I can't even begin to describe for you how enormous the Himalayas are. And the foothills, they appear before the great giants like these ghostly fish rising from the sea."

Denzil had been visiting some old school friends for vacation. He had decided to walk to the top of Tiger's Ridge, and it was there that he met his sister Estelle and her best friend, Alice. He was a gangly man of six feet and four inches; not athletic, not really even elegant but for the steel blue of his eyes. When Alice looked closer it appeared as if a dash of sun had been trapped in the iris of his left eye and when she looked straight into his eyes, the way the Indian looks into everyone, never breaking her stare, never backing down, Denzil stared right back. His hand felt fleshy and hot when she reached out to greet him. His dark wavy hair was already receding from a strong intelligent forehead and his lips, Alice thought, were soft and buttery. *Kissable.*

Denzil coughed and tried to recover the moment. "You ladies out for an early morning stroll?"

"What does it look like to you?" Estelle snapped and tugged on Alice's hand.

"I was just coming to watch the sunrise. And you?" He spoke this directly to Alice, who yanked her hand from Estelle's and wiped the telltale perspiration onto her trousers.

The sun was now in Alice's eyes and she squinted to see Denzil's face in shadow. "I have not identified any of the mountains in the distance and I think one must go as far as Almora or even Kusaini to truly visit the Himalayas."

"I should think one must visit the Himalayas to truly visit the Himalayas," Denzil said as he strolled around Alice and jumped onto a boulder, one long lanky leg followed by the other.

"I suppose, if you are particularly enthralled with proximity," she said smoothly.

His trousers fit him loosely and his arms and legs seemed to be attached by well-oiled hinges as he waved his hand in the direction of the Himalayas. "That peak is Nanda Devi and this large one, in front, is Trishul."

Alice crawled on top of the rock beside Denzil and lined her eye along his arm to find the mountains he was pointing toward. The clouds were already beginning to form over the glaciers and the two of them stared at the jagged horizon; there were hundreds of miles of distance between themselves and the rock faces. The warm orange sunlight poured into the small spaces between them and he could feel her breath on his cheek. He turned to her and smiled.

He had a cocky smile; it was full of arrogance and self-confidence. Alice refused to let it intimidate her. "There is a theory about the collision of continental plates," she said.

"Is that so?"

"A man named Wegener says the Himalayas are a result of one of those collisions. It's been going on for millions of years. Apparently, it still is. Those mountains are actually growing."

They fell silent and circled each other. Denzil had never met such a cheeky girl before and he didn't know if he liked that or not.

"I doubt Sister Dorothea would ever allow us to go that far before examinations were over," Estelle interrupted.

Denzil jumped off the rock and cuffed Estelle lightly across the head. "What on earth are you talking about?"

"A trip to Almora or Kusaini. I doubt the Sister would ever allow it."

Alice joined Estelle, landing just in front of Denzil. "Oh, I suppose I could convince her if we were to be accompanied by one so *brilliant* as your brother." Alice rolled her eyes at him, paused and turned to Estelle. "Come Estelle, we've got to get back for Elocution this afternoon. Will you walk with us back to the college?" she asked Denzil.

"I'd be happy to, but I've got a boat race in two hours and have to meet some chaps at the clubhouse."

Alice dipped her hand into the pond and grinned at her daughter. "He smiled and I thought I might burst. And then he invited us to the races on that following weekend. His and your Uncle Richard's craft was called the *Blue Star*. It was her maiden voyage.

"We had classes that afternoon and had to get back before the Sisters worried about us. The lower road to the college had washed out during the monsoons that year so we had to circumnavigate the entire town. There were tigers in the area and your Aunt Estelle was absolutely paralysed with fear."

"Tigers?"

"Yes, industry on the plains were forcing them into the mountains."

Alice reached across the pond with her stick to pull the boat back into position. Barbara waved her own boat through the air and placed it on the surface of the water. "That day, we were like fawns in a meadow, our ears all quivering, we could feel the tiger watching us as we ran the shortcut over Tiffin top. You see, Barbara, Tiger knows what it means to wait. You ask your Uncle Richard someday. They'll wait for days before they attack their prey."

"Have you ever seen a tiger?"

"Alive?"

"It only counts if they're alive."

"Yes, once, and I'll never forget it. It was from a great distance; the tiger was a blur, really. But the tiger's eyes looked right into mine. Now I dream about tiger. I know tiger. Yes, I know tiger ..."

Wild rhododendrons covered the slopes beneath the pine trees and the families living in the valley below had picked the underbrush clean for their kitchen fires. A green parrot flickered through the forest and giant spiderwebs clung to Alice's braid as she and Estelle jogged along the brick pathway.

Alice finally spoke. "You never told me your brother was so handsome."

"He isn't, you were stunned by the sunrise."

"Oh, but he is ... very."

"He's too old for you."

"Says who?"

"Says me. All that nonsense about collision. Honestly, where do you get that? My brother can see right through that."

"Good."

They walked on a little farther, and descended back into town, then climbed the stairs to the college entrance; the sun was high and bright in the sky and it squeezed the shadows into thin pencil lines around the arches of the chapel windows. Sister Dorothea waved to the girls from behind the lead glass windows and the girls waved back.

As they walked into the front entrance of the school, Alice asked Estelle, "Does he have a nickname?"

"Who?"

"Denzil. Does he have a nickname?"

"He does, but he'd thrash me if I told you."

"I can't possibly go through my life calling him Denzil. Have mercy on me."

"I think you should ask him yourself."

Back in the dormitory, Alice jumped on top of her friend and pinned her arms to the ground. "Tell me or I'll spit on your forehead."

Struggling and giggling beneath her friend, Estelle said, "You are disgusting. What would my brother want to do with you?

Get off me, Alice. Now."

Alice opened her lips as if to spit and Estelle yelled out, "Okay, okay. Chippy, call him Chippy."

"Chippy? Where on earth does that come from?"

By this time, Estelle was laughing as well. "Some comic book character he used to read."

Alice rolled off Estelle and lay on her back. "Chippy? Who on earth named him that?"

"Chippy?" Barbara giggled. "No way, Amma. No way."

"It's true, but you must never call him that. You must promise me."

Barbara brought her hand up to her lips to stifle another giggle, and whispered, "Chippy."

"Barbara." Alice tickled her daughter into submission. "Promise?"

Screeching with laughter, Barbara finally promised.

Alice continued, "That weekend, picnickers had set up lounge chairs along the mall and took their tea in the sun while they watched the sailboats tack their way from one end of the lake to the other. Aunt Estelle and I slipped away from the police demonstration to run alongside the boats on the south side of the lake. After the races, we went into the clubhouse to join your father and his school friends for a drink and some sweets.

"While your Aunt Estelle flirted with Uncle Richard, I stood demurely in the moorghi-khana — otherwise known as the hen house — and stared at the photographs of the great landslide on the wall while I waited for your father to take notice of me.

"It was one moment; a glance, a slight curve in his mouth. I caught his eye and I knew I was in love." She remembered silently how his animal stillness, something uninhabited about him, a foreign place she had always wanted to go, had taken possession of her in the shadows of moths stupid from the lamplight.

That evening, Alice and Barbara lay in the courtyard behind their Pune home searching for shooting stars beneath the night sky. Alice pointed to the sky and drew her finger in a long straight line. "Did you see that?"

Barbara searched for a moment, then shook her head. "Missed it." She was growing sleepy as she curled into the crook of her mother's arms, her mother's heartbeat always slow and soothing. "I think I should like to see Naini Lake again," she yawned and closed her eyes.

"Another one," Alice pointed to the slipstream of another shooting star. "Someday soon, I hope."

Alice lay with her daughter asleep on her shoulder, the child's moist breath dampening her blouse. Pleiades and Cassiopeia glimmered behind a hasty cloud; the stars were always crisper at that time of year and Alice wished she could know their names, draw lines from star to star, recreate the myths of the Greeks. For on that night the universe was a great possibility, bold planets were splashes of red. Jupiter rose slowly on the eastern horizon and she could feel the spinning of the earth.

Later, as they listened for the lazy breath of their children asleep in their nursery, Denzil and Alice sipped gin and tonics on the veranda. It seemed as if life had given them all they needed; Alice was occupied with organizing teas, children's picnics and field trips to the banks of the River Mula or to the waterfalls at Mahabaleshwar. On the surface, it seemed like more than she could have hoped for.

But it soon became apparent that Alice did not fit into Pune society. She cultivated no close relationships with other women and was made very aware of her mixed-blood heritage.

"Alice Spencer?" She had overheard the wives of two prison guards on the grounds speaking to a new arrival. "Well, she's not really our sort," they had said.

Though Alice had never participated in their preoccupation with the preparation of maraschino jelly or boiled turkey, and nor did she participate in their gossip, they were alluding to the fact that Alice was not of the purest British extraction and her presence, it was to be noted immediately by the new recruit, was not, if the truth be known and not to seem too prejudicial on the matter, welcome.

Denzil, with his blue eyes and paler skin, however, passed himself off as being white and though no one would ever challenge him in his lie, Alice began to resent his shame.

The grey landscape of Pune started to depress her and she sought to introduce as much of the colour of the foothills as possible, importing pine trees, mulberry bushes and the jackfruit, bringing tulips into the courtyard. Red, she had decided, was missing from her daily life and it was red she planted in abundance. She had scrambled together oak wine barrels, old bricks and plenty of tulip bulbs she had ordered from a greenhouse in England. And though outwardly she appeared happy with her station in life and her young children, she was constantly combating an overwhelming sense of futility.

Denzil, meanwhile, was dedicated to reform and had no time to fret about the suspicions of his heritage. He had organized the compounds into circles: Circle One for young boys who had committed murder, Circle Two for crimes of passion, and Circle Three for political prisoners. His most recent enterprises were setting up a bakery and library. Though he worked tirelessly on his enterprise, he couldn't escape the knowledge that he was constantly being passed over for promotions. It was a well-known fact that his wife was not white, but Denzil had disguised his own background (having not acknowledged his mother's recent second marriage to a Christian Indian, having discouraged visits from Alice's parents, and shunning all other associations with Anglo-Indians that could possibly lead to any suspicions by his superiors of his alliances). So when Alice petitioned him to vacation with Estelle and Richard somewhere closer to Pune, Denzil balked.

Dear Estelle, Alice had written,
I have found the most perfect compromise. Although it means a farther trek for you, the children would have more freedoms. We could have picnics and the men could hunt.
A.

Dear A.
I hardly think that either of us would be satisfied with picnicking and tossing the children around while the men hunt tiger. In fact, dear sister-in-law, it sounds absolutely primal. There must be something else about this place, Alice, that you are not confessing to me.
Estelle

Dearest Estelle,
You're absolutely right, but I still think it an excellent compromise. The Ajanta caves are exactly what I need right now. I can follow up some research I've been doing on the early Buddhists and I understand the hillsides in a neighbouring valley are an excellent playground for Tiger. The children, with supervision, could play in the river — a stream, really — that cuts below the caves. There is

accommodation in the nearby town of Aurangabad and an excellent Hide in the forest where we can camp out for a couple of nights. You can take the train from Delhi to Monmad and then transfer to Aurangabad. Should take you less than a week to get there. Please, please, please. I need a change of pace. Pune is suffocatingly proper and all of Denzil's colleagues are frighteningly dull. He has been terribly distracted lately, what with the riots in Bombay and all. You heard about those, didn't you? Mr. Gandhi started a huge bonfire in the city and threw silk into the flames. Denzil is feeling personally responsible for this country's plummet into chaos (his words, not mine). Who knows where we Anglos belong now? I was hoping that Richard Thomas might bring him out of his distraction.

Love, A.

Dearest Alice,

Many of our relatives have left for Australia. Our isolation in Nainital has protected us from much of what you talk about. Oh, yes, by the way ... I thought I told you many years ago that Denzil was the sort of man to spend much of his life "distracted" (your words, not mine) ... Give my love to Barbara, the baby and my darling brother, of course,

Estelle

Dear Estelle,

He's just disappointed. He didn't get the posting he had hoped for in Ooty.

We'll pick you up at the train station in Aurangabad. I've got everything arranged. I'm absolutely bursting with anticipation! The baby is healthy and Barbara refuses to wear anything else but that lovely frock you sent her for her seventh birthday. Thank you, by the way. I'm sorry I've been terribly remiss with your children. I promise to pay more attention to them on this holiday.

Love, love and love to all, A.

From opposite ends of the country, the two families arrived in Aurangabad at the end of the monsoon season. Denzil's initial reticence dissolved immediately when he and Richard resumed their old banter and Denzil became aware, for the first time, of the insidious dysfunction of his pretense. He was truly happy to see his old friend and they immediately began their plans for the following few days of the hunt.

That first evening, as the couples sat around an open fire, Alice told the history of the caves.

Tiger Dreams Film Part III Sequence

Long shot of the Ajanta caves. Camera pans to where the river bends and
then rises toward the caves at the far end. Medium shot of me
standing along the railing.

Me: The Ajanta caves had gone undiscovered for almost 1500 years. Vines
had grown over them and they became a convenient refuge for
animals. In the late 18th century a British hunter had cornered a tiger
behind some vines. He was standing on that adjacent hillside.

Long shot rises toward the hillside on the other side of the valley. Jump cut
to view from adjacent hillside. Wipe. Close-up of booted feet running
through forest, across the river and up a dusty pathway.

My Voice-over: When the hunter crossed the river and scaled the hill to
capture the tiger, the tiger had mysteriously disappeared. The hunter
followed the tiger's pugmarks behind a veil of vines.

Pan down the length of the wall of caves.

My Voice-over: Twenty-seven caves in all. No longer a refuge for tiger.

Sound FX. Gunshots.

My Voice-over: Less than 200 tiger remain today.

*

David edits the gunshots and final statement. "Too political, too early in
the film," he says.

Ajanta Caves: The Early Years

Alice poked a stick into the fire and looked across the fire at Denzil. "The early Buddhists carved the caves out of basaltic stone — from the top down."

"Apparently with a spoon!" Denzil remarked. They all laughed. Denzil caught Alice's eye, smiled warmly and nodded, tipping his glass toward her, a gesture of gratitude. He mouthed the words, "Thank you."

Alice lifted her glass to him and wrapped her shawl tighter around her shoulders.

Richard talked about his recent guiding trips, taking the British and their sons north of Kusaini and flushing tiger out by ambush. The British had become quite enthusiastic about hunting and Richard was getting plenty of work from Corbett's hunting lodge and farther into the foothills by Almora. They had all been to Almora before, that first summer Denzil and Alice fell in love.

Alice had organized a field trip for their class and Denzil and Richard had been their guides. It was the summer of 1910 — a languorous hot season of playing tennis and cricket on the lawns of her parents' retreat in Nainital. There were afternoons of lawn tennis followed by claret, served up with lettuce and tomato sandwiches, curry puffs and sometimes, when Alice's father was feeling adventurous, he would order up sorbets. The evenings were occupied with card games of bridge. Denzil remained aloof, engaging in conversation only with Alice's father, briefly acknowledging Alice's presence during tea or as a worthy opponent in tennis, but always feigning excuses to visit with old school friends and sailing partners when activity around the James' household waned.

While Denzil was reading in the garden one afternoon, Alice had approached him cautiously. "The Sister said that if we could find adequate escort to Almora and Kusaini, we could organize a field trip. Are you still interested?"

Denzil put his book down and looked into Alice's eyes. "How many young ladies would I be escorting?"

"Depending on the permission we get from parents, possibly eight or ten. Are you interested?"

"Only if I get some help with the organization," he smiled and returned to the words on the page in front of him. Alice terrified Denzil. She was bold and sensual and very young. Her firm grip on the world intimidated him; her ambitions both excited and frightened him and he thought he might lose her before even possessing her. He felt himself too inadequate, too banal for the "Head Girl" of All Saints College. This pushing and pulling inside him created a tension, like two magnets hovering, one side of him wanting to flip and join forces with her, the other repelled by the similarities they shared.

"Of course I'll organize everything. I'll send the letters of consent out today and we should be able to leave before month's end. Will the timing be acceptable to you?"

"Yes, yes, of course."

"Good then."

"Alice?"

She loved it when he spoke her name and she stopped him with her smile. "Yes?"

Alice's ability to excite Denzil confused him. He studied her lanky, boyish good looks and thought how dramatically her face changed with her moods. He had seen her in foul moods, with darkened eyes, a formidable brow. He had also seen her ecstatic, as she was at that moment, with bright eyes and the creases at the corners of her mouth spread across her cheeks. Her dimple deepened as he sat in his chair and he wondered if he'd ever be able to get over the paralysis he felt when he was close to her. "Nothing."

She leaned forward, opened his book to the page he had been reading and handed it back to him. From his position on the chair he could see the tawny pallor of her skin stretching over her collarbone; she had a lovely triangular shadow between her neck and bone and he thought about touching his lips there. My eyes are perspiring, he thought, if such a thing is possible.

"Let's plan to leave in two weeks' time then," she suggested and skipped lightly over the lawns away from him.

He smiled and called after her, "Keep me posted. I should possibly meet with Sister Dorothea before the week's end."

"Yes, yes, of course," Alice blurted, "and Denzil? Do me a favour?"

He looked at her seriously. "What's that?"

"Don't wear that god-awful shirt when you go to meet her."

She giggled and ran off. Denzil looked down at his shirt. The cuffs were tattered and the seams on the left sleeve were splitting apart. He was not one to be occupied with appearances, having his mind on the laws of physics most of the time; in those days, Denzil could barely brush his hair in the morning, let alone mend a shirt or even bother to purchase another. He laughed and returned to his book. He would go out the following day and buy himself another shirt.

The next two weeks were the longest Alice had ever borne. She had received permission from six of the ten parents of the girls from the senior year. She had organized palanquins into the valley, motorcars along the valley floor. She thought the hike up to Almora from the valley bottom would be a vigorous day's walk and good exercise after a hearty breakfast. Canvas tents, cooks and food had been organized by Sister Dorothea, who insisted that her attendance would be absolutely necessary as she was not willing to entrust her girls to a young man from Malbagong no matter how impeccable his academic record might be. Alice and Estelle worked with checklists, accumulating pots and utensils, blankets and cots, and made sure the other girls had proper footwear and appropriate headgear.

Denzil, on the other hand, remained aloof.

Richard Thomas teased Denzil. "You really haven't had to worry about a thing. Are you sure you don't want company attending ten ripe young schoolgirls, you old dog?"

"No, no, I've got everything under control. No need to worry, my friend."

"That friend of your sister's, that lovely thing, what's her name, Alice? She seems to have taken control of everything."

Denzil smiled when he thought of Alice's enthusiasm. "Yes, and I'm performing my duties adequately, don't you think? Scratch that, I don't care what you think."

"Are you sure I shouldn't accompany you on this trip? After all, I do have a bit of experience in the mountains. Surely you can't have all the girls to yourself, now can you?" Richard Thomas pulled the sail tight and clipped the rope into the clew. Denzil crawled into the back of the boat and the two tacked their way across the lake, green and frothy as a moss bed.

"Suit yourself, Dick. Now it wouldn't be because you've got designs on my baby sister, would it?"

"No more than you have on her friend."

"Don't be daft," Denzil smiled and dragged his hand through the water. "You're welcome to join me, but if you have anything other than noble thoughts about my sister you'll not only answer to me but to that old battleaxe, Sister Dorothea."

"Good Christ, is she still alive?"

"I think she still has a pulse."

Richard Thomas hadn't moved on to Malbagong or anywhere else for that matter. His family managed the Grand Hotel on the mall and he occupied himself playing music and keeping the grounds of Government House. He spent all his money on expeditions, climbing Trishul only a year before and organizing another attempt of Nanda Devi; he also had dreams of hiking into Nepal but finances were problematic. There was a new market opening up for men with Richard's skills, and guides who were familiar with the areas north and west of Nainital were in great demand. Hunting Tiger had become a favourite pastime of the British.

"I remember that trip," Richard stirred his drink.

"Yes, that's right." Denzil turned to Richard. "You found those pugmarks on the banks of the river."

Alice tossed a stone at Denzil. "You never told me that!"

"I didn't want to incite a riot. Crikey, Alice, Richard and I were in charge of — how many girls?"

Richard shrugged. He couldn't remember.

"I think there were twelve of us in all," said Estelle.

Estelle told them about the recent acquisition of land on the other side of town for the expansion of All Saints and the plans of the alumni for Sister Dorothea's retirement party. And Denzil brought out his guitar and sang a recent Roger Quilter accompaniment to William Blake's "Dream Valley": "Memory, hither come, and tune your merry notes; and, while upon the wind your music floats ..."

Alice watched her husband soften in the company of his sister and Richard Thomas, his dearest friend, and rather than mourn the isolation they had experienced since leaving the north, she enjoyed every single moment of that evening when they were all reunited. Denzil had a thoroughly rich voice with an excellent range and she was able to harmonize easily with him, her own voice an excellent complement. That evening she was a happy woman — by the fire, watching, and listening to her husband's good humour.

As the fire quieted, the two couples sat in a circle, grateful, and full of devotion for the comfort of old friends. Estelle retired first, followed by Alice. Richard and Denzil remained until the last ember died and the crickets carried on with their own tunes.

"See you in the morning, old boy," Richard Thomas spoke. "It will be good to show you a thing or two about what it is I do out there all day."

After their tiffin the following morning, the two couples went their separate ways. Richard and Denzil hiked into an adjacent valley, Alice and Estelle hiked up toward the caves, and the children remained with the chuprassi and their ayah to play in some pools along the river. The forest was still wet from the months of rain and Alice's clothes were soaked from knocking the moisture off the leaves of bushes as she led the way up the path. The caves were musty and filled with guano and the two women walked carefully over the slippery stone into the entrance of the caves.

"I fear we've both become a bit more squeamish since having the children," Alice said as she lit a lantern.

Estelle had held a hanky up to her mouth, her eyes as wide as berries. She tiptoed around all the droppings and jumped back at the skitter and rustle of a lizard breaking away from one of the meditation rooms situated in the back of the cave. "I think that I have always been squeamish, Alice. You just have refused to see that in me." Estelle regretted her wardrobe, thinking she should have known to be more practical in her footwear when going anywhere with Alice.

The circle of light from Alice's lantern moved up and down the pillars while she flicked moss from the elaborate paintings. "There are artists from all over India who come here to see this work," she said. "Look, look here. They plastered the pillars and walls of these caves with clay and cow dung, and then painted them with pigment. Frescos."

Alice raised the lamp toward the ceiling. The full face of a woman, her half-lidded eyes and aquiline nose were most certainly Dravidian. "The most beautiful women in the world," Alice said, her voice stretched and thin in the coolness of the cave. "Skin like obsidian, eyes like oceans. Look how she has adorned herself, so full of herself. How I wish I had that confidence."

Estelle moved from side to side and thought the woman's eyes followed her as she came around to one side and that her smile widened as she moved to the other side. "It really is quite magnificent how the artist has managed to keep her alive after all these years," she said.

"You see it too, then?" Alice smiled and swayed the lamp from side to side, animating all the other paintings in the dark hall. "They polished everything with lime to preserve the pigment. Look Estelle, how bold the colours are."

"It seems to have worked wonderfully."

The ring of a distant gunshot hurled passed the cave entrance, carrying with it the echoes it had accumulated from all the other caves on its path through the valley.

Alice felt a lightness in her chest and her lips became numb. She thought it might be from tipping her head back for too long and suddenly she felt a desperate need to get outside. "Come, Estelle," she said. "Let's get some fresh air," and she rushed out of the cave into the sunlight.

Tiger Dreams Film Part IV Sequence

Close-up of panting tiger.

My Voice-over: There are so many ways to kill tiger. A bullet, for instance,
    performs predictably. Upon impact, it swerves to the side, and then
    backwards, splintering the ribs. Every organ ripples from its path.
    Everything gets shredded and then the body simply shuts down.

Ajanta Caves: The First Signs

Estelle had always thought Alice was invincible, but on that day she witnessed the first signs of Alice's vulnerability. "How long has this been going on?"

Alice turned to Estelle, "I don't know what it is, but every so often I get so light-headed I can barely remain on my feet."

Alice leaned against the outside rock wall and watched as the children splashed water on each other in the stream below. The whites of their clothes were brilliant against the deep green of the quiet water, like white moths fluttering over a garden.

"I'm not sure. It is such a vague sensation that I can't isolate it. It sometimes goes on for days at a time. Please, Estelle, you mustn't mention any of this to anybody. I don't want Denzil to fret and I don't, above all else, want this to ruin our vacation together." She pulled herself away from the wall, took a few breaths and blew herself up again. "There, see, I feel fine again." Looking down at the children, she turned to Estelle. "Let's go see how the children are doing. I suspect that gunshot means the men will be regaling us with their exploits this evening."

She jumped from the cave entrance onto a narrow path that led toward the valley bottom. Estelle cursed her footwear again and trundled after Alice. She was grateful for the shortened visit to the caves and wanted nothing more than to return to the camp and have a good stiff drink.

By the time Denzil and Richard arrived at the camp, the children had been tucked in bed and Estelle was sufficiently smashed. The two women were sitting around a small fire wrapped in the kamoan shawls they had had since their youth; they were giggling about the children.

A tigress's large, warm body swung beneath a pole as the men argued about how best to hang it from the tree. Alice felt the heat from the dead animal on her back. It was warm and humid and smelled like peat. A sickly sensation moved through her. She stood up and walked cautiously over to touch the tiger. She pushed her fingers into the fur behind its neck; the rolls of skin loosely attached to the tiger's bones were soft and movable. Alice could feel the pulse of her own heart, skipping and flipping around inside her chest. She swallowed and wetted her lips with her tongue as she moved her palm around to the soft skin of the tigress' belly. There was a movement, something hard and alive. She screamed and jumped back. Denzil began to laugh. She grabbed Denzil's hand and led it to the tigress' belly. "Here, feel here!" she said desperately.

Denzil stared up into the canopy as he palpated the belly of the tigress. "By God, you're right." And then quickly to Richard, "I wonder if we can save it."

Richard seemed impatient. "And what then, raise it as one of your own?" His wife's inebriation had distracted him and he hopped from foot to foot, half-turning to watch Estelle's attempt to rise out of her chair.

"Perhaps, a sanctuary might ..."

"It's suffocating, Denzil!" Alice jumped up and down. "I can hear it crying. Get it out of there!"

Denzil and Richard laid the dead tigress on the ground. Denzil spread her hind legs wide, slipped his blade inside her and cut slowly up the midline of her body. Alice reached into the savaged body and pulled the warm fetus from the tigress' belly. The young cub, barely formed, had her paws pulled up beneath her chin and her tail tucked between her hind legs. It looked as if she was all curled and wet with rain. Alice held the cub like one of her own, cleared the sac from its nose, tearing at the film with her fingertips while Denzil cut the infant's cord.

The cub sighed and gulped at the air, her tiny tongue trolling loosely from her mouth, and then she rolled her head once and fell limp into Alice's arms. Alice stared at the open belly of the tigress. The flaps of skin drooped open; steam rose from her empty cavity. She sat there, for what seemed like hours, just holding the tiny dead animal in her arms.

After a while, Denzil reached over to touch Alice and whispered, "I wish I could take this day back." She pulled her shoulders away from him and placed the dead cub back into the carcass of the tigress. She walked over to a washbasin and poured water over her bloodied arms.

Later that same night, Alice woke Denzil. "Are you awake?" she asked.

"Yes," he lied.

"Today, when I heard your guns go off, I almost fainted."

"Were you worried?"

"No, I think I knew."

"Knew what?"

"I think I knew somehow that she was carrying a child."

He raised his voice. "Don't be ridiculous, Alice."

"Shhhh, you'll wake up the whole camp."

She sat up and looked out the open doorway of the Hide and into the forest. A swath of cool blue light from the full moon took up the entranceway. "Don't laugh at me, Denzil," she said. "I'm dead serious. I think I knew when I heard the shot that you had done something horrible." Before Denzil could defend himself she held her hand up to his mouth and said, "That *we* are participating in something devastating."

Denzil pulled his wife toward him and whispered, "I was mortified, too, and I can't make right what has been done."

"But you can. You can stop killing tiger."

"But Alice, it is what we do."

"Then change your activity."

"Like this?" He placed his hand on the side of her breast and began to rub his palm lightly over her nipple, swivelling the smooth pearl beneath his palms. He experienced a movement beneath her skin like a mongoose tangled in bedclothes, playfully predatorial, all instinct. This was how he wanted them to talk. "Like this?" he repeated.

She smiled down at him and shook her head. "That's not quite what I had in mind."

He brought his hand down the side of her rib cage and grabbed onto her hip. She was breathless as she straddled her legs on top of him and guided him inside her. And when he grabbed her other hip to push himself deeper into her, he could feel all the muscles in her back tighten. Her long black hair, wet from perspiration, fell like a dark scrim around him as she pulled herself up and then lowered herself down in a thirsty, consuming rage. He thought of panicking, of running away; her ferocity was all around him and when he released himself into her, she collapsed on top of him and buried her head — she was quietly keening — into his shoulder.

As he lay there in the dark, fearing the smell that came off her body, he was reminded of the vengeance of beasts. He quietly left the Hide and brought back a wet cloth from the washbasin.

He pulled the cloth along the length of her body, her skin and bone curling away from the pressure of his hand as if each cell of her body were operating independent of each other, their surprise to touch causing her body to shiver. He then dressed and went deeper into the forest to bury her scent. When he returned, the gauze canopy was pulled back and Alice had fallen fast asleep; her body, like a freshly peeled twig in moonlight, was stretched across the bed. He closed the canopy around her, cursing the mosquitoes, cursing his negligence. He crouched in the corner of the Hide and kept vigil over his family for the remaining hours of that night.

Tiger Dreams Film Part V Sequence

Sound. City traffic. Horns. Children's voices.

Medium close-up of old Indian woman (Rita). Blur focus on background.

Rita: "I believe your grandmother was hospitalized in a mental institution for a time."

Me: "For what?"

Rita: "For malaria." Rita frowns into the camera. "But I already told you this."

Me: "Can you remember how they treated malaria back then?"

Woman (Roshon's voice) off camera: "With quinine. The British had set up cinchona plantations east of Pune."

Deep Focus on crowd of picnickers on green lawn. Taj Mahal Hotel in background.

Roshon's Voice-over: "The cinchona bark ..." Reverse-angle shot; Roshon, a middle-aged woman, wipes her fingers on the grass, "was from the South Americas and the British had tried to cut corners by harvesting the seeds from the Americas and developing a hybrid in India. But I think that experiment failed because of the climatic differences of the two countries. I believe there were also problems with pest control."

Claire and David, The Same Day

Margaret sat at the desk in her office, pencil in hand, Claire's chart open and a fresh page to write on. "What happened this time?" she asked.

The seizures, Claire told Margaret, were increasing in both frequency and duration. She would pass out, wake up, couldn't figure out where she was or how long she'd been there. "You'll find the same description on the previous page. I've told you this a billion times before."

"You've told me this a couple of times, yes."

Claire nodded.

"Are you still taking the medication I prescribed?"

"No," and she paused, "no, I'm not."

There was nothing conclusive on the brain scans; Margaret couldn't say for sure that Claire had epilepsy.

Margaret sat back and put her pencil down. She rubbed her chin and stared at Claire.

"Look, Margaret," Claire finally said, "something else is going on here."

"Are you eating well?"

"Yes. I'm doing everything I'm supposed to be doing. What else can I tell you?"

"Not taking any other pharmaceuticals? Cocaine?"

Claire stared at her doctor; the light from the window polished Margaret's complexion a stony white. Margaret could get outside a little more, thought Claire.

"No, no coke, no acid, no mescaline, no horse tranquillizer. Can't remember the last time I sniffed glue."

"No need to get sarcastic."

"No need to get patronizing."

Claire's relationship with Dr. Margaret Barnes had started with Pap smears, birth control and yeast infections. Margaret had begun her career in the north and then became a professor of archaeology at the University of Toronto for ten years. Shortly after her marriage to an Inuit man had gone sour, she'd returned as a student to the university to receive her M.D. She had spent years gathering remnants of those dying northern populations: Frobisher Bay, Cumberland Sound, Ungava Bay, and she clung onto those artifacts mournfully when she couldn't recover her marriage. Claire had eagerly volunteered to help catalogue the artifacts in Margaret's collection for the National Gallery in Ottawa. Skins of beaver, lynx and muskrat had lain in piles alongside curved ribs or clavicles used for tanning. Margaret had collected arrowheads, awls, wooden mallets and soapstone carvings, and Claire had eagerly assisted Margaret in tagging each item.

Skeletons came easily to Claire; they had the habit of appearing before her on hiking trails, in wheat fields or along riverbanks. Perfectly preserved, alabaster skulls of otter, antelope, porcupine and coyote became the bookends, pencil holders and paperweights on the window ledges and bookshelves of her apartment. She had always treasured the trilobites and fossilized fish she and her father had found in the Badlands, and she used a petrified wooden stump — they had dragged it in from the Cypress Hills on one of their

Sunday drives — as a plant stand. So when Margaret needed some help cataloguing her collection, Claire was well suited for the task.

"Our worlds were just too far apart," Margaret had confided in Claire about her marriage.

"How many worlds are there?" Claire had asked.

Margaret had tagged another arrowhead while the two women sat in her basement culling, sorting and categorizing her collection. "Only two that I know of," she had answered.

Margaret stood up from her desk and gestured to the bed in her office. "Sit up here, I want to check something."

Claire sat on the bed while Margaret listened to her chest.

"Take a deep breath, please," Margaret said smoothly. Her hands were soft and warm as they touched Claire apologetically, fluttering against her skin, pressing the cold steel of the stethoscope lightly beneath her shoulder blades, across her rib cage, along her side, over her breasts. "You can breathe out now, please," Margaret said, staring blankly for a few moments. "Sounds pretty as a picture to me, but just in case," she turned and sat at her desk and began to write on a small piece of paper, "I want you to take sixteen Aspirin today, ten tomorrow and eight the following day."

"Aspirin?" Claire laughed. "You want me to take Aspirin for my seizures?"

"It might be what we call pericarditus. The Aspirin will eliminate any inflammation around the heart that may be causing that pain you sometimes complain about. I'm thinking I can hear a rubbing sound, but I'm not quite sure."

"Rubbing?"

"Between the pericardium and the heart muscle. If there is an inflammation, sometimes we can hear a rubbing sound. Anyway, try this over the weekend and we'll set up some tests next week."

"What kind of tests?"

"If I told you now, I'd be improvising. I have to do some homework. Call the office on Monday morning," Margaret said and escorted Claire to the door of the clinic. "You've had a big year, Claire. Your first documentary, the death of your father, moving in with David; these are big things in a person's life."

"Are you suggesting these seizures are all about stress?"

"We'll eliminate all the other possibilities first."

"Meanwhile take sixteen Aspirin and call you Monday morning, is that right?"

"Exactly. Now go home and let David fuss over you a bit."

Margaret hesitated, turned around and began to walk toward the reception desk. Claire stood at the glass door of the clinic and stared outside at the street. Gusts of wind twirled garbage and dust into tornadoes along the gutters, schoolchildren dangled their arms out the windows of a bus, and bare trees, plugged into the concrete sidewalk, bent and twisted in the storm. The school bus lurched forward and disappeared.

"By the way, Claire," Claire could hear Margaret's voice, "I saw your documentary the other night."

Claire turned around to face her, "Oh yeah? How did you get hold of it?"

Margaret winked. "I have connections," she said. "And I thought it was pretty good."

"Just pretty good?"

"Yeah, just pretty good. But I understand you are beginning a new project?"

Claire stopped and stared at Margaret. "Yes. Why just pretty good?"

"I liked it," Margaret said. "I thought the final scene with that one activist sitting there on the verge of tears was perhaps a bit melodramatic, but the rest was very provocative."

Claire closed her eyes and shook her head. "I know, I know. I thought I was pushing it in all the right directions, but I know what you mean."

Margaret smiled warmly at Claire, then turned toward her next patient. "Mrs. Weston? Follow me, please."

Claire pulled her sweater over her head and left the building.

You Dream This:

Your dream is in black and white. It skips along like a badly repaired film. Shadows of hesitant ghosts spill in awkward patterns across your father's face as he stands at the top of the stairwell. A tiger appears and disappears like a mistake; it has a woman's head, long dark hair, a fine nose and slender mouth. Her body, though, is broad, heavy and feline. As if you are filming your own dream, you tighten the focus for a closer look.

Claire and David, That Night

David, smelling of beer and cigarettes from his hockey night, crawled in beside Claire and woke her up. He pressed himself into her back and moaned, pawing at her breasts, holding his breath, waiting for a window of opportunity. Finally, she had to grab his hand and help it over to his side of the bed. David eventually sighed, rolled over and fell asleep. She closed her eyes to the black syrupy underworld of sleep, but could barely reconstruct her father's face and the soft crooked smile he had always had for her. She opened her eyes and lay staring at the bright green digits of the clock radio, trying to recall the tiger and then a few moments later, what kind of animal it was and then, a few moments after that, she couldn't remember any details of the dream other than that of her father standing at the top of a stairwell. Eventually she fell into a thick dark sleep, deep and unrecoverable, the kind that takes sunlight and a shower and a cup of coffee to awaken from.

David left early the following morning, but returned a few hours later to find Claire still sitting on the couch sipping coffee. "How many have you had?" he asked.

She lied and told him that she was drinking the dregs from the first batch and did he want to put another pot on?

"Don't get up, I'll get it." From the kitchen he asked her what was going on.

"Nothing much," she told him.

David poked his head around the corner and sneered. Claire leaned over the coffee table and picked up the bundle of coins that Charlotte Blake had sent. She pulled back the cloth and shuffled through the cards looking for the coin that had the profile of the woman with the slender mouth on it. Tiny and green, the coin was no bigger than her baby fingernail and it filled the absolute centre of her palm like a whisper. "I had this long elaborate dream that I can't recall," she told David. "It's frustrating because I can't remember any details, but I have a sneaking suspicion my father was visiting me last night."

"My grandmother would say that you've been tumbling dry your mind." David said this with authority as he crossed the room and stood behind the couch.

"What do you mean by tumbling dry?"

"Like clothes in a dryer." He leaned over her to smell the top of her head. "You smell like lilacs," he said and walked back into the kitchen. The pot whistled and David ground the beans. He poured the water over the coffee, came back into the living room and saw that Claire was sitting on the couch balancing the weight of coins in her palms.

"I miss your dad," he said.

Claire remembered how she had caught herself the other day in the middle of dialling her father's number, "Just to talk to him, you know, as if nothing had changed."

"I know. I'm always giving myself what I think would be his advice."

"Advice? I've got lots of advice. But have you any more goats?" The two of them laughed. Claire's father had been telling the same joke for years: A young man goes to a Rabbi and asks for his advice. The Rabbi tells him to go kill a goat. The young man returns the next day and the Rabbi advises him to kill another goat. This goes on for a couple of weeks until finally the young man comes back to the Rabbi and says, Rabbi, I've done all you've asked of me, now can you give me some advice? The Rabbi replies, Advice? I've got lots of advice. But have you any more goats?

They sat together on the couch in their apartment flipping the ancient coins over and over searching for dates or names in the script. "This one's a beauty," David said, holding Claire's favourite coin like a disc between his thumb and forefinger. It was the most perfectly preserved of all of them.

David got up to pour the coffee and Claire meticulously replaced the coins in their cards, piled them on top of one another, wrapped them in the cloth and tied the strings around the bundle. Claire called to David, "I'm going to check into flights to India."

She sat there with the coins in her lap waiting for David's unbridled enthusiasm. Instead, David handed her a cup of coffee and sat down in the chair opposite her.

"Not to change the subject," he said, "but are we still going to the mountains this weekend?"

Claire held the hot cup up to her cheek, "Yes, of course." She thought about what Margaret had told her and how she wasn't going to tell David anything until she knew more. "I'm counting on it," she added.

"Good. I've been dying to try my new tent."

"I think they got snow last night. It'll be crisp." She paused, took another sip, and felt the steam on her cheeks. "What I said was this: I'm going to check into flights to India."

"I heard you." David nodded and left the room.

That night, Claire seized in her sleep. She woke drenched in her own urine. After a few moments of a fractured consciousness, she pieced her world back together — bed, bedroom, chest of drawers, bedclothes, bedside lamp, David, wet, soaking wet, smell of urine — and she threw the covers back and jumped out of bed. She whispered to David to wake up. He rolled over to put his arm around her, felt the drenched sheets, and sat up. "Jesus! What happened?"

"I don't know." Claire stood beside the bed and began to cry. "I'm sorry — David — I don't know what to say."

"Don't say anything. Why don't you go have a shower and I'll change the sheets?"

Claire poured herself a bath instead. The old pipes jolted as if relieving a deep cramp in the bowel of the building and she put in some bubble bath and let it fill while she sat on the toilet with her head in her hands. She ached all over and her joints squeaked when she took off her wet t-shirt. Her skin prickled with relief as she slipped into the water.

David opened the door and asked if she wanted some company. No thanks, she told him — he should go back to sleep, she'd be okay. But she looked up toward him and began to cry again. "David, I'm really sorry," she said and slumped into the tub water and buried her face. She could hear the low rumble of his voice and she sat up again.

He was sitting on the toilet seat talking to her, saying something about deep sleep and valerian root. His hair had partially pulled out of his ponytail and dropped in front of his eyes. He tucked the loose strands behind his ears. "What do you think?"

"I know it's not very nice for you, David. I promise, I'll pull it together."

David reached out and placed the pad of his hand on her cheek. It felt warm and smooth and real. "Don't worry about me, Claire," and he leaned over and kissed her forehead. "Take your time; I'll warm up the bed for you."

Claire looked into his eyes and for a very clear moment she truly believed she didn't deserve him. He was too perfectly honest with her, with himself; he had no static. He knew about power and he understood empathy and though he had been civilized to think otherwise, she believed he might be able to think outside of himself, like a woman does in the everyday course of things. She smiled up at him and he backed away and left her alone.

Splashing water over the bubbles in the tub, she drew herself down one more time and lay in the quiet of the water, her pulse racing, a tightness in her throat, the storm inside her head — a gale — the moan of high wind in the trees. And then as clearly as if they were in the same room she could hear someone whisper to her.

I have a story
to tell
of tigers in the jungle
of how steady my hand is when I hold my knife.

Tiger Dreams Film Part VI Sequence

Tiger slaughter. Four, five tiger carcasses piled one on top of the other
  onto the back of an elephant. Close-up of elephant's eye. Long take.
  Jump cut.
Sound FX. Galloping horses.
Medium shot. A veiled woman, silks bloodied from head to toe, in
  sixteenth-century Muslim costume, gallops across an open field.
  Medium long shot. Long shot. Cut. Ancient coin. Squeeze focus.

Claire and David, One Day Later

They drove onto the plateau out of the river valley. Neither mentioned the incident from the night before, but Claire still felt skittish and shy; her hands were cold and she fumbled in the passenger seat to warm them against the heat vent. A dusting of snow sharpened the mountains beyond the copper grasses of the foothills. Thick sunlight poured over the crests of hillsides and horses huffed steam through their nostrils as the light turned their coats golden. Glaciers had once pulled the earth in this landscape back, taking with them layers of till, leaving behind the stony outcrops and rogue boulders — erratics, they called them — that dotted the foothills west of the city. There was a house, one partially finished, empty house that rested on the top of one of the hills to the right of the highway. It had been abandoned before it had been finished. A divorce possibly. Or maybe a death. The children had long since gone; the inheritance, a partially finished home on the outskirts of town, more a hindrance than anything, had been left to the weather and speculation. There were no windows left and Claire could see the sky and clouds through its open spaces.

Wrestling winds and desire was a part of living in the foothills and if she listened long enough she could hear the echoes of buffalo hooves trampling the prairie grasses, turning them over, forcing their roots to renew. She opened her window and let the wind flick her hair against her face. *I am inside something fluid and malleable*, she thought.

"I am the nucleus."

"What was that?" David asked.

She moved her head inside and rolled up the window.

"Nothing," she said. "Nothing important."

The serrated edge of the mountains to the left of the highway remained in reach of the moon, still pale in the morning sky. David turned left off the highway and entered the valley. Sharp-toothed mountains flanked them on either side of the road. Claire sipped her coffee and pulled a poppy seed brioche out of a bag, split it in two and handed half to David.

These mountains were younger than the Rockies, their rock curled like the crests of waves, their anatomy more beautiful and more unpredictable, wilder than any other mountain range in her experience. Her father had taught her that they were the aftermath of the great collision of the Rockies; they were the bent spine of the prairie that in a distant past was cliffs against a sea. She remembered how excited he got that day she expressed a curiosity for his work, how he pulled out hundreds of maps and flipped through them in rapid succession, animating epochs of sedimentation to demonstrate how it was that oil came to the prairies. She had loved that moment with her father.

They drove in silence for another hour. David turned off the side of the highway and parked the car. He remained with his eyes forward, scanning the forest in front of them. "Distanciation." David dropped the word deliberately into the middle of their silence.

Leaning against the door, hand on the handle, Claire mimed the word, "distanciation." Not a particularly smooth word, she thought. Its root possibly had something to do with proximity, though she had learned not to count on Latin derivatives. *Distantia — to stand apart.*

"Nice word. What is it?"

David's eyes remained fixed on the forest, the ferns and hellebore paling in the late season undergrowth. "Bertolt Brecht coined it."

"To alienate?"

"Not exactly."

"To call attention to artifice?"

"Closer."

That's it, she thought. You're getting at my ideas. You want them to stop. You don't like the way I want to put film together. "I know what you are getting at, but I don't mind it. In fact, that's what I like about my work."

"I mind," David said. "I prefer to stay inside the dream."

"What about having both?"

"It's too political."

"Because as a filmmaker I'm asking the spectator to step outside and think about it?"

"What about the sanctity of the story within the film?"

"What if the dis-tan-ci-a-tion is the story?"

"Too cute."

"Not if the story is political."

These gifts didn't always come disguised like this one. Sometimes they were simple, pleasurable. Words like "swale" — the gutters in a road — or "perlin" — the beam that rests on two pillars. Those were the neutral words, words that gave elegance to roads and buildings, words without agendas, words that felt good on her tongue and sounded round and slippery when spoken aloud.

She would carry David's words for days — finding occasions to use them, sometimes with a complete disregard for their meaning —

"Just to piss him off," she would say to friends. David would arm himself with dictionaries and contexts to defend his position and Claire would break into song or recite some ridiculous rhyme using the word in question, mutating meaning into sound. *Distanciation*, she thought, and then shook her head and said aloud, "Now it's you who's beginning to get political."

She pulled back on the door handle and rose from her seat. As she stepped out of the car, autumn rushed against her cheeks; the pleasant burn of pine needles and limestone cleared her sinuses and she felt a fatigue, a kind of breathlessness; probably, she thought, from the pinch of her tights at her waist. On the other side of the car, David yawned and growled and shook himself. She threw her pack on and rushed for the head of the trail.

"Hurry up," she called back to David over her shoulder. "I want to warm up."

"I just think your work could be less self-conscious," he called after her.

"Maybe being self-conscious is the point of my work."

She began to feel better as they climbed higher. David winded easily though, and every time they stopped so he could catch his breath Claire felt the restless animal inside her skittering up and down the length of her body.

The tigress shifts her universe as she migrates.
She is inescapable.

So Claire hurried on ahead and left David behind, wheezing.

David strolled quietly, respectfully, his ears filled with his own breath and the pounding of his heart. He stopped to turn over the deadheads of wood lilies long since bloomed and rotting beneath their leaves, or to pluck the blackened, shrivelled berries of solomon's seal beneath a mess of alder. As they crossed a short avalanche path into the forest on the other side, he was surprised to see the fairy bells still bright red so late in the season, and the blue beads catching scraps of sunlight through the trees. He brought his fingertips up to his nose and smelled the detritus from the forest floor — he liked the way scent could tell him where he had been. For this, he was grateful for his grandmother and her ancient ways.

He came out of the forest, strolled across an alpine meadow swollen with daisies and purple elephant heads and stopped before a small waterfall. A rocky outcrop to his left, still in shadow, ascended a hundred, maybe a hundred-fifty, feet to another plateau.

David scrambled up behind Claire. "Don't even think of climbing that," he said as he removed his pack to reveal darkening moons of sweat on his t-shirt.

She turned back and walked toward him; she was pleased to see him smiling. She loved his smile. Though he used it sparingly, it was simple and honest. She reached across and wiped some crumbs from the corners of his mouth. She was beginning to feel uneasy again and she wanted to keep moving.

"The climb doesn't look that difficult," she told him. "Maybe just a scramble, really. I'm just going to goof around on the rock while you catch your breath. Maybe you should put your jacket on so you don't get cold."

David dug into his pack for his jacket. "Just remember ..."

"Yeah, yeah, yeah," she replied.

David laughed and pulled the zipper up the front of his jacket. He shook his finger at her and sat back down on the boulder. "Distanciation denies the dream," he said casually to her back as she positioned herself along the rock face.

She turned back and smiled. "Maybe some of us are more afraid of the dream than we are of reality."

How many worlds are there?

"Two that I know of," Claire mumbled into the rock.
"Sorry? I didn't catch that."
"Nothing."

The limestone was cool and a breeze came off the waterfall. Claire began to ascend quickly at first, the slope easy, a simple scramble, really. Lichens, black and green, spread fingers of new growth across the face. Spiked moss clung tenaciously to lips of rock where snow would soon rest and Claire carefully placed her fingers and toes so as not to disturb their growth. After ten deft moves, though, the rock began to rise more vertically and handholds took more time to find. As she reached the centre of the rock face, her head pounded and her hand fumbled over the rock blindly as she felt for a hold. Her sweat caused her other hand to slip. She quickly pressed herself into the rough limestone; its crisp alkaline smell stung her nostrils. Her legs began to shake like a sewing machine. She could hear David talking in a slow deliberate voice. He was pacing; she knew this because his voice moved back and forth across her shoulders.

She could die now, on this rock. Her own weight could lift her away from everything solid and send her hurling through open space. Everything slow and falling away from her, arms and legs flailing, clouds shredding across the impossible deep blue. She contemplated — not the accident, but the intention to jump, the absolute conviction of suicide, the determined power of choice, how she might bounce, from one boulder to another, her body loose, her shoulders braced against a rock and like a child's doll, hair knotted before her eyes, expressionless, she would fall face first into the dirt. Broken ribs, punctured lungs, the air hissing out of her. Nothing quite as amateur as the slashing she had taken to her wrists with some broken glass she had found beneath the street lamp; the ragged ends of flesh were hardly deep enough to draw blood so she had milked the wounds and walked into her father's office to drip blood on his carpet. "Listen to me," she had threatened him. "Listen to what I have to say." He had wrapped her wrists in his hanky, and said in a voice almost too calm, "Ridiculous child. My beautiful, ridiculous child." But that wasn't what she had wanted to hear him say. What she had wanted, and she would say this later, was for him to see that with the grace of an artist she could die more beautifully, more exquisitely than he could have ever imagined for himself. She had thought he should admire her. Instead, he had called her "ridiculous" and when he had pulled her into him and held her so tight against his chest she thought she might suffocate and die anyway.

Below the rock face, David's voice began to sharpen and Claire moved her eyes cautiously over the rock so as not to disturb the equilibrium of her body. She had seen a chimney crack earlier in the climb; it was somewhere to the right of where she was, but she couldn't quite find the stretch. Hands slipping, legs shaking, heart pounding. "Damn it," she cursed. She couldn't believe that she had climbed to this height without protection.

She groped blindly for a lip of rock with her right hand and her fingertips finally stuck like sandpaper to an unevenness on the face and she thrust herself quickly forward into the stone and then into the chimney crack that followed the entire cliff band from top to bottom. A thin sliver of light rocketed down to her and she pressed her back into the cold hard stone. God, she thought.

"Jesus!" David shouted.

"Meet me at the top," she shouted back.

Her ribs were barely able to contain the fullness of her pounding heart. Claire pressed her back into the cold stone, pushed her feet against the opposite side and slowly shimmied her way toward the light. She mantled herself onto the grassy outcrop and dragged her shaking body onto the meadow.

"That was close — too close," David said as he arrived from the other direction.

The sun was behind him, his face was in shadow; his hair, in a wild frenzy around his head, made him look like a grizzly posturing on hind legs. She fell back onto the grass, supplicating, purring.

"I'm not amused, Claire," he said. "I would have had to carry you out of here." He ran his fingers through his hair. "Christ, woman, what were you thinking?"

She lay there nibbling the tip of her tongue, her pulse flying through her at a million miles an hour. "Nothing, absolutely nothing."

They hiked over the saddle and scrambled down the scree slope toward the cirque on the other side. She stood motionless and watched the suffusion of colour from the honey-mustard slopes of larch surrounding the lake. The sunlight moved slowly toward the horizon as the wind scudded dark purple ghosts across the face of rock on the north end. All this brought on an uneasy feeling inside her and she focused again on the ground before her to make a steady progress to the meadow below.

David pitched the tent while Claire cooked dinner. They moved silently around one another. Their shadows were perfect. The constellations wrestled for position in the night sky. They had been doing this for a decade now, moving around one another on grassy slopes on cool mountain evenings, perfecting occupations like tent-raising and meal preparation; they were married to their purpose.

But when dinner was served, Claire played with her food like an uninterested child. Her head dropped forward, she lost focus. "It was like a caving inward," she would say later, after it was all over.

David noticed she wasn't eating. "You okay?"

She lied, "Yeah, I think so."

David reached over for her bowl. "Can I finish that for you, then?"

She secured the bowl in his hand before letting her arm drop to the earth. She leaned over and saw that her skin had whitened in the moonlight. Swaying from side to side, she tried to keep her focus on the man; his name she couldn't, at that moment, recall. It was something different, like Dashiell, or Damien, or Denzil. And the deep black of the rock face behind him began to slip like smooth silk onto the surface of the lake and nothing retained its form anymore. Even he, the one who sat before her, began to change shape and she could hear herself whisper something awful like an inappropriate joke, something sarcastic or something ridiculous that even she couldn't believe she was saying. "Help me," she was saying; "I think I'm going to die."

Or perhaps you are already dead. In either case, death is already inside you. You see, Claire, the tiger has this way of reducing us. Like calamities that sometimes occur in the womb: all that will remain of you is your black, matted hair wrapped around two crooked teeth, nothing but a hairball coughed up on the path between here and the river.

Claire coughed, "Who are you?" A slur of ashes filled her lungs.

You cannot see me behind this marble lattice.

She had unravelled in the man's arms as he carried her down the path from the lake. She opened her eyes and could see the canopy of the forest above her and the cold rock of the mountain beyond his face. Then there was nothing.

"I've been thinking lately about how cats play with their food," she heard herself telling him. And then she could smell the pine needles and hear the waterfalls. Her arm flopped out from her body as the man descended into the dark. She tried to find the part in her brain to fold her arm back into her body; its weight was tearing at her shoulder. Blind valleys blocked her thoughts; so much so that she thought the man's wheezing was her own laboured breath. "I can't keep my head up," she could hear herself mumbling.

"Just hang in there, Claire," he huffed. "We're a long way from help."

She tried to speak to him, tried to open her mouth, but the waves kept tumbling over her, pulling her farther under, deeper into sleep. She knew this much: she knew that she was dying. She felt the cold earth against her back, her hair tangled in the brittle underbrush.

The tigress is watching you from the bluff. You can see her tail flicking over the rock.

"Yes, I can feel her watching me," Claire said. Her heart mumbled in her chest without a rhythm. "I'm tired, very tired," she heard herself call out.

She hunts by ambush. You know from the pugmarks in the dirt, feathered and barely visible, that she has been running.

There was a distant echo.

It was the man's voice squeezing through, hurtling itself toward

her consciousness. "Shhh, hang in there. We're almost to the car."
And she felt herself being flung across his shoulders like a lamb
brought in for slaughter.

*The tigress will curl herself around you and sink her teeth into
your spine. Paralyzed, you will watch yourself being eaten.*
"No pain. I want no pain."

The car slowed and Claire rolled forward, almost falling onto
the floor in the back of the Volvo, and then she rolled onto her
back again. She could see the last of the mountains through the
back window; Orion was already in the western sky. It must be
very early in the morning, she thought. She finally remembered
the man's name and she spoke it aloud.

"David?" she asked, and believing for a brief moment that
she wasn't there, she called out, "Can you hear me?"

"We are almost at the hospital, Claire. Hang in there. It is
just over there. Please, Claire. Claire, can you hear me?"

She could hear him. She knew his name. But she couldn't
hear her voice when she tried to answer him, *Yes, yes, I can hear
you, David*, she thought she might have said.

The nurse rolled Claire's veins back and forth beneath the tip of a
needle. They had become hard and impermeable and short of
"cutting-down" to find an entry into her veins, the nurse tried
the top of her foot, in between her toes, the carotid of the neck and
finally she was able to secure a heparin lock in the back of Claire's
forearm. Claire opened her eyes and closed them again. "Just let
me sleep, please," she said.

Psst. Claire?
"Who is that?" Claire said aloud.

The nurse bent her ear toward Claire. "What was that, dear?"

You know how you die. It is already inside you.

Claire reached up and pulled the nurse's hand away from her wrist. "Get away from me!" she screamed.

"Are my eyes still blue?"
Beautiful blue.
"Are the whites of my eyes clear?"
Crystal clear.
"Then I'm still alive?"
Still alive.
"Barely?"
Yes, barely.
"Who are you?"
My name is Nur.

Claire opened her eyes again. Her brother, Ben, leaned into her face. She whispered, "What are you doing here?"

His eyes were full of tears and his smile was weak when he said, "To make sure I get my half of the climbing rack." He squeezed her shoulder. "Doctor says you've had a rough ride. You're not out of the woods yet."

Beyond her brother, David was slumped in a chair, his head bowed forward, his face hidden behind his folded arms. Above her head she could feel her mother's bony fingers trembling through her hair. Claire smiled and closed her eyes. She could hear someone arguing outside the door to her room.

Her father and mother held hands. We are in this together for you, Claire, her father said and then he began to sing, *Bai lai lee lai*. It was a song of his mother's that he had tried to recall. *Bai lai lee lai*. You are dead, Claire thought, you are my father and you are dead. But there were others, too, and their corpses littered the floor around her like flies at the end of the season. Her grandfather was lying prostrate on a train station platform; clouds of sunlit dust lingered over him. And her father's feet flopped as she dragged him from the shower stall; wet and cold, he was wet and cold. You are dead, she thought, you are my father and you are dead. And a young woman, with a surprising resemblance to Claire, was curled on a marble floor; her fingers were gripping the folds of her blue chiffon dress. They were all there — and they were dead. Seems they don't burn anybody anymore? Claire thought. "Someone should clean up this mess," she said aloud.

Her mother leaned down to her face. "What's that, dear?" Claire could smell lilacs on her mother's breath.

The young woman in the blue chiffon dress uncurled her head and looked up at Claire. Mark me in your dreams, Claire, she said. Something simple on the soles of my feet. And Claire asked, Why? Why your feet? And the young woman in the blue chiffon dress spiralling around herself like a fiddlehead in spring said, So when you come to find me you will know it is me. Oh, how I long for my children.

"Nurse? She's trying to say something," Claire could hear her mother call out.

You will come to find me, won't you? said the blue, marbled, infinitely beautiful statue on the cool stone floor, blinking her frozen eyelids and animating her lips to form the words, God, I long for freedom from the father yoke, freedom from the father yoke, freedom from the father yoke. One day you will look out your window and the landscape will lose all its colours; hills will meet the sky without notice, buildings will blend into one another without corners, and your skin, your skin will disappear into the walls of this room; everything, everything will be seamless. Plans, yes, I made plans. I was going to revise old habits but when they found me curled and blind in the orange light of dusk, scraping at myself, excavating, performing my life's work, my fingers like stone claws rippling the hem of my blue chiffon dress, I knew that I had truly died.

It was winter and Claire could see from her hospital window the drifts of snow against a split rail fence. She was cold as she watched her heart's signature on a monitor, hardly a hiccup on the screen, and then a vigorous mess of lines. She went to lean on the voice inside herself and stumbled into her own familiar darkness. A jolt. A smell of burning flesh. The young woman in the blue chiffon dress continued, We are the hunted and the huntress. We are the last of our kind.

Another jolt and the young woman with long dark hair and wide mouth in the blue chiffon dress rose up from the floor on all fours and leapt out the window with catlike efficiency.

The bubbles were starting to weep and her ribs ached from the fractures. They placed the paddles over her chest for what Claire hoped would be the last time. Her eyes rolled from side to side beneath her eyelids.

David is watching you. He is thinking you are watching a car race, or a tennis match, or maybe it is the hydro poles alongside the highway.

Resting in the savannah with the warm sun on her back, Claire lay beneath the voices in the room. She imagined how permanent death would feel, pure and unencumbered. Her heart mumbled aimlessly in her chest.

There is a certain comfort in death, and you think that everything will become so unnecessary, until, of course, no one mentions you.

She stumbled, she puked, she convulsed like an epileptic.

The tiger rises on all fours and her shoulder blades stretch through her skin. Her ears press back and she snorts, pacing back and forth, swiping the air with her paw, hissing. You are so close you can hear her nostrils click. Her sour breath turns your stomach and you can smell your own death on her wind. The wrinkles in her nose are like the ripple marks left by the river. Her teeth are clean and white. She lunges toward you and you feel the warmth of her body in what should be the coolness of her shadow. You think you are in a thousand days of darkness as you stand firm to catch your knife in an angle as tight as the noonday sun. Her flesh tugs and snaps around the three blades of the Kangar widening inside her body and you throw yourself between her hind legs. Her body collapses behind you.

She lies moaning on the ground with the air from her lungs escaping around the silver handle of your knife. You stroke her breast. Waves of steam rise from the loose flaps of mouth that droop around her teeth. Something stirs in you. Something you recognize. Perhaps it is her strained pulse that makes you think of yourself, but while you rest your head on her chest you feel what you believe to be the last beat of your life.

"My life?" Claire opened her eyes and fixed them on the monitor beside her bed.

The wires slid through her arteries and the barbs hooked into the walls of her heart. She felt the subtlety of electricity signalling the first beat and then the next and the next and the next.

"Can you take a breath for me, Claire?" the surgeon asked.

Like a surge channel, Claire's mind rushed toward the shores of the conscious world and from as violent a current as birth, Claire arrived. David leaned over and stroked her head.

"You're back," he said.

"Do you have a straw?"

"Why?"

"So you can blow me up again."

You slice the belly of the tiger open and stuff your hands into her entrails. A fetus curled and blind slips from her womb. You are horrified when you tear at the filmy sac and discover that she is one of your own, interrupted selves — orphaned and suffocated.

Balloons floated into the corners of the hospital room, bouquets of flowers covered the windowsill and cards hung over the curtain rod like flags. David was browsing through a magazine. He seemed older, more tired than usual. Claire sipped her orange juice. She sat upright in her bed. "Distanciation keeps everything from being seamless."

"I like seamless," David said.

"I don't. I like it when images don't match up. It keeps me awake."

Alive, you mean. It keeps you alive.

David looked over the top of his glasses and smiled. "You must be feeling better."

"You know that there are no more tigers."

"What does that have to do with distanciation?"

"Everything, I think."

Fifty-six hours later, while the nurse was writing Claire's vitals on a chart at the central station, Claire called out from her bed,

"Would someone please wash my hair?"

Blood drips from the tiger's teeth and dimples the dust at the threshold of your home. And all you want to do is wash the scabs from your forearms.

And then the weather turned.

Pune 1925

Mosquitoes in the Hide, black eddies in her blood, black water in a chamber pot. Alice's malarial fever burned her from the inside out and she found herself moping behind the gauze canopy of her bed day after day. Sometimes, while sewing or sitting on the bench in the back garden watching the children play, she could feel a slowing, and in a pause as long as it took a shadow to fall across her face, she could see the end of her life. She would drop her head, lean her elbows on her knees and focus her eyes on the ground before her, waiting, just waiting for her heart to begin beating again.

It was as if her lips were the measure of life; their numb, cool state was the colour of death — blue. She would bite and drag their flesh through her teeth, trying for pain, slicing through to the sweet red blood of her heart's effusion; and her breath was quantifiable too, no longer smelling of the coconut creams or the slow-baked turnips (and their caramelized aftertaste) of her youth, but it had become a callowed breath, webbed and rattled from somewhere darker than sleep. She chewed the leaves of parsley and thyme. She steamed cardamom and cinnamon and burned her nostrils with the ambitious heat. She slapped herself and pinched the inside of her arms and bruises flowered beneath the sleeves of her dress. She sustained. And then she slowly resumed.

She took walks at a frail, convalescent pace, to the gate and back, and eventually down the road toward the River Mula. She sat along the banks of the river, plucked the grasses and chewed their whitened roots. An old woman collecting wash water from beneath the bridge inquired after her health. She asked the old woman to fetch her a rickshaw.

And then one morning she awoke with the sunlight warming her body. As she stretched her arms and legs, she felt their sinew recaptured in her muscled reach. She dangled her one leg off the side of her bed and held her fingers against the filtered sunlight.

Alice pulled herself from her infirmary to rejoin the activities of her household. Intermittently at first, and then as the weeks passed, she revived. Barely a trace of the malaria remained — nothing visible except for the way her clothes hung like surrender from her body.

PART THREE
Study of Collision

Tiger Dreams Film Part VIa Sequence

Long take of electron microscope of plasmodium in bloodstream. Violent images of blood cells bursting. Ritardando — Freeze Frame.

Pune 1925

Having finished her exhaustive study of pigments and their import from foreign lands for the early Buddhist art of the Ajanta Caves, Alice was ready for new territory. She began to occupy herself with numismatics, first by beginning to develop a key for the signs of old mints and their decorative symbols. She, Charlotte, Sheila Rana and the children would cross the River Mula, drive into the old part of town and hike the long wide stairs to Parvati Temple where Alice would cull and sort through the artifacts left by the last Peshwa ruler, many of which were the coins found in the temple treasury after the British defeated the Brahmin family in 1817. While the children played along the roof of the temple and Charlotte and Sheila rested in the shade of the Thente tree, Alice engaged herself in the nineteenth-century glories of one of the last stands against the British.

From the top of Parvati Hill, Alice could look over the plains; she was acutely aware that the increasing influence of the city of Pune was gradually beating out the tribal communities for their remaining parcels of land and she couldn't help but wonder if her way of life — the acquiescence to British authority — was Right and Just.

Tiger Dreams Film Part VII Sequence

An arthroscopic camera tracks the path of gold as its molten form washes
through tunnelled branches into cul-de-sacs. The cast is then broken
open and coins are cut from the branches of the tree and they tumble
into a clay pot. The same veiled woman, bloodied from battle with
the tiger, picks a coin from the pot and inspects it. Her profile is on
one side of the coin. She nods approval. Tracking shot of veiled woman
as she leaves the mint and walks past mounds of dirt, the shallow
graves of tiger.

Damodra 1925

Alice's interest in the coins of the temple treasury soon began to wane. She wanted to return to the desert where the commerce of the sixteenth and seventeenth century, during the height of the Mughal Empire, had thrived. She had been very clear with Denzil about her need to escape the confines of the prison grounds of Yeravda and she tried to convince him of her relative good health.

"There is a living fort," she told Denzil. "One that is still inhabited at the edge of the desert."

"Jaisalmer?"

"Yes."

"I am aware of it."

"It was once a great city for trade. And the ruins just west of Jaisalmer ..."

"Damodra. I am aware of that settlement as well."

"Denzil, the desert will simply be lousy with coins," she begged.

"And that is what you are leaving us for?"

"For a month, Denzil. You'll hardly notice my absence."

"I should doubt that very much, Alice." As Alice walked from the room, panic like a breeze passed over the hair on Denzil's arms and he shivered. This had come to him before, disguised as indifference, but now it seemed more flagrant than that, and was beyond self-deception. Since Alice's bout of malaria, he had struggled with the impermanence of his desire.

It had been different when they first met. He paid much closer attention back then. He studied her habits: where she walked, what she read, who her friends were. He concocted lame excuses to visit his sister and timed his hikes to coincide with their picnics. He remembered with absolute clarity that first night they had made love. A piano recital at Sherwood College.

Alice had played many times during the hot at her parents' home, and sometimes he would sit on the stairs of All Saints and listen to her practise in the chapel during the afternoons. He had had a fondness for music and his own guitar playing had received many accolades when he and Richard performed at the clubhouse on Saturday evenings.

He had been determined to settle things with Alice before he was to leave for Malbagong. Back then, determination was one of his most celebrated attributes and one both of them shared. Denzil remembered how she wore her hair that evening, tossed on the top of her head like a mistake, her neck long, and her shoulders narrow. He closed his eyes and refreshed himself with the scent of almond oil she had had on her skin that evening.

After the recital, Alice conversed with the artist by the piano at the far end of the hall. When he could no longer sustain his composure, Denzil grabbed her ungraciously by the elbow and dragged her through the side door into the shadows of the colonnade. Her sweater had fallen over her shoulders and light from the hall caught the white of her shirt; it was startling against her skin. He silenced her laughter with his hand gently over her mouth.

It was as if Alice carried a storm within her, one that could heat up the metal of his watch, and he flicked his hand quickly away from her lips. "Shhhh," he whispered. Her breath smelled like coconut creams and he wanted to devour her. He pressed his thumb into her upper arm and all he could say was, "Be with me, please?"

Those words were all he could bring to his lips, all he could conjure in that moment.

She leaned against the pillar, baring her neck like a doe run down by the dogs. She looked down at his hand, the one that squeezed her arm, and slowly peeled his fingers off her. "Is that a proposal, Denzil?"

"Yes," he smiled.

Her pupils were wide and he could see his reflection in their dark stare. He stroked the skin on her neck with his fingertips and felt the static between them as if the clouds above had something to do with longing. She teased him, moving herself deeper into the shadows of the thick brick arches that surrounded the courtyard outside the recital hall. "You might, in time, grow disenchanted with me," she whispered.

He followed her lead and took her chin in his hand. "Don't be trite, Alice," and he could barely squeeze out the next three words, "I want you."

She took his hand and placed it over one of her breasts, full and round. His palm fit perfectly over her firmness and her deep breaths dissolved him. Animal humidity from beneath the rough woollen fabric of her trousers warmed him as he leaned himself into her and shuddered in complete resignation. The stifled conversations of the gathering inside the recital hall had filled the empty spaces of the courtyard outside.

That seemed so long ago, that storm, those clouds. He knew he would have to let her go to the desert, to Damodra — to restore her, to restore him. He recognized his waning passion, but every bit of his desire yearned to rekindle it.

Alice left Barbara and George with Sheila Rana, and the duties of the household to Denzil's cousin Charlotte. Alice wasn't like the other women of the compound. She didn't take months to prepare nor did she require an entourage of servants to accommodate her wishes. She left without a whisper, one afternoon while Denzil was on an inspection. There was no question of her return so she didn't want to make a fuss of her leaving.

She took the train to Bombay and then from Bombay to Udaipur, Udaipur to Pushkar, Pushkar to Jaipur, Jaipur to Bikaner, and Bikaner to her final destination, Jaisalmer. By the time she arrived in Jaisalmer, Alice was so exhausted she slept for two days before cabling Denzil to let him know that all had gone well and that she should be home within a month's time. *The family will hardly even notice my absence,* she wrote.

"We already do, Alice," he mumbled and tossed the telegram on his desk in his office of the Yeravda Prison.

The following morning, Alice and her camel driver left the fort with food and water for a week and drove their camels directly west from Jaisalmer. The fortress shone golden in the dawn light as she settled into her saddle and felt for the rhythm of the camel's gait. Candles flickered inside metal cages shaped like balls that rolled across the sand as farmers already finished their morning chores before the rising heat of the day, extinguished them and stuffed them into their packs. By noon of that first day, Alice could already feel the heat of blistering sores on her backside.

As she moved slowly through the afternoon, she watched life in the desert circle back on itself, beginning and ending again and again. The desert was good for that: with little distraction, life and death appeared unfettered in their purpose. First, a dead camel, then a bloated one, followed by a belly swarming with maggots, and finally, a camel's bony remains, like exclamations, arced across the scabbed sand. A flock of sheep circled and collapsed like schoolchildren in the shade of a tree while two goats, closer to the path, clawed the upper branches of a brittle shrub. Burned from the sun, leaves of the jojoba plant stretched in rows across the pale terra-cotta sand. Thatch-roofed homes, mud-caked walls and fences, sandstone rails and posts, furrowed red fields of freshly turned soil, and water from recent monsoons floated over the impervious earth as Alice leaned back on the wooden saddle and sipped water from her canteen, the pain from her saddle sores a part of her now. There was evidence of human industry, yes, but not a footprint or whisper anywhere. Camels pulled carts of hay, carts of melons. It was the season of the turnip, of the pomegranate; Nada, her camel driver, offered her the red fruit with tea. She could feel his eyes on her as she peeled its leathery skin back to get at the tart red seeds and she couldn't help but smile as she pressed the back of her hand against the drop of crimson trickling down her chin, the juice spreading down her neck and beneath the white linen of her blouse.

In the pauses, she thought, the body reorganizes. The disorder of her life found order in the simplicity of desert existence. She regretted not having Denzil with her; they might have been able to recover some of what they had lost in recent years. She remembered the first time they had come to the desert together, when they were still fresh and inspired with each other. He had timed the sunsets while she mixed their drinks. It was so easy to think of these things clearly while away from the centre — Denzil, the children, everything usual and ordinary about her life.

It seemed their politics were no longer compatible, what with the Home Rule movement and Quit India campaigns. When she had told him that the British should bloody well pick up their socks or get out, he told her he didn't much like the direction of her politics. He had grown quiet around her, no longer sharing the affairs of his office — not like he used to — not like when she would listen for hours about the languages he was mastering from different prisoners — Gujarati, Konkani, and her mother's language, Malayalam. He would tell her about the developments in the prison bakery, or his plans for apprenticeship programs. Not anymore. Perhaps, she thought, she had been too opinionated.

Alice and Nada arrived at Damodra after dark and slept beneath the stars on a narrow strip of dunes beyond the sandstone ramparts of Jaisalmer. Perhaps it was the stillness of the desert night or the lack of clutter around her, but when she woke in the night to Orion neat and tidy in the centre of the sky, she believed the stars were her blood and the planets her eyes, and she saw clearly what she had not seen before: like the shadow of the needle on a moon dial — deadly accurate, never lying — Alice realized that time had been chasing her all her life. In the desert she understood without naming, without cataloguing and culling, that she was nearing her own death.

She sat up and listened to the crickets rub their wings. Always the crickets. Just like in the foothills. Nada sat quietly stirring the fire with a stick, the yellow glow colouring his cheek green like the veined and pulsing leaf of a plant. She felt hunted and pathetic with hunger, wanting to consume his gorgeous black body, his purity. She lay back down tentatively and watched the sparks from his fire rise and disappear as the sky rotated toward dawn.

The morning sun was like a balloon full of water, heavy on the horizon, and the horizon, like a moat around the earth, was pale in comparison to the dark blue land surrounding her. Flies arrived unwanted, always unwanted, and she wondered if she had settled beside something dead. Coolness came up through the sand and blew across the top of her head, a wind that shifted the grains of sand, tumbling thoughts like landslides through her memory. Red and red and red slid down from the lip on the windward side of the dune. She rose from her sleeping place and felt the solid outline of her footprint as she stepped onto the ripples. Her shadow stretched long and lean across the scalloped sand where she and the camels had walked the night before. *Maybe this is how it will happen*, she thought, *it will happen in pieces, like a trail of stars behind a quarter moon*. She would leave a piece of herself behind, in each footprint.

She wandered over to the fire for her tea.

"Hai, Kulu, hai," grunted Nada. "Hummmph, hummmph." The desert heated up. Nada, in his quiet way, swept his hand gently over the camel's head and Kulu, the camel, unfolded his back legs first and then his front — the soft pads of his hooves spreading weight evenly over the ground — and walked toward a low dry shrub at the edge of the dunes. Over tea, Nada spoke as if the past and future were irrelevant. *I am coming, I am eating, I am thinking,* he said in the essential verbs of his life, and Alice began to mumble beneath her breath, *I am walking, I am riding, I am searching,* relieved that neither her memories nor her premonitions were necessary here — with this man — in this desert.

In the shade of trees at noon, Alice pulled a tick from the back of her neck and spoke frankly with the camel driver. "Nada? Have you ever been in love?"

"I am loving? No, I am not loving."

"Will you ever marry?"

"I am never marrying. Indian woman is not a good thing. Uhhh," and he struggled through the next words, "I am meeting woman in my village. I am meeting, meeting, meeting and they are not liking me." He smiled.

"I can hardly believe that." Alice smiled back at him as she wiped the ticks off the blanket beside her and lay back on the saddle that Nada had placed for her on the sand. A lizard cast a sliver of a shadow and a bird sang a song with phrases that stuttered and slid. Nada — his colour of molasses, his humility — Alice found pleasing. He was such a sharp contrast to the brash arrogance of men in Pune society. He offered her Indian tea and then disappeared over the hillside to retrieve the camels. Alice thought she could love him, that she could disappear into his world and live out her final days and never again speak with memory. *We are existing,* she thought and yes, she was loving him. She knew she was envying him. This was how it was for her now: the desire to speak of love and truth with another man.

She lay back and fell asleep. In her dreams, she got up from beneath the tree and walked over the hillside to Nada. He was walking beside Kulu, pulling him gently from the wooden bridle that had been threaded through the camel's nose. Alice strode over to him and stood in his path. Nada stopped. Kulu halted and threw his head back. Alice leaned toward Nada and kissed him warmly on the mouth. When she felt his fine fingers on her hip she straightened, and made off in the opposite direction, her heels digging and swirling in the sand. She woke, abruptly. Petulant.

She had not come to this place to explore the wetness of another man's mouth. Oh, but her betrayal was delicious, like the taste of fennel or anise. Her dream-kiss with Nada was impulsive, not well thought out, a reprehensible act that she would have to sanctify before returning to Pune. But the slight opening in her heart, like a smirk, something as precocious as betrayal or petty theft, delighted her.

Nada remained in the distance, ignorant of his infidelities, a slim figure kneeling at his camel's hooves — busy with the preoccupations of his service.

A few hundred metres from the oasis were the ruins she had travelled this far to explore. Before her were mud-caked walls flaking off blocks of sandstone strewn over the baked earth. There were rooms as small as a toilet for sleeping and ovens the same size to bake in. Tiny shrubs eked out between the cracks of earth and petrified patties of cow dung lined the doorways and windows of the roofless ruins.

Hot breath passed over the plains and ruffled her skirts as she rummaged through the ancient settlements of the Mauryas, the Guptas or the Mughals after they had been invaded by the Portuguese, the Dutch or the English. Or more than likely, they had rivalled amongst themselves. They had traded trinkets for trinkets, beaver hats for perfume pots or paintings of Mary and Jesus for calicoes and indigoes — all this for the fancy of their women.

Alice's fingers probed tunnels of air in the sand that harboured the dens of scorpions. The thin crust buckled and revealed warm damp sand beneath. She thought herself immune to the dangers of the desert sun, the poison of scorpions, the fangs of a snake. It was only the thickness of her tongue and her split lips that alerted her to the perils before her. Thirst — she must slake her thirst.

The hardened ripple marks beneath her were evidence of a river's current. She knew that beneath her lay the myth of water and, as a diviner would, she bent toward the earth, witching her way toward the deep golden waters of a river as ancient as Saraswati. She had hypothesized in an article for a small publication in Ahmedabad that a fault lay beneath the sands and that a catastrophic event, occurring thousands of years before, had left the area in a constant state of dehydration. Collision: Alice could not leave the theory alone. She had laboured over the concept of a shifting earth for years. Impermanence. Sand always blowing and something always being revealed.

She rolled some perfectly round beads of volcanic rock around in her hands as she watched Nada walk barefoot toward her. His toes flattened against the solid earth. The soles of his feet were like custard, his heels were white against Indian blackness. "You are making up your mind?" he smiled, and handed her a canister of water.

"Yes, Nada. I am making up my mind."

"It is a good thing, to be knowing your mind."

"Yes, I am knowing my mind." She handed him evidence of her find and watched him while he turned the balls around and around in his black hands.

He shrugged and handed them back to her. "I am starting the fire. I am cooking for eating."

She watched Nada walk over the crest of the dune and returned to scouring the earth for more evidence of some other existence. Was there a way to excavate the future to see the woman she could have become? When she was young, she used to bury bits of string in wooden logs, coins in the roots of a tree. She imagined that in thousands of years a scientist would discover the string and speculate about it. She had always left hints behind her, believing that someone, years after her death, would come along and make sense of it all. She imagined that person would experience the same hunger, the same primal desire to understand the beginning and end of everyone. She wished she could reach forward to an arbitrary date in the future so she could see with her own eyes, and not through the filter of her death, her own children grown and profitable in love. How could she possibly do that? For now the knowledge of her own death seemed like a comfortable bedfellow — not so unusual.

Sand poured through her fingers as she worked along a grid staked out with string. Culling chips of clay, silver lids of ewers, and coins, Alice was a conduit between the past and present, uncluttered and free from skepticism, her body intuitive.

Some coins were brutally disfigured, the impressions completely obliterated and the corrosion so violent along the edges they looked like the end of an exploded bullet. Other coins boasted clarity — the exquisite outline of a face or the geometric symbol of a forgotten language or the detail of a garment. There were coins with the blue-green patina of tarnished copper, or the black of ancient gold; their metal had been softened and smoothed by the heat of human hands, their reeded edges were thin and worn.

She turned over one particular coin in the fading light. Its edges were thin and smeared. The distorted figures of three women holding swords were on the obverse of the coin and the profile of a woman's face was on the reverse. Not an ancient coin, no, not ancient, but a coin made of the finest gold, full of the weight that feels like wealth, a decadence coupled with tyranny. Cut from a strip of gold, then hammered into circular discs, the coin was not the seated goddess type, nor did it feature any of the Hindu deities. It had been struck during the Mughals, she speculated — not a rare find, but a coin she would revisit.

The cold chill of the desert rising through the earth made her shiver and she placed the few artifacts in her pouch and prepared to return to camp. Nada would have some tea ready and he would sing his song.

On the crest of a dune, she could see the fire a few hundred metres from where she stood. Nada's sweet song flowed smoothly over the hardened dunes; it was a dissonant raga, something about love and separation. "Hichaki," he repeated, a vibrato of bent notes, sliding and dragging through the air, his canteen of water, a drum, the camel bells ringing haphazardly as Kulu and the second camel, Raju, stretched their necks and chewed, their camel-breath of regurgitated leaves filling her nostrils in a wave of hot musk.

The sun plummeted into the blues and oranges of the atmosphere; it took only moments to rest, a perfect orb fattening as it disappeared off the edge of earth. In the darkness, with the sound of crickets and camel bells and Nada's song, she could feel the stirring of a fetus in her belly. Her third child, she knew, would be a boy.

"You have been too whimsical with your health," Denzil told her when her fever returned the day after she arrived home from Damodra. "People die from malaria, for chrissakes, Alice! This is not a minor ailment to be toyed with!"

Denzil stood at the foot of Alice's bed. She lay prostrate on top of her dampened sheets, her cheeks flushed with fever, her eyes a metallic grey, her pupils wide and vacant.

She squinted, "Could you draw the curtains, darling? The light is just too bright. I have such a headache. Could you get me a cool cloth? I cannot seem to get comfortable. The children? Have they had their tiffin? Is that Barbara in the garden? Where are the children?" Alice flipped over to her hands and knees and began sifting through the bedclothes.

"What are you looking for?" Denzil asked.

"The children. I've misplaced the children." Alice pushed her fingers into the folds of the white sheet. "I've lost the children," she repeated.

Denzil watched Alice in her delirium seeking out the corners of the mattress, and then retreating to the centre, frantic, as if caged beneath the wooden canopy of their bed. He reached over and placed his hand on her forehead.

She looked up and with absolute clarity she sighed, "I'm right dotty, aren't I?"

He sat at the side of the bed and tried to calm her with his hands on her shoulders. In the past he could do that: when it seemed as if Alice was going to spin out of control, he could take her in his arms and hold her, contain her close to him and she would struggle and wriggle until she felt the wildness leave her. But this time Alice stiffened and she resisted him.

"Don't try to calm me. I don't want to be calm."

"Alice, please. You must rest."

"Stop telling me what to do, Denzil! Just stop it!"

Pearls of perspiration bubbled on her forehead. Denzil stood up and walked toward the north window of their room and pulled aside the curtain to see the children in the garden. "What happened to you out there, Alice?"

Alice sat with her back against the mahogany headboard. The flowerheads on the wallpaper were rustling in a breeze, and Denzil's tall frame was shrinking away from her as if she was looking through the wrong end of a spyglass. "I'm going to die, you know."

Denzil swung around and snapped at her, "Don't be ridiculous. You just have to do as the doctors tell you."

"Denzil?"

Denzil crossed to the bed and sat in front of her.

"Will you remember me to the children? I mean, you won't take another woman and forget me, will you?" She smiled generously.

"You, Alice?" he whispered. "How on earth am I supposed to manage you?" He peeled the damp strands of hair from her forehead and spoke slowly and deliberately, "You are not going to die today or tomorrow or even next month. The doctor said you could just as easily go into remission again. You are to take your medicine religiously, lie around for a couple of days, and then you will be your old self again."

"What is my old self, Denzil? I've lost track. What kind of a mother am I? What kind of a wife?"

"You do everything tolerably well, Alice. Perhaps you are a bit impetuous, much to the detriment of your own health, but you are still a spirited woman."

"Is that good? Will you remember that to the children for me?"

"We have to stop talking like this."

"Promise me." Alice's eyes returned to their deep brown again as if the fever had finally left her. "Promise me you will remember what you love most about me," she said in a clear voice.

Denzil turned back toward her. "Answer me one thing, Alice."

"What is that?"

"Did you know you were carrying a child before you left for the desert?"

Alice sat and stared into Denzil the way the Indian stares into everyone, stealing from him, taking his deepest fears and hoarding them. He closed his eyes to recapture what it was she was pulling out of him.

"Did you?" he deliberated, his eyes closed. "Did you know you were carrying a child?"

And Then You Dream This

You are a tiger and you dream you are a woman. The fetus inside you cries; you have starved him of bone. He will be born unmade, interrupted, blinded by what hasn't been said and suffocated by what hasn't been written. He will never forgive your ignorance.

Pune 1926

William Benjamin Spencer was born during the monsoons of 1926. The River Mula had flooded and the rains scattered the tulip blossoms like drops of blood across the courtyard. She lay feverish in her bed, chanting, "It is too hot tonight, it is too hot tonight," and the chuprassi ran down the road to the prison to retrieve Denzil from his office.

He had been working on a scheme to separate the Anglo-Indian and European prisoners from the native inmates, promising English food, mutton and potatoes to the Euro prisoners rather than the curries and rice of the Indian diet. The chuprassi's appearance beyond the curtained doorway of his office was a welcome distraction. He begged his leave and marched down the stairs and out the front entrance of the prison, nodding and cajoling the guards, who understood his mission.

By the time he arrived, Charlotte had taken the other two children into the library and Sheila Rana remained with Alice. It was not an easy birth; William had flipped himself around and tangled the umbilical cord around his neck. In the final stages of Alice's labour Sheila Rana cupped her hand around William's crown and with her other hand slipped the cord over his chin and unravelled him from the complications of his mother's belly. The skies cleared and the River Mula receded. William squeezed his way into the world and curled his brown body into his father's arms like a promise of sunshine. The malaria, no doubt, had weakened his body; his slender legs were bowed in an unnatural way and his tiny rib cage panted uncomfortably with his first breaths. Alice spent the next couple of months stretching the one side of his neck that had shortened during the months it had been wrapped awkwardly in his own cord. She knew now that it was William she had heard crying inside her womb.

"Looks as if you've bred the Indian right out of him," Helen Beverly, the prison doctor's wife, remarked a year later as they watched the children push the old metal wheels of bicycles around the planters in the back garden.

"He'll darken up," replied Alice.

"I should think it will make his life a lot easier when you send him home for schooling." Helen rubbed her bad knee, the one that always got worse at this time of year. "You are going to send them off to school soon, aren't you?"

"Why is it, Helen?" Alice asked impatiently. "I don't understand this: why is it that you call England home when you have never been there?"

Helen looked thoughtfully at Alice. "I've never thought about it much, I suppose. It's just what we've always called it."

Alice didn't want to engage in another discussion about the advantages and disadvantages of the British Education System over the system they all grew up with in India. The trend lately had been to ship the children off to British boarding schools if the family could afford it. The Anglos were being marginalized in the Indian universities and it was thought they would fare better if they were raised with the Mother's English in the British system. Though no one could ever quite articulate for Alice what exactly was so advantageous about sending a young child away from family and India to be raised by nuns and priests, in a country as difficult to get to as any on the map, when there was perfectly adequate, and dare she say, affordable education on Indian soil. "We haven't discussed it yet," she said finally. Her clipped response silenced Helen Beverly, who knew better than to press Alice on certain issues with regard to the British Way of doing things.

Helen Beverly's two girls, and Alice's two children, Barbara and George, had stopped pushing their wheels around the garden. They were now coaching young William to hop up and down along the path. The two women sat quietly listening to the children play.

"How 'bout we get him to hop like a bunny."

"How 'bout he is a bunny and we're his mummy."

"How 'bout you're his mummy and I'm his daddy."

"How 'bout I came 'round the forest like this and was going to hunt you."

"How 'bout we all were hunters 'cept for William."

"How 'bout I was a princess and you had to do everything I told you to."

"How 'bout William wasn't a bunny but he was a bird."

"William, hold your arms like this."

"How 'bout we were in an aeroplane and we saw you on the ground and we waved at you ..."

The children played all afternoon while the two women sat in the garden avoiding issues with one another. Their guardedness was exhausting and by the time Helen Beverly and her children finally left, Alice collapsed on the jula, a broad flat swing, on the porch and moaned at the children to amuse themselves until their father got home from work.

A cool breeze passed over the garden and it began to rain again. Alice longed for the seasons in the foothills, the dusting of snow over the grasses, the clear nights when the stars were close enough to touch, the air thin and precious, and the question of her mother's blood beside the point.

Claire's Recovery, Mid-November

"You're a lucky girl," Margaret Barnes told her.

"Why is that?" Claire asked Margaret. It was the morning she left the hospital.

"Most people with this condition drop dead before anybody gets to them."

Margaret placed her arm around Claire's shoulders, walked her down the hallway into a private room and closed the door behind them. She motioned for Claire to sit.

"You have what is called Sudden Arrhythmic Death Syndrome or I prefer Long QT Syndrome. It is an electrical malfunction in the way the heart beats. According to the information we have now, whole families have suffered with this condition. The gene is passed from generation to generation. Are you aware of any sudden deaths in your family?"

Claire immediately thought of her brother. "Has Ben been tested?"

"Yes, we took a tracing when he was here but he'll need to check it again. We don't always catch it the first time. What about your father's family? Are you in contact with any of them?"

Claire let out a nervous laugh. "No ..." she said. Anatomy posters covered the walls in the room. There were pictures of muscular red men, their organs splayed open in various stages of dissection; profiles of women's breasts; a large four chambered human heart over the threshold of the door; a poster of pace-makers, hundreds of them, generation I, II, and III with names like Cosmos, Galaxy, Solar, pictures of pacemaker leads with barbed ends like some freakish sex toy snaking across the top. There was also a bone man who dangled inanimately from a hook in the far corner. Anatomy and wires and batteries were making her feel fleshy and hot and she lunged for the door to open it and let some air into the room.

"My father's family," she said, panting at the door. "They are all dead, as far as I know."

Margaret signed the bottom of a piece of paper, closed a file and went to the door. "The cardiologist will want to see you every week for a couple of months. We have you as part of a lead study and would appreciate you notifying us if you have any abnormal rhythms. The pacemaker ought to take care of most of those problems but for the first while we'd like to keep a real close eye on things."

"Well, at least we know now, eh?" Claire said.

Margaret leaned against the frame of the door. "I just wish you hadn't had to go through what you went through." She looked up at Claire. "I'm sorry I didn't pick up on it earlier."

"Answer me one question, Margaret."

"And what question would that be, Claire?"

"The one about how many worlds there are."

"Only two that I know of, Claire."

"Which two would those be, Margaret?"

"You've seen too much, Claire."

"Too much of what?"

"Too much of the other side."

"Yes, but there's no going back now. I can't feign ignorance."
Claire smiled and left the room.

David and her mother met Claire at the front entrance to the hospital. "Get me out of this place," she said and crawled into the back seat of David's Volvo. They took her home and tucked her into bed and there she remained, still and fragile as glass.

The burns on her chest healed, her cracked ribs ached with each breath, and the small battery resting underneath her breast steadied her nervous heart. The scar beneath her collarbone was widening, overhealing they told her, like the mid-Atlantic ridge, its soft red chaos bubbling up and cooling, spreading her apart like the torn skin of the earth. She carried Charlotte Blake's coins around like talismans and had commissioned a jeweller to tool her favourite coin, the one with the three women on it, into a pendant. She wore its chain short so as not to interfere with her scar's illustrious healing. She left temporary impressions of herself, the curve of her body on her bed, footprints in the carpet, wet feet on the floor, coffee grounds on the counter. Feeling absent, Claire tiptoed through the next couple of weeks, afraid to move for fear of awakening the deep history inside her. She carried her fear like an afflicted Jesuit, downcast, repentant, afraid to sleep, afraid she might disappear, afraid that David might not notice the body lying beside him had died in the night. She began to refer to herself in the past tense: I came, I went, I saw.

It seemed she didn't need to sleep anymore. Her body was always awake, unable to slow down. In the evening she would read or watch late-night movies. During a viewing of *A bout de souffle*, she'd exclaim in the blue-grey light of 2:00 a.m., "Godard's a genius!" and she'd rewind and play, over and over, the jump cuts between sequences. She'd count the montage cuts in Renais Clair's *Entr'acte*, cast doubt upon the subversion of Altman films, and hurl curses at the comic horror of Tarentino's work.

Later, after she had exhausted herself, she'd crawl in beside David and lie with her head toward magnetic north — to avoid somersaulting into David's incessant hibernation.

The pacemaker had doubled her normal heart rate and to override its power, she ran everywhere, the heel leading the whole foot, a quiet upper body, a slack jaw. She spent most of her time trying to gain control over a body that had betrayed her and she wondered if this was the adaptation the doctors had warned her about, or if it was her pacemaker rejecting her, pushing her out of herself.

She became obsessed with the black hole of her origins — her father's father, his mother, his brother, sister, all dead — information she resented her father for not sharing with her. She phoned Ben weekly, encouraging him to get tracings, and in some perverse way wanted him to share her defect. But Ben did not have the condition; it seemed there were anomalies in her case, it seemed she didn't quite fit the statistics. Perhaps, she thought, the anomaly was because she was still alive. There was an organization the cardiologist had encouraged her to join. They had a bi-monthly newsletter and published photographs of individuals who were described in past tense. They were standing alongside their surviving family members. Claire refused to subscribe.

She felt only the gnawing of daily life, like a tigress on a carcass, scraping life's blood with her teeth, wanting, always wanting, what she could not have — which was, in the simplest terms, to slow down, to sleep, to be ignorant of her own extinction.

David couldn't remember how to touch her and he told her that he thought her body different, more muscular, more transient. When she lay on top of him and he stroked the coolness of her skin, she thought she'd like to draw his blood. There was the constant reminder in the faint whisperings in her dreams that the storms rising within her were not her own. That they belonged to the woman she was just becoming.

Jouissance. He had given her the word before he left for the Maritimes to edit a film. Though she knew the word was French, she thought it must have made it into the English lexicon — but she couldn't find the word in any of her dictionaries. It was a bouncy word, something that sounded like what it meant — to be jubilant — and she had spent the last couple of weeks, in David's absence, searching for a context in which to use it. She saw its reconstruction in images. This was his gift to her. She would only be able to find it by marrying her images together, completing some kind of circle between her subject and her audience. Jouissance — the experience of seeing oneself as unified, rather than fragmented.

On the day David returned home, she walked across the bridge to meet him at the coffee shop. She stopped and leaned over the cement guard-rail of the bridge. The river was in full flood, its current tugged at the grass along the banks, boulders — usually visible — were submerged beneath pillows of pale green water. She preferred the river when it was more forgiving of the land. She pushed away from the railing. The rush of spring run-off was inside her head and she bolted to catch the light on the other side of the bridge. She would make herself interesting to David, she promised herself. She would read newspaper articles and books to help her with conversation. She would leave her preoccupations behind and begin a new, more interesting life with him.

In the coffee shop — where people were immersed in their own rituals of survival — Claire ordered two coffees and sat on a stool facing the street.

David arrived from the other direction and stood before her on the other side of the window; he was unshaven and his broad mouth wrinkled in the corners when he smiled. He came around and sat down, ran his fingers through his greying hair and took a sip of his coffee. Claire thought him decidedly handsome with his broad angular jaw and his nose almost too large for his face. She let her eyes rest on him for a moment as if seeing him for the first time.

"You know what I have missed most about sleeping?" she said.

His eyes, the colour of glaciers, stared at her. "Let me guess." He took another sip and asked, "Your dreams?"

"Yes, exactly. Some of my greatest ideas come from dreams. Now, I only get fragments."

"Jouissance. Did you figure out what to do with it?"

"I'm working on it. I'll have to show you. How was your flight home?"

She focussed on David and listened to him; his observations of the east coast, the storms, the people — their pleasing natures. She could see in his eyes, the way he stopped to gaze at her, the way he held his breath, that she could still enchant him.

"Jouissance is beyond desire," she said after he'd finished describing his trip.

He smiled smugly. "Sex and death are too," he said.

"Beyond reality? Jouissance is imbedded in the dream, isn't it?"

"Remember that point when you cut up your films the way you do."

"Ah, yes. It was only a matter of time."

"What?"

"You always have an agenda."

They sat and sipped their coffee, both wanting to start the sequence again, looping forwards and back until the tension became unbearable or dissipated altogether. Claire felt weak and obvious, as if her own immutable history might be showing through her skin.

"I've been sick, you know. Quite sick."

"I know," he said. "You don't think I know?"

"I know you know. I don't know what made me say that."

They both took another sip of coffee. Loop.

"I have to go to Vancouver."

"Why? I just got back from the Maritimes."

"There's a camera I want."

"Can't it wait?"

"No."

Loop.

David stood up and put his hands in his front pockets and jiggled his keys. He laughed as if he had suddenly become aware of something, shook his head and stretched his hand toward her. "Will you please marry me?"

She stretched out her hand to touch him. He was warm. Claire pulled her hand back quickly.

"Cold," he said. "Your hands are always so cold."

"Poor circulation. I should get back to my research."

"You're rushing."

"I don't know how to do it any other way, David."

"Just what exactly is the problem you have with marrying me?"

Claire sat back and glared at him.

He placed his finger gently over the scar she thought had been neatly hidden beneath her blouse. "This?" he asked.

She recoiled and pulled her collar over the evidence. "I'm on borrowed time, David." She began to speak very quickly about her plans for India, how she couldn't decide whether she wanted to fly into Bombay or Delhi because she'd heard that Bombay had a lot of crooks but that Delhi taxi drivers were the worst, and she'd also heard that there had been skirmishes at the border of Pakistan but that was so far away from where she wanted to go that it shouldn't be a problem, kind of like having some kind of separatist war in Quebec and not wanting to fly into Calgary.

He interrupted her. "Do you want to have children?"

Jouissance — the experience of seeing oneself as unified.

Claire's throat tightened and she thought for a moment the window of the coffee shop was going to collapse in on her. Children? Did she want to have children? She sat there paralyzed. "You know, I think I do," she said aloud. "I thought for a moment, yes. Yes, of course. I'm a thirty-seven-year-old woman. I should have children," and she laughed nervously. "Something just made me panic when you asked that question."

Suddenly, Claire couldn't rid herself of the longing she felt. It was as if she missed her children desperately and wanted to get back to them, wherever they were, whoever they were. She looked at her watch. As if she was coming out of a seizure, she could barely recognize its function. The second hand ticked rapidly around the face and disappeared in the glare of the fluorescent lights of the coffee shop. She felt catapulted into existence. "Shit! I completely spaced it. I'm supposed to be at a production meeting."

David tossed a couple of coins on the counter, picked up her sweater and wrapped it around her shoulders. "Come on, I'll drive you."

"You still haven't answered me," David said as he unlocked the passenger door of the car and went around to the driver's side.

Claire crawled into the old Volvo, pulled her seatbelt over her shoulder and clicked it into place. The shoulder strap cut into her scar and she pushed her right arm through the strap and slipped it behind her back. David eased himself behind the wheel, pumped the gas and started the engine.

"What I said was this: I want you to marry me and I want to have a child."

"Yes, I heard you." Claire took the coin that was hanging around her neck, placed it between her thumb and middle finger and rubbed it in slow easy circles. She reached her other hand over to rest in David's lap. She could smell ashes thick as lilacs through her open window. Mark me in your dreams, said the young woman in the blue chiffon dress. Something simple on the soles of my feet.

Pune 1930

Denzil struggled to love his third child. Hè couldn't know what menace malaria performed on a fetus. And Denzil didn't like not knowing — anything. He certainly resented the child's tax on Alice. The boy hungered for his father, though — children can sense distraction — and William followed Denzil like a shadow, hiding behind doors, under chairs, beneath desks. The middle child, George, was far more independent, perhaps too much so, but Denzil found him innocuous enough. George spent most of his time scavenging the riverbanks or playing football with his school friends. And Barbara, she had that same determined stride, the haughtiness of temper — both infuriating and endearing — that Alice had around that same age. There was something very temporary about Barbara, like a potent colour, undiluted, like the pigment of indigo or powdered lapis. So it wasn't surprising that Alice and Barbara were often at odds with one another. And Alice's deliberate taciturnity didn't surprise Denzil either.

It had been on that first trip to Kusaini, the one Alice had organized during her senior year at All Saints, that Denzil first witnessed that same silence. He couldn't count how many times since then he had had to endure weeks of her preoccupation, her oddly mute reticence.

Barbara whined to her father one day in his office, "Father, she has not said two words to me in over a week."

Ah yes, he recognized that aggravation in his daughter's tone and encouraged Barbara to swallow her pride and break the silence. "Your mother, she gets distracted."

"She can't still be angry with me, can she?"

"I doubt that very much. You mustn't take it personally. She hasn't been in good health and she's very committed to her work."

He tried to explain to his daughter how Alice had always been unable to carry on the functions of love while chasing her other passions. Alice was the kind of person whose life would inevitably become compartmentalized, Denzil told Barbara — children here, husband there, work over there, household down here and friends somewhere else.

"In the beginning, I found it curious that she could be so effusive one day and completely uncommunicative the next," he told Barbara. "She had organized a field trip for her class, to Kusaini, that first year we met. I couldn't keep up with all her plans. She must have spoken to me three, four times a day in the three weeks prior to leaving. But once the trip began, your mother became completely unfamiliar to me."

He recalled how he had watched Alice distractedly from the corner of his eye, catching sight of her hair when she brushed it outside the tent before retiring for the night, observing the way she had tripped and fumbled up the bank carrying water from the river, and the way her shoes were worn on the outsides of the heels when she walked away from him. Denzil had paid passionate attention to these details — the way she threw her head back when she laughed, the dimple in her cheek and the copper colour of her iris when she looked directly into sunlight. She hadn't spoken to him since they'd left.

On the second evening of their field trip, he had followed Alice down to the river. She sat alone on a smooth boulder that had been carved out by the floods during the wet. He listened, from the banks, to the worried river crash beneath both of them. He thought she must be part mineral, as if she belonged to that particular curve of rock, calcified, marbleized.

As the charcoal blue of night in Kusaini had poured over the cliffs on the opposite side of the river, its dark substance deepening into caverns and caves, the outcrops illuminated by hasty dashes of moonlight, Alice was startled by a rustle in the shrubs on the riverbank. Tiger were common at that elevation and her heart jumped inside her breast, anticipating the danger. She strained her eyes to see if the tigress would reveal herself, to get a glimpse of the animal in the spaces between the trees, the pleasurable shape of her own fear.

This time it had been Denzil rustling in the bush, absent-mindedly fumbling around his pockets searching for his pipe, a matchstick and a strike. He emerged from the bushes into the moonlight.

"Do you simply forget from one moment to the next where you put your pipe?" Alice called out to his shadow.

"Nasty, embarrassing habit, I'm afraid." He walked toward her.

"I was hoping you were a tiger."

"I'm sorry to disappoint you."

"Please sit."

He sat. "I noticed you weren't at the fire and Sister Dorothea was concerned for your safety, so I ..."

"Oh, so you weren't concerned?"

Denzil stood up and jumped across to another larger boulder a human length away from Alice. His forehead and cheek caught the cool light as he sat again and struck the match on the stone beside him.

"No, Alice, I wasn't, and I doubt a tiger would find someone of your stature appetizing. They like the more rodent type, more Estelle's shape."

"Is that so? What exactly do you mean by that?"

"You don't have any ... well ..."

"Flesh?"

He felt so incredibly awkward speaking of her body in this way. "I suppose that was the word I was searching for."

He glanced over to Alice, who sat in the full light of the moon; she was smiling and her teeth were perfect and bright, her lips wide and that dimple on her right cheek, deep. He felt bridled, as if the corners of his mouth were tearing against cold steel. He coughed and smoked and tried to slow his racing heart by holding his fingers against the ribs that contained it.

"Denzil?" Alice searched the dark space between herself and Denzil, and could hear a surge of water between their boulders.

He lifted his head to face her, but an uncomfortable shyness made his body seize. He wished he'd had a smash of whisky before coming down here.

"Do you like me?" she asked.

He took a breath and felt the cramp in his jaw beginning to freeze his face so he blurted, "Yes," and then he said, even more quietly, "very much so." He turned toward the river to take another puff of his pipe. Tears were pooling in his lower lids.

"Then why do you avoid me?"

Denzil stood up and shook his legs to get the circulation moving again. "I ..." He put one hand in his pocket and jiggled the coins he had forgotten to remove before the trip. "You think I avoid you?"

Alice pulled herself forward. "You haven't said two words to me since we started."

She stood and he found himself facing her; the sound of the river became louder and more disruptive as if his ears had just popped. He wanted to have the length of her body against his and he drove himself to distraction trying to imagine the taste of her skin. He brought his hand up and ran his fingers through his hair. This woman, this woman had taken away his speech, and his own skin tightened around him as he stared at her body beneath the baggy shirt and trousers, her long braid snaking over her shoulder, and finally her mouth that had closed around her teeth, her lips — he could tell that they were dry and split but all he wanted to do was touch them. He reached out as if he was going to caress her, but motioned toward the camp instead. "We should get back. Sister Dorothea wants to hear your prayers tonight."

"I'll pray for you." Alice slapped his hand with hers and giggled, "Chippy." Then she jumped off the boulder and scrambled back up the bank.

Denzil chased after her and shouted, "I'm going to thrash Estelle!"

"She said that's what you would do," Alice shouted down to him as he scrambled up after her.

They had arrived back to the fire, breathless and confused. As Alice said her prayers that night, Denzil had sat up late beside the fire sipping whisky to settle his desire.

Barbara stood before Denzil; her adolescent scornfulness was firmly entrenched in her brow. "Have you spoken to your mother?" Denzil asked his daughter. He smiled; the irony wasn't going to escape him.

"Well, no." Barbara fumbled with the paperweights on his desk.

"Might I suggest that if both of you insist on playing the same game, neither of you will ever speak to each other again? Take it from me, Barbara. I have learned to break the silence with your mother. She's not waiting for you. She has simply moved on."

The Study of Collision, Mid-December

A blizzard had already hit the south end of the city and ski hills were opening earlier than expected that year. The sky was a cold blue and there was no evidence of clouds anywhere on the horizon. Drifting snow had filled in the low spots in fields, and brown grasses were poking through patches of white. Flanking the spill of tawny prairie to the west, the mountains appeared closer and more magnificent than usual. The plane circled over the city and landed on the long flat strip east of the highway.

"So, is that camera going to do it for you?" David put his arm over Claire's shoulder and walked with her over to the luggage carousel.

"It better. I had to take out a bloody mortgage to buy it."

"You mean, *we*, don't you?"

"Thanks, by the way."

"We have dinner at your mother's in an hour."

"No," Claire pouted.

When it had been brought to Claire's attention that her heart condition might have been inherited, her mother immediately pointed out the longevity of her own mother, now ninety-six years old, and her father, who passed away only a few years before. She seemed to take great pleasure in pointing her finger at the five dead family members on Claire's father's side. Claire and her mother's relationship had become strained, neither of them able to overcome their shock at Claire's illness. For Claire, the shock was associated with the fact that she now had a very intimate association with a bunch of dead family members she had never known; and for her mother, the shock came from losing her husband of almost forty years and almost losing her daughter of thirty-eight years. "Thirty-seven," Claire had had to correct her mother.

"Thirty-eight, if you think fiscally, dear."

"Come on, there's plenty of time for us," David urged Claire now. "My contract is finished with social services, the film is complete, and besides, your brother's in town for a few days."

"Ben's home? What's he doing here?"

"He had a stopover for a couple of days before heading east. Your mom wanted me to keep it a secret." David wrapped his right hand around her neck and pulled her in for another kiss. "I missed you, Claire."

"I've only been gone a couple of weeks."

"Just say you've missed me too, okay?"

"I've missed you too and I love you very much. There, how's that?"

"Not quite as convincing as I'd like, but I'll take whatever you've got to give me. Come on, Dorothy has put one of her appalling meals together. Let's get over there before she has time to make one of her tofu angel food cakes."

Claire picked her backpack off the carousel and threw it over her shoulder. "She's not that bad, is she?"

Claire was regretting her fanatical independence and wished for David to have a momentary lapse of feminism and help her carry her new camera. Instead, he jingled his car keys as she tripped after him to the parking lot. "Your mother hasn't been trying to sell you Barley Green for the past month," he said, looking back over his shoulder.

Prairie winter air strangled Claire as they left the terminal. She could already feel her voice leaving her and her skin tightening across the top of her hands. The wind pitched her hair into her face as she tossed her pack into the trunk and jumped into the front seat of David's '64 Volvo. The cold leather seats crinkled when Claire wriggled to accommodate her new camera.

"Give it a few minutes for the engine to warm up, Claire, before you crank the heat."

"Jeez, it's cold here!"

"Here, put this on." David tossed her a toque from the back seat.

Claire pulled the soft woollen hat over her head and looked at herself in the visor mirror. Why couldn't someone design a hat that was warm and attractive? The toque was always some dreary striped brown-and-orange thing that made a head look too large or too small. She felt suddenly critical of herself. Ben would bug her about the grey hair she now had at her temples and he'd definitely point out the wrinkles in the corners of her eyes. He'd stand back and tell her she'd put on a few pounds, which wasn't true, but he'd say it just the same.

She and her brother were close in age — eighteen months apart. "For the sake of brevity in the childbearing years," her mother had told them. They had spent most of their adolescence sharing friends, drugs, alcohol and truancy, but their relationship had become distant over the years, more as a result of geography than personality. Ben had moved to the East Coast and married a French-Canadian girl. That marriage had soured for reasons Ben chose not to discuss and he was now making every effort he could to get back out west.

"He's here checking out a law firm," David told Claire.

"It'd be nice to have him back in town."

They sat quietly as David drove to the west end of the city. Claire reached up and massaged the back of his neck. He moaned and leaned into her. "God, I love your hands on me, woman." He placed his hand on her thigh. "How have you been feeling?"

"Great. Good. Okay. I don't know. Oh, I think more than anything else I'm just tired." She dropped her arms to her side and let her shoulders relax.

"Well, maybe we can hole up for a couple of days, order pizza and watch Trek reruns." David winked while he shifted down and turned up the long street toward her mother's house.

A leafless cotoneaster hedge surrounded the front lawn of the house. Claire could remember the year her father had put the hedge in, and the progression of more and more sophisticated shearing devices he'd used to tame it. Honeysuckle and mock orange were tied to the front porch; their naked branches were awkward with the clumps of white string that otherwise would be hidden by the leaves and blooms of spring.

Snow blanketed the old wooden democrat her mother had insisted they bring in from the family farm. It sat derelict in the front yard, its wooden deck rotting and bowing from the snow load. Spokes from the front wheels were broken and they jutted through the old crust of a snowdrift. The democrat, like everything else in Claire's life, was getting tired; even David's old

Volvo coughed phlegmatically when he shut off its engine. He sat in the seat beside her and in his most serious voice he said, "I love you, Claire. You know that, don't you?"

She smiled and opened the Volvo door. "What exactly does it mean when you say that?" David laughed and asked if he could take it back and she said, No, he couldn't, and that no matter how much he loved her she still couldn't forgive him for bringing her to her mother's place for dinner rather than taking her home, pouring her a hot bath and waiting on her hand and foot.

"Have you given some thought to what I asked you before you left?"

"Yes."

"And?"

"Later."

"How much later?"

"I'm not sure, but I'm not prepared to discuss it now."

"Fine. But we do need to discuss it soon."

"Fine."

Like all families, Claire's had its pathological dysfunction — insidious, and according to David, kind of creepy. There was a cheerfulness that David suspected was in some strange and perverted way masking something wicked. Claire had to agree with him, but not for the same reasons. The wickedness was in the humiliation of performing at the church chataquas, or in the recitals her mother had hosted on lazy afternoons while Ben and Claire had hammered out some abominable clarinet and piano solo. Wicked because she could see her father wince during her singing recitals, and because her father buried himself in pipe smoke and newspapers during her entire adolescence, claiming that female behaviour was beyond his expertise.

As individuals, their aberrations were comic and Claire found comfort in Ben's excessive comic book collection and her mother's zaniness. She had come to understand her mother and father's marriage agreement and was concerned that in her father's absence, her mother would come completely undone. Nonetheless, Claire objected to her mother's recent obsession with motorcycles and encouraged her to have a more sober approach to her liberation. But Dorothy adored her red leather outfit and thought herself smashing in a helmet. "You can't argue with fashion," Dorothy had told Claire.

The conflict between mother and daughter, according to Dorothy, was a result of Claire's awkward birth and total dependence on her mother's breast well into her third year of life. "You couldn't separate from me," Dorothy would try to explain their relationship, "so you developed a personality so opposite to mine that our differences would be obvious to everybody."

When things got really bad between them, her mother would accuse her of being just like her father. Claire's father had plenty of his own distasteful characteristics, the least of which was his blatant disregard for her mother's ambitions. Claire often caught herself echoing her father, and she hated herself for that.

As she entered the family home, she could smell her mother's famous cinnamon buns. "The secret," Ben had told her long after they had both left home, "is the amount of sugar she uses."

"Mmmmm!" Claire called out as she flicked her boots across a hallway already swarming with shoes and boots, singles and pairs clumped together in unlikely combinations. "Smells pretty good in here."

Dorothy's voice sang out from the kitchen around the corner. "I just pulled them out of the oven and I suggest that you get in here right away before your brother gobbles them up."

"Did you say brother? Do I have a brother?" Claire knew Ben was hiding in the broom closet behind the back entrance because she had heard the fumble and slam of the door when she entered the house. She found herself going through the ridiculous motions of hide-and-seek. "Is he under the table? No. Is he in the cupboards? Noooo. Mother, have you seen Ben anywhere?"

Ben's muffled voice came from the back entrance. "Did you check in the broom closet?"

Claire waltzed over and yanked him out of the closet. "Get out of there. This is embarrassing."

Ben leaped out of the closet, grabbed his sister by the head, and rubbed his knuckles into the top of her skull. He then began to inspect her hair. "One, two, three. Oh boy," he said, "looks bad."

"Shut up," Claire pushed at him. "Looks like you've had the bottle out again."

"Nope, still a natural." He paused and shifted gears, more serious than before. "You look good. How do you feel?"

"I feel okay. And yourself?"

"No seriously, any ...?" And he placed his hand over his heart and thumped a couple of times.

"None that I'm aware of. What about you? David says you're looking for work out here?"

Ben exhaled and went into the kitchen to grab another cinnamon bun. "If something came up."

David was already peeling a curl of bun away from the central knot and drinking a glass of milk. With his mouth full of milk and cinnamon bun he greeted Ben. "Hey Ben, how's it going? She looks pretty good, don't she?"

"Not bad for an ol' filly. You running her good? Warming her up and cantering her?"

Claire's mother piped in. "Okay, you boys, that's enough."

She thrust her cheek at Claire. "Well, are you going to kiss your old mother or not?"

"Sorry, Mom. I had to wrestle your thirty-six-year-old son out of the closet yet one more time."

As Claire kissed her mother she noticed how the bones of her mother's face seemed to be floating closer to the surface. Although her mother had decompressed after her father's death, Claire's heart attack had wound her up tight again. "No parent wants to outlive their child," Dorothy had told her after it was all over. Claire could feel a shiver beneath the looseness of her mother's cheek when she placed her lips dryly upon it. It was as if Claire had already died and her mother was experiencing her ghost. Dorothy broke away suddenly, wearing her fear, moving from counter to fridge and back to the stove, her shoulders bunched up around her neck, the tension in her back almost too much for Claire to bear.

"Mom, relax. Can David do something for you?"

David coughed and stood up. "Yes, Dorothy, can I help you?"

Claire laughed and leaned back on her chair. "Sit down, David. I was just joking."

"No, she wasn't." Ben laughed and then pummelled another bun into his mouth.

"I'm just happy to have all of you here at the same time. The others are so occupied with their own families I never get to see any of them anymore."

The "others" that Dorothy referred to were Ben and Claire's high school friends who had never left town, or the hitchhikers Dorothy had picked up, or some of the patients she had nursed in the hospital before her retirement. Both Ben and Claire knew they had let their mother down — Ben for not being able to keep his marriage together and Claire for not settling down at all. All the film productions in the world, all the successful court battles, couldn't make up for the fact that they had not provided Dorothy with grandchildren.

Dorothy wiped her hands on a tea towel, tossed it on the counter beside the sink and let out a big sigh. "There, now I can sit and enjoy my three favourite people before dinner is ready. Now, Claire, tell us all about the coast. Did you get what you needed?"

Claire told them about the new camera she had bought with David's and her savings and some of her grant money. "Your tax dollars," she pointed out to Ben.

She told them how she was trying to find contacts in Mumbai to help her get into Yeravda. But she didn't mention Charlotte Blake or the coins and she prayed David wouldn't betray her. But David would never betray her. The coins were her secret, the one thing neither her mother nor Ben could claim.

"You are using Bollywood moviemakers to make your film?" Ben asked. "Have you ever seen those Hindi movies, all dance numbers and gyrating I Dream of Jeanies?"

"No, you didn't hear me. I need them to get permission to film in the prison."

"What prison, dear?" her mother asked.

"The prison Gandhi was thrown into after breaking the salt laws. The prison our grandfather supervised."

"Oh, I see," her mother nodded vaguely. The pupils of Dorothy's brown eyes were dilated and she had a faraway look, as if she remained on an island while the rest of the world floated by. Her lips were pursed and they pulled at the rest of her relaxed face.

Sitting close to the kitchen window, Claire pressed her own face against its cold black glass. She could see the snow blowing across the lawn; the wind powdered the hardened cornices, carving smooth arcing waves that crested and fell through the spokes of wagon wheels fencing the entire backyard. The wagon wheels were her mother's idea. Her father had acquiesced reluctantly, forcing Ben and Claire to creosote them — against their environmental sensibilities — and to dig them into the ground the summer before Claire left for university. Beyond the yard was the purple night in the river valley and her mother's reflection in yellow light. She remained like a photograph — frozen in thought, or just simply lost. Claire couldn't know. She couldn't read her mother.

At sixty-five, Dorothy had spent her life caring for others. She had shared anxieties with Ben and Claire as they wrestled with their occupations, their relationships, and their disappointments. She had housed the infirmity of their father's emotional life, and the hordes of other sick or ailing members of the city's elite. "Your mother," her father had confessed to Claire, "she isn't happy unless she is healing the sick, and sometimes I just don't want to be sick."

Dorothy's remonstrations were few but when they did occur they were immediately followed by lavish gifts — flowers, wine, jewellery, or pets — as if she could never justify her occasional need to be heard, to be respected. It was clear to Claire that her mother struggled daily with her sense of self-worth.

Both Ben and David, in contrast, were animated. The colours of their clothing swirled in their window reflections as each took his turn reaching across the table for another cinnamon bun. Claire looked back at her family around the table. David sat on his chair backwards, folding his arms over the back and resting his chin on his hands. Ben was tipping back on his chair, an activity her father would have cuffed him over the head for. Her parents' furniture had the permanent mark of children on it — lampshades tilted haphazardly from the bent wires, the corners of cupboards were worn round from children's foreheads, and the back legs of the kitchen chairs wobbled every time someone shifted their weight. "You children ..." her father used to complain, "have managed to wreck more in a day than I have earned in a week."

Ben was the one who threw the baseball through the living room window and broke the 1920s art deco lamp by tossing his clarinet across the room. He'd burned down the back fence by starting a grass fire, punched in the drywall when his girlfriend dumped him, attracted the cops on more than one occasion by his late-night prowls around the neighbourhood. What was it? Claire thought, ten points for a basement window, twenty for a street lamp, thirty for uprooting the Johnsons' entire garden? He had cost her father more in those six adolescent years than she had all her life. What did she get for her consideration? A heart condition. Nice.

Dorothy broke her gaze and looked toward Claire. "The prison your grandfather worked in? Yes, now that's a good idea. Now Claire, dear, why don't you do one of those nature documentaries they have on television? That would combine your interest in wildcats and film. Are there wildcats in India? Yes, of course, what am I saying? There's the Bengal tiger everybody has been making a fuss over."

Claire, Ben and David sat motionless, staring at Dorothy. Dorothy smiled and crouched over the table to scoop some cinnamon syrup with her forefinger. Brother and sister dared not look at each other for fear of bursting into hysterics and David blinked and smiled, stoned-faced.

After a few moments of silence, Claire turned to Ben, her face aching with restraint, and she asked, "And what about you, Ben, who have you put away recently?"

Ben rested the front legs of his chair down and folded his arms onto the table. "Well, for one thing," he said, "I'm not a criminal lawyer so I'm not all that involved in putting people away. But I have had some interesting cases lately. A witchcraft trial that was kind of interesting."

"Kind of," David turned to Ben. "Was that the one where the guy was libelled for Satanism on some religious talk show?"

"Why, that's like the pot calling the kettle black, isn't it?" Dorothy sniped.

"Almost," Ben smiled at his mother.

While Ben was always able to enjoy Dorothy, Claire struggled daily with her mother's inanity, probably because it was a constant reminder of her own. She searched for a way out, an exit sign or a phone call — anything to get out of her mother's kitchen. She stood up, stretched, and walked toward the hallway.

"Now, where are you off to, young lady?" her mother called after her.

Claire turned on the light at the base of the stairs and as she ran her hands along the smooth rail she said over her shoulder, "I thought I'd wander up to the study and have a look around. Call me when dinner is ready." She turned and left the room, and in the hallway, as an afterthought, she called out, "Please."

To which her mother replied, "That's better."

A permanent swath of muddy handprints greyed the walls on both sides of the hallway. Her father's nutty pipe tobacco — a smell that sometimes appalled Claire — still lingered outside his study. She remembered that first night after his study had been built and how delighted he was to discover that she, too, couldn't sleep. They tiptoed around the kitchen. He heated milk in a saucepan, miming gestures of conspiracy in the shadows of the range hood light. "Hush," and he pointed toward her mother's bedroom when she clattered her spoon against a ceramic mug. "Hush," he said as they ascended the carpeted stairwell and settled into his study to read quietly by lamplight.

Her mother had rarely gone up there during his life. She

thought it important for him to have a room of his own and, at one point in the marriage, had banished him to those quarters altogether, because (and she lied when she told the children), "He snores far too loudly for anybody to get any sleep around here." Now, Dorothy never set foot in that end of the house.

When Claire opened the door to the study, a thin musty darkness poured into the hallway and she quickly flicked on the track of pale yellow lights that illuminated the walls of books inside the room. Dust swirled in lazy circles as she closed the door behind her. In the centre of the room: a large leather chair, the rawhide cracked from the weight of her father's impression, and an ottoman rubbed raw from the shapes of his heels. This was the place where his lap used to be, where she had crawled up and settled while he read, or later, when she was much older, where he sat and lectured her on promiscuity and self-respect. This was where he sat — summarizing her.

She had left this room so many times. So many times, Claire had stood before her father, watching the spittle form in the corners of his mouth and stretch between his lips, and she could still see the darkened nicotine stains on the crowns of his teeth worn down from his pipe rolling back and forth over them while he was deep in thought. He would be saying something to her about respect, something about covering her body properly, wearing a bra, maybe that's what it was, she was supposed to wear a bra because if she didn't then she was just asking for trouble. So she had stood before him, hating him for trying to cover her up, to make her less obvious, less woman.

Then she would leave. She would return his gaze, except she would throw all her hate into it, and she would turn around. *Slam the door this time*, she'd say to herself. *Take your time with this act, move slowly, definitively, and slam the ever-loving door so shut, so perfectly shut that it ruffles that crop of grey hair on top of his head.* And then she would stomp down those stairs, out the back door, crawl into the front seat of her car (not the one he bought for her, because he refused to buy her one, but one she bought herself, with the money she made doing street performances with a remote control car and a mime face, of which he disapproved), and she would squeal out of their driveway and drive dangerously fast until she was out of sight. She knew he had watched her from the window in the hallway and that he was definitely struggling to breathe. "Fuck you!" she would scream in the car, "Fuck you!"

For awhile Claire had thought that all her problems were directly related to losing her father, that she had manifested her heart condition because she couldn't recover from his sudden death. Certainly, when she allowed herself to think of him, the pain in her chest became almost excruciating — like a heart in a constant state of breaking. Now, though, she could see that her discomfort was more because of his oversight in his will rather than her loss. She had got the worst of him. Ben got everything else.

In his study, shelves from floor to ceiling on three walls were filled with the orange-coloured spines of paperbacks, purple hardcover first editions of Churchill's memoirs, Orwell's four-volume set of essays and the entire collection of circa 1923 *Encyclopaedia Britannica*. The fourth wall was covered in maps and a small writing desk piled with books, two and three high. Each book on the desk was marked and unfinished. They were books he must have been reading before his death — Bill Cosby's *Time Flies*, Hemingway's *Islands in the Stream*, James Morris' *Pax Britannica*, and several other titles she couldn't recognize. His reading had escalated in the last couple of years. He consumed books voraciously, succumbing to book clubs and discounts, checking off every other title, reading everything from cover to cover.

In those last moments of his life he must have put one of the books down, finished his pipe, got up and retied his tattered blue housecoat, slipped on his loafers — the ones that were worn out on the instep — taken a final sip of his cold coffee and limped across the hallway into the shower.

She thought how he must have been composing his latest outrage — protesting the war in the Middle East, the Prime Minister's most recent blunder, or some grammatically incorrect editorial — when the blood burst through the wall of his aneurysm. Drooping in the hot shower, he must have lowered awkwardly onto his scarred knees; oh, she thought, how the ridges of tile and grout on the floor must have been uncomfortable on their uneven healings. The water had probably turned cold and he had wished to hell Dorothy had waited for him to finish his morning shower before turning on the bloody dishwasher. His fingers and toes blue, his lips numb, his arms useless at his side, his final moment — cold tile against his cheek. And Claire imagined her mother downstairs, waiting. Waiting for him to finish his shower so she could turn on the dishwasher.

Claire inhaled a tight thin breath and stuffed down her loss as if packing an open wound with cotton. She tilted her head to the side and read the spines of books along the shelves. They were arranged by size, and category, and format, and their titles were as wildly diverse as her father's interests: Stephen Jay Gould's *Wonderful Life*, a book on the Burgess Shale Claire had given him for his birthday a couple of years before, O. Henry's *The Trimmed Lamp*, Melville's *Moby Dick*, all the Massey Lecture Series — Chomsky, O'Brien, Ralston Saul — and a weathered green leather edition of Kipling's *Jungle Book*. Her father's voice was almost audible as she smoothed the palm of her hand over the embossed lettering on its spine. She tugged it from the shelf and the book dropped into her hand and fell open to pages puckered from the wet thumbs of evening baths, and she read:

Then Rikki-tikki danced in a circle to get behind her, and Nagaina spun round to keep her head to his head, so that the rustle of her tail on the matting sounded like dry leaves blown along by the wind.

Claire remembered how her father's weight had caused her tiny girl body to roll into him. Yes, that was when they were closest, when she couldn't threaten him with her gender, when her torso resembled a boy's and she was categorically, simply, a child. It was in those hours of childhood that she experienced his tender moments. He would close his book, turn off the bedside lamp, lie back on her pillow and, as if something was splitting and surfacing inside him, he'd speak in a cracked voice. "She always had cold hands," he told her of his mother. "I remember her long bony fingers."

As a child, she had asked her father, "Was it hot in India, Daddy?" And he told her that it was the fever he remembered most. The typhoid. And that he had to learn to walk again.

She asked him, "What is typhoid, Daddy?" And she draped her little girl arm across his immense father chest.

"A parasite," he told her.

"What is a parasite, Daddy?"

"I had grabbed some fruit she had brought home from the market."

"She?"

"My mother. She hadn't washed the fruit. I grabbed it before she washed the fruit."

"Parasite. What is a parasite?"

"The parasite was on the fruit."

"But what is a parasite?" she insisted.

"Something that lives inside you. It takes from you but doesn't give anything back. Typhoid was on the fruit. I grabbed the fruit and ate it. The parasite wormed its way through my bone and softened it. I couldn't walk for over a year."

He kissed Claire's forehead, or maybe it was just his lips brushing her skin as he mumbled, "My mother would drop water onto my lips from a cloth and sing to me. And the others, the chuprassi, my ayah, they'd come into the nursery to listen to her."

And then he would try to recall his mother's song. It was dark, hesitant, and Claire, now an adult in her father's office, one hand pressed into the top of her father's desk, one in the front pocket of her jeans, her eyes on the carpet, asked herself aloud, "How did that song go, again?" She cleared her throat and attempted the song, "Bai lai lai lee lai lai lai ..." Yes, she thought, something like that. Triads. Keep trying, keep trying, a few more bars, and she sang again, "Bai lai lee lai ..." but her throat clamped shut. She was singing out of tune. That simply wouldn't do.

Then her father would grow silent, withdraw, and try to slip from her arm. "Hush," he would say as she gripped his neck and begged him to stay until she slept. "You must learn to sleep on your own," he'd tell her and then he'd pry her fiercely interlocked fingers apart and she'd begin to cry and reach out for him, his large father frame backlit by the hallway, shoulders drooped, head bent forward, defeated. And she knew, even then in her childlike mind, the flotsam of her father's love.

Pune 1930

George and Barbara coaxed young William from his bed. He had forgotten how to place his feet upon the floor and when his sister tugged at his arm and he felt the dislocation at his elbow, he got very frightened and wanted everything to stop because the nursery began to swirl again in a sinister, mocking kind of fashion. He was determined, though, to feel again the buoyancy of his childhood. His mother at the doorway smiled and nodded to him as if to say that all the pushing and pulling going on was okay, that it would not do him any harm, and he trusted her when she said, "Come Rikki, let your sister walk you to the garden." But he wanted his mother and he stretched his arms toward her while his older brother pushed him from behind. His mother ran toward him, scolding the older boy for being too rough.

She put her hands on his shoulders and looked him straight in the eye. "Now Rikki," she said, "it is time to recover. Fully, completely. You will want to be running around with the other children now."

And he shook his head, not because he disagreed with her but because he had always wanted this. He had always wanted to run in the garden and play football and to build the rocking horse and play in the Santal house with the others. It was the "now" that was difficult.

"But you must try, Rikki. These are difficult things, but you must try."

And he smiled his perfect, crooked smile, his wise and knowing smile, and nodded nervously as he pushed her gently to the side. She stepped away and he grabbed for her skirt and pulled her beside him.

"Not that far away, Mommy," and he pointed to the floor beside him. "Right there, stand right there."

She rested her hand on his shoulders, and Barbara stood before him, walking backwards and coaching him, "Come, Rikki, one foot, then the next. That's right, just lift it off the floor and bring it forward, like this."

She showed him how to do it and he stood with one hand tugging his mother's skirt, the other in front of him, pressing down on the air for balance. He understood the mechanics of motion, that he must lift his foot and move it forward, but somewhere between desire and ambition was a chasm too great to bridge and he looked up at his mother and begged her to relieve him of his chore.

"This is where you must begin, Rikki," she said to him in her kindest voice. "We will catch you if you fall."

"Come on, Rikki," George taunted as he bounced on Rikki's bed behind him. "Come on, don't be such a baby."

"I'm not a baby," Rikki whined. "Mommy, I'm not a baby."

"Baby, baby ..."

"Shush, George." His mother leaned across Rikki and placed her hand beneath his knee. She loosened his foot from its hold on the floor, plucking it up, releasing its suction, and then on its own it floated like St. Vitus' dance over the wooden floorboards.

The very awkwardness of the movement caused Rikki to scream, "Mommy, no!"

His mother urged him like a puppet toward his sister, who squatted and waved her fingers in a come-here gesture. "That a boy, Rikki. Good Rikki."

"No, Mommy, no, I can't walk. I can't."

"You must. I won't let you fall. I won't let you fall."

The Study of Collision, Continued

The door to the study flung open and Ben hopped into the room. He pulled a joint from behind his ear and rifled through his jacket pockets for a match.

Claire pulled on the lever to open the window and its pane groaned as she pushed against the frame to unlock it from its casing. Outside, a blizzard thrashed the brittle branches of a poplar tree against the wooden siding. The wind howled as if from the back of its throat, the river ice moaned and cracked at the edge of the garden, cold rippled throughout the room, and they wrapped their arms around themselves and hopped from foot to foot.

"Congrats on the funding, Claire," Ben said, and he passed her a joint.

"Thanks."

A thin white ribbon raced from the end of the joint toward the open window and the two of them watched as it frayed and disappeared beyond the glass. They smiled at each other, neither able to speak while they held the smoke in their lungs.

Ben cleared his throat. "Dad never got to see your last film, did he?"

Her father had always forgotten to show up for her, she thought; end of story. But, and she knew this to be true, she should not make Ben suffer for her father's neglect.

"It was pretty good, Claire."

"What was?"

"The film. It was pretty good."

"You saw it? How did you get hold of it?" She stuffed the joint into the snow on the windowsill, handed the roach to Ben and shut the window.

"Mom showed it to me." He tucked the roach into his shirt

pocket, twirled around and flopped into their father's leather chair.

Claire gasped.

Ben jumped up. "What? What is it?"

"Nothing — sorry. It's just ... you're sitting in Dad's chair."

Ben had a crooked smile; it was cocky and arrogant and often infuriating. His eyes, though, were like the tawny knots in polished spruce wood, dark and vulnerable like their mother's. "Well, he can't do much about it now, can he?" And with that, Ben began to stomp his shoes into the seat of their father's chair. He danced around, leaving dusty shoe prints across the cushion. Claire's shock shifted to amusement and then to a mild hysteria while Ben carved phrases with his arms throughout the room, "suffice it to say," "forthwith," "with respect to," "clearly." Their father's chair remained unmoved by his violations — as if to say, *I have left this place and you can no longer hurt me.* The two of them fell to the floor in convulsions of hysteria. After their laughter died down, Claire and Ben lay on their backs listening to the rudimentary chords of the piano being played in the room below. Ben stretched his foot up to the bookshelves and began pushing every other book deeper into the shadows while Claire scanned the maps — Leduc, Pembina, Cooking Lake. Red, blue, yellow and black pins were pushed into green and purple shaded areas — fossiled streams beneath the prairie landscape her father, like a sleuth, had spent his life exploring. Thin black tape like ribbons of crude oil caught the light as it curved along contours of descending elevations.

"When I had expressed a curiosity for rock," Claire spoke slowly, "he located for me the ridges and faults where mountains began. He was passionate about his work and I could relate to that. But when I found out about all those women he came to know in his so-called study of collision, I was jealous. Jealous, you see." She leaned up on her one arm and looked down toward Ben. "I was as close as any girl could be to her father, until of course, and you know, I can remember the year, the month, the day, the hour and the moment when he would no longer hold my hand, or take me in his lap, and he told me I was too old for that kind of intimacy. Those are the muddied lines between Dad and me, and I have spent my life trying to reconcile those, those … dilutions, those awkward affiliations." She lay on her back and continued, "My lack of equilibrium disturbs me. I mean, I spent way too much time trying to share his passion. I knew that I should have made up my own. He might have respected that."

"I never let him get to me that way," Ben said.

"When he died, I didn't know who to resent any more."

"And then what happened, Claire? Did you get healed?"

She would never be able to share with him how she had seen her own birth and death on the same day. And then there were the dreams of tiger — Ben would never understand those. Over the years, Ben had become less capable of listening, less interested in what she had to say. They had become too divided — not because her father had been partial to Ben in his will, she saw that now. There were just some things he would never be able to understand about her. But when her heart had ceased functioning and the doctors had sent Ben home because, and they told her this later, he wasn't helping a thing by antagonizing the nurses, Claire knew he had done what her father would have done had he been alive. He had panicked, afraid that he would outlive her, and she felt him now, lying beside her, filling the space her father had vacated.

"I know you won't understand," she said. "That's why I can't tell you what it's been like."

"What? I won't say anything — promise."

"You don't have to."

She kneeled and ran her fingers along the titles at the bottom of the maps. Ben told her the Sinai and North Sea maps were in his office and that their mother had told him to get them out of her sight.

The crux of the matter was this: Claire's father had left everything she loved about him to Ben.

"Dad fired me from my first job," she said to Ben that night in her father's studio, as if to say that she had owned a necessary part of him as well. "Filing all that microfiche was a fate worse than death, so I just stopped showing up." She traced over the Letroset titles of her father's maps. "We never talked about it. I walked into his office one day and he'd hired another kid to do the filing. I asked him if I could just work the maps, but he was so angry he wouldn't let me anywhere near those either."

"He never even offered to give me a job," Ben said.

"That's because you decided to become a lawyer."

"Yeah," Ben giggled. "I don't think he ever forgave me for that."

"You had so much promise."

"Oh, *puhleez.*" Ben pushed himself to a sitting position. "Spare me." Ben rose to his feet. "Well, I'm going to get back down there and save David from Dot's Tarot Reading."

"I don't think he minds, really."

"He's a good man, then."

"Do you think he's too good for me?" Claire looked up at Ben, who had unzipped his pants and tucked his shirttails in, just like her father used to do. At that moment, because of this seemingly inconsequential gesture, she knew that someday she would have to forgive him for being the preferred child, for being something he couldn't do anything about, for being a man.

"Don't answer that," she said.

"Good, I won't then."

Claire's eyes traced the wall of maps and came to rest on a cluster of black and white photographs pinned in the centre of their top margins, their edges curled away from the wall. They were photos she had never seen before — old photographs of a family in a motorcycle and sidecar, another of a woman standing in a desert garden, and a portrait of a young woman not much older than Claire. The portrait was larger than the others and the woman was sitting in a rocking chair. She wore a lace-collared blouse with a cardigan over top. Her hands were unnaturally large and they held in her lap what appeared to be a clipboard. She seemed to have an equilibrium one wouldn't expect from someone that young. She was a woman Claire would want to know. "Who is this?" she asked, pressing her forefinger on the edge of the photo to flatten it.

Ben glanced back from the door. "Didn't you get one?"

"Obviously not, lawyer-boy."

Ben had come back shortly after their father's death to divvy out the remnants of the estate, a book here, prints, photographs, the old Cutlass Supreme, stuff that Claire knew Ben didn't want. He had been hoarding the library, the sculptures, the letters, the fossil collection, and Claire couldn't bring herself to ask him for any of it. She couldn't give her brother the power to say, *No Claire, I don't think so. I don't think he meant for you to have them.*

Instead she stole things: a bookend, a wooden snake, her father's wedding ring. She pretended that her father had given them to her, that they were the precious exchanges between father and daughter, that he had saved them for her or that he had bought them with her in mind. Claire didn't have the courage to ask Ben for anything and true to her nature she hadn't told him about Charlotte Blake's coins.

She looked back at the portrait. The woman's hands rested on the bent arms of the rocking chair and Claire recognized the bony protuberances of her own wrists when she was in the same posture. Suddenly she knew exactly who the woman in the photograph was. "This is Alice, isn't it?"

"Alice Maude James." The words came out of Ben's mouth slowly, as if he was remembering the name as he spoke it. "Alice Maude James," he repeated. "You look like her."

Claire stared at the photograph.

Ben opened the door of the study. The singing voices of David and Dorothy and the artless pounding of piano chords were muffled by the carpeted stairs.

Everything deadened inside Claire's head. An incomprehensible silence hung as large as a century between herself and the photograph. The rounded brow, a soft intelligence, the dark rings of Alice's eyes resembled Claire's own features. As she placed her fingers on the photograph's edge again, she felt a profound loss — not for her father, no, but for Alice, for the mother of her father. Her heart smashed against her chest, and the air sliced like a blade between her ribs. Sitting on the floor, despair hissing out of her, she looked up and saw that tears were pooling in her brother's eyes.

Ben whispered, "He cut a wide swath, Claire."

"I wish there had been more time."

"Time for what?"

"I don't know. Time to get interesting enough for him to have taken notice of me. Time to ask him questions." She turned to Ben. His nose reddened and he shifted awkwardly. She felt a tightening in her throat. "Did you ask him questions?"

Ben nodded.

She swallowed. "What sort of questions?"

His mother, she is so beautiful, thought Claire as Ben paused and thought about his answer. Although she believed that all men were self-centred, she now became aware of her own crude solipsism. Her father had occupied her life for over thirty-six years and she barely knew him, his brother and sister, his mother.

Ben stood at the exit. He shifted his weight and stared at the doorframe. He took a big breath. "Alice had malaria. Dad only found that out when he arrived in Halifax and had to have X-rays in order to enter the country. The doctors pulled him aside and showed him all these micro-fractures in his bones. They told Dad that they must have occurred when he was in his mother's womb, that she had had malaria during her pregnancy. He thought he might have been six when she died. That's when he was sent away to boarding school."

"His brother and sister? What happened to them?"

"They lost track of each other after the war. His sister had become a great actress in the West End and his brother some kind of philanderer. They both died suddenly, only a year or two apart."

"Wow, when did he tell you all this?"

"After you took off for university. Dad and I hung out a lot together. When he had that stroke years ago, I think that kind of opened him up a bit."

She tossed her head back and banged it against the wall. "Why didn't you tell me any of this?"

"You never asked. Besides, I thought he would have told you about Alice, just because you two look so much alike."

You will go and find her.

"She died pretty young — Dad was only six years old."

You have her death inside you.

Claire could hear her father desperately trying to recall his mother's song.

Bai lai lee lai,
Take the moon from your fingers,
Bai lai lee lai ...

She should have paid more attention to him. It was her fault, really. Not Ben's. Not her father's. She should have listened more carefully to what he had said.

Ben slapped the frame of the door. "Well, I'm gonna go down and see if dinner's ready."

"You go ahead."

"You okay?"

"Me? Sure."

She could hear Ben hopping down the stairs into the kitchen as if he was twelve years old. She sat with her back against the wall, rubbing her thumb over the smooth surface of the photograph. Alice's song, lovely for its simplicity, repeated in her head as the door to the hallway eased shut. Claire began to sing:

"Take the moon from your fingers
and let it, let it fall,
Bai lai lee lai, Bai lai lee lai.
Let the sun find your memory
and give it, give it fire,
Bai lai lee lai, Bai lai lee lay."

She stopped and listened as the final notes of the song trembled and then fell silent. Corseted beneath the bony remains of herself, she splintered.

"I know you," she said and as the dust settled in her father's study, she could hear herself quietly sobbing.

Tiger Dreams Film Part VIII Sequence

Music over. Lullaby. A woman's voice.

Medium long shot. Woman bent over ancient ruins. She is digging with a
hand trowel. She sits back onto her feet. Beside her are clay pots, silver
ewers, and in her hand is a small coin. She is humming the lullaby.
Close-up of her face merge to photograph of Alice's face.

Music up and over. Women singing three-part harmony of lullaby.

Medium long shot. Three women digging in excavation site. I am among
them.

Pune 1930

Gandhi's Declaration of Independence, the riots at Chittagong, the Salt March, Gandhi's internment, and hartal, work stoppage, were all great sources of tension in Denzil and Alice's life.

By 1930, there were over 100,000 political prisoners throughout India, and the pressure on the prison system was enormous. Standard disputes over land, or family disputes over love, already stressed the 64 acres within the prison walls of Denzil's domain. The addition of political prisoners, though their presence elevated the prison's status, created a great deal of friction between the surrounding communities and the prison. At the same time, work stoppage was paralyzing the country; the postal service was backed up and the railways in some parts of the country had stopped construction altogether. India was bruising from within.

While Indians struggled for self-determination in a country ruled by a minority, Alice and Denzil had lost the equanimity they had enjoyed in the early years of their marriage. Denzil's increasing power and self-confidence was at variance with Alice's diminishing health; she no longer had the strength to match his determination, though she did take it upon herself to openly protest Mohandas K. Gandhi's most recent imprisonment. It was mystifying to her, she said, that the pure-blooded, chinless British twit thought himself superior to all other races.

"What was it Gandhiji was doing?" Alice questioned Denzil that evening at the Beverlys. "Making salt from seawater, was it? Seems like a perfectly harmless act, wouldn't you agree?"

"Alice," Denzil retorted, "you know nothing of economics."

"Well, if it is economics we are talking about here," Alice said, "then it hardly seems economical to ship bloody salt water to bloody England so the British can lay claim to it. The Indian has been paralysed and is growing hungry and desperate because of it. I should think the British, the great patriarchs that they think they are, might be concerned for our welfare."

Denzil had tried to hush her but she ignored him, "Besides," she continued, "why on earth do the British have to take everything so bloody literally? Surely the Indian should be able to spin his own cotton and make his own salt?"

The evening at the Beverlys deteriorated rapidly when Helen Beverly challenged Alice. "Alice, darling, whose side are you on?"

Denzil slammed his fist onto the table and silenced the dinner party. The cutlery and crystal hopped and clattered in position.

Alice broke the silence. "The fact that Indians have few or no rights over their own economic situation seems an injustice to me and I find it deceitful to be involved in an 'us' and 'them' arrangement with the Indian — 'us' being the British and 'them' being the Indian. Myself, I am somewhere between the two."

She quickly tallied her company's heredity. "Although my own heritage is pretty obvious, you all have suspect lineage. Denzil's mother has just recently remarried to a Christian Indian and has finally come out in the open with her own Indian ancestry. Although you, Edward, are as blue-blooded as they come, the Indian has surely blemished Helen's claim to the Portuguese blood of that Goa fiasco. Portuguese! Honestly, Helen. And the Portuguese, well, they have been having their way with the Indian women since the early fifteenth century. One doesn't have to stretch too far back into history to see that the idea of 'purity' of race is preposterous in a country like India. Or Britain, for that matter. What about the Spanish Armada, for heaven's sake? What about the Moors? Who the hell is 'Us' and who the hell is 'Them'?" And Alice took a deep breath.

Denzil's jaw tightened, and he palmed his trousers with his hot hands. Alice refused to make eye contact with him and she continued. "It just seems to me that the British have gone too far with their policies and that it is about bloody time for the Indian to repossess his country. Surely swadeshi is sound economics, isn't it?"

Alice had participated in swadeshi, using the hand-spun khadi over Manchester mill-made cotton, and she had helped the prisoner, Gandhi, with the spools of thread he had spun during his long internment.

Denzil burst out, relieving some of the pressure building inside him, "Oh, don't give me that 'support thy neighbour over and above quality of goods and services' and 'do without what we cannot get in our own country' that your Mr. Gandhi proposes, Alice! You've never done without anything in your life. Where on earth do you think your shoes come from, the merchants in Pune? Not bloody likely. Those are Italian because the Italians happen to know good leather from the dreadful camel hide they flog in this country."

"Well, then," she replied coyly, "we must send our shoemakers to Italy."

"And slice into the holy cow?" Denzil slapped his hand down on the table again and stretched back into his chair. His crooked smile curled up the side of his face into a victorious grin.

Alice's feet felt cramped and desperate in her leather shoes and she fidgeted beneath the table trying to find a position of comfort. It was true; she had renounced few of her material goods and enjoyed the beautiful silks and brocades of European fashion. Though she lived more simply than most women of her class did, there was a flaw to her voluntary poverty. Her private indulgences were being exposed for the small-minded provincialism that they were.

After a long silence, Denzil finally said, "It's about competition, Alice. If we support our local merchants just for the sake of your swadeshi ..."

"It is not my swadeshi, Denzil. It is a way of life for all the people."

"If we disregard quality over and above availability, the local merchants will not feel compelled to compete. They will grow slothful and indulgent. I can already see the sloppiness in their work, can't you?"

"The Indian does things in a different way."

Denzil rose from the table, walked over to Alice's chair and pulled her chair from the table. "Come Alice, we'll finish this discussion at home. No sense in dragging the Beverlys through all this political dissension in the family."

"Nonsense," chortled Edward. "I love a good spar after a meal."

Alice clasped the table with her hands and slowly rose to her feet. She felt faint with anger and her teeth were clenched so tightly that the skin around her cheeks twitched.

"I know, Denzil, that in principle you agree with swadeshi. You yourself practise it every day with your programs at the prison. You know about self-determination. You know how it works."

Denzil draped her cardigan over her shoulder and squeezed her arm uncomfortably hard. His eyes barely contained his anger.

"She's right, old boy," Edward Beverly said as he escorted them to their motorcycle and sidecar. "You do practise it yourself, you know."

"It's not that I disagree with Gandhi's motives, Edward. I simply wish my darling wife, before she opened her bloody mouth, would see that we Anglos have a great deal at stake in whether India goes to the Indian or whether it goes to the British. We'll be chased out as quickly as the British after all is said and done."

That wasn't the first time Denzil had admitted to his mixed breeding. But he had been passing as British for most of his career, having falsified his birth certificate, claiming to have been born in Wales to wealthy farmers. He spoke of returning "home" for retirement. He had even, at one point, justified his marriage to Alice as a political move — "integrating with the Indian" he had told one of his employers. But as the Anglo-Indian community grew, and more and more of them were admitting the truth of their heritage, Denzil began to soften his own defences, and now with Edward Beverly, and possibly to bolster his argument with Alice, he openly admitted to his Anglo-Indian status.

Denzil had won the argument. He could always reduce an issue to its lowest common denominator. In this case, it was about survival, and who could argue with the basic facts of survival? In the early years it had been what Alice admired about him, but now she realized that she, too, had become the essence of an argument. She too had become one of his reductions.

Rumours had been circulating about Alice's relationship with Gandhi since his arrival at Yeravda and until that evening Denzil had remained silent about it. Alice and Denzil remained inside their own thoughts as they rode through the old part of town, past the open fields, across the River Mula and down the dusty lane to their home. Alice tiptoed into the nursery to check on the children and returned to the parlour where Denzil sat silently observing his nightcap, a good stiff whisky. She moved over to the piano and began to play a nocturne while Denzil rolled his pipe between his teeth. He sat beside the window and smoked quietly as Alice played. Out of the corner of her eye she could see the white ribbons of smoke shred into the air above him. She knew his tension. It had become her own.

"Your Mr. Gandhi is on another hunger strike, you know," Denzil said softly.

"I know that," Alice replied.

Over the past few months, he had watched Alice become inspired again. He had calculated how many times she visited the old man in a week, observing her entrances and exits, and he watched with great anxiety their increasing frequency. It wouldn't have been such a problem, Denzil convinced himself later, if she hadn't become so distracted — touching Denzil in vague and unfamiliar ways, making him desperate for her to want him. He wanted things to return to how they'd been in the early days, when she'd laugh and tug at him before he'd leave the bed in the morning. He remembered the effort she'd make with candles and crystal and late-night walks to the river and back, listening to his plans, his work, sharing his ambitions with her. He wanted Alice returned to him. He would even take her restlessness, her outbursts. Although he knew his greed was ugly, he was incensed that his wife was rejecting him for the company of another man. He wouldn't stand for it. He could hear his voice crack when he asked her, "Do you love him?"

And Alice, without hesitation, told him, "Yes, of course I love him. What Indian national doesn't love him?"

He pulled his pipe from his mouth. Fireflies trembled and glissaded like buttery stars in the dark night beyond the window. He could see Alice's reflection in a pool of yellow light as she sat at the piano. The edges of images, the piano, the bookshelves behind her, the piano light — they all cut into her, breaking her thin angular body into slivers. And though it was only a reflection, and its inaccuracy was obvious, he thought he could see Alice sneer when he said, "You think I don't have a clue how to love."

"We all do the best we can," she replied, as she rested her hands on the piano keys, searching for the memory of another piece.

Gandhi's prayer that had begun before they left for the Beverlys reached a climax as they sat in the parlour. Other prisoners had joined him in the high-pitched whine that the British would never grow accustomed to.

"I wish to hell he would stop that incessant yodelling!" hissed Denzil.

His head throbbed from the spirits they had consumed at the Beverlys earlier that evening and Alice stopped playing the piano for a moment while she watched Denzil rub his brow.

"Denzil?" she said suddenly. "What if he dies here? In your prison? What then?" She turned back to the piano, shaking her head. "The British can be so bloody daft when it comes to this country. It is absolutely ludicrous to think that by holding him hostage the British can isolate the movement. It can't be done."

Alice began to play another piece — softly, like a ghost, not giving enough weight to some keys and missing others altogether. Her coolness was unbearable and Denzil wanted to antagonize her, frustrate her into knots. She hovered her fingers over the keys and Denzil could tell, by the way her face softened and the way her back straightened, as if to make more room in her heart for the contemplations she had permitted herself of Gandhi, she was thinking of him.

He threw his pipe onto his desk. The legs of his chair scraped across the wooden planks of the floor when he stood up to cross the room. "And I suppose you think that after the Indian achieves self-government, there will be a flood of prosperity? Well, dear Alice, this country is about to descend into chaos, the Hindu and Muslim will slaughter one another, and your man Gandhi will be thrashed by his own men. Is that what you want?"

He could see his body chasing his shadow as he strode toward the piano. His anger was so thick and impermeable it crowded the space between them. He could never have anticipated the violence of his arm when he reached out and grabbed the edge of the piano board, and he would never understand how he could have deliberately slammed it onto the fingers of Alice's right hand. And later, years later, after she had died, he could still see the shock in her eyes as she looked up at him before she fell to the floor. His whole body would shake when he thought he could hear the sound of crushing bones beneath the weight of the mahogany piano board. He would recall his remorse when she woke later in her own bed and whispered to him, "We won't speak of this again." And then, when she finally reached out to him as he wept in the chair beside her, her swollen hand caressing him lightly on his shoulder, "I love you," she said," I forgive you," she said, he had felt powerful again for she had finally touched him in all ways necessary.

PART FOUR
Interminable Prairie

Tiger Dreams Film Part IX Sequence

A series of archival stills. Couples of the Raj. Playing croquet, having tea on
lawns, tennis, gymkhana, a wedding, a bored couple doing nothing.
Hold frame on last still of a tiger hunt.

Music Up and Under.

My Voice-over: Tiger fat cures hemorrhoids, their eyes will improve your
vision, their whiskers will heal a toothache, their bones will increase
your intelligence, his penis is an aphrodisiac, the stomach eases
cramps, the brain cures acne and if you sit on the skin of a tiger for
long enough, you'll become its ghost.

Continue endless photos of tiger hunts. A sickening parade of conquests.
Speed frames. Last frame. Tiger. Dissolve slowly.

The Interminable Prairie, Late March ...

The interminable prairie, the kind that neither stops nor begins, had spread itself like an animal across Claire's back. She could feel the needling of a tooth in the back of her neck and thought, *I am paralyzed and I am watching myself being eaten.* Spooked by her own uneasiness, she entered that communal Prairie disturbance where whole populations watched and waited impatiently as the chinook winds gathered on the western horizon. Suicides and the eccentric behaviour of children increased during those times. But when the cold snapped and the warm winds cracked the sky open, people emerged joyously from their homes. They wore t-shirts and shorts in spring colours of green, pink, and yellow; they rode their bicycles along the gravelled shoulders of roads, or bled the brakes on their cars.

But in that nutmeg wind, Claire began to consume herself. She was cannibal.

"I imagined the moments before losing consciousness would be similar to my own death," she would say later in an easy style, before her own camera. "Colours were more vivid and I was more enamoured with myself, more aware of my beauty. The world was saturated with blues and greens."

She was what David called a seasonal creature, fickle with temperatures and landscapes, always aligned with change, and he tiptoed behind her, hoping not to reawaken her instinct to leave, the runaway theme Claire carried with her during the warm winds. But it was no use, she had made up her mind that she was going to die and she had told David to get on with his life without her.

He told her he wouldn't sleep in their bed until she came back. And she told him that if that were the case, he would have to sleep on the couch for a while, and then she packed some clothes into a bag and made her move toward the door.

"But, what about my back?" he asked as he leaned against the frame of the door holding everything together inside him, keeping his cool.

"Maybe now, you'll get a new couch," she told him and walked spiritedly out the door. I am shredding my life like silk with a razor, she thought as she ran down the stairs and onto the street. She ran until she could run no longer, covering half the city, and as she walked along the riverbank toward her parents' home, Claire felt a part of herself renewing. Or maybe her life was repeating itself, or she was repeating someone else's — she couldn't tell for sure. Since she had discovered the photograph of her grandmother in her father's study, she had become fascinated with the durability of likeness, feeling that the bones of her face, her limbs, even all her soft tissues, mirrored those of someone else. For the first time in her life she felt a kinship to someone. Before, she had thought of her family as separate from her: her father, a male; her mother, an alien; her brother, well, he was left to speculation. All this had left Claire feeling freakish and solitary in the confines of her family. But now, there was Alice.

She arrived at her parents' home early in the afternoon. Her mother hugged her and scuttled her bag off to her old bedroom down the hallway.

"He's a good boy," her mother said as she put the bag down at the end of the bed. "I'm sure you'll work it out."

Claire grabbed her mother by the arm. "Mother, he's a great guy. I just need some space to figure things out for myself."

Her mother stared back at her, lips pursed and brow furrowed. "It doesn't happen like that, Claire," she said. "You don't just leave someone because you need your own space — whatever the hell that means."

Claire sat down on the bed while Dorothy remained standing at the doorway. She picked up one of her mother's "fetishes" — a tiny embroidered pillow — and brushed her fingers over the design. "You haven't a clue what I've been going through."

Dorothy leaned against the doorframe and folded her arms. "You aren't the only one suffering from this condition. We all have been deeply affected by this. Perhaps you won't understand until you have children of your own … Don't forget, Claire that I almost lost a daughter." Dorothy stopped, her eyes narrowed and her head tilted to one side, as if sounding her own inclinations. "David needs to stop letting you walk all over him," she continued. "He loves you and he thinks he's doing you a favour by letting you have your way, but you," and she paused as if to catch herself from saying something she might regret and then she said, her voice rising in pitch, "how on earth can you be so arrogant as to believe no one else suffers?"

Claire threw herself against the other pillows on the bed and stared at the ceiling. Dorothy was shaking; her hands fluttered around her like butterflies blown out of the poppies. "He needs to ask the world of you."

Claire placed her cold hands on her hot cheeks. "Thank you for your honesty, Mother. Now may I please have some privacy?"

"I hate to disappoint you, but you're not going to die today, Claire. It's not in you. You're going to have to figure this one out." Dorothy stopped, cleared her throat and then spoke again.

"You," she took a deep breath, "you and your father." She stepped back into the hallway. "There was always this urgency with him, like he had to live everything in a day."

The house was silent, suspended in an unrecoverable past. Claire looked up and saw that the walls had been painted a different colour. She could hear her mother's steady determined voice. "You may stay here for a couple of days, but I expect you to go back to your own place by the end of the week."

And then Claire could hear the door close and the squeaky soles of her mother's shoes as Dorothy marched down the hallway and into the kitchen.

Claire remained on the bed and plucked at the words on her mother's pillow: "Home is in the Heart," sewn in red thread, framed by a green border. She severed one thread by chewing on it and then feverishly unravelled the rest of the design. Always the unevenness of love, thought Claire, as she dismantled her mother's work. She knew that her mother would never have pushed Ben out. Dorothy always cut the men in her family so much slack — forgiving their adolescent behaviour as if it were a permanent disability like blindness or deafness. However, for Claire, there were no allowances, only consequences that Dorothy carefully administered like some kind of parental torture — for daughters only.

She stared out the window of her room. The crab-apple tree in the backyard clawed the air in sharp staccato reaches. A warm breeze passed over the polished snow and blew into her open window. Its smooth creamy texture was as familiar as David's breath.

Later in the dark, while she watched the moon colour the snow blue and she was alone, truly alone in her thoughts, she knew it wasn't really time to die, that her mother was right. She was going to have to figure this one out.

The following morning, Dorothy dropped Claire off at the hospital and asked her if she wanted some company. But Claire said, no, that she'd be fine and that she'd make her way home after the clinic.

In her last conversation with the cardiologist at the pacemaker clinic he had alluded to some link between quinine, the anti-malarial drug, and SADS, Claire's heart condition. As the technician placed the leads over her chest and ribs and one around her ankle, the cardiologist told Claire that recently they had isolated quinine as one of the drugs that caused a prolonged QT, even in patients who had shown no prior symptoms.

As Claire lay on the bed, the technician placed a magnet over her pacemaker and tapped the monitor with a wand. The cardiologist put his glasses on and stared at the screen. "Okay, let's see what this baby can do." The technician turned a dial on the machine beside Claire, increasing her heart rate with each increment. "One hundred fifty … one hundred sixty … one hundred seventy beats per minute. Don't worry Claire," the cardiologist said kindly.

In the wild drumming inside her chest she could feel the beat of another, as if within her were two hearts or maybe more, and in the buoyancy of thought she could hear herself warmer, richer, darker.

You are running and your pulse is flying and you feel as free from death as ever. You can hear the soft pads of your paws as you gallop through the forest, the dry grass, the desert sands. You are running away from your own extinction.

Your spots have evolved into stripes, sabre tooth into eye; you are white and black, or black and gold. Your eyes are planets, and your pupils are as cold as the dark side of the moon. You are the tiger.

The technician quickly dialled Claire's pacemaker back down to ninety beats per minute. Standing beside her, the cardiologist looked down at Claire and smiled gently, and then returned to looking at the monitor. "Okay, let's shut it off," he said and then counted aloud as Claire's heart began to slow, "Eighty ... seventy ... sixty ... fifty ... forty ..."

"When you're lying there," Claire would say later, "and you can feel your pulse dropping away bit by bit, just disappearing into nothingness, and you know you can barely laugh, because you're thinking not that you are going to die but that no matter what happens you're going to live because they've got this battery inside you, like the Energizer Bunny, and that you'll just keep banging the drum, you won't have any choice in the matter, you'll be ridiculous in life anyway. And in those moments, all that you will have ever wanted in your life is control."

"Thirty-five beats per minute, okay, better turn it back to ninety."

Claire exhaled.

"Let's see if the ventricular lead is working," the cardiologist said. The technician turned the dial, click, click, click, and Claire's heart mumbled and throbbed beneath her breastbone, her throat tightened, her lips numbed.

You migrate deeper and deeper into the forest until your back is against the last stand of trees and all you can feel is the breeze whistling across the open meadows behind you. In the valley below, you can hear the stomp of the elephant, the fall of trees and the mournful cry of the langur, and you panic because you have seen your mother dismantled on the path between the edge of the forest and the river, her claws and bones scraped clean and ground into medicine, and you are convinced that you are next so you cry and then you charge ...

"Stop," Claire begged. "Stop that, please," and she began to cry.

"Okay, change it back into AAI mode." The cardiologist smiled and put his hand on her shoulder. "Sorry, Claire, we just wanted to make sure we could use it — if we ever needed."

Later that same evening, Claire asked her mother about her father's family history. Ben had mentioned that Alice had died of malaria, was there some kind of link between quinine and Alice's death?

Dorothy had many theories about her husband's past, none of which supported Claire's theory. "I believe Denzil murdered Alice," Dorothy said that night at the dinner table.

"Who murdered who?" Claire asked.

"I believe Bill's dad murdered his wife." Dorothy poured some more tea into a cup and stirred in the honey. "Your father used to wake up in these sweats. He had these dreams of his mother. She was being dragged out of the parlour where she played the piano. By the way, she was quite an accomplished pianist. You know, if you would have kept with it, you ..."

"Mom, please. Tell me more about the dream."

"Well, he'd tell me how he could see her through the crack in the door, that she had dropped to the floor and that his father dragged her from the room. He couldn't remember anything after that. After those dreams, Bill always fell into one of those terrible depressions for days. I think Denzil killed her." She paused, stirred some more honey into her tea. "I sometimes think Bill had that same kind of violence inside him."

"Oh, Mother, don't be ridiculous. Dad never raised a hand to you."

"No, no, I don't think that's what I'm talking about. I'm talking about that rage of his. You, of all people, should know what I'm talking about. You could always get his blood pressure up."

Tiger Dreams Film Part X Sequence

Mise-en-scène. I sit on a stool and lean into the lens of my camera.

Me: "My father's eyes were like two perfect crimes. Something tragic
would emerge in their blue, something like love, something like loss.
And when I dragged him from the shower that last time, I thought I
could see his history in the dulled blue iris of his eyes; it was like sea
foam after a squall."

The Interminable Prairie, Early April ...

"You and your brother both have that kind of rage, you know." Dorothy kept stirring her spoon in the hot tea. "Your little brother used to turn pitch red and throw knives down the hallway. And you, I had to stick your head under a cold tap just to get you to calm down."

"What about his brother and sister? Did you ever know them?"

"Yes, yes. We met his brother in London. Not a friendly man at all. Bill had wanted to introduce you kids to him but his brother wanted none of it. Your father was destroyed, Claire. He had no one from his childhood to share his family with. His sister died very suddenly toward the end of the war. She had been quite a famous actress in the West End when one day she just up and died, right there on the stage. All very dramatic, I suppose. But your father's brother, well, you know I don't know a thing about him, other than Bill couldn't reconcile how his only brother had no interest in meeting his family. He never got over that rejection."

Dorothy stopped stirring the spoon and touched the hot metal on the back of Claire's hand. Claire jumped back and rubbed her hand. "Mom, I can't believe you still think that's funny."

Dorothy laughed. "I know, I know. I guess I just like the predictability of it. It's kind of like comedy, don't you think?"

Tiger Dreams Film Part XI Sequence

Medium long shot. A young boy sits upon his travel trunk on an empty
train-station platform. Out of boredom, he begins to unpack the trunk.
Medium shot. It is full of clothes, some books — a complete collection
of Shakespeare, tiny blue clothbound books that could fit into a young
boy's lap during a long journey — a wedding photograph of his
mother and father, another wallet-size one of his mother, and some
small river stones. Close-up of boy's eye. Cut.
Mise-en-scène. He tiptoes into a room and climbs the tall chest of drawers
to retrieve the stones. He rubs his fingers over their smooth, tumbled
polish.
The bed in the room is vacant, the covers pulled tight across the mattress,
the pillows stiff and uninhabited. He fills his pockets with the stones
— something, anything of hers that might bring her back to him. Cut.
Medium shot. From the trunk in the train station the boy surreptitiously
pulls out a tattered blanket and he smells it. Unmatched shots. The
earth during the monsoons; a woman's torso, in her arms — a blue
dress; spices — nutmeg, cinnamon. Jump cut.
Medium Close-up. He brings the blanket to his cheek and brushes it gently
against his skin. He puts everything back into his trunk and struggles
to close it. He sits down, waiting. Pan to the rest of the station. Men in
uniforms sweep the stairs that go up and up. The spectator sees
something Escher-like, staircases going everywhere and nowhere.
My Voice-over: My father, at the age of six, began to feel his own wilderness

grow inside him — something like solitude, an indefinable space. He would be a grand soliloquist. So tangible was this absence, like something sweet, that it would lure people to him all his life. My father, a child of six, sat in that train station waiting for someone to claim him, for someone to fill him up.

Space: An Interval, Early May ...

Dorothy insisted Claire attend her book-group meeting on Wednesday night and what she referred to as her "woowoo sessions" on Sunday afternoon if Claire was going to live under her roof for any length of time. Her mother had invited David for Sunday dinner but he declined gracefully, saying Claire needed her own space.

"What exactly is this space thing you and David keep talking about?" Dorothy asked Claire.

"Space? Space, Mom, has something to do with time and distance. It's how our generation measures love, I suppose. It's the continuous extension of an interval."

"I always thought it was when you kids just wanted to get high."

"That too."

David had brought her clothes and the books he thought she might need. He had clipped out ads from the newspaper on cheap flights to Asia, and old photographs from his personal black-and-white collection began to appear mysteriously on her pillow: the first, a bombed-out building; the next, of a young boy crying on a crowded street; the latest, a photograph of a man sitting alone in a park. He romanced her in the only way he knew how. Carefully. Metaphorically.

Meanwhile, Ben got a job in a law firm with an old school buddy. The job was a lateral shift, he told Claire and Dorothy, and he moved back into his old room down the hall from Claire's, bringing with him the dregs of his marriage, a lavender-coloured duvet, three boxes of books, his album collection and a CD player.

"I got desperate," he said. "I just wanted to get away from there." And as Claire and Ben stood in the doorway of his room looking at the collection of albums and the compact disc player, Claire began to giggle.

"Yeah, Ben, you sure told her. You've got a bunch of albums that you can't play on her CD player. Radical." Claire kneeled down and read aloud the titles of the record albums. "Chicago, Black Sabbath, Moody Blues. Nice relevant collection, Ben. She must have been choked when you took off with these."

"Your sarcasm can be so tiresome, Claire." Ben turned around and walked down the hallway toward the kitchen. Claire followed him. He opened the fridge and stood in its light. His shoulders sagged; the vertical lines in his forehead deepened.

"I'm sorry, Ben." Claire opened the cupboard behind her and pulled down a box of cereal, dug her hand in and popped some into her mouth.

Ben pulled out a carton of milk, spread back the spout and drank out of the corner. He swallowed, closed the spout and put the milk back into the fridge. "Do you suppose they are making milk differently? I mean, it always seems a bit sour nowadays." Ben hopped up to sit on the counter between the refrigerator and stove and looked at her very sternly. "I'm not sure you'd see my marriage the same way I do, Claire."

"Why is that?"

"You operate differently than I do. I mean, I want to have a family, have children, a more traditional life. You don't seem to want any of that."

"What makes you say that, Ben? How on earth do you know

what I want or don't want? You've always been so busy talking about yourself that you never bothered to ask me. You're just making assumptions." Claire walked across the kitchen and sat at the table with the cereal box in her lap. "You think just because I don't have children, because I'm not married, that I've chosen that? Well, it just so happens that at one time having a family was all I wanted. But I also have ambition and I'm not quite sure how I can combine the two."

Ben remained at the fridge, put his hand into his pocket and jiggled his loose change. His mannerisms were strikingly like her father's, the way he slouched into a thought, dropping his head forward and staring at his feet. He spoke into the floor, "I couldn't decide what colour of socks to wear anymore. I kept getting my hair cut. I obsessed about keeping the house clean, thinking that I'd begin to feel ordered again." He looked up at Claire, his dark eyes sorrowful. "I loved her as much as I could love anybody, I think. But I wasn't big enough to share her with somebody else."

Claire and Ben sat quietly in their mother's kitchen.

"That's too bad," Claire finally said and then immediately regretted it.

"What? Too bad that I'm not big enough or that the marriage didn't work out?" Ben stared at her and she could see his face twisting.

"Both, I suppose. I mean, I think monogamy is highly overrated. Look at Dot and Bill and how long they lasted."

"And I suppose you are still under the delusion that what they had was a good marriage?"

"It worked, didn't it?"

"Yeah, Dad got to do whatever the hell he wanted and Mom ..."

"... got to do whatever the hell she wanted."

"I'm just saying that I think she would have preferred something different."

"Have you ever asked her? I mean, do you know that for a fact?"

"No, but I look at how happy she has been lately — the opera, the trip to Egypt, the ..."

"She's just filling in space, Ben! She hasn't a clue what to do without Bill around. Look, I'm not saying they had this perfect marriage, but they figured out a system that worked."

"Yeah, for Dad."

"Mom had free will. She could have done something else."

Claire got up, went to the fridge and pulled out the carton of milk, spread back the spout and took a big swig, swallowed and then said, "Dad was restless; she knew that when she married him."

"Christ, Claire, can you hear yourself justifying the way that Dad treated her?"

Claire replaced the milk in the refrigerator and closed the door. "You know something that always astounds me? How antagonistic you always were with Dad."

"And it always astounds me how you idolized him."

"If Dad and I had such a great relationship, Ben, then why did he leave ...?"

"He didn't leave everything for me, Claire. You're in there, too."

"Two parts Benjamin D. Spencer, one part Claire A. Spencer. How would you read that, Ben?"

They stood opposite one another. Ben unzipped his trousers and tucked in his shirttails, then zipped his trousers back up. "He probably thought I'd find more use for his stuff than you would. Maybe he loved me more than you. Is that what you want to hear? I don't know, Claire. Who knows what Dad was thinking? You can have anything you want. You know that, don't you?" He kept his head low as if stuck in the middle of a thought.

"That's not the point, Ben."

"When are you going to grow up and enter the real world, Claire?"

"I have, Ben, and the real world is divided into two parts you and one part me."

Ben stared coldly, his warm humour reduced to a frightening mix of rage and helplessness.

Claire continued to badger her brother. "You're the one who doesn't live in the real world, Ben. You don't have to, because you can carry on being an ass and it doesn't matter — it never did. Everyone always defers to you. Why do you think that is, Ben? Because you're incapable of taking care of yourself? I don't think so. It's because you're a boy and boys still get to have it all ways."

"Oh, go ahead, Claire. Make this political. You're good at that because it makes it someone else's problem. Well, you're just some spoiled cowboy chick from the foothills who cranks out bleeding-heart liberal bullshit about human rights issues of which you know nothing."

Claire got up from her chair, put the cereal box back into the cupboard, went to her room, grabbed her jacket and the photographs from David, left her camera on the bed, and walked out the front door.

The Anatomy of a Seizure, First Movement

You lean against a pillar and your lower jaw feels like pure mercury. You feel absence, as if your heart has left you. And like colour without love, you pale. You think if you could just laugh more often you would never feel this vacancy again.

Stony, Early May

Claire ran out to the edge of the city, hitched a ride to a small town twenty kilometres down the highway and then she hopped into an old pick-up truck that took her to the reservation just east of the mountains. She hopped out of the truck and walked through the gates and down the dirt road, leaping over muddy swales that crossed the road in irregular intervals. "Swales," she said aloud, emphasizing the "w," elongating the "a." She had been dying to use the word in context and now in her solitude, as she wandered across the fields where she had first met David, his gentle words came to her, comforting her, occupying her mind, distracting her from those horrible moments when she thought she should be more than what she was. Ben could do that. He could reduce her.

She stopped before an open field when she realized what she had been doing for the last hour of her life. Leaving. Like she always did when the chinook winds arrived.

On the other side of the fence, one of the last remaining herds of buffalo in North America clustered. The buffalo, twenty, maybe twenty-five of them, were pushing the brown grasses aside with their noses and greedily chopping and grinding the new growth with their teeth. Their moulting coats clung to the barbed-wire fence on all corners of the field and the young buffalo calves bounced around like carousel horses in the late afternoon light. Claire rested against a wooden fencepost and inhaled the animals' scent. *I will have to film this someday*, she thought.

By a stand of poplars just up the hill from where Claire leaned, a buffalo cow was calving. The cow stood awkwardly, her neck stretched out, her hind legs stiff, the hooves of the calf appearing and disappearing as the cow pushed and moaned. Within minutes the calf slid onto the ground behind the cow and dangled like an anchor by its pulsing cord. The cow licked the filmy sac from the calf's nose and Claire marvelled at the speed with which the calf rose onto its feet and began to suckle. She brought the back of her hand up to wipe the mucous from the tip of her nose and she thought, *It takes only moments for a calf to achieve what has taken me almost forty years. How is it that I am still alive?*

It was chilly and she didn't have a clue what she was going to do for warmth once the sun disappeared. She had nothing with her, no matches, no blankets, not even a snack to get her through the evening, but when she looked up at the deepening sky and smelled the fresh sweat of birth from the buffalo, she felt safe and sure of her life.

She walked down the hillside toward the river and crawled in behind a cliff that had been warmed by the sun. The river crashed and tumbled from the spring melt. Its eddy lines roiled beside the standing wave below her; its trough stretched the width of the river where two narrow tongues of water plunged into the wave on either side. David had taught her the anatomy of that river in the first year of their courtship and now she knew its every bend and weir intimately. Downriver from the reservation was a quiet inlet where the water pooled and hushed beside the raging current. Clear rocky cliffs above and below the surface reflected a perfect symmetry between air and water; the only difference between them was that certain animals have the ability to breathe in one world and not the other. In the kayak, the eddy-in had to be precise — one powerful paddle stroke, lean, pull, brace, brace, and everything suddenly still. They'd pull out their kayaks and swim.

Leaning against the wall of rock beneath an overhang, Claire brought her knees up to her chest. With each breath a new star or planet emerged. Venus. Saturn. A sliver of moon. She understood now that she would never be able to describe a universe without David in it.

That evening she slept beneath the bluff with the cold fully inside her.

When the Cold Is Inside You, This Is What You Dream:

You etch mandalas into your grandmother's callused feet. It is a darkly feminine ritual, performed between two women, and in your seamless sleep you ask, "What happens when women like us die? What is it that we leave behind? I know I am the last of our kind." As you place the soles of your grandmother's feet onto the cold stone, you say, "But will no one mention us to our children?"

Stony, the Following Day

Claire woke and hitchhiked back into town. At the door of their apartment she pulled out her keys and began to fumble with the lock, her hands so cold she was unable to still them.

David opened the door and smiled. "Your brother called last night. Said he was worried about you. Said you guys had a fight. Where'd you go?"

"Stony," she said and walked into the room.

David had seduced Claire at Stony ten years before. It had been a hot summer evening after a branding party. He had taken her shirt off to look at the muscles in her back. And on that hot summer evening with the smell of burnt flesh and smoking fires, it had taken David forever to kiss her on the mouth.

She walked into the living room of their apartment; her fossils and skeletons were in their places along the bookshelves, half-finished coffee cups sat on the old water-stained side tables, and there was a new couch in between them.

"Eaton's?" she said.

"The Bay," he answered.

"Nice. I like it."

She tossed her things onto the couch and turned around to look at David. He was still standing by the open door.

"You going to stay for a while?" he asked.

"If you'll have me."

Claire felt a burning around her eyes as if wind had flicked sand into her face.

David shut the door and moved closer to her. "You're not coming back because Ben told you I bought the couch, are you?"

"No," she laughed and pointed to the pile of black-and-white photographs strewn across the dining table. "I know you have an endless supply of those." She inhaled a few short breaths and took his collar into her fingers. "David?" The next thing she was going to ask him was not at all what she thought she might say or do when she had rehearsed this moment. "David?" she said again and recoiled a second time.

"Yes, I'll come to India with you."

"Mom says that you have to stop making it so easy for me."

"I'm sorry," and he brought his hand to the middle of her back. "What was it that you wanted to ask me?"

"Will you come to India with me?"

"Hmmmm," he smiled. "We'll see. We've got some things we need to discuss first."

"That's better." Then she kissed his chin, his cheeks, the skin around his eyes, the scar on his forehead, and finally his mouth as she pulled him down to the floor. She wanted his blood and the soft centre of his heart. She unzipped him, reached inside and whispered, "I know, David, that I have made you suffer."

He held her firm; his fingers dug into her. He was angry, hurt, rougher with her than usual and he astonished himself with his greed, finding his way into her. He could hear himself growl and he bared his teeth to his woman when she begged him to eat her.

In the stillness after, he thought he could hear her ask, "David, will you remember me?"

Pune 1932

While Chandrasekhar stood on the bridge of an ocean liner calculating the gravitational collapse of stars, Denzil was suppressing the riots in Bombay. He had received the Order of the British Empire for his vocational rehabilitation program and his gift for languages made him indispensable to the British during the negotiations of the Quit India Campaign. One day in the spring of 1932, he told Alice that he was to be posted north to Karachi. He urged her to travel a couple of days ahead of the rest of the family to Bombay, where they would meet up and travel to Karachi together. That way, she would be spared the stress of the move.

Admittedly, political power was shifting out of Pune, Alice argued, but surely the Karachi of 1932 was no better a position for a Superintendent of Prisons, what with the city being so far on the other side of the proposed boundaries of the Muslim homeland? Karachi was unbearably hot during the month of May and she found it odd that the transfer should occur before the wet season. In deference to her ill health, Denzil had assured Alice that he would take care of all the details of their departure — the packing, the children — and that Charlotte would accompany her to Bombay. The children would remain with their ayah until the family was reunited in Bombay for the voyage north to Karachi.

It wasn't that Alice was particularly enchanted with Pune or even their home in the gardens across from the prison, and in many ways she looked forward to a change of scenery, but her life had certainly become much more inspired since the return of the Mahatma. Leaving Yeravda meant leaving him and the women who had been arrested with him, and she found herself already missing those afternoons when she and the women walked together. Those were the afternoons when Alice felt epochs away from her convalescence; when she walked along the dusty path to the prison entrance, bringing news to the women, bringing gifts of fruit, nuts and curd into the fenced-off garden where Gandhi and the Nehrus, both father and son, greeted her openly. She wanted to fill them up in all the places the British had been absent, hoping that by her simple acts of love, they would free her of her own exquisite isolation.

Alice had ensured that large marble slabs would be laid around the mango tree she and Gandhi had planted when he was first interned two years before. Its trunk had increased in girth considerably since then, and the three branches radiating from its centre provided the shade where Alice and Gandhi would sit.

Gandhi had been trying to unite the high- and low-caste Hindus to sign an agreement to eliminate untouchability. Alice had seen him racked with sadness to hear the fights in the streets, to know that there were still millions of Hindus unable to break the code of their caste.

She had permitted herself to love him, to enchant him, catching his eye at just the right moment, smiling in such a way that it made her cheeks dance — the way in which she had seduced her own husband so long ago. She sat in his cell, often muted by his butterfly gentleness, trying to think of worthy things to say while he pulled the thread from the spinning wheel, curling the shiny thread around his fingers, and carefully organized it around the spool. She confessed her daily struggle with luxury, her passion for European silks and the comfort of good Italian shoes.

The women in the next compound had laughed along with her, telling her that consistency wasn't the point. It was the truth of her actions that counted. What she had desired most was to become indifferent to luxury, to be perfect in her religion. The women had told her that she must become indifferent to her poverty, and then perhaps she would be perfect. But she knew that perfection meant she would need to be ready for her own death and that idea was too uncomfortably close for her.

It had been so refreshing to sit within their intelligence, their thoughtful application of ahimsa, of matters of the heart. When Alice asked the oldest woman, Sajani, about the truth of her motives for being imprisoned, Sajani told her the story of Tolstoy's recalcitrant soldier who had refused to perform military service because it was against the teaching of Christ. He had been imprisoned for this and yet his soul felt good. "Our Lord endured," he had said, "and He asked us to do so as well."

"But you break the law," Alice said.

Sajani nodded and curled another loop of thread around the spool. "We believe the laws of love and laws of violence are mutually exclusive. The lords of our nation believe differently than we do. They have created these laws to enhance their own commerce and not their own truth."

The long silences between the women and Alice occupied the space between her Indian self and her British self. After hours of spinning cotton, her bent fingers frozen, pain shooting through her shoulders, she would leave the women and return to her home across from the prison entrance. As with most Anglo-Indians, Alice had adapted quickly to the crossing over between the Indian and the British, and the places she created in her own home were an expression of something uncorrupted by either. She was able to forgive the deficiencies of both the British and the Indian. It was because of this peace of mind that she knew Gandhiji's philosophies were saving her.

Alice had felt the modulations of her love for the Mahatma

like the cool extension of a yellow flame. When she thought of him, she felt an ache in her heart. She swallowed and clicked her tongue in silent disapproval of her thoughts, for she knew of the inappropriateness of her alliance. Denzil had witnessed her reading Tolstoy and Thoreau and had challenged her on the contradictions of these men who boasted simplicity and love from the comforts of their country estates.

"The luxury of intellectuals," Denzil had scoffed.

She knew that her relationship with Gandhiji and the women who walked beside him was part of the reason she and Denzil were leaving for Karachi.

The punkah hung silent above Alice's bed on that final day at Yeravda, and when she tugged its cord, it swayed woozily between the bed and the ceiling. Cobwebs billowed out from the punkah's clogged latticework. She slumped onto the linen spread that lay crisp as a wafer on the bed. A lizard dropped onto the canopy with a soft thud and its weight stretched the fabric so that she could see the scales of its belly, the perfect symmetry of nature's design. She sighed lazily, sat up and walked over to the vanity, leaned over the washbasin and splashed a cup of water over her face. Liquid dripped down her neck, and her silk blouse clung to her skin like wet tissue.

She could hear the dog bark and she walked over to the window to catch a glimpse of the children screeching and giggling in the west garden. The branches of the mulberry and jackfruit trees that had been forcibly wrapped around one of the pillars on the veranda were now animated in a mutinous capture of the Yeravda House. Beyond the veranda, the plowed earth in the garden looked like curdled chocolate pudding around the thente tree, and the roots of the pippol trees stretched their thickened branches toward the earth along the boulevard that led to the prison. Everything seemed gripped by some kind of gothic memory, tunnelling into the darkness of the earth, hiding, remembering.

Charlotte Blake and Molly, the housecat, who was slurping milk out of a shallow bowl in Charlotte's lap, sat swinging in the jula on the veranda. Alice poked her head out of the open window and smiled at the younger woman. "Charlotte?"

Charlotte turned slowly and smiled back. "Yes?"

"I suppose we should have the pani-wallah refill the dishes of water under the bedposts in the nursery." Like a moat around a fort, the water dishes prevented scorpions from invading a child's haven. Gauze draped over the beds protected the children from the malaria mosquito that had infected Alice. "Charlotte? Did you hear what I said?"

"What was that, Alice?"

"The pani-wallah and the dishes?"

Charlotte looked blankly at Alice and cocked her head to the side.

Alice repeated, "Could you please have the water boy refill the dishes in the nursery?"

"Yes, of course, I'll call right away."

The white figure of Charlotte Blake passed in front of the open window and Alice returned to her room to finish with packing. She had packed and repacked her wardrobe every day for a week. Waking in the early hours, she had tiptoed to the wooden cupboard, quietly unhinged the latch, opened the door and pulled out the dresses she had placed there the day before. On this final day she took out each of her dresses and shook the fabric to release any scorpions that might have snuggled into the folds the night before. She draped each dress on a hanger, pushed the other dresses aside and hung it back on the wooden pole. She thought how similar she was to her dresses — on the cusp of Indian and British fashion; her Indian heritage always suppressed for the culture of the British. She knew she wore a sari with traditional finesse and there were times when she thought saris the most elegant fashion, but she reached for her blouses and skirts more often because of their simplicity. In truth, she still preferred the woollen trousers of kamoan wool she had worn until their inappropriateness in Pune society made her more controversial than she cared to be.

She turned to herself in the mirror and pulled the waist of her skirt around so the seams lined up along her hips. The skirts these days had a pretty fluted shape to them if they fit properly; when they didn't, as with this particular skirt on her slight figure, they drooped and waned like a tired orchid. Her silk blouse, now almost dry from splashing water over herself earlier, hung open at the collar, and her tawny skin stretched over a sliver of collarbone beneath. Too much evidence, she thought. I have the appearance of someone so much older than myself.

Her whole body had become a confession of her ordeals — stretch marks from child-bearing were etched across her belly; her knees were scraped and mottled from scrambling around excavation sites. She held up the fingers of her right hand and pulled at the bent fingers folded in toward her palm. They straightened for a moment, then slowly began to fold back in. She was not so smug anymore that she believed herself above the trials of other women her age — women who were married to drunks, women who were thrashed nightly by their husbands. In the early years of her marriage she had thought she would bring about change, she would be a woman to rise above the confines of her gender and class. She knew herself fortunate to have a husband who permitted her a certain latitude of judgement she saw lacking in other marriages. She had a husband who recognized a depth of intellect in his wife, while other men simply disregarded their wives as trite and inconsequential — so much so that the women themselves began to believe in their own insignificance, began to turn on each other and feed off their dull-wittedness. But Alice had been determined to change all that, to alter a man's perception of himself and of the women around him. In a sense, she had been devising her own Pune Pact, not for the untouchables, but for women. But India had too many other distractions, and ironically, the very man she had thought might help bring about the necessary change for her gender was distracted with achieving the rights for the Untouchables. Women, for Gandhiji, were merely an addendum to the addendum. A country had to begin somewhere, she supposed, but why was she always the last one on the list?

Meanwhile, the admiration Denzil had for Alice, and she for him, had been eroded. While the India that was working toward self-government was filled with anticipation and promise, their marriage would never recover from Gandhi's campaign. He had divided them. "Don't forget, Alice," he had told her one night recently, "that you are only one woman and an Anglo at that. You have no power. You've completely romanticized a world that doesn't and won't exist — I guarantee it."

Why was self-determination a romantic notion? she thought. Alice looked back over the room for errant scarves, stockings, and blouses to pack away and then she latched the wardrobe shut one last time.

Tiger Dreams Film Part XII Sequence

Me: "Neither of my grandparents would live long enough to allow for the
    years of confusion and self-doubt that came after liberation."
Tracking shot of me. David assembles the camera on a rickety old go-cart
    with some boys who live down the lane from the prison. I walk the grey
    powdered pathway toward the prison gates and stop at the rod iron
    gates of Gandhi's prison cell. Medium close-up shot of me.
Me: "Instead, Alice and Denzil must have come to believe in the
    permanence of chaos, that there could be no calm after the storm."
    Cut.

Pune 1932, Departing for Karachi

Charlotte poked her head around the doorway. "Devaki has watered the dishes in the nursery. Is there anything else?" Charlotte had a breathy voice that gave the impression of fragility, but Alice knew that there was something sinister about this presumed frailty. She just couldn't find the words to openly disapprove. As she fumbled with her hair, she asked Charlotte about the children. "Do you know if they have had their tiffin yet?"

"Yes," Charlotte said. "Sheila Rana has fed, watered and scrubbed them. Shall I summon a rickshaw to get us to the station?"

Alice could see Charlotte swaying from side to side in the doorway while she looked into the mirror. "Yes, Charlotte, now would be fine."

The younger woman swivelled on one heel and left the room. Alice returned to the mirror and fussed with her hair. She had cut off her braid after William was born; she had found her hair too difficult to maintain, especially with the frequent bouts of malarial fever that now plagued her and her difficulty in handling a comb with her right hand. She felt a familiar twinge of sadness as if parts of her were being snipped away — gradually and without much protest.

Why was hair such a defining factor? She had always kept her hair well, oiling the roots, candling the frayed edges of her braid, applying hennas in the old way, something she had learned from Sister Dorothea years before. Her bobbed hair looked comical to her now. It was as if fashion mocked her features — her jawline was too wide, her cheekbones too high and her eyes set too deep to suit this new masculine design. She licked her thumbs and ran them along her temples to dampen the loose strands of hair that trembled in the air around her. She called to Charlotte, "Is Denzil going to join us, then?"

Alice didn't think Charlotte as dim-witted as Denzil considered her to be. He was harsh with his younger relative and often alluded to what happened when cousins married each other. "Charlotte, are you there?"

She had thought that Charlotte might be a bit deaf, but Denzil disagreed. "Not deaf, Alice, daft," he had said. "The woman is daft."

"Will you call me when the rickshaw arrives, please? I'm almost finished packing."

"Yes," and Charlotte remained in the doorway as if to say something more.

Alice smiled at her and waited for her to leave. "Well? Charlotte, is there anything else?"

"Pardon me? Oh, no, I'm sorry." Charlotte backed away and straightened her skirt; she turned and disappeared down the hallway. The heavy soles of her shoes clumped against the wooden planks on the veranda and faded as she walked around to the back of the house.

Alice had weakened since the first bout of malaria six years before and with the miracle drug from the Americas, the quinine, it seemed as if she was deteriorating even more rapidly. But the doctors would hear none of her complaints, believing that her malaria had advanced too far into her brain for her to be clear on her judgement.

"It seems," her doctor had told Denzil, "that you were remiss in reporting your wife's illness earlier. I'm afraid there is nothing more we can do but wait."

Alice had become like all those women she had thought herself so different from — understated, insecure, and frail from exhaustion. She began to doubt herself; the doctors had convinced her of her weakness of mind, and her protests about the possible failure of the quinine were being overruled. She felt herself drifting into obscurity.

The final bag to pack contained her jewellery: a string of pearls Denzil had given her the previous year on her thirty-seventh birthday; a topaz ring from her mother; a ruby necklace from the desert; a lapis hair comb to accompany her braid of hair; and finally, her collection of rare coins.

She opened the cloth bundle that housed her coin collection and pulled her favourite coin out, the one she had collected in the desert the year William was born. It had the worn impression of Nur Jahan, the great Mughal empress who was famous for her beauty and power. A thousand dust storms since Nur's time had pitted the gold coin and its edges were as thin as a knife blade. She handled it as little as possible, as the salts from her skin could erode what was left of the impression.

Her friend Sajani had enjoyed having the coin in her hands. She said she was flattered that Alice shared her preoccupation with her. History was the architect of their life experience, Sajani had told Alice as she flipped the coin over and over in her fingers. "This coin tells me about the gifted power lying dormant within all of us."

"Us?"

"Women." Sajani handed the coin back to Alice and smiled. She picked up her cotton and began spinning again. "I pray that there will be a thousand like us to take these ideas and carry on with the battle."

"Why does it always have to be a battle?" Alice asked.

"Because there will always be doubts, Alice. Men have thousands of years of forgetting before they can move beyond weapons. It is our responsibility, as women, to teach men to fight, not with weapons but with love. But," and she took Alice's chin in her hand and shook it, "we must be patient, Alice."

We must be patient, Alice. How many times had she heard that in her life?

To Alice, the coin represented a dream of the woman she would never come to know, a woman she could never be. As she carefully positioned the coin in the centre of her palm she had a perfect thought, the kind that comes maybe once or twice in a lifetime, intractable but transitory. The thought was that her life *could* reach beyond herself, that death, like time, had different locations, that it was not always located at the end. It had a fulcrum to balance upon, or a centre where life could be gathered into it. Her death would mimic her life, like the perfect reflection of the mountains in a lake. Which is truer?

Nur Jahan's face pressed through the milky film of rice paper Alice used to protect the coin, her cheek still youthful and rounded, the profile of her lips like a half rose; her lidded eye was large and saw more than most. The image of Nur, or the image of herself. Which is truer?

Alice smoothed the wrinkles and folded the frame back over the parchment. She placed Nur's coin on top of the other coins in her collection, wrapped the square green cloth around the bundle and tucked it into her bag.

Charlotte appeared at the door. "The rickshaw is ready," she said.

"Thank you, Charlotte. I'll be there momentarily."

The room seemed still, as if Alice's absence had already happened and she was looking back on it in her memory. There was a severe ascetic quality to the room now. Taupe linens lay rigid across the bed. White gauze curtains hung straight and unresponsive to the warm breeze. The chuprassi had dampened the khus-khus tatties and was now hanging them throughout the house. The room darkened as the tatties unravelled down the open windows, flapping against the lintels and engulfing her home like the body of an armadillo. Insects scurried across the floor and she could hear the pat pat pat of the spiders' feet.

Alice felt perspiration trickle down the middle of her back. She wished she could wash herself down one more time before the journey. It would be days before she could adequately bathe again and on those journeys there was always a scarcity of fresh water and an abundance of humidity. With a final glance into the mirror, Alice hoped to surprise herself with a sense of newness. She was met with barely presentable pallor. *The image or the woman, which is truer?* she asked herself.

September, Departing for India

Flooding from the monsoons had almost completely wiped out Bangladesh. There were rumours of widespread cholera outbreak in Varanasi. India and Pakistan had been testing nuclear bombs along the border, Sikh extremists were blowing up automobiles in Connaught Circle, and Kashmiri kidnappers had lopped off the head of an unsuspecting tourist. Ben couldn't reconcile himself to the fact that Claire would be throwing herself at the mercy of a country in the midst of religious turmoil.

"It's all about land," Claire told Ben the night they came back together after their fight. They were both tentative, the difficult question of love cracked open and dangerous between them. They were finishing off the heels of their father's Scotch bottles when Claire called the drinking to a halt. Ben had brought out the Schnapps. She waved her hand at the bottle, rejecting it, and watched while Ben took a swig of the liqueur.

"It's all about land," she repeated. "Religion just clouds the issue."

"Aren't those religious wars they are having over there?"

"Under the guise of religion, yes, but the common denominator is land ownership. Kashmir is lakefront real estate, you know."

"Holy wars?"

"Yeah, they call them holy wars because that somehow justifies the killing, but really it's about appropriating land."

They sat on the floor in their mother's kitchen. The only light came from the digital clock on the stove; it was 2:00 a.m. Claire spoke slowly; her speech had become laboured through the haze brought on by her father's Scotch. "Aren't you at all curious about Dad's family?" she asked.

Ben stretched his legs out in front of him. "Curious?" he asked. "Not really."

"Are you serious?" Claire swung her head around and squinted at him. "You are serious, aren't you?"

He nodded, took another swig and balanced the bottle on his knee. "You're right. This tastes like shit," he declared, and he placed the bottle on the counter behind him and shifted around to face Claire. Ben had a genuine faith in himself and Claire envied him his self-confidence. His smile was broad and warm as he told Claire he thought their father was a great guy — an enigma, really — but that he had somehow known their father would be dead for the majority of Ben's (and Claire's) adult life.

"I'm not saying I don't care, Claire. I think, to be honest, I moved beyond Bill long before he died. Nice guy. Really smart. But way too complicated for me to even try to understand."

Claire felt herself once again being swayed by her brother's opinion, thinking that perhaps he was right, perhaps her curiosity had been misplaced and her whole project was a pathetic reflection of how incomplete she was. Maybe it was her love of the macabre that brought about her interest in India and her need to be involved with something greater than Canada. Or, and this was probably closer to the truth, Claire needed to find something good about her father inside herself. Though her father had left her free will (although she still struggled for independent thought), he had also left her with India, and if Ben was to get everything else of her father's that was near and dear to her, she was going to inherit India.

Ben drove Claire back to her apartment that night and slept on their new couch. He was to drive Claire and David to the airport in the morning. All three were hungover, David from partying with his hockey buddies, and Claire and Ben from finishing off their father's liquor cabinet once and for all.

"E-mail me at the office as soon as you can," Ben said and handed them both packages of wet wipes. He hugged Claire and shook David's hand. "Don't take any shit from her," he said. "You're a better man than I'll ever be for doing this with her."

"Don't worry; I'm already working on payback." David gripped Ben's hand tightly and patted him on the shoulder. "Besides, I might find some truth in that Bering Strait Theory and find out where my people really come from. What if, after all of this, we have been laying claim to the wrong tract of land?"

"I thought your people came from some primal soup right here."

"Ah yes, but nobody really knows for sure."

"Well, good luck with your own pilgrimage, then, and take lots of pictures," Ben said, and he kissed Claire on the forehead.

They stayed overnight in Bangkok and flew on to Delhi the following evening. Claire brought her camera, sixty tapes, a few changes of clothes, her passport, a bedsheet, antacid, antibiotic cream and some painkillers. David carried his camera, black-and-white film, passport, water purifier, and the plane tickets in a separate bag on his shoulder. The planes were packed full and the lack of legroom unbearable for both Claire and David. They paced the aisles and stretched by the emergency exits during the long flights.

A sallow tinge covered the walls, floors, chairs and counters throughout the Delhi airport. As David exchanged his U.S. traveller's cheques for some rupees at the State Bank of India window, Claire carefully perused the city map in search of their guest house. David handed a man behind the window at one of the pre-paid taxi booths a two-hundred-rupee note that was quickly exchanged for a fifty-rupee note.

"You have not given me enough, Sir. Taxi is two hundred-rupees."

Feeling inadequate with the new currency and too overwhelmed by the alarming number of taxi wallahs lined up to take their baggage, David didn't bother to argue the injustice.

"Ripped off before we even get out of the airport." David admonished the taxi wallah, who drove around the same block a couple of times until David told him that he would get paid the same amount of money regardless of how long it took to get to their guest house, and no, he was not interested in the fact that their guest house had burned down only yesterday, they would take their chances, and no, he didn't want a nicer accommodation for just a little bit more money. How much more money? he asked out of curiosity. No, he didn't want to just go and find out, he wanted to know now. Oh, for only $150 US? Well, no thanks, and would he stop driving in circles and if he wanted to have anything that resembled a tip that he might want to think about arriving at the guest house in the next couple of minutes.

The horns in the traffic were thick as bees, bony arms flailed through the open windows of buses that crawled like millipedes along the grey streets and the grey streets were coloured by refuse, Pepsi labels, chip bags and green banana peels. Hawkers sitting upon piles of refuse at streetlights were selling year-old editions of *India Today*, little marble elephants, miniature chess sets and silver anklets.

In the chaos of Delhi streets, Claire retreated into the centre of herself; her core, like a pebble, tumbled around inside her ribs. If a part of her was Indian, she thought, then she was a stranger to herself. She was, for the first time in her life, immigrant.

A European businessman smoked a cigarette while he stared out the window of the Pizza Hut in Connaught Circle. David asked directions from an Israeli who was sitting outside a travel agency browsing maps while his partner wrote postcards. A faded poster of the sandy beaches of Goa was taped to the inside window and the Caucasian model dancing on the beach against a pale blue ocean wore 1970s bell-bottoms and bare feet. An Indian woman in blue jeans spoke into her cellphone as she dashed out from a glass building and crawled into a taxi. These images were almost familiar scenes for Claire — the fishing lines of Western influence tugging on this otherwise indefinable universe.

Freshly coloured saris fluttered like blossoms against the hazy side streets. White kurtas, and peach, ocean-blue and emerald-green salwars, sparkled on the Indian men and women. Straight-backed women blew snot from their jewelled noses at the intersections as their children drooped passively in their arms; shadows from the crumbling ruins beside them fell across their faces.

David stared through his camera lens. "Feels like I'm cheating," he said. "It's like this country wakes up every morning and moves toward a dramatic composition."

Claire spoke through the cotton scarf she had draped over her nose and mouth to avoid the fumes puffing into the rickshaw from the exhaust pipe of the bus idling beside them. "How on earth am I going to organize a film in this country, David?"

David laughed, put his arm across her shoulders and shouted over the thunder of Delhi traffic, "That's kind of an oxymoron, isn't it?"

They spent the first couple of days sleeping in their guest house and venturing out to various restaurants to eat. Claire bathed twice a day. David spent most of his time negotiating prices for beer.

With every movement she made, she felt like she was slipping away, and she struggled daily with gathering her courage to face the many, many people of India. "Maybe this was a mistake," Claire confessed.

"Don't sweat it, Claire. I'm sure there are some very nice people in Delhi." David paused and nodded his head, "But let's get the hell out of Dodge."

Claire wrote Ben from an Internet café situated in a back alley off Connaught Circle.

Dearest Ben,

I am in a level 10 video game and I've only played to level 4 before.

We spent yesterday navigating the streets of Delhi. What can I possibly say about this city? It is big and ugly and polluted. Very polluted. It has reached the point of no return. The only thing that can happen to this city is that it reaches maximum entropy — maybe an outbreak of disease from some wild strain of virus. My sinuses are a mess and I dare not take a breath. I am in a sort of stasis, just wishing I were somewhere else. Our luggage got lost in Bangkok so we are waiting for it to go to Kurdistan, Madagascar, and God knows where else, before it arrives in Delhi. Next time we'll keep our luggage with us.

Anyway, it took a day to find this place so that we could e-mail you and I don't know what's in store for us in Bombay or Pune. My health is good and David hopes to get a parasite so he can drop some weight. It shouldn't be too difficult, judging from his appetite and questionable food purchases from street stalls.

We leave late tomorrow night on a train for Bombay. Off for another adventure. Please let Mom know everything is fine and that I mailed a postcard to her from Bangkok. It should get there by the time we get home.

Claire

"Hi Mom?"

...

"The connection is bad."

...

"What? I can't hear you."

...

"I love you."

In India everything moved very quickly; Canada, by comparison, was a dull rumour. The train station in the Paharganj area of New Delhi was confusion in an orderly fashion. The porters looked at Claire's and David's tickets and plucked up their bags. Claire wrestled with one of the porters to keep her camera bag and the porters placed the other bags on top of their heads and began trotting through the train station.

"Seems ridiculous that all I can think of is home," she confessed to David as she ran after him down the stairs and onto the station platform. "And while I was at home all I could think of was being here. It must be such a struggle for you to know whether I'm coming or going!" she shouted.

"Yes," David shouted back as they waltzed down the platform behind the porters.

"The numbers," Claire called to David. "The numbers of people, cows, cars. My God, I can't do the math."

"Two hundred million cows in India, Claire. What did you think it was going to be like?"

They walked half a mile to their compartment and found their name on a sheet of paper taped to the side of their railcar. They followed the porters into the train, tipped them generously and settled themselves into their sleeper.

"It's the number of people my imagination can't come to terms with," Claire shoved her luggage under the bottom bunk. "How many people are there in this city?"

"Fifteen million, I think." David threw his backpack onto the top bunk and sat down to have a drink of bottled water.

"That's half the population of the entire country of Canada, Claire. Didn't you do your homework before you came?"

"I wonder how many of them watch documentaries?"

Passengers walked by their compartment, checking their tickets. Two more passengers joined Claire and David. A woman Claire's age, dressed in blue jeans and a plaid shirt, arrived with her adolescent daughter, who wore headphones and was decidedly uninterested in the presence of two obvious foreigners in her compartment. The woman's daughter swung herself onto the top bunk opposite David's, folded her legs up and flipped her tape over. The woman spoke immaculate English. "I assume you are American?"

"Canadian, actually. My name is Claire and this is David."

"I am Mridula."

"Rithula?"

"No, MmmmriDu-la."

While David read and Mridula's daughter listened to music on her headphones, Claire and Mridula burst open with confidences Claire had forgotten could be shared. They began with the usual exchanges: how long are you here for, where will you be going, where are you coming from; my daughter plays tennis, she was in a tournament this last week, we are going home to Bangalore; that is a long way from Delhi; yes, thirty-six hours on the train; you must be a dedicated mother; well, you get them involved in these sports and before you know it, they become very good and their coaches want them to compete nationally; tennis is a very big sport in this country; yes; how many children do you have; two, the other is a dancer; oh, is there a national ballet; I suppose there is, but she dances for weddings; what does your husband do; we have a very popular restaurant in Bangalore on MG road; what is the MG for; Mahatma Gandhi; every city in this country has a Mahatma Gandhi Road; yes, he was a very important man.

"You want to know about our arrangements of marriage," Mridula smiled. "North Americans are always curious about our arrangements."

"You might be confusing me with an American," smiled Claire.

"But you are curious?"

"Deadly curious."

Mridula slapped her thigh and laughed. "You see, I told you. We will trade. I'll tell you all about arranged marriage, and you will tell me about premarital sex." They both giggled and looked over at David, who grinned over the top of his book. "No boys allowed," Mridula called out to David. David lifted his book higher and turned away.

"So? Did you have to sleep with a total stranger?" Claire asked.

"No, nothing like that. In fact, he left me alone for the first couple of months of our marriage. I didn't want him to touch me. It took me a long time to feel comfortable with the idea that he was my husband and I would have to sleep with him. He was very patient with me."

"But you obviously have worked it out." Claire gestured to Mridula's daughter.

"We have no choice but to work it out. If we don't and we divorce ... well, that is not a very good thing in our society. He was very gentle with me. I am grateful for his kindness and I have come to love him very much."

"So, was he your first?"

Mridula glared at Claire. "Of course he was my first. My only. Sometimes I am very curious about other men, but in the end I don't think it would be worth it. That is not to say that I don't flirt, though."

Claire cocked her head to the side.

Mridula continued, "I flirt because I know with whom I am going home at night. It is very cut and dried in our society."

Claire thought of how much she missed the freshness of pursuit but lacked the savvy to recoil, and she told Mridula she wouldn't know how to flirt, that it had been so long ago she had forgotten.

"Indian women are very good at flirting. Observe while you are here. You might learn something from us."

"I already have."

"Oh," Mridula whispered, "you mustn't think what I have is ideal. There are many women my age who are very restless. We married so young, our children need us less and we think about some other kind of life." She placed her dark hand on Claire's leg. "I will come to Canada someday, maybe."

"Could you?"

Mridula smiled. "Of course, but I would be afraid to get lost in your wilderness."

Claire talked about filmmaking and showed Mridula how to hold her camera, how to focus, the differences between blue light and orange light, and zebras. Then Mridula took the camera and began to film Claire.

"It must be very lonely for you?" Mridula asked. "All that space and so few family around. It must be so very lonely."

"Lonely?" Claire had to stop and think about whether she was ever lonely and she didn't think she was. "No, not really," she said into the lens, but later, when Claire and David were editing the film, Claire thought she could detect a lie in her voice. She asked David if they might keep the footage, maybe dissolve it over some of the landscape footage Claire had taken earlier that summer at Stony.

"Lonely?" she said to Mridula while on the train. "I don't think what I have experienced is loneliness, though after coming to India I can understand now how empty it must feel for the Indian coming to Canada."

"Yes," Mridula agreed with Claire. She had heard of friends who couldn't wait to get home. Mridula stopped filming and put the camera down on the bed beside her. She reached over and touched Claire on the top of her hand. "This is good, isn't it?"

Claire looked into Mridula's eyes and tried to achieve the same depth the Indian achieved with hers. For Mridula, it was nothing for her to stare, but for Claire, her eyes watered, she blinked, she rubbed her eyes, looked down, looked away. She told Mridula, yes, that it was good for her too, and they pulled their blankets over their shoulders and stretched their legs across the compartment.

Claire teased Mridula about how the middle class had the same symptoms worldwide, so many servants, and so little time.

"Indian cooking takes all day, Claire," Mridula said. "If I didn't have a cook, it would be myself in the kitchen all the time. I wouldn't have time for my children or for my husband, let alone me. All I would be doing in my life is cooking. The poor, they have no life but to cook and clean."

"I have always thought Indian women were in the dark ages. Our Western emancipation seems to have bypassed you. We work, raise the children, cook, clean *and* take care of our men."

"But you do not have any children?" Mridula raised her hands in the air and looked around. "Why is that? You are not so young anymore."

Claire said she didn't think herself too old to have children, that she was considering the possibility. There were some complications far too detailed to get into.

The women talked about other things: dinner parties, sleeping habits and travel plans, until their throats were too sore to continue. They exchanged addresses in silence, pulled blankets over themselves and lay staring at each other across the compartment.

Claire closed her eyes and rolled onto her other side. It came to her slowly, as the train rocked on the tracks, that Mridula was the first woman friend she had made since high school. Her life had been cluttered with men — David, Ben, her father. All these men and no women, thought Claire, except for her mother, and she wondered why she couldn't make that count. Most of her other friends had married and had children; their lives were occupied with raising their families and enjoying the normal course of life. Claire had lost contact with most of them, finding herself either envious or appalled by the lives they led. She was unable to reconcile the fact that their attentions had been diverted to lactation techniques, playschool traumas or divorce trilogies.

Over the years, Claire had let herself become tough. She had learned how to spit with the wind, hunt gopher and hurl a football. She expressed strong opinions about world leadership, the war in the Middle East, the refugee situation in Afghanistan, the Serb-Croat crisis, and she had become an aggressive interrogator if anyone dared oppose her. She practised sarcasm and abuse until it became second nature; she showed no mercy in a heated argument. She dismissed her mother and continued to participate in demeaning what was true and honest about herself as a woman — just to become a part of her father's world. Now lying beside this woman who was soft, feminine, witty and charming, Claire could see the softened edges of the woman she had left behind, or the woman she had never allowed to surface. At that moment, something shifted inside her, like the quarter turn of a planisphere, the east and west of her rotating. India, with all its wildness and chaos, enlivened something she had always feared — the woman she wanted to be.

On the Indian Decca, outside the windows of the train, the reflection of the full moon appeared in irregular pools of water left over from the monsoon. And beyond — there was a desolate, featureless prairie. A raven landscape. Peopled. Always peopled.

The city of Mumbai, formerly known as Bombay, began at 5:00 a.m. and the train slowed for the next two hours through seven islands that had been joined together into a single landmass. The first railway in Asia had been built from Bombay to Thana in 1853. Cotton mills, reaping the benefits from the American Civil War, began to spring up all over the city, sparking the first industrial influence in that part of the country. Finally, the opening of the Suez Canal in 1869 sealed Bombay's future as India's major trade centre.

Mumbai also had a history of political unrest; its multicultural communities of Parsis, Gujaratis and Hindu, and the linguistic divisions of Maharashtra and Gujarat, had divided the city for over half a century. It was the city where Gandhi had burned foreign cloth and where Claire's grandfather had suppressed the riots during the early Quit India campaigns. And it was the first city her father had visited after staying away from India for nearly fifty years.

... *Since there are 55,000 active cases of leprosy in the city*, Claire's father had written her mother in 1970, *one stays confined indoors throughout the visit. It has occurred to me in the past that I could have been slightly less maladjusted if my parents had not sent me to the U.K. as a youth. These visits to India in the past year have not altered my opinion about my father's motives in incarcerating his children at an early age, but I am certainly more appreciative of the fact I did not grow up in this unhappy subcontinent.*

love,
William

Claire remembered the afternoon her mother had handed her the letters from her father. Dorothy had stood at the edge of the raspberry patch. "You might find these useful," her mother had said. The letters were in her hands. She was gleeful, with an almost unnatural thrill in her voice. "I love the smell of freshly turned soil, don't you?" Dorothy had said.

And Claire had to agree that yes, she did too; she looked forward to the cosmos in bloom.

"There are some letters from India in there," her mother had said.

Claire wiped her face with the tail of her shirt, rubbed her hands down the backside of her shorts and took the letters from her mother's hands.

"Thank you," she had said. "I'll look at them later."

She then stuffed the bundle of letters into her back pocket and resumed weeding her mother's garden. Dorothy, Claire thought, must have flung the seeds haphazardly from the banks of the river to the edge of the lawn — the garden spiralled toward its edges in ever-weakening stands of carrot to ever-increasing stands of quack grass. The rows of peas and beans were squeezed together; the asparagus stalks were now in seed. The garden was over-lettuced and under-tubered and mounds of potatoes surrounded by circles of onions were interspersed with the troubled shoots of lilacs or raspberries. The feathery leaves of cosmos, yet to bloom, were strewn haphazardly throughout the mess of foliage, making the pulling of weeds a tedious, if not impossible, task. Claire had dropped to her knees and had dug her fingers into the crowding plants, slowly extracting the roots of thistle and dandelion that thrived on the chaos. Claire had been attempting to organize her mother's garden for years. Her mother's lack of predictability was apparently a well-thought-out collaboration of species — "companion planting," she had heard her mother's friends say as they wandered the periphery of Dorothy's yard with their painted fingernails and polyester white slacks, offering polite support for Dorothy's "unique" and "unconventional" ways.

Claire had continued throughout that afternoon, digging up the hardened soil, loosening the crust and breaking the clumps into something soft and penetrable. She had pounded wooden stakes into the ends of rows and stretched chicken wire across vines of yellowed peas, taking peaceful, still moments to wind their tendrils away from each other and onto the wire.

There were two letters he had written from India. The rest were from his Texaco days in the Amazon — eloquent, loving letters he had written to Dorothy in their early years of marriage. Now, Claire held the two letters from India in her hands as she stared out the window at the endless slums of Bombay that bordered either side of the tracks. There were corrugated cardboard roofs propped up like cards over crumbling brick or concrete walls, and standing outside these makeshift homes were bare-bottomed children who stared blankly while they peed into the dust, and women who crouched over small fires poking embers with a stick, their knees up around their ears — a position, for Claire, agonizing to imagine. Claire tried to imagine the magnitude of the poverty, but her eyes were too full of the monotony and duration of the images that passed by: two hours of constant movement over the landscape and Claire never once took her eyes away from the window.

"Scopophilia," David said.

"Scopo what?"

"Scopophilia. The voyeur. The desire to see."

"I am forcing myself to see all this. I did not *desire* to see this."

"Are you sure?"

She wasn't sure. Was she identifying with the women cooking over the fire, or the naked children in the dust? *Through a glass darkly*, she thought. These victims — for they were victims of a strange life — they had no agency, and she was granting them no more than a sheepish gaze from her safe place on a train. She was one of many who cruised by their wretched lives, removed and lost in the meditations of her mother's garden.

"Do you think they ever imagine?" she asked David.

"Imagine what?"

"Something different for themselves?"

PART FIVE

India Gate

Tiger Dreams Film Part XIII Sequence
— Cut from final film.

Medium shot of me through the window of the train. I am staring outside.
   I press my forehead against the glass. Zoom to close-up. I look right
   through the lens of the camera as if the world beyond me is only in my
   imagination. Cut to medium shot in an attempt to neutralize my gaze;
   point of view is from behind a smoking fire. The train passes; my
   forehead is pressed against the window of the train. I look disengaged.
The sequence is not entirely successful.

Mumbai, Twelve-Hour Train Ride from Delhi

The Victoria Terminus was densely packed with the weak and hungry: a woman's milky white cataracts stared up at Claire while her infant, whose soupy excrement was smeared across the concrete floor of the station platform, bellowed frantically; a bony old man pulled himself along the floor, his bent limbs twisted from back to front; and an amputee on a furniture trolley rolled by David and Claire to offer them a boost in exchange for a few rupees. Claire smiled at him, pretending deference. "No, thank you," she said. "No."

They had booked a room at the Lawrence Hotel, which was down the street from the Museum of Modern Art and across from the Jahangir Gallery. Bombay was littered with the old buildings of British Rule and its gothic architecture was what Claire had always imagined India to be. Mossy vines of green ivy climbed up and around many of the buildings in the city. Some vines had successfully dislodged stones and brick, levelling whole structures. Monkeys and the beggars now occupied their ruins.

A child prostitute, probably from the district of Kamathipura, Asia's largest slum, taunted David. She had beautiful teeth inside a stunning smile. Her dress was too large for her nubile body, her breasts were barely formed and one arm had been hacked off, either for fetishes or possibly, thought Claire, discipline. While the child pursued David in a weak seduction, a hawker descended upon Claire, called out to her, followed her up the street and shoved boxes of saffron and incense in front of her face. She slapped the young man's hand, took off her sunglasses and stared into his chocolate brown eyes.

"No, thank you, I said. No, thank you!"

The young man backed away and ran to some other travellers across the street. Claire ran after him and tapped him on the shoulder. "No, thank you, I said. No, thank you!"

He turned to her and said, "Okay, okay!"

And she continued to harass him until he turned and ran the other way. She ran back across the street to David, who was now taking a photograph of a praying mantis.

"Amazing little fellow," David said. "How on earth do you think he got here?"

Claire leaned against the corner of the building and crouched down by the insect. "I suspect he's asking himself that very same question."

The hotel was in a back alley and up a couple of flights of stairs. It was really only a few rooms on one floor but the shower was hot, the toilets were Western style and the bed was comfortable. Claire lay awake that night listening to the ticking of the ceiling fan and the noise of traffic. She returned to her mother's garden in her mind and smiled when she thought how her definition of chaos had changed since arriving in India. She thought of her grandparents coming to this city for vacation, staying in some fancy hotel — maybe even the Taj Mahal Hotel, just down the street. Claire's grandparents would have had tea in the afternoon and wandered around the shipping docks buying goods that had come in from the West. Her grandmother would have worn a flapper dress, the drop-waist kind, and a big floppy hat and white linen shoes. Her grandfather must have worn a topi and a white linen suit. They might have had friends they travelled with, and languorous afternoons by some poolside, sipping gin and tonic and making idle conversation about how difficult it was to get anything done in this country. They were young, she thought. Younger than she was now. But their lives were almost over.

There would be an aging population of people of her grandparents' generation who were still alive, though — people who had seen the burning of cloth and the making of salt. They would have been the ones to escort the British out of India and bid their farewells to the Anglo-Indians. They would have had to reacquaint themselves with the fallout of Home Rule, formalizing the division of property and taxation to benefit the Indian.

As David scoured the streets for a couple of bottles of beer, Claire lay beneath the fan's erratic overdrive on the ceiling of their room. She imagined a nation on fast forward. What must it have been like for those who began with Gandhi and those who finished with the nation that India had become now?

Pune 1932: Departing for Karachi

Alice and Denzil took their tea on the veranda while the rickshaw driver took tea with the servants in the kitchen. The children played fetch with Sebastian, the terrier. Biscuits, sweet and dusty like the air, and made by the inmates in the prison bakery, were dipped into saucers full of sweet Indian tea. Denzil had headed up the bakery as one of his rehabilitation programs in the prison and it had met with great success. They were shipping biscuits all over

Maharasthra now, and a grocer in Bombay was ordering dozens of the baked goods on a weekly basis. The grocer, a large jovial man, had travelled all the way from Bombay to visit the prison bakery and Denzil had been surprisingly friendly with the man, speaking fluent Gujarati with him during tea and inviting him for a quick game of cricket before heading back to the city. Alice had watched, with great amusement, Denzil's immediate affiliation with this unlikely fellow and she remembered thinking how strange men were for the way they negotiated their easy, non-political contracts of friendship.

Sitting opposite Alice, Denzil sipped his tea quietly and gazed down the lane where the muscular roots of the pippol trees stretched doggedly from their branches toward the dry soil. The red blossoms of the geraniums had crinkled and faded in the heat. Clouds of dust were kicked up from the clusters of prisoners playing football in the field across from the prison entrance; their whistles and shouts were like radio static in the otherwise silent morning. To Denzil everything was reducing, changing form — even the lovely Alice, his wife of twelve years, with her illness, the seizures, suspicions of opium addiction, her consumption of spirits. Yes, they were all changing form. He recalled Alice in the garden last evening, delusional, searching for the key to the house, her nightgown streaked with mud. Thorns had torn her feet, and her eyes, how could he describe her eyes? They were astonished. Hot. Conflicted. And he carried her — for she had grown so thin in the past year — back into the house and bathed the blood and mud from her feet.

"I am Denzil," he had repeatedly assured her. "I am your husband, Denzil."

And when she finally recaptured her senses, she had winked at him and said, "He loves you, you know. He loves you."

Alice reached out for the pot of tea and he winced as he

watched her reddened knuckles, like the broken wings of a bird, wrap around the handle. He would never forgive himself for his violence. Even long after her death, in the middle of another marriage, after he finally ordered her headstone to be properly built, he could never come to terms with the rage that caused him to slam that piano board down upon her fingers. To take her music away — that was simply reprehensible.

His mind clouded with excuses and defences for what he was about to do. The Beverlys would think him too rash, Alice's parents would accuse him of neglecting the wishes of his wife, Estelle would never speak to him again if anything happened to her on the voyage and Richard Thomas would certainly question his motivation. But she was becoming unmanageable.

Denzil was in an utter state of turmoil as he sat opposite his wife of twelve years, sipping his tea from his saucer. *We Anglos*, he thought, *we have such a way of concealing ourselves.*

Alice lined up her three children to inspect them. She groped at the two wriggling boys, licking her fingers to clean their faces and smooth their hair. She fumbled her hands around their bony bodies to memorize them, and then she rubbed her cheek against theirs, a gesture that made them squirm.

Denzil watched his wife embrace the boys' faces. He saw how much they adored her and he felt weak. He wiped his brow with his handkerchief.

Alice took her daughter's shoulders in her hands and stood back to get a look at her. Barbara was getting tall and quite elegant; her thick bottom lip and dark eyes were a combination of both Denzil and herself — a perfect combination really, both of personality and form. "You'll help your father with the boys, now, won't you?" she said.

"Yes, Mother. But, I don't understand why I can't come with you and Charlotte and leave the boys with Father?"

Alice turned to Denzil as if to say, now that's not such a bad idea, but Denzil had hopped up and waved his hand for Barbara to get along and play.

"I have something fun for us to do before we get on the train. A surprise," he said, and patted Barbara on the back to send her on her way.

Barbara's eyes lit up and she cocked her head to the side. "A surprise, Father? For Mother?"

"Perhaps. Now kiss your mother goodbye, wish her good health and run along."

Denzil's hand found its familiar place in the middle of Alice's back. She turned and curled into him. *You can be very sweet,* she thought. She turned and called after her daughter, "I'll see you tomorrow, darling," and then said quietly to Denzil, "She really is growing too quickly. I suspect I won't recognize her tomorrow for all the changes she is going through right now."

"You've been away from her for longer than a day before, Alice," Denzil reminded her and they both spoke at the same time. "Damodra, 1925."

Alice looked away. "Yes, you never cease to remind me of Damodra."

"I only bring it up to illustrate to you that I should think the two of you will survive this separation."

"I suppose," Alice sighed. "Though I feel strange about leaving this time. Something isn't quite right. Perhaps I've got a fever coming on again. I don't know."

She turned to him and smiled, and from his look she knew she warmed him, and that his heart was for her. "I'll see you tomorrow?" she said. "We'll stay at the Bentley. Is that right?"

"Yes, we will be there tomorrow afternoon. I thought you and Charlotte might like to shop without the children."

"Shopping?" Alice said incredulously. "Goodness. Why on earth …?" She stopped herself. Best not to question the generosity of his spirit. Alice took her husband's hand in both of hers and brought it between them. He stroked his thumb over the bent fingers of her right hand, and his jaw tightened. Alice could see the vein on his forehead pulsing. "Thank you," she smiled, and pulled her right hand away. His eyes frightened her — not because his rage sometimes consumed them, but more because of their containment. His corneas were frozen like porcelain behind perfectly cold blue irises. They were startling for their contrast to the dark rings around his eyes; they were like beacons in the dark.

Denzil grinned and gently pulled his hand from hers. "My pleasure. Now you must go and I must get some business completed at the office before heading into Pune. Are you sure you have everything you need, darling?"

"Yes, but if I've left anything behind you'll bring it with you, won't you?" And then, with one of those sudden bursts of energy that characterized Alice, she smiled and grabbed his arms. "Oh Chippy, everything is going to be so much better away from all of this. I just know it. We'll be closer to the desert. Remember the desert? The stars? Maybe we just need to figure out where we are again."

She felt an inkling of desire, a pinprick of a flame, and she knew that she would have to make more of an effort with her husband when they reunited. She would cultivate the romance that had lagged since William was born, since she'd become ill with malaria. She would touch him more, stroke his back in the night. She would find different, more interesting ways of loving him. She'd become confident again, less needy, make new friends and have garden parties. She wouldn't rely on him so much. She would begin her research again. Surely he would want her then.

"We'll go to Nainital during the hot!" she said excitedly.

Denzil took Alice into his arms and held her close to him. He could feel her breath on his neck and he stroked her thick, black hair with his hand. She smelled of cinnamon and cloves, and her body, though thin and weak, had the same slow pulse that had always soothed him. He held her and then he let go of her and walked backwards and down the steps.

She smiled at him and shook her head, trying to right the image she saw before her. There was something awkward about the way he backed away from her, as if he shrank before her, his knees buckling, his shoulders caving in. Something hideous, something unmistakably twisted, occupied his shadow.

He turned and walked down the lane toward the gate while she remained on the veranda. She could feel the coolness of the eaves casting shadows across her face as she turned and went back into the house.

Alice had left the logistics of transporting the luggage to Denzil. She had labelled two trunks "Baggage Room," for the articles not needed for the voyage, three carry bags were labelled "Present Use, Baggage Room," and she and Charlotte carried the small chintz bags, topi boxes and provision baskets with them in the rickshaw.

Alice turned one last time to look at the children. Barbara was tall like her father, well on her way to being a woman. She is confident, thought Alice. She'll do well for herself. And George, the middle child, popped a football into the air with his knee and ran around to the side of the house to finish his game. The youngest boy, William, stood on the stairs and waved vigorously. His crooked smile embraced a soft, gentle kindness, the sort of look given to chosen ones, and she thought maybe William would be the one to change the world. She blamed herself for the typhoid. To not have washed the fruit; her distraction was unforgivable. William. A perfect psalm. Providence, really.

She turned around, slumped into the seat, and pouted as the rickshaw driver turned the carriage and ran down the lane. Deep within her she could hear herself asking the one question that had been pressing against her, squeezing her so tightly that she had found it difficult to breathe. *How do you explain to your children that dying is not an act of desertion?*

Charlotte and Alice caught the train to Bombay when the sun was still high in the sky and the dust hovered like clouds of insects around their heads.

Every conversation Alice attempted with Charlotte was met with monosyllabic grunts and groans.

"Where shall we go first?" she asked Charlotte.

"Not sure," Charlotte replied, and then squeezed her eyes shut.

Charlotte felt her body move in pillowed lurches as the train cornered out of the station. The imperceptible murmurs of servants in the hallway outside their cabin grew to a menacing pitch as she tried to retrace her steps. The transfer had been Denzil's idea. Packing up the house had been hers. She thought it best to give Alice the impression that everything about the transfer was under control. After Alice was hospitalized in Karachi, she would be able to return to Pune and begin the transformation. She might look for some chintz to replace that dull fabric on the punkah in the main parlour, maybe even add a flounce and some flowered calico to its frame. And the veranda, well, she would replace the grass chairs with wicker ones from England. Repotting the bignonia and adding bamboo trellises to the south side of the veranda would certainly give that room a cooler feel. She would bring in some more achimenes and begonias and violets and have a block of ice placed in the centre of the room every single day. Charlotte opened her eyes, her reverie disrupted by the slowing of the train. Alice was moving her head from side to side like a cobra, dipping down, bobbing up, trying to make eye contact, but Charlotte closed her eyes again and made every effort to disregard her cousin's wife.

There was such an absent-mindedness and general lack of interest on Charlotte's part that Alice eventually turned her head to watch the landscape. Through the strange soupy glow of the yellowed windows, the land appeared to have been flopped down like a large canvas tacked to the skin of the earth with dry tufts of grass. A lone cyclist navigated the ditch and the Marathi's thatched-roofed homes were stuffed in between the trees and shrubs alongside the tracks. The sun fell rapidly below the clouds that gathered like snow-capped mountains in the west. There were places in the earth's crust where the insides were pushed outward into perfectly shaped thumbs pointing skyward to God, or hills that appeared like the lapping and overlapping of a series of race-horses pressing for the finish. Alice longed for the foothills and the mountains of Nainital.

The brakes — like the claws of a cat scratching rock — slowed the train as the hills joined together and closed in around them like a great walled fortress. *Where is the moat, the drawbridge?* she thought. *I am leaving this place forever.*

Along the valley floors, black puddles with frilly ridges of grass dotted the fields to the left of the tracks. Startling white lilies transformed into egrets and flew like secrets behind the olivine mesas. The edge of day was the colour of burning butter and Alice traced the horizon with her finger, wondering if she was the only one who saw how truly round the earth was. Hot wind puffed through her opened window as the train deliberated before a climb.

This was Alice's dream world before she died: the ponderous horn of the train, the swishing of metal wheels against tracks and then, a break in the land and a softening of sound, a distant hiss, and always, always the constant prattle of the Indians. As darkness descended, it hid the earth's blemishes, the lost grasslands, the deforestation, and the fluvial scars of the wet season. She could hear herself gasp at the sight of a large cat leaping into the remaining forest.

A liquid night now surrounded her and the sky was the colour of her mother's skin; and then, a nomad's oil lamp flickered against the purple hillsides. There, a sleeping place. There, a waking place. There, a place to die. The horn said, come quickly, and the train sang solo into the night.

Lonavla. Vendors were selling coconut sweets and dried fruit cakes. *Chai, Paan, Samosa,* they called out. Oil lamps dangled from posts and shed pools of light on the tatty orange-haired children digging in the dirt beside the train. Paan-wallahs passed before her window and she dropped her head behind the rim of her topi to avoid the insistence that seemed as much a part of Indians as their religion. Red gums against a black maw.

Beyond Lonavla the train began to climb, an agonizingly slow ascent into the thick night. Then the earth heaved and cracked, leaving deep gullies where railway tresses stitched the land together. Yellow lights came and went like holes poked through black paper. And then it came to her — pauses in her pulse, like ellipses on a page, metal filings between her teeth, a sea surging and receding inside her ear — and she bit down hard upon her lips.

Charlotte turned to Alice and cried out, "Dear God, Alice, you look wretched!"

"I'll be fine, just give me a minute. I'll be fine." Alice grabbed Charlotte's hand and tossed it off her knee. "I said, Charlotte, I'll be fine."

She hesitated as she slipped her handkerchief from the wrist of her blouse and dabbed the moisture purling on her upper lip. Time was swallowing itself in one rapid tidal sweep and she chanted quietly to herself, "Six respirations equal one vinadika, sixty vinadikas equal one dhata, sixty dhatas equal one day and one night."

The frail moments of her life were jostling for position and suddenly the fact that her children were not with her was a dreadful error in judgement. Waiting to be reunited in Bombay could prove unbearable. She dropped her head between her knees and there she remained until the tingling in her lips stopped.

The Anatomy of a Seizure, Second Movement

Your body heats up. Synapses arc and miss because things have separated and become disorganized. You lose consciousness; that is, the world in which you reside becomes another. Sometimes you can still sense the living and you watch the people around you rush here and there and shout orders at each other and you can hear the rustle of clothing and you can feel the warmth of someone's panicked breath on your face and you purse your lips to suck in all the available oxygen, but mostly you are absent and you wallow around in some dark timeless place where the rules of your human existence no longer apply. You float or hover or slither toward bubbles of thought; they are like beacons or lights at the end of a hallway. Sometimes the breaststroke works and you can swim toward something that sounds and feels rhythmic and reliable. Those are the good days. When you can pull yourself through the aperture and recognize colours and smells and the shapes of things and your lips tingle as your body reacquaints itself with your mind. Yes, those are the good days. When your lips tingle.

Bombay 1932

Alice and Charlotte arrived at the Victoria Terminus in Bombay and waited around for a porter to help with the luggage. Charlotte held Alice's arm as they stepped onto the station platform. Harbour bats swooped and screeched high in the metal trusses above their heads. Trains from the north and trains from the south arrived, uniting families from all parts of India and Alice looked on enviously as fathers held their children in buoyant embraces and mothers herded their families toward the station's entranceway. Alice searched the eyes of the poor as they stared up at her from their weakened bodies, and in them she thought she could see God. This made her panic.

She and Charlotte walked out of the station into the frantic nightlife of Bombay. Alice snapped at the porter for mishandling her luggage and gently pushed Charlotte away as she pulled herself onto the carriage. The two women sat quietly as the bony old horse trotted along the streets of Bombay. Lungis adorned half-naked brown bodies of merchants carrying baskets of mangoes. Pomfret gasped and wriggled across the stone ground and chickens flapped furiously in cages. The smell of rotting fish had now become overwhelming and the two women brought their scarves out to cover their noses. A leper appeared out of the dark and held his residual fingers into the air, their skin white and shiny over their rounded tips. His other hand, half-dissolved, held a basket. He nodded his head toward Alice's purse and mumbled a prayer. This man with no limbs, begging for coin, seemed to Alice to be some kind of joke being played upon her from another lifetime and she stared deep into his eyes searching for God's love, but she had found herself unable to rise above her immobility. Having no power left to push the leper away, she ignored him. When he finally turned away, she watched his ragged profile walk down the back street, alone and miserable. *I should have loved him*, she thought.

She climbed down from her carriage and stuffed a few coins into the palm of the driver's hand and walked straight into the hotel lobby.

She was already forgetting the details of her life in Pune: the smell of her bedclothes, the wooden design on the dining room chairs. She couldn't even remember the colour of the walls. They were probably white, she consoled herself, although she did remember at one time talking about having them repainted. Did she have them done? She couldn't remember. She had crossed over the moat. The bridge had been drawn. She was never going back. She knew this in the way someone remembers a detail later and then describes it as premonition.

She lay awake that night, listening to cats tromp around on the metal roof and pigeons fluttering their wings below her window. She rocked herself to sleep trying to recapture the soothing motion of the train. Six prana equal one vinadika, sixty vinadikas equal one dhata, sixty dhatas equal one day and one night ...

India Gate

David and Claire ate porridge and cold toast in a very expensive restaurant on Dubash Marg. They strolled to the far side of Calaba Causeway where David bargained with a Muslim shopkeeper for a sextant and Claire fondled homespun khadi in the tiny corner shop. David left the shop, returned to the shop, made an offer on the sextant, left the shop again, returned an hour later and finally settled on a price with the shopkeeper. For the remainder of the afternoon, he flipped the green and blue filter lenses and twisted the screws of the protractor. He polished and adjusted the instrument while they sat on the lawns before India Gate. Claire filmed the gathering crowds of the Gate, a yellow basaltic edifice constructed to commemorate the arrival of King George V and Queen Mary in 1911. Ironically, this was also where the last British troops were escorted out of India after Independence.

She focussed her lens on a man standing against one of the pillars of the gate. He was unusually tall and his greying hair distinguished him from the mostly black-haired crowd. He wore an eye patch and puffed on a pipe, his large shoulders stooped forward, and when he turned to greet someone his profile startled Claire away from her lens.

She had felt startled like this sitting beside, walking toward, or standing across from many people of India, who carried in them a part of her father: their dark eyes, large noses, wide jaws. This was a brief belonging for her, her body a part of the geography.

Claire pulled herself away from her camera. The image was a fabrication of her imagination, a resurrection. A wish. The man met up with another and the two of them began to stroll toward the hotel. Claire thought she could see him limping. She felt peaceful and sad at the same time, wishing that this man was her father and that he could see her now, in front of India Gate, waiting for him — more made, more put together, than the last time they spoke.

They had gone out for dinner a couple of weeks before he had died: David, her mother, her father, and herself. It had been a pleasant evening, her father entertaining everyone with his stories, the ones she never tired of — the cheesy accommodations in Brazil where a little boy sucked his fingers while smiling up at him, and piddled on his pant legs; or the hilarious spaghetti westerns he contrived about the incompetence of the Mexican police; or stories of Claire's and Ben's rivalry. He had leaned over to David and winked. "She couldn't wait until I got home to tell me all the nasty things her little brother had done, so she'd call me at the office."

Claire had never called him at the office, but the story always sounded better that way. She never bothered to correct him.

"I would get home," he had said, "and take Ben into the back room. Ben would yell out and I would beat the bed while Claire remained outside the door listening gleefully while she thought I was beating her brother to a pulp."

She remembered pressing her ear to the door and listening — perhaps not gleefully, he had exaggerated that part of the story, but she could remember being suspicious.

"One day, Ben and I came out of the room and there was this beautiful, little devil of an older sister standing in the hallway with her arms crossed, a squint in her eye, and you know what she said to me?" He paused, not for any kind of response, just because he knew how to deliver a story. " 'Next time,' she said, 'next time, I want to watch.' "

They had all laughed uproariously at Claire's expense. That was a good thing, Claire thought in retrospect, not because she liked to be the brunt of anyone's jokes, but for the very fact that they had laughed together.

Later that same evening, her father went down on his knees before David and told him how eternally grateful he was to him for taking his daughter off his hands; he could tell David was a good lad and he wished him all the best.

That evening had been the last time she had seen her father, and she remembered that when she had hugged him goodbye that night, she could smell his death like rank perfume on his skin.

She began to pan the crowd with her camera, focussing on individuals, watching the movements of their eyes, the freedom in their smiles. Through the lens of the camera the country appeared clean and unpopulated. Couples stood in sparkling salwars, men in white, women in peach, children in shirts and trousers. They stood around in organized crowds, laughing and cajoling each other as if they all belonged.

It is a playground scene, shot from a young girl's point of view, and the audience experiences her alienation, thought Claire. She was always scripting scenes in her cinematic consciousness, little mini dramas that had no plot, telling compositions where characters were triangulated into positions of power or feebleness.

Further along the causeway, teenage boys were jumping into the ocean from the seawall; the tide was high and the water was the colour of creamed coffee; floating refuse, and oils and tar from the traffic of ships in the harbour, splashed against the seawall.

None of this deterred the boys. They seemed oblivious to the contamination, or perhaps, thought Claire, they were so highly evolved, they had already adapted.

David had moved across the lawn and was leaning against the wall. Claire suspected he was plotting the azimuths of their journey, leaving crumbs on a trail to ensure his safe return home. She caught his eye and he mockingly kneeled down to the earth and sniffed. She knew he was looking for the scent of his beloved Canada. He then stood up and dramatically looked longingly across the water. He was her Tonto, her faithful servant, the one who would take her home at the end of the day. She laughed and waved, and the crowd filled in around him in the shadows of the archway. In many ways he belonged here more than she did. David had roots deeper than the earth's mantle; he simply belonged wherever he was.

She returned to look through the lens of her camera. It was a large obtrusive camera and it drew a great deal of attention from the children, who hopped in front and made faces, their soft eyes as round and dark as blueberries, their complexions like smooth chocolate milk, light and dark, light and dark over the roundness of their small faces. The youngest child, a little girl around six years old, hid behind an older boy. Claire zoomed the lens back in — the little girl's nose ring flickered as she poked her head around to the lens of Claire's camera. Their family had come to picnic on the lawn, and while their mother sat with sisters and grand-mother and great-grandmother in a cluster, nattering and taunting each other in waves of laughter, the children ran around harassing foreigners like Claire.

"Where are you from?" the oldest boy asked in an impeccable British accent while his little sister tugged at his jeans.

Claire put her camera down. "Canada."

"Canada is a very big country," said one of the other boys.

"Third largest country in the world."

"Do you have a Canadian coin?" asked the first boy. "I collect coins from all over the world."

Claire looked toward the women, who were now all staring and laughing at her. A beautiful young woman stood up and walked over to the boy.

"You go and leave this woman alone," she said as she swept him with both hands across the lawn.

"I just asked her for a coin, Amma," the boy pleaded and dug his heels in to resist her.

The woman turned to Claire and smiled. Her teeth were perfect and white. They sat properly in her mouth and presented a full radiant smile. Claire's own mouth felt awkward; her teeth were too large for her mouth — one of the consequences of mixing up the races, her orthodontist had told her.

"Do you have a coin for my boy?" the woman asked. "I assure you he will stop being so annoying."

Claire reached into her money belt, brought out a one-dollar Canadian coin, a loonie, and gave it to the boy. He took the coin and enthusiastically ran off to show his friends. His little sister stood quietly and stared at Claire. Claire reached into her money belt again and pulled out the two-dollar polar bear, motioned for the little girl to come closer. She placed the coin in the little girl's hand. "This is worth twice as much as your brother's coin. Besides, I think it is prettier. Don't you?"

The little girl stared at the coin and nodded. "Now don't you dare give this to him," and Claire couldn't help herself as she stroked the tiny fingers of the girl's hand. They were like a baby bird, exquisitely formed and naked. Claire delayed releasing the coin for as long as possible. She resisted brushing the child's cheek, agonizing over her desire to feel the smoothness of her skin with the back of her hand — oh, she thought, if you were my daughter I would never leave you, I would spoil you with time, I would give you all of me and forget myself. You would crawl into my arms, your skinny legs wrapped around my waist, ribs like blades digging into my breast, your knuckled chin grinding into my collarbone and in all my pain of being the furniture of your life, I would ask myself again and again, how is it possible to love this much?

A big evil smile grew on the little girl's face and Claire recognized it immediately — it could have been her own. The little girl took the coin and ran over to her brother and his friends. She looked back to Claire, smiled and raised her eyebrows. Claire winked, held two fingers into the air and mouthed the words, "twice as much."

"Thank you," the young woman said.

"She's beautiful," Claire said.

"She's a little rat," the young woman laughed and walked back to the group of women and sat down. *How confident a mother can be about the nature of her children*, thought Claire.

An older woman leaned over and spoke to the younger woman and she glanced over to Claire, smiled again and waved for Claire to join them. Claire hesitated and looked over at David, who was still polishing all the little parts on his sextant while he sat on the grass a few metres away. She decided to leave him to his occupation. She got up, carried her camera with her, and walked over to the women.

"Sit. Sit," said the older woman. "Tell me, what are you doing here? You have a film camera. Are you a filmmaker?"

"Yes," answered Claire. "I'm going to Pune to work on a film about my grandfather."

"Your grandfather? What is he?" asked the shorter woman, who was wiping her fingers on the grass.

"He was the superintendent of the prison Gandhi was thrown into."

The women looked at each other and nodded. They began whispering to each other and Claire began to feel uncomfortable.

The oldest woman, grey-haired and almost blind, leaned forward and snapped at the others. "Radha! Roshon! Shame on you." She turned to Claire and smiled. "I apologize for their manners. I obviously have not done such a good job. They whisper about coincidence."

"Coincidence?" asked Claire.

"You have come a long way in a very big world, but really the world is very small, and my daughters discuss the coincidence of you and myself on this lawn together — now."

"I don't understand."

The younger woman, the mother of the boy, spoke. "I apologize for my grandmother's cryptic ..."

"I am not being cryptic," snapped the older woman. "You shush. I'll speak," and she turned toward Claire. "You know, there were many women serving time during those years? That would be a good subject for a film, too."

"Women in the prisons?"

"Of course," and then she paused and twisted her old lips around her yellowed teeth. "Superintendent of Prisons, you say?"

"Yes, he was Gandhi's jailer after the Salt March of 1930 and during the Pune Pact of 1932." Claire said this proudly, as if infamy elevated her in some way.

"You will continue to attach yourself to the canons of men until you find your place amongst women," said the old woman as she patted Claire on her knee. "I was in Yeroda at that time as well."

Claire stared at the old woman. "You were there in 1930?"

"I marched with him to the sea."

"Do you still practise ahimsa?" Claire asked the old woman.

Tiger Dreams Film XIV Sequence

Freeze Frame on Rita.

My Voice-over: To ask a woman who had marched with Gandhi if she still
practised ahimsa, the law of love, was asking for a different kind of
intimacy. Even though I had never been undressed before it by the
vagaries of war and prejudice, I knew of the fundamental solicitudes of
love. True — I have been loved well and I suspect, though I can't say
for sure, that I know how to love, but would I die for it? Would I even
go to jail for it?

India Gate

"It is not that I practise ahimsa anymore — it is my way."

Claire sat before the women, completely at a loss for words.

Rita teased her, "You should close your mouth, dear girl — it is so unbecoming."

Claire closed her mouth and laughed along with the other women. "I was just thinking last night how there must still be some of you alive," she said without thinking. "I mean, I'm sorry, I didn't mean to imply ..."

"That grandmother is old? May God be on your side," said the youngest woman.

"Shush, Radha. I am an old woman but I still have my wits about me. Your grandfather was an Anglo-Indian, wasn't he?"

"I think so. I don't know for sure. I don't have a lot of information about him."

"Then what will your film be about?"

"Home Rule."

"What did your grandfather have to do with that?"

"Perhaps it is more about what he didn't have to do with it. He was awarded the Order of the British Empire for suppressing the riots. Wasn't that a good thing?"

"For whom?"

Claire sat back on her heels and stared at the old woman. She looked around the group of women. "What do you women do, that you speak such impeccable English?"

The middle-aged woman introduced herself. "My name is Roshon, I am a research agriculturist from Ahmedabad. I studied at Cambridge. This is my little sister, Madhu, and she is a very accomplished artist, her work is in the Jahinger Gallery right now and this is her daughter Radha, whose children took your money. And this is my mother, Rita, and, well, she is a dissident."

They all laughed and Rita swirled her head from side to side, "It is true. I cannot keep myself away from trouble. I should have been a vaishnivite."

"A vaishnivite?"

"Free agents, women who danced and sang for a meal. The British thought them to be whores so they outlawed them. I only write about it now."

"Oh, so you are a writer?"

"Of sorts — yes. But mostly just to protest. Why do you make films?"

"To understand protest."

"Your name, dear child, is?"

"I'm sorry. My name is Claire."

"What was your family name?"

"Spencer. My father was born in Pune and my grandparents both died there."

"Was your grandmother an Indian?"

"I believe so. From what I can tell, her mother was an Indian."

"Yes, yes of course, and her name was Alice."

"Yes! Her name was Alice. My God, you remember my grandmother?"

Tides pulled at Claire's skin and split her open. *Imagining, I have always been imagining this moment,* she thought, *or a moment just like this and all I can do is pluck at the grass.*

"Your search agrees with you," said the old woman.

"My grandmother? Are you sure?"

"Rita never forgets a face." The youngest woman wearing the peach salwar spoke. "We think that is perhaps why government officials are always trying to have her put away."

They all laughed and Rita shushed them again and then shifted to face Claire. "She would visit the prison every day, bringing the women prisoners fruit and nuts. Very beautiful woman. She was like you." Rita shook her head. "She was very thin, though. They said she had malaria. I understand she died shortly before we were released in 1932."

"Yes, yes. I think so too." Claire was fumbling with her camera, unloading and loading another tape. "Do you mind if I get this on film?"

The women began to speak amongst themselves. They laughed and nattered back and forth while Claire released the lens cap and checked the battery power of her camera. The women stopped talking and Roshon spoke to Claire. "My mother is uncomfortable with a camera, but ..."

"Nonsense," Rita spoke. "I would love to see myself broadcast across this country."

Rita took a sip of tea and began to speak. "Your grandmother ..."

"Wait!" Claire turned on her camera and tightened the focus on Rita, her glasses reflecting the descending sun. Claire stood up and moved to the other side. "Okay," she said. "I am ready." And she settled down beside Roshon and Madhu. "Tell me what you remember."

"She would come on the rounds without her husband and stop to chat with us outside our compound. She was very well-spoken and always dressed simply. We thought her to be a very practical sort of woman compared to the other wives."

"Do you remember what she looked like?" Claire asked.

"Like you, dear child, that is why it is easy for me to remember. There were rumours that her husband sent her away, that he was jealous of the growing friendship between she and the Mahatma and that he didn't much approve. But they were rumours and you can well imagine the kind of rumours that would circulate amongst prisoners."

Claire thought she probably hadn't heard Rita properly. "Alice and whom? You said the Mahatma. You mean Gandhi? She was a friend of Gandhi's?"

"It wasn't unusual. He was a very amiable man, particularly with the women. Your grandmother was in a very good position to visit with him and he most certainly wasn't going anywhere." Rita smiled at her joke.

Claire pulled away from the camera and smiled too. "No, I guess that's right."

"I also said that those were just rumours. Imagine if you will, the long hours of idleness we had to tolerate in the prison. Your grandmother would have been a wonderful respite for Gandhiji. I know she was to us."

"Yes, of course."

Claire had focused her camera on Roshon and was now panning over the other women's faces before she came back to rest on Rita's face. Rita was luminous against the dark green lawn. The fading light worked against Claire and she kept rising and moving around to catch residual light. The weight of her camera was becoming unbearable, and while Rita seemed to have no objection to the camera, Claire was beginning to feel its intrusion. She put the camera down and shut it off.

"There was something terribly desperate about Alice," Rita continued. "She was always in such a hurry."

Claire stared at the old woman. *I am bleeding*, she thought, *I am sure of it*, and she looked around at the other women to see if they were going to panic. "There has been an accident," she muttered, but the women had begun to speak amongst themselves. She felt all the seams of herself ripping open, as if she had cut herself deeply, and she feared she would come undone, that her flesh was simply going to fall away from her bone. All her scars began to burn and she was reminded of her auspicious survival. She looked at her arms, then her hands, and finally her fingers for evidence of the disaster but there was nothing — only the imprint of grass on the heels of her hands. "She was desperate?" Claire repeated and she could hear nothing but the waves slapping the seawall and the rise and fall of laughter across the lawn.

Bombay 1932

Alice woke rested and hustled Charlotte, who was not much of a morning person, out the doors of the hotel and onto the cluttered streets of Bombay.

A young man insisted he repair Alice's shoes, which weren't in need of repair at all, another wanted to sell her saffron, another, a compass, and another, a gramophone. All this and they had only walked as far as one of the quiet side streets behind the Taj Mahal Hotel.

In a shop on the corner of Best Marg and Calaba Causeway, a stooped seamstress smiled and waved her hand over some Manchester silk. Alice ran her fingertips over the silk.

"Homespun khadi?" she asked.

"No, Mem, in the back, in the back, plenty of cottons for Indian in the back of shop." The little woman motioned to Alice to follow her into the darkened shop stuffed to the ceiling with bolts of smooth finished silk. Silkworms of the western Bengal region were coveted worldwide for their fine threads and traders had gone so far as to transport the worm to countries in Europe. The climate there was too cold, though, and the silkworm had become dormant. The East India Company settled for shipping the spittle of silkworms in large vats to Manchester, where it was spun into cloth. The seamstress and Alice wandered to the back of the shop.

"Seems ridiculous, don't you think?"

"What is that, Memsahib?"

"Please, don't call me that."

"What should I call you then?"

"Call me a lackey."

"Oh no, that would be unkind."

"But true."

The woman looked down over the cloth she stroked. "Oh no. I don't think so." And then to change the subject, "What is it that is so ridiculous?"

"All that fuss the British make so their sons can have work."

"If you like, I will show you some homespun silk?" The seamstress, obviously uncomfortable with Alice's conversation, changed the subject again. "I will make a beautiful dress to match your beautiful figure."

"What about cotton for the children?"

"Oh, yes, plenty of cotton in the back for your children. Dropped the price just for this morning. You can give me sizes of your children and come back this evening for pickup."

"Can you send them to me?"

"Oh, no, no, no. Post is behind for months. Your children

will have grown out of them by the time they get to where they need to go. Can I interest you in raw silk, spun locally, good personality — to take to your own tailor?"

"Raw silk? I don't think I've ever felt raw silk."

Charlotte was pacing back and forth in front of the shop while Alice negotiated a fair price for the bolt of raw silk.

"Charlotte, can you come and help me with this fabric, please?" Charlotte gladly left the busy street for the coolness of the fabric shop and picked up the bolt of fabric. Alice held up some different cotton fabrics. "These colours are magnificent, aren't they, Charlotte?"

"It is the new vegetable dyes," said the seamstress. "They are having much success. It is the coarseness of the weave."

"Ahh. See, Charlotte, there are many advantages to going completely Indian."

"Yes, Alice." And then Charlotte said impatiently, "I think we should make our way to the ship now."

Charlotte removed herself from the shop and stood in the street again. Alice paid the seamstress, thanked her for her time and joined Charlotte on the street. The two women made their way back to the Bentley. Alice's mood had changed from that of ease to one of extreme agitation over the course of the morning and Charlotte's fidgeting had begun to irritate her. "For goodness sake, Charlotte, what is it?"

"What is what?" Charlotte asked.

"What on earth is bothering you? You seem so — so irritable."

"That's funny, Alice. I was going to say the same about you," Charlotte retorted.

They packed their bags in silence, paid their bill and hailed a rickshaw to take them the two blocks to the ship. The hollow clop of the horse and the jingle of the tiny bells from the horse's halter were the only sounds Alice could hear. She was inside something soft and pliable, as if the slip and thud of her pulse generated the images before her, a montage of men and women stepping into their shops and pulling their shutters to the ground, lovers embracing, women laughing, children chasing other children, then a silence, an overwhelming, isolating sadness.

The carriage came to a halt in front of India Gate. No dramatic light, no sharp angles, just a slow oozing into the night, a mottled and unsettled sea. She walked through India Gate and up the gangway to the quarterdeck of the ship, each deliberate step more distant than the last, as if her footprints were removed from her — peeling away. She placed her gloved hand on the freshly painted railing to steady herself in the uneasiness of the moment. The ship was in shadow now; almost cool enough for a cardigan. The sea stretched in vexing crests and troughs before her.

As Alice spoke, she could hear her voice aching. She hovered somewhere between body and sky. "Charlotte, William will want his doll for sleeping. Can you remember which trunk that got into? Charlotte, are you with me?"

The air cleared, her ears popped and she could finally hear the clatter of the crowd spiralling in and around India Gate below. The park was peppered with families picnicking in the warm evening; the streets were full of automobiles and horse carriages. Still no sign of her family.

"Yes, Alice. I'm not sure where William's doll might be. Perhaps, William has it with him, or Sheila Rana has placed it somewhere safe."

"Good lord, Charlotte. Where could they be?"

Alice worried her chin with her forefinger as she searched the crowded landing for a sign of Denzil, the three children and Sheila Rana. Every tall man in a black suit, every child, every family of three children, every ayah in the whole of India were boarding the ship except for Denzil and the children. She wrung her hands around the railing and hit it impatiently. She stepped back and turned away. No sense in fretting about a few errant minutes in one's life, Denzil would say. She thought to herself, *How many prana would that be?*

The fading sun saturated the colours; whites were luminescent and reds bled into the stones of the buildings behind the crowds. The Taj Mahal Hotel took up most of the frontage along the causeway like a ship, opposite and defiant. Someday, thought Alice, Denzil and I will indulge in a bit of extravagance once all this political mess sorts itself out. But the minutes in her life fluttered and flattened before her, wasting away into tiny specks that floated in front of her eyes. Like a grainy photograph, the magnificent British architecture in the buildings lining the streets remained stalwart against the rough textures of Indian sensibilities, and everything before her eyes began to crumble. She looked out beyond the forecastle and watched as the sea turned frightfully black in the night.

Things had a way of working themselves out — the slowness of the sun's descent would somehow give Denzil and the children a shorter distance to travel, and her family would arrive, frantic — because Denzil was such a stickler for time — and he would rush up the gangway and apologize for worrying her, it had all been a mistake, he should not have let her go ahead, and the children would gather around her skirts and somehow all this anxiety would seem silly and she would feel like a fool because any minute now, they would arrive in a taxi. Any minute now.

The Anatomy of a Seizure, Third Movement

Sometimes you think you can avoid losing consciousness and you throw yourself to the floor, thinking for some reason that it might have to do with elevation. You sip water and gulp air. You focus on an object before you, preferably something red, because red is easiest to find in a crowd when the scene blurs. You convince yourself, because you've managed to remain lucid and can add and subtract odd numbers, that there is nothing wrong with you, that it was all an accident of identity, and that the woman on the ground before you has nothing to do with you.

Dreaming the Tiger

Roshon, Rita's daughter, gave Claire the address of her brother, a musician for Bollywood movies. Bombay had a bustling movie industry, the Hollywood of Asia, and Roshon's brother had a connection to the film industry that could possibly help her get permission to film inside the prison at Yeravda. Namesh was a very busy man, Roshon told her, but he had many friends in Chicago, so she was sure he would be pleased to help her.

Claire thanked the women for their kindnesses and kissed Rita on the cheek. "You have made my whole trip worthwhile."

Rita nodded and said, "Call your mother."

"My mother? Why?"

"Tell her you love her. She's your mother and she has suffered in many ways." Rita slowly stood up with the help of the two young girls who had rejoined the picnic after the sun went down. "You will send me a copy of this film, will you not? Although I'm as blind as a bat, I would like to show it off to my sighted friends. They are always bothered by my popularity with the government so I think this ought to put them right over the edge."

"Yes, of course, I will send you copies." Claire held Rita's hands and looked right into her clouded eyes. "Only if you keep out of prison."

"Oh, nobody listens to me. I'm just an old woman now."

Claire and Roshon exchanged their personal addresses and again shared amazement at their unusual encounter in a country as vast as India. As she backed away from the women packing up their picnic, gathering their children, laughing and sparring with each other, Claire glanced down at the business card Roshon had handed her: Centre for Environment Education, Nehru Foundation for Development, Director.

"Roshon," Claire called out to her. "Where does one find tiger in this country?"

As the crowd began to fill in around her, Claire could see Roshon shrug and then call out, "Good luck," as she disappeared into the darkness.

David leaned back on the lawn and watched some children taunt a beetle as Claire arrived and sat down beside him. She had too much of her own excitement inside her to make any sense of it to him, and when she smiled at him, he brought his hand up to her arm, squeezed it gently.

"You're having a good time, aren't you?"

And she told him yes, she was having a very good time. David pulled his hand back, stood up and brushed his slacks off.

"Me too," he said. "Except this guy told me the sextant I bought is a fake."

"Take it back."

"Yeah, right," he said sarcastically. "Come on, let's eat."

"I want to call Mom tonight," Claire said.

"Why?"

"Did you know that there are no more tiger left in India?"

David stared blankly.

"The film Mom wants me to do — remember that night at Mom's place when we were sitting around the table with Ben?

I'm thinking that tiger should be the topic of my next film."

"You're kidding, right?" He stepped back. "You're not kidding."

"David, there are no more tiger left in India. Don't you think that's significant?"

He took her hand in his and pulled her toward the street. He shouted over the growing noise of the traffic, "Significant? Sure." They were now walking quickly along an esplanade of smooth rounded pillars. "But I thought your gig was Protest."

"Still is. I'm just feeling more feral these days. India has done that to me."

They had arrived in the middle of a traffic circle and stood watching as the inhabitants of Mumbai circled around them. Claire swung her camera onto her shoulder and filmed the oncoming traffic, the beggars wandering across the road, the young prostitutes dropping to their blankets like bright blossoms wilting in between the spin and slur of traffic. "Maybe this film *is* about tiger," she said.

That evening Claire and David hung out at the STD/ISD office down the street from the Lawrence Hotel and waited for Claire's mother to return Claire's call. She left her mother the number to call her back, but the lines were probably busy and the shopkeeper was anxious to close. They left before Dorothy could get through. Later that same evening, Claire made a note in her journal: *Close-up of tiger's eye. Reverse angle shot to tiger watching from the branch of a tree. A river.*

The following morning, while David checked out the Rhythm House near the Jahangir Art Gallery, Claire arranged to meet Namesh at his apartment. She found him up three flights of very steep stairs in a room about eight feet by fourteen feet. There was a metal locker at one end of the room. A double cot, with thick brown ticking piled high into a corner, was scattered with magazine and newspaper articles, and the walls were covered with tattered posters of animals: elephants, gazelles and tiger. In the corner to the right of the open door were a small television, a hot plate, some metal pots and a stereo. The whole room had a utility about it, as if those who inhabited it were only tourists passing through for the night.

Namesh was a soft-spoken man with wide round cheeks and smart eyes. "I live here part-time with my wife's family," he said, leaning against the wall.

Claire glanced around the room for another door leading into more rooms. "You live in this room? All of you?"

"Yes, of course." He tilted his head from side to side. "I have friends in Chicago. My band and I tour in America every other year."

Namesh handed Claire a cup of tea and pushed a bowl of raw sugar toward her. She spooned some sugar into her tea and told him about her project. He sat and listened quietly while he filed his fingernails.

"So would you be able to help me?" she asked.

"I will send you to Trishpal Singh, a fellow who works at Aga Khan's palace. It is now the Gandhi Memorial. He will know to whom you must talk in order to get inside the prison, but you mustn't tell them about your connection to my grandmother, or to myself, for that matter."

"So she really is a problem?"

"It depends."

"Does this go as far back as Gandhi?"

"Yes, it seems everything political in this country goes as far back as Gandhi, but my grandmother has never learned to keep her mouth shut about anything. Now it is all about women's rights. She is quite an extraordinary person, really. But her politics have made it difficult for all of us. She wrote a few defamatory papers on the regression of women's rights since Independence and there were some people in government who thought her very unsupportive."

Namesh put on some music and turned up the volume on the speakers. They pounded and fizzed as he shouted out to her over the music, "Now, do you like this? I just composed this for another movie."

"What is the movie about?" Claire shouted back.

"Terrorism," he shouted over the music.

"Oh," Claire shouted back. "Are you all troublemakers in your family?"

Namesh winked. "Every last one of us."

She pointed to the poster above the speaker. "Do you know where there are tiger?"

Namesh turned down the music and looked closely at Claire. "I thought you were making a film about your grandfather."

"I understand there are some tiger in Kanha. Is that true?"

"Tiger? In Kanha? Maybe a decade ago."

"Well, where can I see tiger?" Claire asked.

"Tiger," Namesh said sadly, "are almost finished. Maybe Ranthambhore, I don't know." The brightness of his eyes seemed to darken and Claire felt a black cloud settle over the two of them.

Tunnel like a poet back through the history of your words and search for the absences, for the dream to bludgeon.

You will find within your own body a movable centre, impossible to grasp, hermetic and veiled. But if you speak the dream, you will remember the dream. And in India, we begin where we end.

"I have dreamt of tiger," Claire said aloud.

"Then you must pay very close attention," Namesh said and poured her another cup of tea.

Tiger Dreams Film Sequence

Caesura: There is a pause where the screen goes blank and the spectator
has time to consider and separate from the text. Loop: Everything
begins again.

PART SIX

Confessions of
an Old Woman

Tiger Dreams Film Opening Sequence

Sound FX. The steady drumming of wheels against the tracks.

Music up and over.

Extreme Long Shot. 90 degrees. Train curving around a bend in the
landscape.

Medium Long Shot. Arms hanging from open windows.

Medium Shot. I am pulled into focus through the barred windows of
the train. I am searching through my bags. Pause. Medium Close-up.
I touch my fingers to my ears, the buttons of my blouse, the pockets
of my skirt. Cut.

Pan to the red coach car on a curve around the blurred grasslands of the
Decca.

Life Work, Diwali

Green parrots swooped over vines tangled around the latticework and chipmunks darted over the ribbed branches of lemon trees heavy with fruit. Claire stretched her legs out and nudged the golden cat away from her leg. It leaned back into her and dragged its oily fur across her calf muscle.

She tied the string around the bundle of letters Charlotte had given her earlier that day, walked over to the camera bag and stuffed the bundle beside the coins. She could see David and Charlotte standing in the hallway before a bookshelf. Charlotte was nodding and pointing at objects on the shelf. She pointed her finger toward the top shelf and David reached up to pull something down. She then swung around and wobbled toward the terrace door while David retrieved the tea and followed. She opened the glass door and entered. The cat hissed and scurried into the garden.

Charlotte's busy manner, and the way she huffed and wheezed around a room, reminded Claire of Joan from the university archives. Tucked into her arms like a pile of autumn leaves was another collection of papers. "These belonged to Alice, too," Charlotte said. "They were the articles she had written for the Archaeological Society in Aurangabad. Those two Italian boys had started up the society. I can't remember their names."

Charlotte licked her fingers and pressed them onto the curled edges, separating and scanning each page from the corners of her cataracts.

Claire took the cup of tea from David and quickly put it down on the table. "The Archaeological Society? She worked, then?" Claire wiped her hands on her skirt and reached toward the papers Charlotte was holding tightly.

"Of course she worked. We all did."

"Well, you know what I mean." Claire tugged at the papers in Charlotte's hands. "May I?"

Charlotte released the papers. She looked down to her own shaking hands and began twisting the ring around her thickened knuckle. "Yes, dear. She worked. That was another thing I think your grandparents couldn't agree on — Alice's work. Alice ..." Charlotte paused and looked straight into Claire's eyes and shook her finger in her direction. "Are you a tyrant? Do you break all the rules?"

Claire shrugged. Did she break all the rules? *Yeah, sure,* she thought, *I break the rules. Does that make me a tyrant?* She flipped through the article that had been handed to her — "Colour and the Buddhists: The Use of Foreign Pigments in the Ajanta Caves" by Alice Maude Spencer, 1925.

"These Ajanta Caves," Claire asked. "Are they around here?"

"Yes, just north of Aurangabad. About a seven-hour bus ride from here. Your grandmother came down with malaria shortly after that expedition."

Claire continued to unfold clippings, photographs, and a small pouch of blue powder. She held up the crudely sewn pouch for Charlotte to see. "What's this?" The powder had bled in irregular patterns up the front and back of the pouch; its deep parasitic blue continued to suck light from the rest of the room.

"Your grandmother scraped that from the walls of the Ajanta Caves. That was also the year she found the fetus of a tiger."

Claire's eyes widened, and she could feel her pupils dilate. Time swooped past her head like wings and she could smell the tawny hide of an animal cornered in her mind. She stood up to breathe in some air from the garden. Rubbing her thumbs across her moist palms, Claire turned toward Charlotte. "I have a camera," she said hungrily.

"I know that, dear."

"I want to film you."

"You have been filming all along."

"You knew?"

"Yes, of course, what do you take me for?"

"Why didn't you say anything?"

"I was waiting for you to ask permission."

"I didn't think you'd give it to me."

"So you thought you'd take it instead."

"I'm sorry. I should have asked."

"Oh, don't worry about it, dear. If we had to ask permission for everything, we'd never get anything done, now would we?"

Claire picked up her camera and placed it on her shoulder. She adjusted the white balance and leaned back against the wall of the courtyard. "Tell me about the tiger," she said. "Tell me everything."

Charlotte studied Claire carefully. "You look like her — except for the eyes. The eyes are Denzil's."

"My father's as well."

"Yes, of course. Tell me something first."

"What?"

"What kind of woman did your father marry? What is your mother like?"

Claire carefully considered Charlotte's question. She turned to David and tilted her head as if to say, *This is where you come in.* "You can probably answer that question better than I can, David?"

"Sorry, what was the question?" David had been deeply engrossed in reading Alice's article.

"What kind of woman is my mother?"

"Oh, your mother? Well, she's a lot like Claire."

David looked at Charlotte and then returned to the article.

"She is not! My mother and I are nothing alike."

David looked up again and flipped the article over in his lap. "What's the matter with you? I should think you'd be flattered."

"To be like Dorothy?"

"Why not? She's great."

"She's nuts."

David turned toward Charlotte. "Bill said he fell in love with Dorothy because she was the first woman who knew how to love him."

"He never said that."

"That's what he told me."

"When did Father ever say that?"

"Shortly before he died, Claire. He and I were in the study and he was telling me about the early years of exploration and then somehow we got onto the topic of women and he said he didn't know love before he met your mother."

The wall behind Claire was rough and uncomfortable on her shoulder blades and she moved over to the small table in the corner. She wanted to say that she was the only woman who knew how to love her father, and then she thought how ridiculous that would sound. How could a daughter possibly know how to love her father — not in the way he needed to be loved. "I'm more like my father, Charlotte. I look like him and I think like him. Dorothy is ... well ... she's different than I am."

David laughed aloud and Claire glared at him. "Don't tell me I'm like my mother when I'm not."

"But you are, Claire, don't you see it?"

"No, I don't see it."

Diwali, the Festival of Light, a celebration dedicated to Lakshmi, the goddess of wealth and plenty, lasted for a total of five days. That evening, on their way back to their hotel room, deadly explosions of firecrackers accompanied flashes of red and white lightning in the streets. Shuddering and cringing with every explosion, Claire brooded. Why had she never seen it before? She was like her mother? And as if the fireworks were beating reluctance out of her, she began to mumble beneath the harassment of explosions, "What if I am my mother's daughter?" There were no streetlights, only the sudden glow and flashes on sidewalks, back alleys, under the bridge, along the River Mula. Women were screeching in delight and fear, and boys and men were running through the streets tossing burning fuses this way and that. She thought, *This must be what a war zone is like.*

Later, in the relative quiet of their hotel room, David stood in the doorway to the bathroom towelling off his hair. Claire lay on the bed rubbing her favourite coin with her fingers.

"What are you thinking about?" David asked.

"Irony — mostly." Claire opened her eyes and propped herself on her elbows.

"Ah, my specialty." David threw on a t-shirt, pulled up a pair of shorts, sat down on the bed and flicked on the television. "You should go with it. If your grandmother is stealing the light, let her. Makes more sense, anyway."

"Seeing those papers she wrote ... I felt as if it was me that was dead, and I was watching her work, you know, collecting samples, chiselling away at some piece of stone. And it drives me crazy that Father never spoke of her."

David lay back and began flipping through the channels on the television. "I have to admit, that was pretty cool watching you put on those pearls."

"Yeah? In what way?"

"Wowa! Hey, Claire — Star Trek. Can you believe it?"

David fluffed up the stiff foam pillow, tossed it onto the foot of the bed, lay on his belly and turned up the volume. "This is the one where Picard meets the Metamorph." He popped open a bottle of beer from the base of the bed, offered it to Claire and opened another for himself. "She hatches out of a cocoon and is supposed to fall in love with the first man she meets. It just so happens Picard is the first one on deck."

Claire leaned her back against the wall and crossed her legs. David flipped his feet into her lap and started toeing her thigh. She took his foot into her hand and pushed her thumb against his arch. He moaned, looked back over his shoulder and smiled, then turned back toward the television. It was like that with David — he remained on the periphery, refusing to participate in or even become the author of any of her afflictions. She sipped her beer and circled his heels with her thumb, trying to remember what it was that she had forgotten. Something had gone missing and she couldn't for the life of her remember what it was. She touched her earlobes, the buttons on her shirt, her necklace — everything was in its place.

You Are Constantly Dreaming This:

You dream of the Canadian winter — an alpine meadow stiff with snow in a crystalled night. Hoar frost casts fractal shadows across the sloping bellies of drifts, slick blue ice fields moan with calving seracs, and the stars are so incredibly bright they must be moons.

Life Work, Diwali

David whispered the word: "Suture." He lay on his side staring at Claire when she awoke.

"What was that?" Claire asked. It was still dark outside.

"Suture." His lips softly formed the word as he dragged his fingertip along her scar, exploring the flow of tissue as it spread on either side of the incision toward her breast and collarbone. He repeated the word one more time, "Suture," and then rolled her over on her side, pressed himself against her back and wrapped his arms around her.

"Thank you," she whispered and then fell fast asleep again.

Aga Khan's Palace, a Couple of Days Later

Trishpal Singh, Namesh's contact in Pune, picked up Claire and David at their hotel and took them to what was once Aga Khan's Palace. It had now been converted into the Gandhi National Memorial. "After Gandhi had delivered his Quit India Resolution in Bombay 1942," Trishpal told them, "'the British interned him in Aga Khan's Palace rather than at the Yeravda Prison. Gandhi's wife, Kasturbai, died in the palace."

As they drove through the gates and along the roadway to the palace steps, Trishpal told Claire and David how his grandparents had been farmers just north of the city. "The British had sold them cinchona seeds and they cultivated the tree for its bark. The bark was used for an anti-malarial drug. But then the British found a cheaper, easier way of getting the bark directly from the Americas." This destroyed his grandfather's farm; he couldn't pay his taxes so the British took it away from him. "My father was forced to go to the city to find work."

"So they used that drug during the '30s?" Claire slammed the door of the Ambassador and swung her camera, like a carpenter hauling a two-by-four, onto her shoulder.

"Oh, yes, many many people died of malaria every year. My grandfather had sold his crops to the medical laboratories before the British took his land."

Trishpal stood back to allow Claire to go before him up the stairs. He had the look of an Indian cricket star; he dressed well and carried himself like an athlete. He toured Claire and David around the museum, showing them articles of clothing, photographs, and a spinning wheel, all belonging to Gandhi. "But this is not why you are here," Trishpal said. "Come, we'll have chai, and talk about your plans for your film. You drink chai?"

The moisture from Claire's palm made her hand slip from David's. "Yes, please, we'd love some tea."

Trishpal disappeared from the front room and David wiped his hand across his shirt. "How are you doing?"

"I want to go to the prison," Claire said impatiently.

"We'll get there. Trishpal seems to know what he's doing."

"Have you got any money for him?"

Claire and David had spent what they eventually decided was too much time trying to figure out equitable tips for tour guides, porters, taxis, and rickshaws. Claire couldn't escape the feeling that she was being too cheap or that the people who had given them service had different expectations. She still couldn't read these people, what they wanted from her, what they expected. "Oh, why don't we just ask him? I'm tired of second-guessing this kind of thing. These guys spend all day with us and then when we give them what we think is fair they look at us like we're out of our minds. Let's just ask him right now."

Trishpal came back into the room with the tea and had them sit in the shaded corner by the tree.

"Trishpal? I want you to help me get my camera into the Yeravda Prison. How much money do you want for arranging that for me?"

"Oh, you decide. I help you because you are a friend of Namesh. You decide, please. If nothing, that will be okay. If something, that will be okay, too."

David shrugged. "How soon can we go?"

Claire sipped her chai and nibbled on a biscuit.

"Those biscuits, madam, are from the prison bakery." Trishpal offered her another. "You like?"

"Yes, they are very good, thank you." Claire took another and dunked it into her chai, then popped it into her mouth. "How soon can we go?"

It wasn't that he ignored her, nor could his behaviour be construed as rude, but when Trishpal turned to David and began to make plans to go to the prison the following day, Claire resigned herself to the invisibility of women. Initially, she had resisted when men asked her questions and then verified her answers with David. She had acted indignant — repeating her answers and complaining about their disregard, but after a few weeks of invisibility she was beginning to feel worn down. She had spent her life trying to get her father's attention, trying to get him to listen to her, but like Trishpal, her father always favoured the man. Her brother and David were the ones to whom her father chatted on lazy afternoons, entrusted his business affairs, and imparted his philosophies, his wisdom, the secrets of his love for her mother. Her own complacency was new to her and she felt pathetic compared to women she had met since arriving in India, women like Roshon, or Rita, who had spent their lifetime asserting themselves in a world that so blatantly ignored them. She began to feel like a cousin once removed, or an aside in a script, finding it more and more futile to assert herself. Ben had accused her of being someone who had never had her freedoms taken from her, but now, inside her quiet resignation, she considered the possibility that freedom was a question of perspective. The expectation that she should be grateful for the freedoms granted to her only angered her more. Why was she supposed to settle for less? She looked down to see that she was holding David's hand again, and that his fingertips had turned a deep purple.

The following day, Claire, David and Trishpal stood outside the prison gates while the guard went in and out of a small metal door. The door had been inset with rivets into a larger metal door that had been inset into a larger wooden door that had been inset into a concrete wall.

"Her grandfather used to be Superintendent of Prisons," David had told the guard. "We would like to come inside to see where he worked."

After the young guard had retreated inside to talk to someone about their request, he came back out through the small metal door. "What do you want to see inside for?"

Trishpal and the guard launched into a long dialogue that

neither David nor Claire could understand. Trishpal pointed to Claire several times and the young guard nodded as if he understood. He went back inside the small metal door and Claire and David stood outside on the pale sandy courtyard in front of the prison gates.

A large white cinder-block barricade surrounded the prison grounds. A guard's house to the right of the prison entrance had the typical red, clay-tiled roof of Pune architecture, and the filigree in the eaves cast shadows on the prison guards as they stood idly, smoking and waiting. It looked cool behind the green wooden lattice; the place had a clean, immaculate, cruel tension. She fancied that her grandfather led the double life of a perfidious dictator — impotent and desperate with his woman, volatile with his prisoners, charitable and loving to his children. These fictions were dangerous for their proximity to truth. The guards in their shadows, their hands lightly upon their weapons, turned their heads in unison toward her.

This would have to be choreographed later.

Tiger Dreams Film Part XV Sequence

Sound FX: Drumbeat.

Close-up: Five dark men with their yellowed eyes, sunlight across their
noses and brows. Cut. Photograph of women marching beside
Gandhi. Wipe. Rita standing with daughters. Wipe. Gandhi entering
prison. Cut. Five dark men with their yellowed eyes, sunlight across
their noses and brows, turn their heads in unison toward the camera.
Cut.

Yeravda

The young guard came out of the small metal door and approached David. "You may come with me."

David and Claire moved toward the door, but the guard shouted something to Trishpal. Trishpal touched Claire on the shoulder. "He wants only David to come inside."

"Well, that is ridiculous." David turned toward the guard. "Please, ask your superintendent to let the woman inside. It was *her* grandfather who worked here, not mine."

The guard looked at David and at Trishpal and then over to Claire. "One moment, please."

He disappeared into the small metal door again.

Claire held her camera low in her hand and turned it on. David saw that it was running and nodded in the direction of the guard's house. He whispered, "Get those guys smoking on their break."

She smiled at the guards as they stared and she whispered under her breath, "They can see her inside me."

Maybe you are Alice and it is here that you enter the end of your life.

"If I splice this scene with how I am feeling right now, is that what you would call 'suture'?"

"I don't know. How do you feel right now?"

"I'm thinking that there are wounds that need sutures both

inside and out. Big jagged wounds from falling on rock, and if you take the two flaps of skin and stitch them together, eventually the skin will begin to knit together miraculously, in that one-cell-at-a-time kind of way. Take the word 'suture,' for instance. Could it be the vehicle by which we heal? The catalyst?"

"It is also a moment of recognition, when we realize we are not who we thought we were, that we are someone else. Suture is for the audience, really."

Another guard opened the small metal door and the younger guard stepped over the threshold with one foot and motioned for both Claire and David to come in.

"We're in," whispered David. "Better turn that thing off."

Trishpal lit a cigarette and nodded to David. "David, sir, come here for a moment, please."

David walked over to Trishpal, who turned away from the guards to speak. "I have not mentioned the camera, sir. You get in to see the boss — then you ask, okay? Then you ask."

David nodded. "Hey look, if you've got somewhere else to go — we understand. We'll catch up with you later."

David put a hundred rupees into Trishpal's hand. Trishpal pushed it back toward David. "No, sir. I have not done anything. You keep it. You are like a father to me."

"Okay, but don't wait too long for us. We'll find our own way back to the palace."

"Yes, sir." Trishpal took a drag on his cigarette and sat down on one of the oak barrel planters that framed the entrance to the prison. He wasn't going anywhere.

David turned and walked back toward the small metal door. "Great," he mumbled under his breath. "Now, I'm a father."

Once inside the prison entrance, David and Claire were asked to show their passports and their backpacks. Claire hugged her camera and showed the guard what it was. He shook his head and motioned for her to put it on the desktop. Another guard was writing down all the articles inside their backpacks in a large ledger.

Nothing had been balanced for this scene. The darkness in the hallway — skin and uniforms — meant only voice-overs could be used. In the end, David recommended discarding the scene that followed.

"I would like to take this with me," Claire said.

The guard looked past Claire toward David. "What is this for?"

Claire stood back and let David speak. "It is my wife's camera," he said. "Her grandfather used to work here."

The guard asked again, "What does your wife want with this camera?"

"She would like to take some pictures of where her grandfather worked for her mother back in Canada. We are from Ca-na-da." David spoke this loudly and he exaggerated the formation of each syllable. "Ca-na-da. Do you know," he repeated and nodded his head emphatically, "Ca-na-da?"

"I know Canada," the guard replied, somewhat annoyed. "And you look Indian."

"Yes, I do, don't I?" David kept smiling and nodding.

Claire bowed her head and spoke to David. "Darling, can you ask the nice young man to let me have my camera back?"

The guard rose from the desk. "One moment, please."

He walked over to the young guard who had been negotiating their entry. They spoke for a few moments and the young guard ran up the stairs. A few moments later, he arrived at the base of the stairs and motioned to David and Claire for them to follow him.

"May I bring my camera?" Claire asked.

David put his hand on her shoulder. "Here, let me interpret for you." He called out to the guard who was still standing at the base of the stairs, "Can my wife please bring her camera?"

"Yes, yes, please come." The guard at the desk handed Claire her camera and Claire and David followed the guard up the stairs to the superintendent's office.

"Please wait here," the guard said and went into the office. David and Claire stood outside a curtained doorway. The guard returned immediately and he motioned for David and Claire to enter the room. "Please come in."

Several rows of wooden chairs filled one half of the office. This was where the morning role call took place, where daily tasks were assigned to the guards: Which prisoners needed discipline? Who needed amnesty? What is to be done about the Christmas concert?

The room was well-lit and the glass in the windows had been freshly cleaned. A man called out from behind a large desk that filled the other half of the room. "You like Indian tea?" he asked.

"Yes, thank you," David replied. He had finally resigned himself to tea and he even found himself craving it now.

Photographs of past superintendents covered one wall and a large photograph of Gandhi was placed between the two windows overlooking the prison grounds. Claire scanned the photographs but couldn't see her grandfather. "How far back do these photographs date?"

"Only since Independence, madam." The superintendent stood briefly and gestured to the chairs in front of his desk. "My name is Mr. Bahti. Please, sit."

He sat down again and a buzzer rang. A sepoy arrived with tea and biscuits. David and Claire both took a cup and saucer along with a biscuit.

"You like our sweet tea?"

"Oh, yes, very much so," replied Claire, whose head coincidentally ached from the sugar she had consumed since the morning.

"Your grandfather, madam, was superintendent at this prison?"

Mr. Bahti signed a few pieces of paper. Another sepoy, not the one who had delivered the tea, took the papers away and left the room.

"Yes, I believe he would have been here during Gandhi's internment."

Claire surreptitiously sat back far enough so that the angle of the lens might catch Mr. Bahti's head. David spliced what followed onto the previous guardhouse scene.

"Have you any records that go back that far?" Claire asked.

"No, madam. We didn't keep records from before Independence. But we do have the registry that was kept when Gandhi was interned. You might find something in there. If you like, I will take you on a tour of the prison grounds. We will take you to Gandhi's prison cell. We have made it up very nicely."

Claire responded enthusiastically and Mr. Bahti asked her to leave her movie camera behind. "We have a law against photographs inside the prison."

"I'll just carry it with me, if you don't mind. It is a very expensive piece of equipment and I would hate for it to go missing for one reason or another."

"International incident and all that." David winked at Mr. Bahti. The man nodded his head. "As you wish," and a buzzer went off again.

A different sepoy, not the one who delivered tea and not the one who had brought papers for signing (it was as if the previous sepoys had been terminated after each task), arrived and Mr. Bahti spoke quietly to him. Claire shut off her camera and looked around the room where her grandfather must have worked. She walked over to the window and looked out. He would have stood before this window, she thought, watching the prisoners in their daily exercises; the grounds below were impeccable: white stone curbs contained circles and ovals of sparse green grass, sandy walkways skirted thick walls dappled with broken shards of glass. There were several sepoys, dressed in white lungi, walking beside prisoners dressed in greying kurtas. It was this sinister arrangement of an immaculate universe, a certain facile predilection for symmetry, that made Claire want to rip her clothes off and scream maniacally. She thought of her father and his tantrums, of her own.

Mr. Bahti approached the other window. "We have a theatrical society in the prison," he said. "They put on very, very good plays, really quite entertaining, you know."

Neither David nor Claire failed to notice that when Mr. Bahti spoke, he spoke directly to Claire. He spoke with pride when he told her about their rehabilitation program, how some prisoners went into the city for theatrical productions, even for some of their studies. No, he replied to one of her questions, they no longer had women prisoners. There were too many complications in having women in the same compound as men. The women prisoners were kept elsewhere.

"Come," he said, "we will go for a walk."

Claire followed David and Mr. Bahti out of the office and down the stairs. A large photograph of Jawaharlal Nehru hung in the landing. The colours of the photograph were bleached from the sun and the paper had rippled beneath the glass. "Jawaharlal Nehru." Mr. Bahti waved his hand in the direction of the photograph as he continued down the stairwell. "He picked up where Gandhi left off and led India into Independence. He preferred persuasion rather than force. These are values I try to adhere to myself."

Mr. Bahti then turned and walked down the last flight of stairs, through the tall archway and into the prison courtyard. The sun whitened everything, bleaching the green grass and leaves, paling the crushed red gravel of the pathways. "We will take you first to Gandhi's cell. As I said earlier, you might find your grandfather's signature in the registry."

The thirsty earth flicked into the spaces between her toes, balling up in slurries between her feet and the black rubber of her sandals. As she strolled behind David and Mr. Bahti, Claire could feel the eyes of the guards inspecting her and she turned quickly to see someone in the window of the second-storey office move back and away from view. She caught up to Mr. Bahti and David just as Mr. Bahti was telling David that most of the prisoners were in Yeravda for murder.

"Really?" David asked. "Crimes of passion?"

"Yes, mostly," said Mr Bahti.

"Claire, did you hear that? Crimes of passion."

"Or drugs," added Mr. Bahti and he pointed to a European dressed in a prison kurta. "That fellow is from Germany. He has a life sentence with us."

He stopped before a wrought-iron gate and waited for Claire to catch up. "Here we are. We take much pride in the fact that the Pune Pact was signed right here."

He pointed to the thick trunk of a mango tree that dominated a small courtyard inside the gate. A bench surrounded the tree and a bust of Mohandas K. Gandhi was positioned directly behind it. "Malak, one of our life prisoners," Mr. Bahti continued, "made that statue during his imprisonment in the 1950s. He was a very famous artist, known throughout the world. He got his start in our art school."

"Is he still here?" David asked.

"Oh, no sir, he died in the sixties — before my time."

Time, in India, was a highly refined concept. There had been episodes in India's history where the Muslim triumphed over the Hindu, or the Hindu triumphed over the Buddhist, or the Buddhist triumphed over the Christian, for not just ten or twenty years but for hundreds. Time had its own special relevance for the Indian people — or so it seemed to Claire — where an individual need only be accountable to his or her contemporaries. With each dynasty, the Indian universe had escalated into such chaos, the individual or even the community couldn't possibly be held accountable for the crimes of their ancestors. According to Mr. Bahti, the State of India — the India he knew — had begun after Independence from the British. He permitted himself the luxury of living in the perpetual present. For the Canadian, it was different: Government existed outside of time. Though the players changed and new policies were introduced, old policies thrown out, Government was something sentient, something that had been given the power to determine life and therefore flowed freely through every Canadian's life. To say, as a Canadian, *that was before my time*, was considered irresponsible.

The white walls of the prison glared from the sun and Claire casually fingered her camera, turning it on again. To the right of the small courtyard were three prison cells. Mr. Bahti extended his hand graciously to the passageway that led to the doorways of the cells. "These were the prison cells of Gandhi and Nehru and Nehru's father."

As Claire stepped onto the path that led to the corridor, her sandal rested briefly, comfortably, in a curve in the stone. She took another step and paused.

Beads of perspiration had appeared on Claire's forehead and she had lost colour in her cheeks. "Are you okay, Claire? Why don't you sit for a moment?"

"No, no, I'm okay." The scar across the top of David's left eyebrow shone in the light. "I'm just paying attention, that's all."

In an unconscious gesture, fore and middle finger resting lightly across the inside of her wrist, Claire felt for her pulse, the steady, predictable rhythm of her heart: she had never known it could be so soothing. Slowing and rocking like a somnambulant, hypnotized by her own mimicry of life, the science of her blood flowed like warm butter through her.

She took another step and paused. The stone had been worn smooth.

Suture, she thought. How many worlds are there?

Two that I know of. And as you walk over this stone you are stitching them together.

David read aloud from the registry that lay on a wooden card table to the left of the entrance to Gandhi's cell. "Two pairs of sandals, one walking stick, eyeglasses, spools ..."

Mr. Bahti pointed toward the registry. "That is where your grandfather's signature might be."

"Thank you." Claire walked over to the registry and began scanning the pages for her family name.

Her camera weighed heavily on her right shoulder and she asked David to hold it for her. David was just about to swing the camera onto his own shoulder when Mr. Bahti pointed to it. "May I see?"

"Uh, yeah, sure." David hesitated and brought the camera down to eyeline. He focused the lens on Claire and then called Mr. Bahti over to him. "Here, look through here." David pointed at the viewfinder.

Mr. Bahti took the camera and was immediately surprised by its weight. He smiled. "Very heavy instrument for a woman to carry." He looked through the viewfinder at the image of Claire and then looked closer at the camera. "This sounds like it is on."

"No, no — just charging the batteries," David said hastily.

"Ah, yes. Yes, yes."

Claire turned back to the pages from 1929 and began flipping forward. The signatures in the ledger were small and sometimes only the initials appeared in the right-hand column. "My grandfather's signature can't be that difficult to find. I mean, how many possessions did the man have, after all?"

The room to her right was in darkness and had a silk theatre rope tied across the doorway. Inside, there was a spinning wheel and a glass cabinet, and inside the cabinet were a broken pair of glasses and some worn leather sandals. Beside the sandals, draped over a wooden box, was a white lace doily. She returned to the registry and began scanning the pages under the column "Articles or Gifts." The lace had been registered under September 1932 as a gift from someone with the initials AMS, and beside those initials were the initials DBGS.

"Alice Maude Spencer," Claire said aloud. "AMS, Alice Maude Spencer. These are my grandmother's initials. David, look!" She pointed to the signature of the signing officer. "And these are my grandfather's initials, Denzil Benjamin George Spencer. My grandmother must have given Gandhi that lace over there. That one in the cabinet. My God, David, that's my grandmother's lace!"

Suddenly the black soles of her sandals were unbearably hot. She kicked them off and placed her feet onto the cool surface of the stones. She stared into the camera; her eyes were like rare blue pearls, almost frightening for their clarity. "That, Mr. Bahti, is my grandmother's lace."

Mr. Bahti continued to move around Claire, pretending to film her. She was ghostly through the fabric of her green silk salwar. The filtered sun etched a line around her small breasts and slim hips.

She spoke again, this time to herself as she turned away from the camera. "Lace — she gave him white lace." She leaned against the door frame and curled to her knees before the prison cell.

Whir, click, fade to black.

Voices Only:

"This sounds like it is on," said Mr. Bahti.

"No, that just means the battery is charged. Here, I'll take that for you."

Confessions of an Old Woman

The following morning, David and Claire watched Charlotte wind up and throw her leg in a wide painterly arc, swinging her other hip forward to stumble toward the screen door.

"Come. Come in. I have tea and biscuits ready."

Charlotte felt lighter in spirit than she had for years, she told them. She had dusted and primped, swept and organized, all morning. She had even re-alphabetized her file boxes, the ones with the index cards of names and addresses of everyone she had ever met in her life, and in the process had found a few more photographs of Alice for Claire to take home with her.

"That photograph. Have you seen that one? It is of your grand-mother giving a concert at the Prison Cultural Hall. That must have been around 1930 — before that dreadful accident she and Denzil had coming home from the ... Oh, what were their names? They emigrated to Australia shortly after that."

"What accident?" Claire asked as she set her camera down and tried to position the lens.

"Oh, some sort of collision that broke your grandmother's right hand. See. Look at how she holds that parasol in that pho-tograph. Shame, it was. Such a shame."

Charlotte hesitated to tell Claire what she knew about the accident, how the young William had seen his father carrying his mother into his parents' room. How the following day Denzil and Alice never came out of the room and she could hear weeping, a sorrowful, remorseful weeping, and not that of a woman's. In the end, Charlotte prudently decided not to bring up the complications of Denzil and Alice's marriage.

"What is it?" Claire asked.

"Nothing, dear. Nothing. I thought I remembered something but," she shrugged, "I can't recall it. Poof, gone just like that." She laughed and then returned to the other photographs. "And here. This photograph was taken of all of us just before Alice and I departed for Karachi. Goodness me, she looks rather underdone there, wouldn't you say?"

Alice was slouched in her chair; her shoulders scrunched up around her neck, her hands on the arms of her chair as if she had just arrived, or perhaps was just leaving. She appeared almost demure and apologetic for her presence. Claire's grandfather, Denzil, had a broad formidable forehead and a thin moustache. He had the nineteenth century look of a melodramatic villain. Her father, a young boy, sat at a lace drawn table; he was the only one in the photograph smiling. His bony knees collapsed together like the poles of a teepee and he held a cup and saucer as an offering to the photographer. Beneath the table was the blurred image of a white dog.

Charlotte stood up to stretch her leg. "I wasn't always this crippled, you know."

"Looks like you get around fine," David said kindly.

Tiger Dreams Film Part XVI Sequence

The camera pans the room of Charlotte's home slowly. Cats scurry behind
a couch, cut-glass decanters and crystal wine goblets sparkle through
the glass of a cabinet, curtains shiver before an open window. Cut. A
series of black and white stills are introduced in rapid succession.

My Voice-over: Charlotte's anachronistic charm seemed odd in the social
chaos of modern Pune. It seemed as if she clung to the order of the Raj
and believed it would all be returned to her someday, altered perhaps,
but maybe better to suit her needs.

Reverse-angle shot — that is, it is apparent I am in the room listening to
Charlotte. Close-up shot. Charlotte curls her lips around her crooked
teeth.

My Voice-over Charlotte's Muted Voice: When she spoke of the past her
voice became hollow as if someone had come along and scraped the
pulp out of her words.

Charlotte's Voice Up: Denzil confided in me. He had made me his ally.
While others found him terribly arrogant, I found him self-confident,
exciting. He shocked me out of my constant longing for something —
I don't know what. I was stupid. I had convinced myself that his deceit
was an affirmation of love for me.

Charlotte's voice is muted. She continues to gesticulate silently.

My Voice-over: My grandfather's deceit, like so many lies, was more about
self-loathing, about his own feelings of inadequacy, his inability to pay
attention to the details of Alice's gifts than it was, at all, about her

illness. Charlotte had thought, and this is how foolish she was, that she would escort Alice to Karachi and return to Pune to the loving care of my grandfather and his children. It is creatures like Charlotte who are as innocuous as mice. They attach themselves to the creative natures in men to avoid their own irrelevance. By their compliance, though, they participate in deceit and threaten our existence.

Confessions, Continued

Charlotte stopped scuffing her foot. She straightened her back and moved her shoulders from side to side. "You know, my hip feels much better today."

She looked down at Claire, whose profile was an overlay of the past, just as carefully crafted as Alice's. Claire looked up and smiled gently at the old woman. Charlotte brought her fingers — knuckled and reddened — up to her cheek and steadied her jewelled finger on the thin scar that divided it in two. "We were somewhere between Karachi and Bombay, 1932," Charlotte began. "Her cries were so beastly I couldn't bear it anymore. I attempted to assure her that the children would be safe with their father and that after a well-deserved rest at a very reputable hospital in Karachi, she could return to the children renewed. He's a good man, I told her. He simply wanted what was best for her, you know."

Charlotte squinted her eyes, gritted her teeth. She mimicked a slow, easy walk: "Alice circled around me, like this, she circled me. I see, Alice said to me. Let me get this straight, she said. You think that taking me away from the children is best?"

Charlotte stopped circling and turned back to Claire. "Well, of course, I assured her that we would be in Karachi soon and that she could cable the children to let them know she was fine, but she just continued to circle and pace like this." Charlotte began to walk in circles around Claire. "Every muscle in her body twitched. I'm not bloody fine, she yelled at me and she said she wasn't about to lie to the children to save my face."

Charlotte stopped and turned around. She spoke right into the camera. Her eyes watered and she continued, slowing and pausing, remembering, repeating. "She had been vomiting every day, I think from that medication she was taking. I remember the stench in that cabin was unbearable. Unbearable. I wanted to help her clean up, get her straightened out, you know, but she would have none of it." Charlotte paused and clicked her tongue. "She wasn't bloody fine, she told me, and how dare I think I could tell her what to do?"

You listen to the confessions of an old woman and you know, just by the tone of her voice, that she has been with something wild.

Charlotte clawed the air with quick furtive gestures. "She batted the air in front of me, like this, like a cat, like this. I told her that the hospital wasn't a permanent condition of her life. That she would only be in Karachi for a couple of months — until she was feeling better. I told her she should calm down and let me do something for her." Charlotte nodded her head. "Oh, she told me what I could do for her, all right." Charlotte's eyes widened, the clouds of her cataracts were raised off her corneas like the artful embossing on a frontispiece. "She told me to get out of her sight!" Charlotte threw her head back and shouted, "Get out of my sight! she screamed. And when I tried to convince her that it was for the best she twisted around and dug her claws in my face." Charlotte drew her finger down the scar on her right cheek. "A great bloody mess it was."

Charlotte sat down in the chair opposite Claire. She shook her head. "After that, Alice just collapsed onto the floor. I left the cabin and locked the door behind me."

Freeze frame on scar. Whirr Click Fade.

Arabian Sea 1932

A great sadness whistled through her bones. Alice clung onto consciousness by staring at the floor, hoping and praying she would not lose sight of the world. No, not now, please, she begged herself. Not now.

Charlotte's black-laced boots turned and left the room. The door closed. A sliver of light like a sword beneath the door flickered and animated the dust as it settled into the cracks of the floorboards, and Alice could hear the tongue of the lock clicking into the door frame. Charlotte's shoes — her hard wooden heels — scuffed as she stumbled down the hallway of the ship.

The cabin seemed close. Close in the sense of almost being inside her, as if something dark and musty pressed against her ribs. She felt a tightening in her throat and numbness in her lips and she experienced a kind of blindness — a darkening around the edges of her vision. Inside her were all the contradictions of her generation. She had been the subjugated and the emancipated, the captive and the free. Her life was barely made. It had yet to be created. She prayed aloud, "Oh, God, please take care of my children."

The curtains were tall and the bed unusually narrow. It seemed difficult to reach as she navigated her body toward the bed and pawed her way onto the mattress. She thought she might lie back for a moment. She covered her eyes with her forearm and kicked her shoes from her feet. A spot between her ribs felt broken and she brought her fingers up to feel the stretch of skin between the two narrow bones. Her heart threw itself against her rib cage in angry pulses and she was pleased that the touch of her fingers seemed to calm it.

The activity beyond the stillness of the room — jangling keys, the tick tick of the wooden heels of shoes and the muffled conversations of other travellers — gradually faded as she fell asleep to the slow rocking of the ship at sea.

Hours later, or it could have been days, feeling puffy-eyed and weak, Alice rolled off the bed and stood up. She had no idea how long she had slept nor whether she had really slept, only that her lower back ached from the position in which she had lain, and the cabin was now dark. She looked out her window, but could only see the black water against an even blacker sky.

"I will not be traced back to this horrible end," she said aloud. "I will not be remembered like this." And she pulled off her clothes, crumpled them into a ball, filled a washbasin with the remaining water in the bucket, washed her hair, and followed this by washing every inch of her body. She then splashed herself with rose water and talcum powder, washing away her essence, the culmination of all that was right and wrong. She could feel the disparate parts of herself collide — her eloquence, her awkwardness, her love, her sex, her anger, her youth, her age. She had been alive and dead again and again.

She slipped her favourite blue chiffon dress over her head and pulled on new silk stockings and her new shoes. Then she began to tidy the cabin. The smell of vomit was still strong and she splashed water from the basin onto the floor and used her bedclothes to mop it up. She piled the wet clothes into a corner and sprinkled rose water over the entire cabin.

"Fresh air," she spoke aloud. "All I need is fresh air."

She sat down in the cane-backed chair in the cabin. Oh, she craved fresh fruit, fresh water, fresh sheets, anything that smelled of the mountains: jasmine, night queen, and the bhabhar grasses of the foothills. She closed her eyes and listened for the sound of crickets, strained to feel the cool breeze off Naini Lake. Holding the palms of her hands together, she lowered herself to her knees and prayed.

Christians Bury Their Dead

The Hindu burn their dead and the Christians, they bury theirs, and since there were only three Christian Churches in all of Pune, Charlotte told Claire and David, they ought to be able to find out where Alice had been buried. It had taken Denzil almost a decade to have a proper headstone made for Alice's gravesite, Charlotte recalled.

"All his finances had been tied up in the children's education," she said. "He had insisted to Alice's parents that this is something she would have wished for, and it prevented him from paying attention to the details of Alice's headstone. But I think, in the end, though I can't quite recall the end result, someone took care of it for Denzil. Anyway," she snapped her tongue, "hand me those Yellow Pages, will you?"

David grabbed the telephone book from the shelf beside him and placed it on Charlotte's lap. "Now, can you stretch the cord to reach over here?" Charlotte pointed at the telephone sitting in the corner behind Claire's camera. "Let's telephone one of these churches, shall we? See if you can pay a visit to your grandmother's grave?" She then smiled at Claire and said, "You know, I feel good, really good."

Charlotte talked to Reverend Patak of St. Mary's Church and he pointed them in the direction of St. Sepulchre Cemetery, which was on the other side of the racetrack. If they turned right on Sholapur Road, they should see the gates of the cemetery a quarter of a kilometre on the left-hand side. Many of the Methodists had been buried there. "If she has no luck there," the reverend told Charlotte, "there is an Indian cemetery across the road."

"I won't be joining you," Charlotte announced to Claire and David. "My arthritis simply cannot bear one more rickshaw ride in my life, but do come by and let me know if you find her, would you?"

David and Claire assured Charlotte of their return and thanked her for all that she had given Claire, all the information she had imparted, especially since they had only just met each other.

Later, when Claire found Charlotte in her bed, she wouldn't touch her. She stood in the doorway — the smell causing her head to spin — and she bit down on her lip to remain conscious. David pushed her aside, wedging his shoulders against hers in the threshold of the door as he moved toward the body to cover it up. On Charlotte's bedside table lay the topaz ring Claire had seen on the woman's finger a few days before.

The street was unusually quiet as they headed toward one of the main thoroughfares, Mahatma Gandhi Road.

"Don't you find it odd that Charlotte would hang on to that stuff for so long?" David asked as they loaded their bags and Claire's camera into a rickshaw. "She must have loved Alice very much."

"And Denzil, apparently," Claire replied as she climbed into the rickshaw. "St. Sepulchre Cemetery, please," she said slowly and loudly as if speaking through a megaphone.

The rickshaw jumped and jostled along the potholed road and a morning fog lifted as they crossed through the old part of town. Claire inventoried the memories anchored within her grandmother's possessions. Though the pearls gave her a sense of her grandmother's elegance — of the way she must have held her head high upon her shoulders the first time her grandfather had draped them on her, a slight, delicate tilt to the head as she pondered possibilities — they also hinted that there once must have been love between Alice and Denzil. This helped Claire to reconcile herself to her grandfather's deception. He must have thought he was doing the right thing by sending her away.

But it was the collection of coins and the archaeological studies that inspired Claire most. These were the chronicles of her grandmother's mind, the meticulous contemplations of a woman curious enough to break through the codes of her gender. Claire thought again of her own legacy and she turned to David. "Will you remember me to our children?"

David stared at Claire suspiciously. She took note of how his lips were pulled together and his eyes were soft and grey. He was a big man for this country. She knew that she was going to have to take him home soon — the diesel and the crowds and the relentlessness of India were beginning to wear on him. His lips parted and spread into a wide grin and he laughed. "Is this part of the contract?"

"Shouldn't it be?"

"Where do I sign?"

Claire blurred the focus on her camera and bleached the images of the streets of Pune. Their rickshaw circled around the open fields of the racetrack and turned up the street to St. Sepulchre Cemetery.

Tiger Dreams Film Part XVIa Sequence

Medium long shot from the inside of a Muslim tomb (Fatehpur Sikri has a
good one). Delicate filigree of carved marble lets light in from
courtyard. Images of coloured robes pass before the latticework. Cut to
Medium shot of latticework from outside tomb in the courtyard.
Movement behind the latticework, a figure in black robes. Pull focus as
beautifully manicured fingers hook through the marble lattice.

Karachi 1932

As Alice bided her time in the hospital in Karachi, letters from Denzil regaled her with the children's activities: his impersonation of Santa Claus on a camel, Barbara's latest success on the piano, George's truancy and young William's impressive recovery. *We all look forward to your return, and I heard,* Denzil wrote, *that your recovery is imminent. The doctors have boasted of amazing results.*

Estelle, upon Alice's insistence, had come all the way from Nainital to accompany Alice back to Pune. She had been appalled, outraged, by Denzil's decision to send Alice away and made it very clear to Charlotte that Alice would return to Pune and that she should not get too comfortable in Alice's home. She thought it necessary to remind Charlotte that she retained her position in the Spencer home because of Alice's charity and not due to any exceptional skills the younger woman possessed. Estelle had written Alice's parents in Bangalore and begged them to accompany her to Karachi, but Alice's mother had taken ill and had grown so blind that her father couldn't possibly manage such a long journey with her in tow, and nor could he leave her alone. He promised Estelle that he would meet them in Pune upon their return.

Shade was scarce in the gardens of the hospital and Alice sat dully in the full glare of sunlight while Estelle huddled beneath a parasol. Flies dangled like emerald green blisters in the air. A fat moth clung to the trunk of a tree — its gold and silver wings drew together and eased apart in slow fanning arcs. Alice stretched over the back of her chair to cup her hands around the moth and felt the brush of its wings against the palms of her hands. Her throat was dry and her lips were split and sore. She spoke softly as she tugged gently on the moth and sent it into the sunlight, the flies chasing it across the lawns.

"I was supposed to change things," Alice said distractedly.

"You have acquired more than most of us, Alice," Estelle said almost impatiently.

"What does that mean? Acquired? You speak as though I consume freedom like a commodity."

"For many of us, that's what it is. It's costly and much has to be given up to attain it. I've never had your strength."

"Well, we can hardly say that. Look at me now."

Estelle watched some of the other patients shuffling slowly in the arched shadows of a colonnade and she could hear laughter from a room behind her. *It must be exhausting to be Alice,* thought Estelle, *to constantly be battling complacency.* "Did you ever follow up on that coin?" Estelle asked.

Alice brightened and leaned forward. "Yes, and thank you for asking." And with barely a breath in between she continued, "When Jahangir had pretty much done himself in with arak and opium, Nur took over the affairs of the state. Imagine running a country from a zanana. Very impressive, really. To think a woman could govern with only her voice must have meant her presence was quite extraordinary, don't you think?"

Estelle revelled in Alice's enthusiasms and when she heard the animation in Alice's speech she was reminded of all that had gone missing in her life, all those moments when they were young. Normally, she did not allow herself to remember these things.

"I brought you these." Estelle produced coconut sweets she had purchased at the marketplace in Nainital.

Alice reached across and rolled one into her fingers. "You didn't?"

"I did." And the intensity of Estelle's feelings for Alice came flooding back to her.

When they were teenagers, Alice and Estelle had traded their secrets in the blue light of the moon, wrapped in the traditional kamoan shawls, eating sweets they had purchased that day at the marketplace on the mall. After removing the maggots that had burrowed their heads into the sweets, the two girls would quietly nibble into the soft centres of their candy. They would speak in sticky hushed tones while perched on the sills of the tall arched windows at the far end of their dormitory. They'd stop to listen to the horses slip and trip on the brick pathways that circum-navigated Nainital. And they had made up conversations from the chatter of monkeys digging through the cook's refuse outside the school cafeteria, and identified different concertos that the crickets played in the grasses outside their dormitory window. They spoke of tigers as if they were myth.

By the time the girls had reached the age of sixteen, they had spent what seemed a lifetime together. And though they were different in everything from the fundamentals of personality — Estelle was shy, Alice was not — to the way they presented themselves to the world — Estelle was round, Alice was thin — they were attracted to one another, laughing at each other's jokes, reading each other's poetry aloud, and sharing the secrets of their deepest fantasies.

Out of curiosity, perhaps, or simply to keep themselves warm on that first cold winter night in the foothills of their sixteenth year, the girls had found solace in the warmth of each other's bodies. After all the other girls had fallen fast asleep, Alice crawled onto Estelle's cot and beneath the heavy woollen ticking of her friend's bed, Alice had slipped her hand under Estelle's nightgown and felt for the soft skin of her breasts. Estelle lay still as a mouse, her nipples begging for a wet mouth. She moaned and squeezed her thighs together, unable to reconcile the cramping she felt in her lower belly.

Charged with the sweetness of her own excitement, Alice took her mouth away from Estelle's breast and whispered into her ear so that none of the other girls in the dormitory could hear, "My turn." And then she lifted her body from Estelle's and lay on her back, waiting.

Estelle had repeated this scene many times over in her mind — how she had gathered Alice's nightgown up and around her hips and pushed her hands over Alice's breasts; how they were the size and shape of apricot seeds. She had felt the ribbony curves of Alice's body, the very dialogue of her skin. And how exciting it had been to have Alice shudder and guide Estelle's hand down her belly. She had been insatiable and Estelle could never rid herself of that kind of desire. She had been ambushed by Alice — and even now she felt it. Most especially now, as Estelle contemplated Alice in the landscape of Karachi.

"Did you find other coins of that vintage?" Estelle offered Alice another coconut cream.

Alice rolled it into her fingers. "Nur had that coin minted along with a whole series of coins. The signs of the zodiac were printed on the sides. I don't think they were used for trade, though, and that's why it was so curious to find that one in Damodra. They had been taken out of circulation immediately and became collectors' items for the embellishment of private treasuries. I'm thinking that Nur herself was in Damodra and that she carried her fortune with her."

"She must have been quite a woman."

"Or maybe not," Alice said defiantly. "Maybe her natural propensity for ruling over an empire was in the everyday course of things and our contemporaries — I mean, women our age — have just been fooled into believing we have no station and no capabilities. The minting of coins was as symbolic as the issuing of farmans. She had power, dear Estelle. Real sovereign power."

Alice leaned back into her chair and stretched her legs out before her, pointing and flexing her toes.

"Will you go back there? To Damodra?" Estelle asked. Though it seemed as if the air had been taken from Alice's words, there were still hints of what delighted her in Alice so long ago.

"I'd like to go to Agra first. That is where the coins would have been distributed. Then, I will go back to Damodra." Alice paused. "But first," she shifted in her seat, "we must get me back to Pune and to the children."

Estelle talked about her own daughter's malaria. The child had contracted the disease in the forests north of Nainital during one of Richard's expeditions. Her daughter, named after Alice, had been too small and too young to battle the disease, and she had died in a fevered sleep only a year before. "Blasted mosquitoes," Estelle cursed. "I can't think of any good that comes out of their existence."

"You needn't stay with me, Estelle. Really, I am fine to travel alone."

Alice said this not because she believed it to be true but more in an attempt to relax the mounting tension she could see in her friend.

"I don't doubt that for a minute," Estelle smiled kindly. "I think I do this more for myself than for you."

After young Alice's death, Estelle's drinking had escalated to the point of embarrassment — even for herself. She became ashamed of her infirmity and isolated herself in one of the rooms in Richard's hotel. While she had cultivated what she might refer to as good friendships with some of the other wives in town, she couldn't share with them the agony of her loss. And now, sitting across from her daughter's namesake, the excruciating memories of those final days came rushing back to her: the child too hot to be in her arms, too cold to be without cover, her complexion as smooth and shiny as porcelain, her hair damp and tangled at the base of her neck, Estelle combing the knots, combing their wet, black mats. Young Alice gave not even a whimper, just a soulful smile, a tired, wise smile, as she slipped from life's net like a tiny minnow escaping capture. Estelle gasped after realizing she hadn't taken a breath for quite some time. "I must have a drink," she said.

Alice nodded to the Sister across the courtyard. As the Sister walked over to the two women, Alice whispered, "The Catholics are very good at taking care of the ill. I remember very clearly Sister Dorothea's careful consideration when we all had chicken pox that year."

The Sister arrived and asked if there was anything she could do for them.

Alice replied cheerfully, "Would it be possible for my sister-in-law to have a gin and tonic? Would it be possible to ...?"

"I'm afraid," the Sister interrupted, "we have a policy that prohibits the consumption of alcohol." The Sister turned to Estelle apologetically. "You understand, many of our patients suffer from that affliction. I am sorry for the inconvenience, but there is a lovely hotel not far from the hospital where you might freshen up."

Alice could see very clearly Estelle's growing discomfort. "You go, Estelle. I'm not going anywhere. I'll be here when you get back and we can speak of better times."

Estelle held Alice's hand and stroked her arm, feeling for the fine muscles beneath her skin. But she felt only a vacancy, as if there was only air between skin and bone, as if disintegrations had already taken place. She had spent a lifetime trying to forget what Alice felt like to her fingers. Now she spoke hurriedly, anxiously. "I have never stopped loving you in that way, Alice." Estelle stared into Alice's startled eyes and then turned and disappeared through the large wooden gate that led to the main thoroughfare into Karachi.

Alice, with the help of the Sister, retreated to her room and slept. When she awoke, Estelle still hadn't returned and when Alice sent an orderly to find her, he came back with news that Estelle had spent the afternoon drinking and was now sleeping it off in her hotel room.

Alice stood before the window of her hospital room and ran her fingers along the soft fabric of her dress. She could have been wrong. Maybe death's fulcrum had shifted. Or maybe she was already circling back into life. It was hard to tell. But she had begun to make plans, the plans someone makes when returning from an extended vacation, changed, refreshed, and ready to revise old habits. She knew about urgency now and she suppressed the flutter of anticipation she had in her breast. She stood before the window, her dress brushing against her legs as if a breeze had blown up from beneath her, and she thought for a moment that she was standing in sand because the floor shifted like the desert and eased her closer to the window. Outside the hospital room the landscape had lost all colour, hills met the sky without incident, buildings blended into one another without corners, and as Alice waved her hand in front of her face, her skin disappeared into the walls of the room. Everything was seamless.

Tiger Dreams Film Part XVII Sequence

Close-up on a polished marble floor. Its sheen ripples like heat rising. Long
Take.

My Voice-over: It was difficult to go back to that place.

Sound FX Up and Under: A heart beating slowly at first and then the
rhythm picks up until it sounds as if we're driving through a tunnel
with the windows down.

My Voice-over: To imagine my life ending in that way. That steady
drumming of life inside me, something wild and untamable
scrambling to get out, the final resignation, exhaustion, without a
voice, no longer able to open my eyelids and watch as the world
carried on without me, to know everyone was forgetting me, my life's
work, all that defined me, oh, Claire did this, and Claire did that, and
me lying there cooling as the blood pooled in my body, and me trying
to get out of my body, caesareaned, conscious in my permanent sleep,
and remembering those dreams where a tiger loved me like I was one
of her own and through all of this I tried to remember how it felt to
have the warmth of my mother's hands on my face and the way she
stroked my back as I wept over my father's ways. My mother, she never
left my side.

The camera remains focussed on the marble floor. Flicker of shadow and
light, a body collapses into the frame and a breeze blows strands of
thick black hair across blue lips. Freeze Frame.

Karachi 1932

Estelle found Alice, curled and blind in the orange light of dusk. It appeared as if she had been scraping at herself, excavating, performing her life's work. Her fingers, like stone claws, rippled the hem of her blue chiffon dress.

St. Sepulchre Cemetery

The entrance to St. Sepulchre was just behind a pile of refuse at the end of a series of shops displaying Levi t-shirts, Limca soda, and Chips Marsala. The chips had become a recent favourite of David's and he ran across to buy a bag before they entered the cemetery.

Later, when they were editing the film, Claire could not recall the actual circumstances of the search — getting to and from the cemetery — only what she had found. Even her memories of Charlotte became blurred between the fact and fiction of her journey, all the missing pieces contrived, made up, and she thought how similar she was to her father, how convenient her memory had become. It had eclipsed the sorry facts of Charlotte and Denzil's conspiracy and that of Alice's lonely ending — even though she was convinced that she had made all that up as well. She went back to the cemetery later — to film the statues, the sun rising on her grandmother's headstone and the garden reconfigured, luxurious with bloom. She would falsify the landscape — romanticize death to compensate for her grandfather's total disregard of it.

The entranceway to the cemetery was made of granite, and the chinking harboured green moss and black lichen that oozed out of the walls in eerie disarrangement. Claire and David walked cautiously through the damp, cool archway into the unkempt gardens of toppled headstones and vandalized cenotaphs. Claire noted a white marble statue of the Virgin Mary, her head bent slightly to the side, a bald-eyed, gentle Englishwoman. Mary, Mother of Jesus — it was as if she was governess of all the Anglo-Indian dead. Her stone was wet and her robes carried the black disintegrations of diesel.

A toothless old man dressed in a lungi, a tattered Western shirt, and a turban, limped up to Claire and David and nodded in the direction of a small brick building. He went into another building, came out with a key and unlocked a padlock to the small brick building.

"Reverend Patak has contacted you, has he?" Claire asked.

"Haan, haan," the old man mumbled and circled his head from side to side. He led them into a tiny room with a small desk and old wooden shelves that were stacked with large brown and black leather-bound ledgers. He began to pull them down and pile them on the desk. "Saal?"

"I beg your pardon?"

"Saal?"

"Alice." Claire spoke more loudly than usual. "Her name was Alice Maude Spencer."

He looked blankly at her and brought his crooked fingers up

to the ledger and etched in the dust the numbers one and nine and dotted two spaces after. "Saal?" he asked.

"Somewhere between 1930 and 1932, I think. But let's start farther back, please, just in case."

Claire drew 1926 into the dust, the very year her father was born. Perhaps Alice had died during her father's birth; he would have been too busy with the tragedy and guilt of his own beginning to have remembered anything of his mother. Then Claire could possibly forgive him for not remembering Alice to her. Still, she had to face the fact that her grandfather had successfully wiped out any memory of Alice to his children save for Charlotte's greedy appropriations, of which he knew nothing. Claire might, in fact, have to exonerate all the men in her family for all time, since it was a woman, Charlotte Blake, who had ultimately been responsible for erasing the memory of Alice — and not, as she had believed for so long, her father's deliberate omission.

You hunt like a man. You must learn to dream like a tiger.

The old man nodded his head once to the side. He opened the top ledger and pointed to the first page. He then left the room and limped into the gardens of the cemetery behind the other brick building. There were others in the gardens, women gathering shrubs, carrying piles of grass on their heads. It seemed to be an endless task for them to keep the cemetery clean. Claire pressed her forehead against the window to see the rest of the garden. Nothing had been done for years; the dried shrubs and grasses tangled the pathways between the headstones and it seemed as if the trunks of trees encroached upon places where the dead lay, their grey and dried roots fingering the soil around mounds churned up by rodents.

Claire sat down at the desk, David opposite her, and they both began to scan down the pages of each ledger. On the left margin was the "Date of Burial" followed to the right by a column that showed where in the cemetery the grave could be found, "Number of Grave," "Christian and Surname," "Age of Deceased," "Signature of Officiating Minister," "Class of Monument (if any)." The last column was titled Cause of Death.

People had died of consumption, malaria, gastrointestinal disorders, typhoid, and there were plenty of infant deaths, stillborns, unknowns. As the pile of ledgers increased to her right and decreased to her left — 1930, 1931, 1932 — without a sign of Alice's name, Claire's spirits began to fade.

Claire not only required Alice to have lived, she also needed her to have died. Without Alice's death, the death Claire carried inside her could only be her own migrant self — transitory and fleeting. She was a fiction then, not really even a memory, but something made up and incomplete.

David finished his pile of ledgers and began to grab from the top of Claire's pile. He seemed as anxious to confirm her reality as Claire was. Sadness and gloom began to seep into the small dark room as they neared the final ledger. "I don't know why I thought we'd find something here," Claire moaned. "It was a long shot, I suppose."

Closing the final ledger on her side, she sat back in her chair and began to cry. David continued to trace his fingers down the final page of the final ledger. He stopped in the middle of the page. Claire watched his lips forming words like a child learning to read. "Here we go," he whispered. "Claire, look. Right here."

He swung the ledger around to Claire and she saw, in the middle of the page, what looked like a child's first attempt at printing. There were the words — Alice Maude Spencer. She read the words again, not believing her eyes. Then she took her finger back to the first column and scanned across the page: Date of Burial — 1932, Oct. 25; Portion of Cemetery in which the Grave — M.E; No. of Grave — A-a-3; Christian and Surname, and age of deceased — Alice Maude Spencer, 38 years. Claire looked up at David. "This is her, isn't it?"

David stood up and started to breathe deeply. He nodded and exhaled. "Yes. Yes, it is."

Claire wiped her eyes and searched the column for Cause of Death. It had been left blank. Why was that, she wondered? According to Ben, Charlotte, even Rita, Alice had died of malaria. Why, then, wouldn't that have been written in the column? For a brief moment, Claire indulged herself with the notion that maybe Alice never did die; maybe she simply left her circumstances. Maybe she was a seasonal creature like Claire, and would return when the weather changed. What if Claire had actually met her — or had seen her on the street, like Hitchcock in his own films? Maybe Alice was auteur, narrating her own life, leaving the camera occasionally to pass before its lens? Perhaps she was capacious, her spirit strident and full, and Claire was only projection — ghostly and suspect? Claire felt for her pulse, finger to wrist. She hesitated for a moment, finding nothing. She quickly touched her neck just below the jawline and felt the faint pulse of the animal beneath her skin, clawing its way back from extinction.

She scratched on a piece of paper the location of Alice's gravesite and they left the small room to re-enter the gardens. Claire stumbled behind David onto the dirt path that cut the cemetery in two. "She died at thirty-eight, David. Thirty-eight." Claire had just celebrated her thirty-eighth birthday. "I'm thirty-eight," she said.

"Come on. Let's go find her," David said excitedly.

He charged on ahead and began to clear away branches and grasses from the stone markers at the edge of the path. Scrawny roots, whitened with death, wound their way up and over headstones. Claire pulled and yanked at the branches of dead rose bushes and the thick grasses that bound the stones to the earth. The names of the dead had dropped away from their headstones; their letters had plummeted into the dirt below and nothing in the graveyard was where it should be. It was as if someone or something had come and deliberately shaken the dead around, confusing them in their passing.

Tiger Dreams Film Part XVIII Sequence

Long Shot. People dressed in black, marching past mounds of dirt at the
    edge of a forest. Cut. Tracking shot of entering St. Sepulchre Cemetery.
    Long shot of statue of Mary, Mother of Jesus. Pull focus of Mary's
    bowed and humble stature. Pan cemetery, women pulling weeds,
    women planting seedlings.
Sound FX. Wailing of woman, yowling of tiger.
Music.

St. Sepulchre Cemetery, Continued

As Claire scuffed the dirt from another headstone with her toe, she could hear David's voice calling her from behind a hedge on the other side of the lane. She tripped over a granite block as she turned and began to run toward David's voice. Behind the huge trunk of a tree that had twisted to the spin of the earth, David stood with his hands in his pockets. He grinned and nodded to the headstone. "Here she is," he said, and he backed away.

Claire walked around to see the inscription; the stone inlays of Alice's name had been removed and her name was transparent in the marble: Alice Maude Spencer. Below her name were her date of birth, 12-11-1894, and date of death, 21-10-1932, and below this read:

Love thou the sorrow Grief shall bring
Its own excuse in after years
The rainbow — see how fair a thing
God hath built up from tears

We thank our God upon
Every remembrance of her
       Philippians 1:3
       DBGS

Claire remained at the foot of the grave and rubbed the coin of Nur Jahan that hung on a chain from her neck. How graceful Alice's fingers must have been, how strong to have dug through the stone ruins of the ancients, to brush away the dust from glass, to tear away the tyrannical roots of plants and pull up from the deep earth the heavy remains of past indulgences, and then to take the gentle moments of the Indian evening and stroke the piano in the clean melodies of the Romantics — Chopin, Debussy, Schubert. Claire was not so impractical as to expect Alice's spirit to rise up and embrace her, but as the warmth of the sun lowered on her back she felt a moment as full and as excruciating as the first breath of an infant, and just as surprising for its truth. She understood her father, his loss, and his fear that had sprung not from her own awkward birth, as she had always let herself believe, but from his mother's early departure. He had become petrified of desertions, and even though he must have known that daughters had to leave their fathers, how many times it must have felt like death to him — the way she kept leaving him and leaving him, slamming the door, squealing out of the driveway in a fury, only to telephone later begging his forgiveness, weeping and professing her love to him. God, how she loved him.

She felt her bones beginning to soften and she started to sing in a wavering inaccurate voice, "Bai lai lee lai, Bai lai lee lay ..." a song to call up her dead father, to let him know that his mother's death was not an act of desertion, it was an accident, just a bloody unfortunate accident.

David paid the gardener two hundred rupees to clean up the gravesite. After some negotiation and misunderstanding, the old man offered to place bricks around the perimeter and plant fresh seedlings across the top.

"Fine," David said. "Now please leave us."

The gardener hung around, curling his fingers over the black lines of his palm and nodding his head. "Three hundred rupees, three hundred."

David stood behind Claire. He was anxious for her to have her peace so he paid the gardener another hundred rupees and told him to go. The gardener hung around for another couple of seconds and then David stomped his foot and chased the old man away.

Pune 1932

Denzil stood before his office window listening to the phonograph — a recording of Alice's last concert at the Prison Cultural Centre. The music was confident, clean, each note clear and without confusion — she played Bach as if all the voices lived inside her, as if she played with six hands instead of two. She was a community of notes cooperating, moving aside for one another, joining and parting, mimicking playfully. She was so much more than One.

That morning he had received the telegram informing him of Alice's death, and he had been standing for hours watching the sun pass through the broken glass that had been set into the top of the prison walls. Coloured geometric shapes, red, green and blue, stretched onto the pathways in time to the rhythms of Alice's music.

Would it be like the absence of weight in the crook of his arm? Or would it sound like the hum of the piano after a sonata? Was it all an illusion, this unfolding of Alice into his life, the dark contours of her body, her skin muscled tight to the bone? He had watched her hungrily as she slowly removed herself from him, dressing and knotting her hair, then disappearing into the heat of the day. Was she something made up? Something he had gazed upon once? Perhaps he was just a tourist. An uneasy conflict postured inside him. He felt her absence like a cool wash.

He had stood before that window every morning for the past seven years and watched her cross the compound to visit the prisoners. He had been observing her walk since she was a young woman in the foothills of Nainital, pretending to be preoccupied with other things as she waltzed along the ridges of mountains, the walls of ruins, or the garden of their home. In truth, he had carefully observed the length of her stride, the way her arms brushed her sides like the tick and tock of time, the way she busily acquired the world around her. And now he stood before his office window staring down to where she had once passed, a throbbing in the base of his spine, suppressed emotion overwhelming him.

Every morning at half past ten, Alice had strolled down the pathway, first to visit the women prisoners; next, the young boys in Circle Two; and finally, Circle Three, Gandhi's Circle. A headache — the early spasm of it — cowered behind his left eye and he rubbed his brow in preparation for the unpleasant visit with Mr. Gandhi, to tell him of Alice's death.

He walked out the office door and down the two flights of stairs. A photograph of the viceroy, Lord Willingdon, hung on the freshly painted yellow walls of the landing. Denzil paused before the photograph and stared blankly at the viceroy, blaming him and the whole bloody British Empire for Alice's death. A guard stood up and tugged at his uniform as Denzil passed. Denzil blamed him, too. And as he walked uneasily into the sun and toward Mr. Gandhi's cell, a sickly pallor fell over the buildings of the prison.

Alice's father would later reproach Denzil for his lack of concern about Alice's headstone. He would offer money and Denzil would refuse, and even though his finances were in a shambles, he would send the children home to England rather than invest in a headstone. He convinced himself that that was what Alice would have wanted. In truth, he was searching for ways to erase her. There would be a battle of correspondence, demands for Alice's belongings, a proper burial, and eventually, years later when the children were away at school, Denzil would order a headstone and be done with the matter once and for all.

He knelt down to pluck an errant weed from the chalk-white path. Rising from his knees, Denzil could see the older man standing before him at the iron gate of his courtyard; he stood up and walked toward him. Gandhi held both his hands out to Denzil, and like an oyster closing around a pearl he took Denzil's hands into his. The younger man looked at Gandhi incredulously, turned and began to walk away. *Not today*, he thought, *I have been mistaken. There has been an accident of information. Alice is on her way home from Karachi. I must get to the station to meet her.* But when he glanced back, the older man was watching him. "I'm afraid ..." Denzil swallowed, then repeated himself, "I'm afraid that I've lost my bearings." He closed his eyes and began to shake. He felt the warmth of the old man's fingers on his shoulder; their fine, perfect strength gently stilled him.

Tiger Dreams Film Part XIX Sequence

Medium long shot of grand piano in a great empty hall. Tall windows let
 light in and bleach the image.

Sound FX. Footsteps of someone approaching piano.

Camera tracks with the sound. Cut.

Medium shot of piano tuner's toolbox.

Pull back to Mise-en-scène. A piano tuner, tapping notes that are terribly
 out of tune. He has the sound board open and begins to tug each
 string, adjusting the pitch. The image vibrates and then the image
 resolves. This is repeated as the tuner moves up the scale.

The audience experiences the purity of each note, clean and precise in
 tone.

Pune 1932, Continued

Denzil, a casualty — adrift — reached up and squeezed the old man's hand so tight that his own began to ache. *I blame you, too,* he thought as he removed the gentleness from his shoulder. Tears dampened his cheeks and he opened his eyes and searched the grounds beyond the older man's face. "I haven't a clue where I am," he said. "Not a bloody clue."

He turned his back to Gandhi, walked along the path and through the entrance of the prison. He could hear the needle on the phonograph scraping through its last groove in his office on the floor above him. He tripped over the threshold of the guards' exit and hastened homeward along Gaol Road. *Yes, there had been an accident of information.*

The children were playing in the backyard and Charlotte was busily repotting a plant. Denzil arrived along the east side of the house. "Take the children to the lake today. I must be alone," he ordered Charlotte.

"Don't you think it wise that we tell the children?" Charlotte looked up from the overgrown roots she had been snipping from a plant. The scar on her face had healed, but it felt like a reproach to Denzil. She repeated, "Denzil, I said …"

"I heard what you said. But it will not be 'we' who tell the children. It will be 'I' who tells the children and you shall not utter a word."

Charlotte furiously stuffed the plant back into its pot, stood up and stomped around to the back of the house. She had felt unsure of her role upon Alice's return, and was secretly relieved that Alice was now gone. She had nursed and cared for the children, bathed them, made sure they ate their meals, looked after their education, tutored them in Latin, and had loved Denzil to completion. But he had not once returned her affections, never once uttered an endearing word to her, and now she was not even permitted to share in his despair. How could she have been so daft?

Denzil stood behind her, feeling absolutely wretched. His head pounded as he spoke. "I've been abominable to you, Charlotte. You have always been so loyal."

When she looked up he could see her reddened nose and eyes; she had the look of someone who had already been crying for quite some time. His voice cracked. "I'm sorry if I ever misled you."

Charlotte felt ridiculous standing at the corner of the house — her hands filthy with soil — and all she could think was that her nose was runny and her eyes were puffy and that she must have been a fright for Denzil to look upon.

William came running around the side of the house and stopped when he saw Charlotte and his father standing before each other. "Cousin Charlotte," he gasped. "Why are you crying?"

"Run along, William." Denzil spoke in a short clipped manner. "I'll toss the ball with you in a moment."

"But why is Cousin Charlotte crying, sir?"

"Run along, Rikki," Charlotte sniffled. "Your father will be with you in a moment."

William stood at the corner of the house; his tiny legs, still weak and bony from the typhus, poked out beneath his knickers. He tilted his head to the side and squinted his eyes. "When is Mother coming home?"

Denzil started at the young boy. "I told you to run along."

William recoiled for a second and then stood absolutely still, eyes filling with tears, face reddening, and hands working the fabric of his knickers. There was something so horrible about that moment that William would spend his life in a constant state of forgetting — using unpredictability like a blank verse with which he constantly invented a fantastic history, fictions that he would tell so often they would become truth. But he would never return to that agonizing moment when his mother was no longer with him. He whispered inaudibly, "I only want to know when my mother is coming back."

Charlotte ran to William, took him by the shoulders and led him away.

The pain behind Denzil's eyes was now surgical in its precision. He turned, climbed the stairs into the front room, across the parlour and into his bedchamber. He stretched toward the bed and slowly settled down on the edge. His eyes darted around the room and he made mental notes of the furniture. He would read his life backwards to find its errors, to edit his pain.

He would become incapable. Shaving and bathing, the everyday functions, would elude him. In the evenings he would organize his socks, shoes, tie, trousers, and shirt. But their obvious functions would baffle and overwhelm him. His despair would be so profound that he would return to bed and not rise again until the following day, when he would attempt to dress again, and fail.

Now, he sat and brushed his fingers along the lace ruffle that Alice had crocheted from the spools of cotton she brought home from her visits with Mr. Gandhi. Imperfect patterns from the sun fell onto the bedspread and across his face. He shut his eyes to the light and tried to hush the clamour inside his head. When he opened them again, the room rocked from side to side. As if intoxicated,

Denzil stumbled across the room and opened the latch on the trunk Alice had packed before leaving for Karachi. He had never sent it on to her. Was it because he believed she would recover, or because he knew she never would? He gasped like a landed pomfret as he pressed his face into the smell of her clothes. He pulled out her braid of hair, a ruby necklace, her mother's topaz ring, and the string of pearls he had given her for her birthday the previous year. A thousand times in his dreams he had played his fingers over that thin smooth ridge of collarbone where the pearls had rested like perfect drops of icing, that place where he had kissed her so effortlessly. He lifted his fingers and let the pearls slip around his knuckles into a milky white pool on the linen bedspread.

There were photographs: the whole family gathered in the motorcycle and sidecar; the family having tea on the veranda; the children in their school uniforms; Alice in gardening clothes; Denzil in his uniform; one of her and Estelle on the new garden bench they insisted on bringing home from Aurangabad; and the one with Denzil and Richard Thomas standing proudly over their tiger kill. That was the year their lives began to leave them, and he blamed all of them — Estelle, Richard, Charlotte, the children. For what, he didn't know, but he blamed them nevertheless.

The light grew dim in the room as he gathered up the traces of Alice's life and placed them onto her pillow. He lay down beside them and tried to calculate the exact distance between himself and Alice. He drew triangles in the soft fabric, connecting the imprints of his fingertips with the shadowed valleys of linen. He remapped their world, their India, gazing upon it as if from a great expanse, and then he buried his face in the linens and wept like an infant. He blamed himself.

PART SEVEN

The Tiger Dreams

Tiger Dreams Film Final Sequence

Mise-en-scène. It is obvious to the audience that the camera is on a tripod
and I am filming myself because I drop in and out of view as I pick up
my grandmother's pearls and drape them around my neck. I begin to
braid my hair.

Me: "I am clawing my way back from extinction."

The Tiger Dreams

Mr. Bahti had invited Claire and David to sleep in his home. "It was probably the home of your grandparents," he told Claire as he escorted them down the road to what was now his family home.

Claire clutched her camera in her hand and trekked up the long lane toward the house where her father was born.

David had been arguing with Mr. Bahti about the nature of democracy. Mr. Bahti claimed that India was the greatest democracy in the world. David tried to interject, saying that India might be the largest democracy in the world but that in actual fact, he thought the system flawed, if only because the Hindus and Muslims were unable to resolve their land issues. Mr. Bahti asserted that the Indian had nuclear capabilities and that they were the strongest army in the world. David agreed that they were possibly the *largest* army in the world, if only because of their numbers, but argued that many countries had nuclear capabilities, one of which was Pakistan. And didn't that make him rather nervous?

"You look Indian," Mr. Bahti said to change the subject.

"Yes, yes I do, don't I?" David smiled and sauntered toward Claire who was sitting on a wooden garden bench. She was stroking the armrests; they were wreaths of metal ivy. "Apparently I look Indian," David said as he leaned against the large thente tree behind the bench.

"Oh, David, it's just their way." Claire reached up behind

her and caressed his arm. "This bench is in a photograph with Alice and her friend."

"No kidding." David pulled out his camera. "You sit."

Mr. Bahti approached the bench. "You will come and meet my wife and daughters. They will have tea with you. Come, come."

David snapped a few photographs of Claire on the bench. Claire smiled for the photograph — her wide mouth was her trademark and she knew the exact angle and definition her lips required to deliver the perfect smile every time. At that moment she was very aware of how she must look to Mr. Bahti. White, North American, and vain; she wished, just once, that someone would say that she looked Indian.

Mr. Bahti looked back and waved his hand for them to follow him. "That bench was here when we moved in. Come, my wife is very anxious to have tea with you."

Mr. Bahti started to walk again toward the house. Claire could tell that his authority in the prison had spread through his whole life. Both she and David jumped to attention and followed him up the front steps, onto the veranda and into the front room of the house.

The central room was painted a pale blue and the floors were a soft yellow. The ceilings were high, and small arched windows let smoky light into the whole room. Large swaths of colourful cotton divided the rooms.

Mrs. Bahti and her two daughters bowed and nodded their heads from side to side. Mrs. Bahti stretched her jewelled hand toward a wide couch that sat against one wall. "Please, come and sit."

Servants moved in and out of the curtains at frequent intervals. Everyone nibbled on biscuits from the prison bakery and sipped their tea in awkward silence.

Claire would recall later that she had felt uncomfortable wandering through the home of Mr. Bahti and his family. It was difficult to remain reverential about every step she took into her grandparents' world and she'd eventually lost herself in the ordinariness of their life. She asked to see the bedrooms and the studies, and Mrs. Bahti, having been surprised with the announcement that there would be visitors only that morning, was obviously uncomfortable with the state of her home. Mr. Bahti had told Claire he thought it inappropriate for her to film inside their home and she had agreed with him. She turned her camera off and put it aside for the evening.

Many lives had passed through the premises since her grandparents had lived there and she doubted that much remained from their time other than the garden bench beneath the thente tree and the general layout of the house. She could see the seams like thickened scar tissue on the floors, walls and ceiling where there had been a room added onto one end of the house. There were pockets of silence, the smell and taste of the history of places; Claire tried to fit herself in. But there was something hollow about the place, as if all its inhabitants had vacated long ago, and nothing that anybody did now to the place — paint the walls, put up fabric — could escape the absence.

Dinner was served very late into the evening. David moaned and groaned throughout the meal in appreciation of the dishes that were presented to him. "Allu Mutter, you say? This, Claire, is the best." He pointed to a potato dish that swirled around in green peas and a thick tomato sauce.

Claire agreed with David, as she always did when it came to food, and she snapped off another piece of naan bread and dragged it through the korma sauce from a chicken dish.

"Mr. Bahti," she asked. "How would it be possible to take some footage inside the prison walls?"

"That is not possible. We have very strict rules about photographs."

"What if I just wanted very specific areas of the prison, Gandhi's cell, my grandfather's office? The prison is so immaculate." Flattery, she thought, use flattery. "And the grounds are so well kept."

Mr. Bahti held his hand up and began to shake his head. Claire interjected, "I was wondering what you thought ..." Advice, always ask for advice, she could hear Father coaching her. "I was wondering what you thought about a few shots from the inside of Gandhi's prison cell? You know — what he would have been looking at for all those months in prison? I would not film anyone, or betray any of your prisoners. I simply want a sense of place, a setting for the story."

"And what is your story, madam?"

Claire improvised. "Part of my film will highlight the rehabilitation programs initiated in Yeravda during my grandfather's time — the bakery, theatre, and concerts."

"And the other part of your film?"

"Land reform and its role in self-rule."

He took a drink of his beer and waved his hand to stop the conversation until he swallowed. "The Canadians, they are so serious, don't you think?"

"Just a day. That's all I ask. A day in the prison."

"A sunny day," said David.

"Yes, a sunny day."

Mr. Bahti sat back and smiled at Claire. "One day," he said very sternly. "You may have one day."

After finishing their meal, they drank tea, and Claire and Mrs. Bahti chatted about saris and how the art to wearing them was in the folding of the fabric.

"Like an accordion around the waist," said Mrs. Bahti, and she dangled her fingers in the air to show the motion of folding the fabric. Mrs. Bahti wanted to get a pair of blue jeans, she said, but she doubted that her husband would tolerate them.

Claire stifled yawns that were coming with alarming frequency. She announced to Mrs. Bahti that she needed to retire and turned to say goodnight to David and Mr. Bahti. They were sharing a bidi and some Bagpiper whisky David had bought earlier in the day.

"I'll be right behind you." David nodded and returned to his discussion of land reform with Mr. Bahti. "These zamindars," she could hear David saying, "they still have land in Bihar and Bengal?"

Claire was too tired to bully her way into bidis and whisky with the men in the drawing room, so she bid them all good night and thanked Mr. Bahti for everything.

"Yes, yes, my pleasure, madam. Sleep well."

Mrs. Bahti showed Claire into a bedroom just off the dining hall. "This might have been your grandmother's room," she said. "We do not sleep in it because of the early morning sun. But it is the largest room in the house so I am suspicious that it was meant to be the master bedroom." She turned to leave. "If there is anything you need, please do not be afraid to ask."

"So sorry, I think I'm just exhausted." Claire yawned and clasped her mouth with her hand. "Thank you so much for your kindness."

"Nonsense. You will write to me from your home in Canada. That would be lovely."

"Yes, of course, I will write to you."

"May you be a mother someday. Namaskar." Mrs. Bahti clasped her palms together, bowed graciously and left the room.

Claire was finally left to herself. Hot air puffed through the closed wooden shutters and shifted the soft white curtains hanging on either side of the windows. She flicked a spider off the crisp linen bedcover, lay back and fell fast asleep.

You Dream This Only Once:

You are dropping into a thick green tongue of a river. You swim effortlessly in fathoms of water; a wildcat claws at your shoulder and you take the waterfall together, and everything is warm and growing inside you.

On the Other Side of the River Mula

Charlotte, in her bedroom, unrolled her stockings and left them in neat little crescents on the wooden floor beside the bed. She unzipped her skirt and wrestled to get it around her broad awkward hips. She pulled her slip up over her head and caught a strap on the pins in her hair; she fussed and pulled and finally dislodged them, releasing a slow, tumbling cascade of grey hair. The straps of her brassiere, always loose, dropped over her shoulders and she squeezed her baggy arms; their dried, brown wrinkles raked against the cotton fabric as she wriggled her arms through to twist the brassiere around. She unclasped it from the front; her thin, tired breasts fell lazily over her ribs as she set herself upon her mattress and lay back on her pillow. Charlotte twisted the topaz from her finger and set it down on the side table. She closed her eyes. She became indifferent to her poverty. She was dead. She was perfect.

But You Dream This Quite Often:

You stand by an open fire in blue jeans and white t-shirt. You hold your child in your arms. The wood is dry; it sputters and sparks, flickering red and orange light over your child and you. You see this because you are dreaming and you can be all places at once. The child has rested her head on your shoulder. Her skinny legs barely wrap around your waist and you thrust your pelvis forward to catch the constant pull of gravity on the child's body. David, or someone who feels like David, reaches for the child; he will lay her down for the night. You are uncomfortable, your back aches and your arms are tired, but you will not surrender the child to her father yet. You have a story to tell, of tigers in the jungle, of how steady your hand is when you hold your knife.

River Mula

David's breath was heavy; he was chugging like a train, his dreams cloaked beneath his eyelids. Claire lay beside him, watching him struggle and writhe inside his disturbance. She rose from their bed and stood before the window. It was dark and the moon was soft and hazy through the city air and she could hear the scrape of rickshaw wheels, the horns in the distant traffic and the chirp of crickets — there was always the chirp of crickets in India. She would miss their constant dialogue.

Through the kitchen and out to the garden surrounding her grandparents' home, she tiptoed in her bare feet. The blue light on the sandy earth, the charcoal grey of her skin and the deep, deep purple of the leaves gave the landscape a coolness, a sense of remove.

There are places in the foothills just west of Claire's home where the forest meets the grasslands. In those zones of tension, fescue and cinquefoil assert themselves in the stands of aspen or pine. Shrubs of willow and disenfranchised yew attempt to create their own colonies within the golden grasses of barley and wheat. Hybrids occur in alarming numbers and their success recreates new, imagined landscapes. When Claire returns to those places where the red-tailed hawk hunt mice from wooden fence posts, the coyote circle sheepishly in the ditch alongside the gravel road, and the horizon is unattainable in the night, she listens for the crickets and remembers that night, the slow easy flow of the River Mula like blood through her veins, the comfort she finally felt in a foreign land.

She circled over her own footprints. The soft dust parted like waves as she placed the soles of her feet into her own tracings, repeating and repeating a predetermined perambulation. She had marked the soles of her grandmother's feet, carving radiating patterns into the hard calluses of her heels, hoping that on this night, this blue night in October, she might meet with her.

Her father had drawn her maps all her life. He had drawn her maps of his dreams and had traced pathways for her. He had come to know the earth with a certain intimacy, as if the curvatures of landscape would reveal for him his own longing. He had told her about the land of Quivera, a land inhabited by a miraculous people. Quivera was where the sun set, it was the end place, the residence of the dead. It was supposition, a mirror of what already had been. And as Claire understood what it meant for a parent to prepare a child for the longing of life, she thought maybe India had been part of her father's dreams, the land where he began and where she would end. Quivera was the "other" of the two worlds, and in a mercurial way she had brought him back here, to this place of imagined territory. She had cracked open something inside herself and discovered an ever-widening circumference of truth. I am now within the mother yoke, she thought. I have attained freedom.

And these scars that spread across your body are from your own battles. They are the puncture wounds and claw marks you have inflicted upon yourself. You are the hunted and the huntress. You will never be seamless. You will always be sutured.

"But I will heal," she called into the darkness.

Yes, you will heal.

Denzil had seen Alice pushing at the edge of her garden, drawing a map with her feet, cornered and anxious, unable to leap out of herself. She had pulled his children from her womb, had cut their ribbons, and let them suckle from her breast. She had been mother, sister, lover, and daughter to all of them, and though she died before she had time to reveal her complete devotion, she had been a woman rising — fully made in a time compressed.

Sudden quiet: the cricket without wings, the cars without horns, the rickshaws without wheels. Claire stopped to listen. Strings tightened inside her spine, aligning pitch, tuning her into a single note. On that night in October, at the edge of her grandmother's garden, she could see her own bony white ribs harrowing the soil. Revealed. Extract. She was the last of her kind and she trod carefully so as not to disturb the bone. "Alice must be remembered," she whispered.

Sudden quiet: the crickets, the horns, and the wheels in the traffic seized. David startled from his sleep. He stretched his arm over the bed and felt the crinkled imprint of where Claire's body had been. He dressed and walked out of their room and onto the veranda. From where he stood, he could see Claire walking in tighter and tighter circles, her eyes to the ground, her hair loose over her shoulders, her long legs bare and perfect in the light. The only sound — the soft thud of her feet on the dusty earth. Time allowed for this moment. Claire held her hand to her breast, bent her knees, and kneeled into the earth. She swept her other hand down so her fingers could fallow the fine powder, and David whispered a prayer, the palms of his hands together. As she raised her fingers to her lips, a zephyr passed through her blouse and the moonlight, her consonance. Beside her, a skeleton. Something wild. Its ribs picked clean, elegant trusses above sharp, perfect shadows.

Acknowledgements

In loving memory of my father Norman W. Cowper. So too for my late aunt, Elaine Lysne, and my recently deceased grandmother (Nana), Almeda Lysne. A moment of silence for all those individuals who died suddenly, without warning, from Sudden Arrhythmic Death Syndrome. I survived you, but I wake each morning with devout thanksgiving for my life. Thanks Charlie Kerr and the medical teams at Denver Medical Centre, Foothills, VGH and St. Paul's hospitals.

My heartfelt thanks to Michelle Benjamin for soliciting my manuscript and Lynn Henry for exquisitely editing it, the Raincoast team for their great energy, B.C. Arts Council for giving me the kick-start on graduate studies, Eastern Washington University for graduating me, and all the students who have endured my curiosity for story. Verna and Tom, thanks for letting me drive fast.

My utmost respect goes to John Keeble, who challenged me from the beginning. You are truly a great friend and teacher.

A special thanks to my Aunt Babs, Glenn Chase, who gave me the seeds for the story. To the women and men of India for their generosity of spirit, namáste and bahút bahút dhányavaad.

Thank you, Colleen, for running, skiing, and riding with me while I worked through the complications of my imagination. Your call for subtlety made this a better story.

Jill, I miss you. How many times can a woman read a story? Thank you for your extreme intelligence. Garrett, thanks for being my Buddhist-Guy reader. Hey Barb, what a way to get to know a gal? And Sally and Jenilee, in the end, after battling and finally succumbing to your early observations, I believe I have built a better story. Thank you. Thanks to the community of Rossland.

Mom — you have all the best lines in the script of my life. Geoff and Karen, you have been invaluable in my search for Truth. Glen, thanks for those late-night laughs. Bruce, thanks for all the arguments. And resolutions. To my sister, Lillias. This story has been written with you in mind at all times. This is ultimately for you.

And finally, thank you, Terry, Sharmila, Sadie, and Tika, for the laughs we have every day. Hey Milty, thanks for the metaphors.

About the Author

Almeda Glenn Miller wrote this novel for her grandmother, a woman she never knew. Almeda is of Anglo-Indian descent; she grew up in the foothills of the Canadian Rockies. She is the former owner of Goldrush Books in Rossland, British Columbia, and teaches creative writing at Nelson Fine Arts Centre and Selkirk College. She lives with her family in Rossland, British Columbia.

This book was set using Trump Mediäval. Trump Mediäval was designed by Georg Trump for the Weber foundry and released between 1954 and 1960. Trump was a prolific type designer who considered himself first and foremost a teacher of the graphic and lettering arts. With its crisp angularity and wedge-shaped serifs, Trump Mediäval appears carved in stone. It is a strong, highly legible text typeface.

The sans serif (used for the film script in *Tiger Dreams*) is FF Scala Sans, designed by Martin Majoor, who wished to enhance his elegant serif FF Scala with a companion sans-serif family. Despite its sans serif starkness, Scala Sans's evocation of traditional text forms makes it easy to read.

At Polestar and Raincoast Books we are committed to protecting the environment and to the responsible use of natural resources. We are acting on this commitment by working with suppliers and printers to phase out our use of paper produced from ancient forests. This book is one step towards that goal. It is printed on 100% ancient-forest-free paper (100% post-consumer recycled), processed chlorine- and acid-free and supplied by New Leaf Paper. It is printed with vegetable-based inks by Houghton Boston Printers in Saskatoon, Saskatchewan.